INVASION

ROAD TO THE BREAKING
BOOK 6

CHRIS BENNETT

Invasion is a work of historical fiction. Apart from well-documented actual people, events, and places that figure in the narrative, all names, characters, places, and incidents are the products of the author's imagination, or are used fictitiously. Any resemblance to current events, places, or living persons, is entirely coincidental.

Invasion

Copyright © Christopher A. Bennett – 2021

ISBN: 978-1-955100-04-5 (Trade Paperback)
ISBN: 978-1-955100-03-8 (eBook)

Cover Image Photo:

"Union Soldiers in a Field"
Copyright © Garrison Gunter
(https://www.flickr.com/photos/ggunter/1398495842)

Publisher's Cataloging-In-Publication Data
(Prepared by The Donohue Group, Inc.)

Names: Bennett, Chris (Chris Arthur), 1959- author.
Title: Invasion / Chris Bennett.
Description: [North Bend, Washington] : [CPB Publishing, LLC], [2021] | Series: Road to the breaking ; book 6
Identifiers: ISBN 9781955100045 (trade paperback) | ISBN 9781955100038 (ebook)
Subjects: LCSH: United States. Army--Officers--History--19th century--Fiction. | United States--History--Civil War, 1861-1865--Fiction. | Confederate States of America. Army--Drill and tactics--Fiction. | Women spies--Southern States--Fiction. | Militia--Southern States--History--19th century--Fiction. | LCGFT: Historical fiction.
Classification: LCC PS3602.E66446 I58 2021 (print) | LCC PS3602.E66446 (ebook) | DDC 813/.6--dc23

To sign up for a
no-spam newsletter
about
Road to the Breaking
and
exclusive free bonus material
visit my website:

http://www.ChrisABennett.com

Invasion [in-**vey**-zhuhn] noun:

1. An act of incursion, as an enemy, with an armed force into a country or region for conquest or plunder.
2. Advent of something troublesome or harmful that affects life in an unpleasant and unwanted way, as disease.
3. An unwelcome intrusion into another's domain.

Dedication

To
Patricia
for loving, encouraging,
and supporting me all the way.
And especially
for putting up with me!

Contents

Chapter 1. The Best-Laid Plans 1

Chapter 2. Baiting the Hook 29

Chapter 3. A Web of Deception 50

Chapter 4. When Truth Is a Lie 82

Chapter 5. Prison Break 100

Chapter 6. Roads to Harpers Ferry 133

Chapter 7. A Rapturous Meeting 172

Chapter 8. The Evil That Men Do 193

Chapter 9. Backs Against a Stonewall 226

Chapter 10. The Fateful Lightning 258

Chapter 11. Empty Homecoming 292

Chapter 12. Joyful Surprise 338

Acknowledgments 356

Recommended Reading 356

Get Exclusive Free Content 358

*"Dead men don't
kill the living."*

– Evelyn Hanson

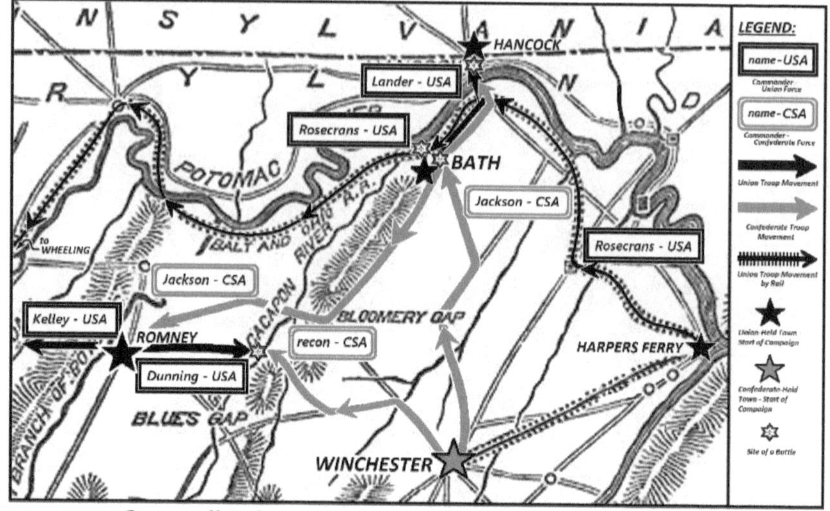

Stonewall Jackson's Romney Expedition – January 1862

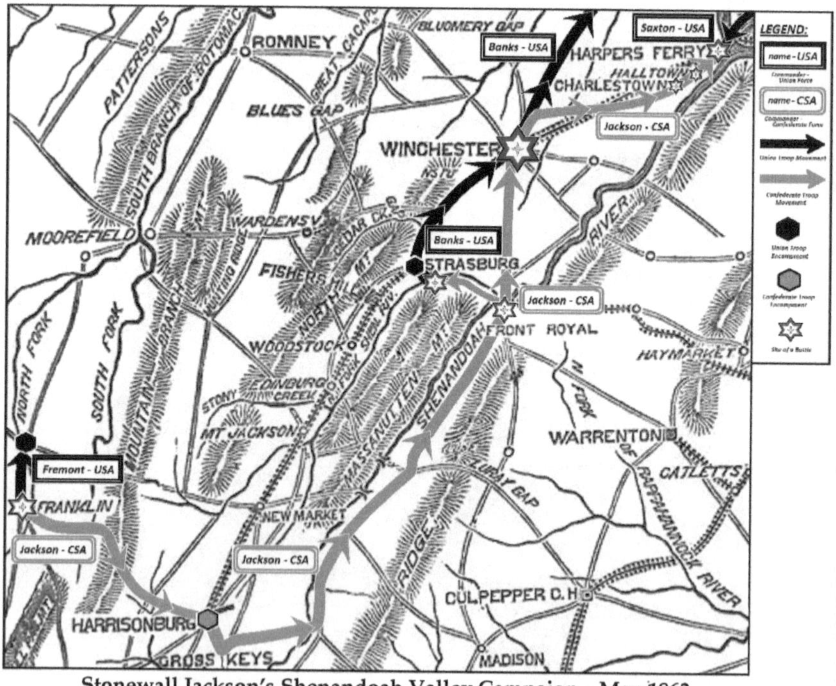

Stonewall Jackson's Shenandoah Valley Campaign – May 1862

Chapter 1. The Best-Laid Plans

*"The best-laid plans of mice
and men often go awry."*
- Robert Burns

Wednesday January 1, 1862 – Washington, D.C.:

"You're telling us after traveling all this way, and waiting four days to speak with General McClellan about our critical plans for the spring offensive, that we aren't even being allowed to see him?!" Nathan said, rising partway out of his chair. "General Porter, this is not acceptable!"

General Rosecrans put a hand on Nathan's arm and the two shared a serious look, before Nathan sighed, and sat back down. But Nathan noted Captain George Hartsuff, Rosecrans' chief of staff, seated on the other side of him, had turned red in the face and was slowly shaking his head, though he refrained from commenting.

Brigadier General Fitz Porter, Major General McClellan's staff executive officer, a handsome man about Nathan's age, with the rugged, hawkish look of a soldier, leaned back in his chair and gazed across the table at Nathan and Rosecrans with a frown.

When they'd initially met earlier in the week, Nathan had been pleased to see Porter, and as a result had held out high hopes for the success of their present mission. They'd known each other at West Point, and Porter had also served with distinction in the Mexican War. He had even been one of the heroes of the battle at Molino del Rey where Nathan had earned his gold medal and heroic reputation. But Nathan's previous good feelings for Porter had suddenly soured, now believing McClellan's ill influence had likely rubbed off on the man.

"As I have already explained, gentlemen," Porter said, in an even tone, "General McClellan is still sick in bed with typhoid fever and is not taking any visitors at present. But I have discussed your plans at length with the general, and he is now fully versed."

"With all due respect, General," Rosecrans answered, "I don't see how you could have possibly discussed our plan in detail, when we have only shared with you our brief, high-level overview of said plan, when we met with you for less than an hour, three days ago. We anticipated spending half a day at the very least going over the strategy with General McClellan."

"As I said before, General, that will not be possible," Porter answered mildly, then smiled. "But you may be pleased to hear the general has already made his decision on the matter, so you need wait no longer."

"Oh. Well, that's good, then," Rosecrans said. "And which divisions is he assigning to our campaign? I should like to speak with their respective commanding generals as soon as possible that we might organize our assault and get a jump on Stonewall Jackson."

General Porter didn't immediately answer. Rather, he sat and gazed at Rosecrans, and unreadable expression on his face.

"General … I'm afraid you are proceeding under a false assumption," Porter finally replied. "The commanding general has *not* approved your request for an additional two divisions. In fact, he believes the planned offensive, to take the town of Winchester from Stonewall Jackson, as you have laid it out, might have the unintended consequence of shifting the focus of the war to the wrong theater: away from the more important objectives further east."

Nathan snorted derisively, "You mean General McClellan fears someone besides himself may steal the thunder? Take some of the attention away from him and thus deprive him of his anticipated glory? And here I thought this was about defeating the enemy and winning a war …"

"Whomever gains the ultimate glory has nothing to do with it, Mr. Chambers," Porter answered, sounding a bit miffed. "And may I remind you, *sir*, you are only a civilian here, and have been allowed in these meetings as a courtesy to your state's governor, and at the sufferance of the Army. Kindly refrain from overstepping your bounds, sir."

Again Nathan began to rise from his seat, and again Rosecrans restrained him. Nathan sat back down, reached into his pocket, pulled out a cigar, and bit down on it, a scowl knitting his brow.

"General Porter … this is exactly why we wished to meet with General McClellan in person … that we might have the opportunity to explain our thinking on the strategy … to answer any questions or concerns he might have. To go over the details that he might feel comfortable with what we are proposing, and so he can see that it *does* meld with the general's overall eastern strategy—in fact it serves to support and strengthen it."

But Porter waved his hand dismissively, "General McClellan has already made his decision, General Rosecrans. So, unless there is some other urgent matter you wish to discuss, I have important duties to attend."

Rosecrans scowled at Porter, but could see he was getting nowhere, so he rose to his feet, collected the papers he'd laid out on the table in front of him, and pivoted toward the door, foregoing the customary salute or other courtesy he should have offered General Potter.

Nathan and Rosecrans' other staff officers also rose, likewise ignoring Porter, which was, strictly speaking, a serious breach of protocol. And Harry the Dog lifted his prodigious bulk from the floor where he was resting, and followed after Nathan.

General Porter seemed to take no notice of the slight, already gazing down at a stack of papers he'd brought to the meeting with him.

But even as Rosecrans reached out for the doorknob, Porter said, "Oh, Mr. Chambers … would you kindly remain a moment? General McClellan wishes for me to have a word with you—in private, before you depart."

Nathan exchanged a look with Rosecrans, shrugged, and turned back toward Porter.

"We will await you in the outer hallway, Nathan," Rosecrans said, as he went out the door.

Nathan returned to the table and sat across from Porter. Harry sat next to him, not lowering himself to the floor this time, but watching the interaction of the two men intently.

"General Porter … what is it I can I do for General McClellan?"

"Let us speak plainly, Mr. Chambers, shall we?"

"Certainly, General. Such has always been my preference."

"Mr. Chambers, to be perfectly blunt, the commanding general was *not* pleased when I informed him you had accompanied General Rosecrans to Washington. And he was *not* pleased to hear you had assisted in the planning of the spring campaign in the west. He believes … it is not your place to involve yourself in military matters since you are no longer in uniform."

Nathan snorted, "Again I say, isn't the important thing trying to defeat the enemy and win the war, rather than who wins the glory?"

But Nathan could see Porter was getting red in the face. "Mr. Chambers, I will remind you to keep a civil tongue. I will not allow General McClellan to be denigrated."

"General, I tire of this conversation. Please state what you were told to say, that I might be on my way."

Porter leaned back in his chair and smiled. It was not a pleasant, friendly expression to Nathan's way of thinking.

"Mr. Chambers, the Major General McClellan, in his capacity as commander of all Union armies, has instructed me to tell you to stay out of this war. Entirely. He has asked me to be very clear and explicit on this point. He says, don't bother to enlist nor to seek an officer's commission in the Union army. If you do, General McClellan will see to it you are permanently stationed in the most remote backwater on the continent, or the most mundane possible desk duty at the War Department. Is that clear, Mr. Chambers?"

Nathan rose to his feet, "Yes, it's clear, Porter. It's clear that McClellan is the simpering coward I always suspected he was, not even man enough to say those despicable words to my face. He's a glory-seeking peacock who would rather lose the war than risk another man receiving more praise and recognition than him. And as for *you* … you *disgust* me, sir! You are nothing but a bootlicking toad—shamelessly doing McClellan's dirty work for him."

Porter sprang from his chair, "You dare insult me, sir! I'll not stand for it."

But Nathan, who towered over the general, reached across the table, grabbed the front of Porter's uniform coat, and slammed him back down in his chair.

"Sit down, and shut your mouth!" Nathan leaned over and glared into the other man's eyes. "You've conveniently made sure there were no witnesses to your general's treachery. But that's a double-edged sword, my friend, for now there are no witnesses to what I might do in response ..."

General Porter's earlier confident smirk and his most recent angry scowl were replaced by a look of abject fear.

Nathan took a deep breath and briefly closed his eyes, then said, "Now ... keep your slimy mouth shut, and just sit there until I am out the door. Or I swear by God, I will crush you like the insect you are, and like you so richly deserve. Do I make *myself* clear, sir?"

Porter nodded, wide-eyed, but said nothing.

Nathan turned, marched to the door, and exited, slamming the door behind him, narrowly missing Harry's tail and startling General Rosecrans and the other officers who were quietly conversing down the hall.

೫෧෮෪෫෯೫෧෮෪෫෯೫෧෮෪෫෯

"So, Fitz ... after you gave Rosecrans the news, did you speak with Chambers as I'd instructed?" McClellan asked, sitting up in his bed.

General Porter, who sat in a chair next to the bed, nodded, "Yes, sir. I gave him the message, even as you'd ordered."

"And?"

"And ... as you can imagine, sir, he was ... none too pleased by it."

McClellan smiled, "Yes, I should think not. But what was his response?"

"I ... I would rather not say, sir. It was *not* something I wish to repeat, General."

"Come, now, Porter—I'm an old soldier, and certainly capable of absorbing crude and irate language. Out with it, if you please."

"Yes, sir. But only because you insist. Mr. Chambers called you a coward for not speaking the words to his face ... and he called me a bootlicker for repeating your message to him."

McClellan frowned, "*Coward?!* You did explain to him I was in my sick bed with typhoid fever, else I would have been there in person to say those words myself? By God! Coward! How dare he! The unmitigated gall!"

"Yes, sir. The man is nothing if not brazen and contemptible."

"Well, you at least defended my honor and yours to the scoundrel, I presume?"

"Oh, yes, sir! In no uncertain terms. I told him straight out I wouldn't stand for him denigrating you, nor insulting me. Yes, sir, you can be sure after upbraiding him, I sent him packing, straight away out of the office."

"Good. As it should be! Good man, Porter. The only way to deal with such arrogance and insolence."

Porter nodded, but no longer met eyes with the general.

McClellan scowled, and looked thoughtful for a moment before continuing, "Porter ... there's little enough I can do about Chambers' insulting behavior for now, him still being a civilian. But Rosecrans ... that's another matter. The man may as well have insulted me himself, bringing that incorrigible *civilian* into my offices for an official Army meeting about military business. I don't have to stand idly by and allow such behavior."

"No, sir. But what will you do then about General Rosecrans, sir? Call him in for an official reprimand?"

"No ... I think not. He'll likely just laugh it off, as he is even now laughing at Chambers' insulting behavior toward me. No, I am of a mind to have him replaced. Yes ... I believe I will strip him of his command of the Department of Western Virginia."

"Oh! But, sir ... I was under the impression he had done quite well running that command this past year."

"Humph! Don't forget I practically handed him the region already conquered after our success at Rich Mountain. A lowly private could've led the Army as well as Rosecrans after that."

"Yes, sir."

"Porter, I will give it some thought, and once I'm up from this insufferable sick bed, we will discuss the matter further. We must figure out a way to reorganize the department, so it sends Rosecrans and his staff the proper message, while not looking too obviously punitive to anyone at the War Department. He likely still has friends there."

"Yes, sir. That does sound most prudent."

⁀⁀⁀

After the disappointing meeting with General Porter, Nathan and Rosecrans decided to stay positive, and agreed to revise their plans for the spring offensive to make do with the men they already had. They also agreed that the conundrum of Commanding General McClellan was likely a problem that would resolve itself in due time; either he'd succeed with the vast army given him and the war would be over, or he'd fail and the president would be forced to sack him.

But when Nathan greeted Rosecrans at the train station the next morning, the general's mood had soured.

"You look like you ate a rotten egg for breakfast, General," Nathan said as Rosecrans stepped up to him.

"Good morning to you too, Chambers," Rosecrans said, scowling as he handed Nathan a sheet of paper. At a quick glance Nathan could see it was War Department letterhead, and the next thing he noticed was the signature at the bottom of the page: *Major General George B. McClellan.*

He looked back up at Rosecrans, "New orders from McClellan?"

Rosecrans nodded, "Go ahead … read it for yourself."

Nathan quickly read through the orders, then looked back up at Rosecrans, "I can't believe it. He not only turns down your request for two additional divisions … he … *damn it, William!* He's taking *away* 20,000 men already under your command! Of all the slimy, backstabbing schemes …"

"Yes … this little expedition to Washington City has turned out even worse than we'd feared. I am effectively stripped of my command, having only … hmm … roughly 3,000 men left under me, and those scattered all around western Virginia guarding various facilities. Hardly an effective fighting force …"

Nathan was fuming as he read the orders a second time. "Doesn't say when this takes effect … perhaps there's still time to take some action."

"No, in fact there isn't. The lieutenant who delivered the orders informed me I needn't hurry back to my command in Wheeling to implement these new orders; that General McClellan had already communicated the orders directly to my subordinates … out of courtesy and for my convenience, of course …"

"Of course," Nathan said, agreeing with Rosecrans' heavy sarcasm. "But the orders say your men are being transferred to General Lander … is this the same *Frederick* Lander who was a colonel under you at Rich Mountain?"

"Yes, the same. Back in August he was promoted to brigadier general, backdated to May. And in October he was again promoted to division command, having been one of the few commanders who'd come out ahead after the debacle at Ball's Bluff."

"Hmm … McClellan's new darling? He didn't strike me as the bootlicking type back at Rich Mountain. In fact, he seemed a very gallant and admirable fellow during the battle. Brave, aggressive, and intelligent, as I recall."

"He *is* a good fellow—all that you say and more. I remember before the battle he and I were out reconnoitering the enemy's log fort when a rebel sharpshooter shot his horse right out from under him. I feared he might've been injured in the fall, but he jumped up, fiery mad that they'd shot his favorite horse. He immediately jumped upon a large rock, shook his fist at them and shouted, 'Go ahead and shoot me too, you yellow bastards!' but no more shots rang out. The man has unwavering courage under fire, from all I've seen and heard.

"And he's not overly fond of our commanding general either. No, Nathan, I very much doubt any of this was his doing."

"Well, that's good to hear, at least. But *damn it*, William! This is a bitter pill."

"Yes, agreed. Let's get back to Wheeling, shall we? I suddenly find I have had quite my fill of Washington," Rosecrans said with a scowl, gesturing toward their train car.

Nathan nodded and headed up the stairs. Harry the Dog squeezed in behind him, forcing Rosecrans to wait for the large, four-legged body to pass. Rosecrans couldn't help but chuckle and shake his head, lightening his ill humor, as he mounted the stairs behind the gigantic hound.

ഇഇഈ൪ഈഇഇഈ൪ഈഇഇഈ൪ഈ

"Captain Hill, what's going on, sir?" Confederate Lieutenant Jubal Collins asked his superior as he strode up to Bob Hill's tent. Jubal saw that the captain's gear was stacked outside and the tent was being dismantled by two privates.

"Ah, there you are, Lieutenant," Captain Hill answered. "While you were off at the quartermaster's, posting your latest missive to your lady friend, word came down we're to move out within the next few hours—the entire Stonewall Brigade along with the rest of General Jackson's division. Hurry over and get your men packed up and ready to march."

"Yes, sir! But … where are we going? If you don't mind my asking."

"North. The general's going on the offensive."

"Whew …" Jubal whistled, tipping his hat back and scratching his forehead, "on the first of January?! I never expected us to fight again until spring."

Bob chuckled and held out his right hand, palm up. The skin of his hand fairly glowed in the bright sunlight. "Guess the general likes the look of this weather. Likely the Yanks are thinking the same as you, that we'll not make a move 'til spring. So I'm guessing General Stonewall wants to catch 'em by surprise."

"Hmm … now that you mention it, sir, we are having some mighty nice, unseasonable weather at the moment," Jubal said, gazing up at the bright, sunny sky. He noted that only a few scattered, puffy clouds disturbed its otherwise perfect blueness. Then it occurred to him it'd been so warm first thing that morning he'd not bothered to don his jacket. "Well, should be a pleasant hike, anyway. Likely beats sitting around here for months on end," he said, and smiled at his Captain.

Captain Hill nodded his head and returned the smile.

But later that day, as the sun was setting, Jubal was becoming convinced this was *not* going to be the "pleasant hike" he'd predicted. Shortly after noon a cold front had rolled in, blotting out the sun and dropping the temperature like a stone. And despite the exertions of their march, he'd soon called a brief halt so the men in his company could pull warm coats and jackets from their packs.

And he realized, with a sinking feeling, that they'd moved out so quickly that morning, and had made such good progress that they'd likely left the supply wagons with their tents, food, and cooking gear far behind. He now thought it unlikely they'd see any of their baggage before morning, which would make for a long, cold, hungry night sleeping outdoors in nothing but the gum blankets they had stowed in their packs.

But even as he was thinking these depressing thoughts, he suppressed a groan; snowflakes were suddenly swirling through the air on a gusty breeze.

𝕰𝖃𝖆𝖅𝖈𝖅𝕰𝖃𝖆𝖅𝖈𝖅𝕰𝖃𝖆𝖅𝖈𝖅

Nathan was enjoying the relative warmth of the train car after a frigid day of travel by horseback and a night spent sleeping in a cold tent. The hundred-some miles of track Stonewall Jackson had destroyed on the B&O line at the beginning of hostilities the year before still hadn't been completely repaired. There remained a forty-mile gap in the line, starting with the destroyed bridge across the Potomac at Harpers Ferry.

Nathan, Tom, and Harry the Dog, along with General Rosecrans, his staff, and several companies of Union soldiers, had been forced to debark at Sandy Hook, on the Maryland side of the Potomac, just across the from Harpers Ferry, and take turns being ferried across along with their horses and baggage. Fortunately for Nathan and Tom, General Rosecrans could pull rank allowing their party to board the first ferry. From Harpers Ferry they'd followed the gravel path of the now defunct rail line to the point where the tracks were back in service again, near Cherry Run, Virginia.

And it had been a very unpleasant ride, and an uncomfortable night spent sleeping out in tents, as the weather had taken a decidedly nasty turn. Snow mixed with sleet and a biting wind during the day had given way to a bone-chilling drop in temperature at night that'd turned the ground to a solid sheet of ice, making footing treacherous for both man and beast.

But Nathan's enjoyment of the train car's warmth was short-lived. They'd only been on the train a dozen or so miles when its whistle blew and Captain Hartsuff jumped up, staring out the window to the left side of the train. He turned toward General Rosecrans and said, "Look, sir! A large column of Union soldiers—a brigade at the least."

Rosecrans and Nathan were immediately on their feet, along with Tom and the other officers, rubbing the accumulated fog and frost from inside the train car windows to get a better view.

Nathan saw that the captain had spoken truly: a large contingent of Union soldiers, on the march headed north on a snow-covered dirt road, were paused at the edge of tracks, apparently to allow the train to pass. The train engineer clearly had seen them as well, blowing his whistle and slowing the train perceptibly. It now crept slowly past the waiting troops. Though most of the soldiers were afoot, Nathan saw a group of a half-dozen or so officers sitting on horses at the head of the column, their breath coming out in puffs of steam whenever they conversed.

As the train approached the group, Nathan noticed the man in the center wore a single gold star in a gold-trimmed patch on each shoulder—a brigadier general.

"Hey—*I'll be damned!* That's Lander," Rosecrans cried out. "Hartsuff … stop this train!"

❧❧❧❧❧❧❧❧❧

A few minutes later, Nathan was once again shivering. A cold sleet pelted the brim of his hat and tried to slip down his neck past the collar of his coat as he strode briskly down the tracks next to Rosecrans, with Tom and the staff officers in tow.

General Lander had clearly seen their approach, though likely he did not yet know their identities. He rode his horse slowly toward them alongside the tracks, two of his officers following behind.

When the two parties approached close enough for recognition, Lander's face lit up in a broad grin and he immediately leapt down from the saddle, tossing his reins to the captain riding just behind him.

Except for the general's stars on his shoulders, Lander looked the same as Nathan remembered him from their time together at Rich Mountain six months earlier. Only a few years older than Nathan, Lander was tall, lean, and handsome, with long, flowing light brown hair and short-cropped beard. Nathan decided if one were asked to portray the very image of a heroic, young general he might describe Frederick Lander.

General Lander trotted toward them, coming to a stop a few feet away, standing straight and snapping a salute in front of General Rosecrans, who returned the gesture smartly. Nathan had to resist a very strong urge to salute also.

"General Rosecrans," Lander said, "what a pleasant surprise, sir!"

"Well, I will say it's pleasant to see *you*, Frederick, but this weather? Not so pleasant," Rosecrans responded, shaking hands with Lander before wrapping his arms around himself and shivering for emphasis.

"You'll get no argument from me on that point, sir!" Lander responded, continuing to grin.

Lander then greeted Nathan and Tom warmly, remembering them from their service together at the Battle of Rich Mountain.

"General," Rosecrans interjected, "shall we return to the warmth of my train car to make the introductions of our staff officers in a more pleasant setting? That is, if you have time to speak with me for a few moments ..."

"*Do I?!* General, you have no idea how many times I have wished for your sage counsel these past few months. I am delighted at the prospect of sharing a few moments in your company. Please ... lead on, sir."

⸙⸙⸙⸙⸙⸙⸙⸙⸙⸙⸙⸙

Back at the train car, after the introductions were made all around, Lander turned to Rosecrans and apologized emphatically for taking away command of so many of Rosecrans' troops, per General McClellan's recent orders, reassuring him he'd had no say in the matter, nor any foreknowledge of the event.

Rosecrans waved off the apology dismissively, telling him he'd known it was just more of General McClellan's nonsense.

Then Lander's expression turned serious, and he said, "As you gentlemen have clearly been traveling the last few days, you've doubtless heard nothing of what's happening here in the Shenandoah Valley ..."

"You are correct, General ... we've had no news, so were more than a little startled when we saw you and your troops out on the road—especially in this horrific weather ..." Rosecrans answered.

"Well, you can believe me we'd not be out here if it weren't for the most dire necessity," Lander said. "Two days ago, we received word from our advanced scouts out of Bath, that General Jackson was on the march toward that town with a large contingent."

"*What?!*" Rosecrans exclaimed, shaking his head. "We knew the man was bold, but a winter offensive in such weather?! The man is asking for a disaster."

"Well, hopefully we can grant him one," Lander answered, flashing a wicked-looking grin. "But his actions may not be as ill-conceived as it may seem at this moment ... you see, we now know he started out on the morning of New Year's Day. And if you recall—"

"It was sunny and warm that day, a fair, cloudless sky ... at least in Washington," Nathan said, looking thoughtful.

"Yes, exactly, Mr. Chambers. The weather here was likewise quite pleasant. I presume the prospect of a spate of fine weather emboldened him to make a move he'd doubtless been planning

13

for some time. But he may be regretting the decision by now ... or at least his men are, I'll wager. Even that very night on the first, the weather suddenly turned frightfully cold. I can only imagine how his soldiers out on the march suffered it." He shook his head sadly, as if he really did feel empathy for them, despite them being enemy combatants.

"And your march to the north then?" Rosecrans prompted. There was an unspoken component to his question, and everyone present knew it: why was the Union army moving north if Jackson was attacking from the south? Even the *thought* of the most obvious answer was more than a little disconcerting.

"I know what it looks like, gentlemen. And believe me, it galls me to retreat before the enemy like this. But once I explain my circumstances on the ground at the moment, I believe you'll agree with my decision."

"I'm listening," Rosecrans answered, noncommittally.

Lander sighed, "As you know, General, the estimates we receive from our scouts on the number of advancing enemy soldiers tend to be wildly inaccurate at the best of times. In this weather ..." he shrugged. "The reports I've received say Jackson has anywhere from seven thousand to twenty thousand men. Seven we might handle with the few men you've seen here — if we had a good, defensible position — but twenty?

"And unfortunately, Bath is *not* an easily defended town. Further, my men on the north side of the Potomac are presently spread thin, guarding bridges and other possible fording points and will take a good week or more to gather ... never mind the formations of yours I've recently been handed that are spread all over western Virginia at the moment.

"No, gentlemen, I have cursed the bad timing that has rendered me impotent to do anything other than withdraw in the face of Jackson's bold offensive. If I'd have had another week of warning, I might have swept down on him from the north, catching him out on the road, and annihilating his entire command. But as it is ...?" he shrugged.

"I feared our garrison of 2,500 or so officers and men stationed at Bath would be quickly overrun and would be lost to our cause if I ordered them to hold the town. So, I am withdrawing them to Hancock, across the Potomac on the Maryland side, leaving only a skeleton force to harass and delay the enemy. In Hancock they will join with the brigade that is currently garrisoning the town, and there we can make a stand against the rebels."

"But … there are no bridges for many miles in either direction, general," Nathan said, recalling the maps he'd seen of the Potomac, and the B&O Railroad which roughly paralleled the river's course, "and the river is … hmm … five hundred or so feet wide at this point, and at least six feet deep. Too far to swim, and too deep to ford. So, how will you get your men across to Hancock before Jackson arrives? It will take days to ferry so many across in boats."

Lander grinned, "Ah … I'm happy you ask, Mr. Chambers, as it allows me to brag somewhat—if you'll forgive my doing so—on the scheme I've come up with, along with the engineers. Have you heard the term *'bateaux'*?"

It was Tom who answered, "It's the French word for *boat*," he said, recalling the French he'd learned at school and that he'd used to good effect with Adilida down in New Orleans.

"Exactly so, Mr. Clark. And in this case, a very particular type of flat-bottomed boat of the kind used on the Seine in Paris. But we will not be using these *bateaux* to ferry our troops; these boats have a peculiar rectangular shape—that is, they are flat across the bow and the stern, rather than pointed—much like a barge—so they can be lashed tightly together end to end in a continuous line. When anchored to the river bottom, planking can be quickly laid across them to create a bridge stable enough for men and horses to cross, and even light artillery. And the bridge can be pre-built and installed on a moment's notice, unlike traditional pontoon bridges, or more permanent structures.

"I'd intended to use the *bateaux* to launch an attack to the south, but so far General McClellan has forbid it. At least my *bateaux* have proved their worth by providing me with the means to evacuate Bath and save the garrison. Once we've dismantled our floating bridge our friend General Jackson will be left scratching his bum on the other side, wondering how to get across."

"Do you really think he means to cross into Maryland?" Rosecrans asked. "Wouldn't it be more sensible for him to turn west, take Romney, and then threaten Wheeling and our efforts to build the new state and its regiments?"

Lander shrugged, "I would've thought so, but if he meant to take Romney, why didn't he just attack to the west from Winchester to begin with? Why attack northward and take Bath? It is of no strategic importance that I can think of."

"I know what he intends," Nathan said, looking thoughtful, and absentmindedly reaching into his pocket for a cigar before sticking it in his mouth unlit.

"I believe he *does* intend to take Hancock before turning west for Romney … for two good reasons. Firstly, he wishes to damage the C&O canal, which passes between the river and the town, and put it out of action for an extended period of time. After the damage he did to the railroad last year, the canal has been a critical lifeline for transporting men and material for the Union, and he means to disrupt it if he can."

"Hmm … yes, that makes sense," Lander said. "And the other reason?"

Nathan smiled, "A feather in his cap. He wants to be the first Confederate general to capture a Northern town, in a Union state. It'll enhance his reputation down south and make it easier for him to recruit troops and requisition supplies, even if he holds the town for but a short time before returning to the Virginia side to continue his march."

"Makes sense," Rosecrans said.

But Lander frowned and said, "Gentlemen, I fear General Jackson is going to be sorely disappointed on both counts. I swear by God, on my sacred honor, he will *not* take the town. Not while I live and breathe!"

Nathan smiled, then leaned across and patted Lander on the shoulder, "Good man, Lander. Good man." Nathan decided he liked Lander even better now than he had back at Rich Mountain.

When Nathan sat back in his seat, another thought occurred to him. "General Lander ... am I right in remembering you're now in command of the garrison stationed at Romney ... some 5,000 men, I believe, including our own Seventh West Virginia?"

"Yes, just so, Mr. Chambers. Why? Do you have a thought as to how I might best deploy them, given the circumstances?"

"Yes ... as a matter of fact, I do. When General Jackson stands across the river from Hancock, 'scratching his bum,' he'll be farther away from Winchester than our own garrison at Romney will be." Nathan turned and looked at Rosecrans, "Our original plan for this spring was to take Winchester away from Jackson ... now with him presumably emptying out the place to launch his attack—"

"It may be but lightly defended—ripe for the picking," Rosecrans completed his sentence for him, and beamed. "Nathan, I like your way of thinking."

But Lander slowly shook his head, "I like it too, but, as I said, General McClellan has issued explicit orders *not* to advance, even now with Jackson on the march. I can't order an offensive against Winchester without openly disobeying his orders. Whatever our feelings about the man, he is still the commanding general."

But Rosecrans was undeterred, "General Lander ... when you've been around the army as long as I have, you'll understand there are always ways to get around orders."

Lander raised an eyebrow at this, but said nothing, allowing Rosecrans to elucidate.

"Just don't call it an offensive, or even an attack ... call it rather ... a 'reconnaissance in force.' Your men aren't attacking Jackson, they're just going to have a look. To make a determination as to the state of the defenses he has left behind in Winchester."

Lander gazed up at the ceiling of the train car for a moment, then looked back down and smiled, "And if they find those defenses entirely lacking ... well, who could blame them for taking advantage of the enemy's poor judgment! I *like* it, gentlemen. Besides, if nothing else it will make *good old Stonewall* nervous about having his supply lines cut, and might make him hesitant to push his attack farther to the north or west ... perhaps even forcing him to withdraw altogether."

The impromptu train car meeting was winding down when the door on the back end of the car suddenly burst open, and a thin, baby-faced lieutenant stepped in, immediately coming to attention and snapping a salute at General Lander. "Pardon the intrusion, General!" he said, between gasps for breath. "A scout has just arrived at the gallop from Bath. He reports the rebels have reached the town, and the remnants of our garrison are engaging them as ordered. They are vastly outnumbered but mean to attempt a fighting retreat to slow the enemy's advance. They expect the enemy to soon flank them and cut off their escape."

Lander nodded his head, then gazed down toward the floor and sighed. For a moment no one spoke. Then Lander sprang to his feet. Nathan could see a look of fire and determination in the young general's eyes.

"Then we shall not forget their sacrifice, and strive to ensure that it has not been in vain. Lieutenant, spread the word among our officers; there is no time to lose. We must be across the Potomac and our bridge dismantled before Jackson and his rebels arrive, and they are now less than five miles away."

"Sir!" the lieutenant snapped another salute, then turned and raced out the door.

Then Lander turned to Nathan and Rosecrans and said, "Though my exodus is now all the more urgent, I fear you gentlemen may be in grave peril; the rail line heads south from here and passes within two miles or so of Bath. It is only a matter of time before Jackson destroys the tracks in the entire area. If he thinks to do it before completing his conquest of Bath and of Hancock, you may be cut off and at his mercy. Perhaps you should debark, along with all the companies on this train and join us in crossing over the river to Hancock. You are certainly welcome, and I would find your presence a great comfort and a blessing in this hour of need."

Rosecrans and Nathan met eyes for a moment, then Rosecrans turned to Lander and said, "Thank you, General … that is most gracious of you. But my place now is back at Wheeling organizing what's left of my department to defend that city. Should Jackson continue west, we must do all in our power to stop him from reaching Wheeling, or I fear the new state will be doomed."

Then Nathan said, "I too have urgent obligations back at Wheeling. We will take our chances with the train, General. Hopefully our friend Stonewall will be focused on the fight and won't give thought to the railroad until after."

Lander nodded his head, then reached out to shake hands with Rosecrans, and then Nathan. "I pray you're right, Mr. Chambers. General … it has been a pleasure, sir, but I must now urge you to tarry no longer. And Mr. Chambers … I look forward to seeing you in uniform when next we meet, ideally with a couple of gold stars on each of your shoulders."

Nathan smiled and nodded, but could think of nothing to say in response to that; there wasn't time for a lengthy explanation, and anything abrupt would seem disingenuous. So he just said, "Thank you, General, and good luck to you."

"Godspeed, gentlemen," Lander said, then turned and strode out the door, his staff officers fast on his heels.

Even as Lander was exiting the back door, Captain Hartsuff was heading for the front. As he reached for the door, he turned back to General Rosecrans and said, "Already on it, sir. Train will be moving again post-haste."

"Good. And pass the word throughout the train—all soldiers, and any other able-bodied men, are to arm themselves, load their weapons, and prepare for battle."

"Sir!" Hartsuff said, nodding by way of salute, and ducking out the door.

⁎⁎⁎⁎⁎⁎⁎⁎⁎

True to Captain Hartsuff's word, a few moments later the train lurched into motion. And even as it was building up to speed Hartsuff re-entered the car with the train conductor in tow.

General Rosecrans quizzed the conductor on the most vulnerable places where the rebels might disrupt the rail line within the next ten miles or so, in a place closest to the town of Bath. The conductor thought a moment, and decided it would be the small bridge over Sir John's Run, where it emptied into the Potomac.

The general then ordered the conductor to stop the train at the point closest to the bridge where it could not be seen by any rebels that might be there. He also ordered the train to proceed with the least amount of smoke and noise possible in their approach.

"Captain Hartsuff, what're our numbers and current troop disposition?"

"Sir, the first two passenger cars contain a rifle company of just under a hundred men, and their officer, a lieutenant, from the Forty-Fifth New York Volunteer Infantry Regiment. Per your orders, they are armed with weapons loaded, keeping an eye out for rebels and awaiting further instructions.

"There are also a half-dozen civilian government and train company officials armed with pistols in the second car. They are … a bit more *aged*, shall we say, than I would prefer, but otherwise I have no knowledge concerning their possible fighting prowess or capabilities.

"Next comes us: five officers plus Mr. Chambers and Mr. Clark … all of us carrying only sidearms. Oh, and Harry the Dog, of course … well-armed with some rather wicked-looking teeth," he added, glancing over at Nathan, who nodded in acknowledgment.

"The next car carries the horses, and the one following that, the baggage. Oh, and of course, the caboose at the end, with two unarmed B&O employees."

"Hmm … how many horses?"

"Just ours, sir. The rifle company are all afoot, and I understand the civilian officials came out from Wheeling by the train to inspect the damaged line, so didn't figure to need any other transportation."

"Well, they may regret that choice if the line ahead has been taken out," Rosecrans said with a wry smile. "It's a long walk back to Wheeling."

"Yes, sir."

Rosecrans looked over at Nathan and said, "Well, I guess that's about all we can do until we reconnoiter the bridge and see what we're up against. Hopefully General Jackson has had his hands full—what with this continuing nasty weather and all—and he hasn't given a thought to the railroad yet."

"One can hope," Nathan said, and reached into his jacket pocket for a cigar, which he proceeded to light. After a few puffs he said, "General, when we get to that bend and come to a stop, Tom and I should go out and scout for you."

"Oh? Don't think my men are up to the task?" Rosecrans asked. Though he kept a straight face, Nathan detected amusement in the general's eyes and in his tone.

"It's not that, William … I'm sure your men are more than capable. But Tom and I are dressed as civilians … if the enemy were to spot us, they might think we're just a couple of local citizens making our way along the tracks, and looking at them out of pure curiosity. Whereas any of your uniformed officers or men would likely catch their attention right quick."

"Ah, good point, Nathan. All right; agreed. And thank you kindly for the offer."

Nathan grinned, "Never mention it, General."

ↇↈↂↇↈↂↇↈↂↇↈↂ

A half hour later, Tom and Nathan knelt behind snow-covered bushes that seemed to fill every possible gap between the dense tangle of trees through which the rail line had been cut.

Nathan held a brass spy glass to his eye as he gazed out at the bridge, less than a mile away down a very straight stretch of tracks. It was their first glimpse of the bridge since leaving the train and heading out along the tracks on foot. And what they saw was *not* encouraging.

After a minute, Tom could not refrain from asking, "Well, sir?"

"Rebels all right. A cavalry troop—forty or fifty I'd say. They've felled at least two good sized trees and laid the logs across the tracks. And they're busily chopping more."

"But what about the bridge, sir?"

"Still there for the moment, and no sign of … wait … what's this? Ah, *damn it!* Men lifting small heavy kegs from a wagon … and now they're carrying them toward the bridge."

Nathan turned back toward Tom and handed him the spy glass, reaching over Harry's back to do so.

"I'm guessing that's not whiskey in those barrels," Tom said with a wry grin as he took the spy glass and lifted it to his eye. He quickly spotted the things Nathan had described.

"No, I think not. Come on, Tom. Let's get back to the train as quick as we can. I fear we've got little time to lose if we want to save that bridge!"

ஐ๛๏ଔଔஐ๛๏ଔ๛ஐ๛๏ଔଔ

Damn it! Forty to fifty cavalry you say?! Though we have them outnumbered, with nearly a mile to cover on foot out in the open against cavalry we'll never get to that bridge before they can blow it. Then they'll just ride off leaving us stranded," Rosecrans said, slowly shaking his head. "If only we had more than a handful of horses ourselves and could mount a charge."

But Nathan had a thoughtful look as he gazed at the ceiling of the train car. When he looked back at Rosecrans he grinned, "Ah, but, General … we *do* have cavalry, and I think … it may be just what we need."

"What do you mean, Chambers? What cavalry?"

"General, it just so happens, we have at our disposal a hundred-ton iron horse!"

"Oh …" Rosecrans said, then let the idea sink in for a moment. "Oh, I think I see where you're going with this, Chambers. Hartsuff, please just go fetch that young lieutenant from the rifle company. I'm ready to give him his marching orders … or rather his … *riding* orders," he said, and looked over at Nathan—the two exchanged a grin.

22

Tom and the other officers looked at their respective commanders in puzzlement, wondering what secret language they might be exchanging.

ꕥꕥꕥ

"How much longer, Sergeant?" Lieutenant Simmers asked the engineer, who was currently up to his knees in ice cold water, tying a keg of gunpowder to one of the bridge supports.

The sergeant looked up and scowled, "As long as it takes, Lieutenant. But if you think you can blow this bridge any quicker … be my guest," he gestured toward the cold water of the creek.

Simmers shivered involuntarily at the thought; the weather was already icily cold, and the precipitation couldn't make up its mind between snow and sleet, so had apparently decided to do both at the same time.

Theoretically the sergeant's answer was disrespectful to the point of insubordination. But he was an engineer, doing a difficult, nasty, dangerous job, so Simmers decided a little leeway was likely in order.

"Just hurry it along, Sergeant," Simmers answered, and turned his horse away.

"Oh, yes sir! That I will most certainly do, sir, now that you've asked so nicely!" the sergeant answered in a tone that could not be mistaken for anything but heavy sarcasm.

Lieutenant Simmers was debating turning back and snapping at the man when he was interrupted by the arrival of one of the privates, who pulled up on his horse at the top of the riverbank in front of him.

"Ah, Private Jeffers … how is the barricade coming along?"

"Good, sir. Should be finished within the hour. But I came to tell you there's a train coming. From the North, sir."

"Oh … all right, I'm coming," Simmers said, and kicked his horse into motion, up out of the shallow embankment.

When he reached the top, he could see for himself what the private had reported: a locomotive coming slowly toward them down the tracks, great puffs of steam and smoke fighting to rise against the best efforts of the bitter wind and sleet. The engine was still about three quarters of a mile away, and not seeming in a great hurry. Likely the engineer had seen the activity on the tracks, including the felled logs, and was slowing so he'd not suffer an accident.

Why he didn't reverse course and run away, Simmers couldn't imagine, unless the line was also cut further north. Whatever the cause, it was likely their good fortune, as a train on the B&O line was probably carrying supplies for the Union army: food, clothing, and equipment that would be a Godsend right now to the men of the Stonewall Brigade. And even if empty, the capture of a Union locomotive and cars would be a feather in his cap.

Simmers ordered the engineers to continue their work but organized the rest of his men in a defensive position in the open area on the east side of the tracks away from the river, next to the small platform and hut that served as the train stop. He would have preferred to place men on both sides of the track, but the trees on the river side came right up to the gravel of the roadway, allowing no room for cavalry to maneuver, if necessary.

He waited as the train approached, reflexively unbuttoning and loosening the pistol in its holster on his right hip. He looked around to make sure his men were likewise prepared, and was gratified to see pistols and rifles at the ready.

When the locomotive came to within a hundred feet of the bridge it came to a hissing stop. Though it pulled three passenger cars, they were dark inside and appeared to be empty. There was no movement nor any sign of occupants.

Maybe just carrying cargo in those two box cars, Simmers decided, excited at the prospect of those much-needed goods. He kicked his horse forward having a mind to go over and quiz the engineer about the train's contents.

But he'd not moved ten feet forward when he heard a sudden, inexplicable sound of breaking glass. A window on the first passenger car had exploded outward. Simmers looked and saw a man standing in the window, holding a rifle, butt forward. The man wore the blue frock coat with brass buttons of a Union soldier!

They met eyes, and the man grinned before turning the rifle around and pointing it out the window. At that moment dozens of other windows suddenly shattered, spraying glass out across the gravel of the train tracks.

And even as dozens of riflemen appeared at the broken windows inside the passenger cars, rifles suddenly appeared on top of the box cars as well.

The world erupted with the thunderous noise of hundreds of Union rifles firing from the train, mixed with the sporadic, mostly ineffectual return fire from the weapons of the mounted rebel cavalry, whose horses were bouncing and shying at the sudden, unexpected cacophony.

Though a dozen or more of his men were already down, Simmers tried to rally his troops, shouting encouragement, urging them to fall back in good order to the tree line. But even as he did so, a new threat appeared. Half a dozen horses came charging out from the river side of the train, around the front of locomotive, led by a man wearing a blue coat with gold stars on his shoulders—*a Union brigadier general!*

Simmers turned to face the new threat, even as the enemy horsemen threw ropes around the logs and began dragging them from the tracks. Then he noticed two of the riders—also Union officers—break off from the others and head toward the bridge. There they paused and fired multiple pistol shots down toward the river. Simmers aimed his pistol at them, but never fired; they were too distant, and from his moving horse it would've been a waste of precious rounds.

Simmers said a quick, silent prayer for the surly engineer he'd just recently had words with, then turned, intending to target the Union general, if he could. But he was momentarily distracted by a large animal moving among the horses. At first glance he thought it a small bear, but then decided no, it must be a hound, but the largest ever.

Then even as he turned his attention back to the Union general, he noticed a tall man in civilian clothing spurring toward him. Simmers flinched when he saw a flash of fire spew from the man's pistol. A second later something hit Simmers hard in the shoulder, like a hammer blow, sending his own revolver spinning off into the snow and nearly knocking him from the saddle.

In that moment he knew he must flee or die. He gritted his teeth at the pain, turned away from the train, ducked low in the saddle, and spurred his horse up the gravel road that led back to the town of Bath—back to the safety of General Jackson's army.

ઠઠ૭ૠ૭ઠઠ૭ૠ૭ઠઠ૭ૠ૭

The moment the wagon came to complete stop on the gravel drive at the Belle Meade farmhouse, Stan jumped down from the front seat where he'd been sitting next to Georgie.

He was immediately mobbed by the farm's happy residents, both black and white, patting him on the back, shaking his hand, and greeting him warmly. Stan beamed, laughed, and joked, in his usual loud, boisterous manner, as he returned the warm greetings of men, women, and children. The entire farm of well over a hundred souls had turned out to greet them, despite the frosty weather, after Jamie, who'd ridden ahead, had spread the good news of their imminent arrival.

When Tony finally managed to work his way through the throng and reached out to shake Stan's hand, he found himself scooped off his feet, a thing he'd not experienced since being old enough to remember. Stan kissed him on both checks and gave him a squeeze that nearly knocked the breath out of him, before he was back on his own two feet.

Rosa, who'd been next to Tony as he worked his way through the crowd, laughed out loud, covering her mouth at the humorous sight of Tony, no small man himself, being lifted like a child by Stan. Tony looked down at her, shrugged, and grinned, enjoying the sound of her laughter and the sparkling of her eyes in her mirth.

"Is good to be seeing you again, Tony! And all of you," Stan said gazing around at the gathering. "Hello Miss Abbey … hello Miss Megs … Miss Margaret," he said, waving at the three women where they stood up on the farmhouse steps a few feet back from the gathered crowd.

From the rumors Tony had heard—that Billy and Stan had been wounded in a gunfight with the Captain's old enemy Walters somewhere way up in the bitter-cold mountains—he had expected Stan to look a bit "worse for the wear" as the big Russian was fond of saying. But such was not the case. Stan seemed as strong and vigorous as ever, as if gunshots and privation had no effect whatsoever on the gigantic man. Tony just shook his head in wonder at the thought. *Stan is just Stan*, he remembered hearing Mr. William say once.

But when Billy came around from the back of the wagon where he'd been riding, walking deliberately next to a concerned looking William, it became clear they had indeed suffered through a desperate, dangerous situation. Billy's face betrayed a good deal of pain as he slowly stepped up to the crowd. In deference to his obvious discomfort, his greeting was less boisterous, if no less warm.

And after a few moments William took him by the arm and led him toward the house, "Thank you, everyone," William said, "but Billy needs to lie down and rest for a bit after our travels." And surprisingly, Billy didn't object to being led away into the house. When he stepped up the stairs, the three ladies of the house stood aside to let him pass.

"Welcome home, Billy," Miss Abbey said, smiling warmly. "We are so very happy you have returned safely to us, and hope you will be feeling better soon."

Billy looked at her and nodded, but said nothing.

William stepped ahead of him to open the door and met eyes with Margaret. He paused a moment, smiled, and tipped his hat to her, "Miss Margaret … a pleasure to see you again," he said.

She returned the smile brightly, "William … welcome home."

He nodded, still smiling, then turned to hold open the door for Billy.

But as Billy approached the door, Margaret stepped up to him and said, "Billy … there are no words sufficient to thank you for all you have done on our behalf … risking your life selflessly to keep us all safe. I, for one, shall ever be grateful."

Then for the first time since arriving home Billy smiled. He nodded, and said, "You're welcome," then turned and entered the house.

CHAPTER 2. BAITING THE HOOK

"Bait the hook well.
This fish will bite."
- William Shakespeare

Saturday January 9, 1862 – Unger's Store, Virginia:

"Goddamn it!" Lieutenant Jubal Collins swore, as he rubbed his bruised knee and wiped the snow and frozen mud from a badly scraped elbow. He'd been pushing a wagon up the icy road with a half-dozen other men when his feet slipped out from under him, and he landed hard on the frozen roadbed.

He scrambled to get back up but slipped again, this time landing on his backside, as the other men continued to push against the heavy load, which stubbornly refused to move.

Jubal had spent the last two hours and more trying to help a long stream of wagons get up the small hill on a sheet of ice that was supposed to be a road. Each wagon was pulled by a team of four horses, but the horses hadn't been shod for the weather, and they continually lost their footing, often falling completely to the ground in their traces. First one, then another would slip and fall—sometimes all four at once. So, the men had been forced to get out behind and push.

As Jubal sat, catching his breath, a man stepped up to him and stretched out a helping hand. Jubal reached out for it even as he looked up at the man's face and suffered a shock—it was General Stonewall Jackson himself!

The general wasn't a man anyone would particularly notice if he were dressed as a civilian. But even though he wore the casual kepi hat of a common trooper, there was no mistaking the two gold stars on the shoulder patches of his fine gray coat, marking him as a major general. And there was no mistaking the intense, commanding gaze of his eyes, nor the vigor and purpose in his stride.

"I don't generally agree with using the Lord's name in vain, son," the general said, with a serious expression on his face. He gazed up at the heavy sky, then down at the icy road and said, "but today ..." he slowly shook his head.

Jubal tried to stand erect and salute, but the effort nearly made him fall again, and the general reached out to steady him.

"Never mind about that now, Lieutenant. Let's see if we can't get this wagon moving, shall we?"

"Yes, sir, General!" Jubal said, and turned back toward the wagon. As he stepped forward and placed his hands against the cold wood of the tailgate, he couldn't decide if he was surprised or not when the general stepped up next to him, put his shoulder into it, and pushed.

"C'mon men ... give it all you've got," the general said, "we've got to get off this road and into camp. And the only way we're going to do that, is to move these wagons. Heave!"

Jubal pushed with everything he had, careful this time to keep his feet up under him. From the grunts and groans he could tell the other men were also giving it their all. At the same time, men out front were pulling on the horses' leads, coaxing them forward. Ever so slowly the wagon began to move, until the men could stop pushing and the horses were able to keep the momentum going on their own.

Jubal turned toward the general, and not knowing if it was appropriate or not, decided to say the thing on his mind, "Thank you kindly, General. That was just the push we needed. But ... don't you think, sir ... well, that it ain't right you bein' down off your horse in the road with us regular soldiers?"

Jackson tilted his head thoughtfully, then said, "No, Lieutenant ... I believe this is *exactly* where I should be. Come on, men, there's another wagon behind this one, and unless I miss my guess, it's also going to need our help." He turned and strode briskly down the road toward the next wagon in line, as if he were entirely immune to slipping and sliding on the ice.

Jubal shared a wide-eyed look with the man next to him and shrugged. Then despite their fatigue and the biting cold, they shared a grin and turned to follow their general.

Captain James Hawkins half slid, half scrambled back to the roadway before standing up and brushing the snow and brambles from his pants and coat sleeves. He'd been up on top of a rocky ridge with a pair of binoculars borrowed from Colonel Samuel Dunning, of the Fifth Ohio, who was in charge of the operation — a so-called "reconnaissance in force" toward the rebel stronghold at Winchester.

Hawkins had volunteered to climb the steep embankment, him being the youngest and most rigorous of the senior officers present. Besides, he had the honor of leading three hundred men of the Seventh Virginia Infantry, "leant" to Colonel Dunning for the operation, and wanted to make a good impression on behalf of the regiment.

"Well, Captain?" Colonel Dunning asked, returning Hawkins' salute from where he waited atop his horse, in front of a group of a half-dozen other mounted officers. Snow swirled around them in the half-light of pre-dawn, making for a surreal image to Hawkins mind.

"Not much stirring in the rebel camp, sir. I expect the weather's not to their liking. Only a few pickets up and about, otherwise it appears they're all still in their tents."

The colonel smiled at this news. "And their force size, Captain?"

"I make it out to be a brigade, sir. Approximately 2,000 give or take. Seems like they may have only arrived last night, as I see no fortifications nor any signs of digging in. And from this vantage point I can only make out two six-pounder cannons, though there could be others on the far side of camp out of view."

"Well, our numbers may be about even, but it seems we have the element of surprise," Dunning said, looking back at his officers. "Gentlemen, let's give our rebel friends an *extremely* rude awakening, shall we?"

An hour later, just as the sun was cresting the eastern ridgeline, the rebel camp was indeed rudely awakened by the sounds of gunfire and pounding hooves, as two-hundred cavalry poured in through the gap along the road, followed closely by several hundred infantry, coming at the double-step in two columns, bayoneted rifles in hand.

But even as the rebels roused themselves from their sleep and attempted to get organized to face this unexpected assault, hundreds of Union rifles opened up on them from the hillsides to their right and left, catching them in a deadly crossfire. James Hawkins and his three companies of the Seventh Virginia were among those on the left.

Most of the Confederates pouring from their tents saw what was happening and fled. Others lay on the ground and raised their hands over their heads. Only a handful managed to load rifles and prepare to fight, but these were quickly shot down by their attackers.

Within fifteen minutes it was over. It had been a complete and thorough rout, with fifteen rebels killed, over a hundred wounded, and twenty captured, along with the two cannons that Captain Hawkins had spotted before the battle—artillery the rebels had never had time to load, much less fire. There had been no Union fatalities, and only minor injuries.

The remainder of the Confederate force had fled the battle, headed east, back toward Stonewall Jackson's headquarters at Winchester. With the snow thickening, and visibility worsening, Colonel Dunning called off any immediate pursuit, fearing his forces might become spread out and scattered, leaving them open to counterattack or ambush.

But two hours later, Captain Hawkins' elation over the easy victory and the acquisition of more than two dozen fully laden supply wagons turned to dismay when Colonel Dunning announced they were to turn around and march right back to Romney. Dunning calmly deflected the complaints, protestations, and entreaties of the other officers, explaining he had no orders to march all the way to Winchester, and even if he did, he'd be forced to ignore them at this point, and pull back.

"Look, gentlemen," he calmly explained, "I understand the sentiment, and … frankly, the feeling of having the blood up after such a heady victory … But we must face facts. Though we routed the enemy, we did not destroy him. Somewhere out there on the road there are more than fifteen hundred soldiers at least, whom we must presume are still capable of fighting. And those are only the ones we know about; likely there are others back toward Winchester whom we have not yet encountered.

"And don't forget, we gained our victory this morning through total surprise. That will *certainly* not happen again on this campaign. So … enjoy our victory, gentlemen; after all, we have accomplished what we came to do, which was to make General Jackson think twice about sticking his neck out too far to the north or west. Now we must accept reality and return to base or we shall leave ourselves exposed to the same type of treatment in reverse."

Though he didn't like it, Hawkins had to agree the Colonel was using good sense and good judgment. He went to tell his men the sour news.

಼಼಼಼಼಼಼಼಼಼಼಼

The night after Jubal's encounter with General Jackson, it was a bone-weary Stonewall Brigade that finally made camp in an open, snow-covered field just outside a small town called Unger's Store, which was not much more than a general store with a post office and a few scattered farmhouses nearby.

Despite his near exhaustion, Jubal made the effort to seek out Captain Hill to see if he knew anything about what might come next. He found his captain's tent only a few yards away from where he'd pitched his own. The captain had already lit a small campfire in front of his tent and was standing in front of it, warming his hands.

"Ah, Jubal, there you are. I was about to send for you. Had a pleasant hike today?" he asked, with a wan smile.

"None better," Jubal responded, returning the sour look. "I did get to meet General Jackson, though. So I guess it wasn't all bad."

"Oh, did you? And did he happen to tell you the news of the day?"

"No, sir. He neglected to do so, though he surely had good intentions. We were a bit busy … with some stubborn wagons and an icy hill."

33

"Yes … heard about that. Good work getting over that hump, Jubal. Sorry I wasn't there to help. Anyway, word is a large Union force under Brigadier General Benjamin Kelley has launched an attack from Romney toward Winchester even while we were trying to take Hancock."

"Oh," was all Jubal could think to say. He tried to picture a map of the area to figure what this news meant. He found it helped to think of it as a triangle—Winchester to the south, Bath and Hancock to the north, and Romney the third point off to the west, almost equally distant from the other two. "So … while we were moving out from Winchester to attack the Federals up at Hancock, they were moving to attack the very town we just left behind?"

After a frigid march, and the relatively easy investment of the town of Bath, they'd been frustrated at Hancock. Somehow Union General Lander had made it back across the Potomac with nearly the entire garrison from Bath, even though there were no bridges nor any decent fording places for miles. They still couldn't figure how he'd done it. And then to make matters worse, Lander stubbornly refused to surrender despite being badly outnumbered and having to endure two straight days of artillery bombardment across the river.

"Well, I can see how it might look that way," Captain Hill answered, "but more likely they launched their attack in reaction to ours … hoping to draw us off from our objectives. And, depending how well they do, it just might work."

"You mean us trying to take Hancock? Seems like we already failed at that one."

"No, that was just a target of opportunity. The general's main goal from the beginning was to take Romney, which gives us a strong foothold in western Virginia from which we can threaten their attempts to break up Virginia. And it gives Winchester, our district headquarters, a little breathing space from General Rosecrans, who'd likely use Romney as the launch point for his own offensive come spring."

"Ah … now it all makes a bit more sense," Jubal said. "So … then what now? Do we beat it back to Winchester to drive off the Federals?"

"I don't know. I'm sure General Jackson and his staff are discussing that question even now. Guess it's a question of who flinches first … if they take Winchester our supply lines back to the south may be cut. Likewise, if we take Romney, then General Kelley's brigade could be cut off from their side, even if they manage to take Winchester."

Then Bob Hill grinned, "But if I were a betting man, from what I know of General Jackson, I'd bet he'll not take their bait and will opt to attack rather than retreat. My guess is, we will continue our march on Romney."

ഓഴ)രുഗ്ഗഓഴ)രുഗ്ഗഓഴ)രുഗ്ഗ

"General … I just heard the news—that Lander has ordered the evacuation of Romney, without even giving Jackson a fight!" Nathan said, as he entered General Rosecrans' office in the downtown Wheeling house the Army had rented out for his headquarters. "I questioned him pulling back from the attack on Winchester, but this?!" he continued. "I thought Lander had more backbone than that."

"Yes, it's not the happiest news, but calm yourself and have a seat," Rosecrans said, gesturing toward the empty chair opposite his desk.

Nathan stood for a moment scowling, then sat heavily with a sigh.

"I know it's a bitter pill, Nathan, but I agree with Lander on this one. He just doesn't have the numbers gathered yet to take on Jackson in a place like Romney, which has little to offer in terms of defense. He's got to play it smart and preserve his troops … keep them just out of Jackson's reach so he can't close with them and destroy them. Keep pulling back, lengthening Jackson's supply lines, making him feel exposed.

"We now finally have a more accurate count of his numbers— we know he had only about 8,500 at the start of his march and has lost a good number to cold and illness along the way. So, he knows he can't possibly make it all the way to Wheeling, and now *we* know it too. If we're lucky he'll be foolish enough to pursue the Romney garrison as it withdraws, and then Lander will have time to bring together enough men for a counterpunch."

"Hmm … I don't expect Jackson to be that careless. He's aggressive, but not a fool. With those numbers, I'm sure you're right, General. He'll have to stop at Romney, and likely won't even be able to hold it for long. Not if General Banks finally gets off his lazy backside and brings his division across the Potomac."

"Agreed. So, ironically, it seems as though our evacuation of Romney will actually signal the end of Jackson's offensive, what the press is now calling his 'Romney Expedition,' and will likely have cost him much more than it has cost us."

Nathan again scowled at Rosecrans, "Hmm … seems to me, General, at the beginning of this month you were determined to attack Jackson *from* Romney and take Winchester. Now you're trying to convince me you're happy about *only* losing Romney? Seems a bit disingenuous, General."

But Rosecrans took it in good humor, and shrugged, "Things change, Nathan … things change, as you well know."

ↅↈↂↃↇↅↅↈↅↃↇↅↅↈↃↇↅↅↈↂↃↇↅ

"Ah … there you are Billy," Nathan said, as he came around the side of one of the outbuildings and found Billy sitting on the ground leaning up against the back wall, warming himself in the sun. He resisted the urge to say he'd been searching all over the farm for the last hour or more trying to locate him—that was hardly Billy's concern, after all.

"How are you feeling today?" Nathan asked, kneeling down next to him.

But instead of answering, Billy gazed at him with an odd look, then tilted his head as if pondering the question.

"You must stop doing that, Captain," he finally said in a flat tone.

"Stop doing *what*, Billy?"

Billy frowned at him. "Stop worrying over me. You are being worse than my mother ever was …"

Nathan smiled and nodded, "Well, I suppose I'm feeling responsible for getting you wounded and nearly killed, and I—"

"No! Stop, Captain … stop talking now …" Billy said and leaned his head back, closing his eyes.

For the first time in their long relationship Nathan heard anger in his friend's voice directed at him. It was puzzling, but he was wise enough to do as he was bid, so he shut his mouth and sat down next to Billy.

They sat silently for a long while—so long that Nathan began to wonder if Billy had nodded off. He'd not been his normal energetic self since returning from the snake hunting mission almost two weeks ago, and Nathan wondered if this was another symptom of his slow, painful recovery.

Finally, Billy sat up straighter, looked over at Nathan and said, "You must stop insulting me."

"*Insulting* you?! I would *never*—"

"You insult me when you say you are responsible for getting me wounded. No man is responsible for my actions … I chose to do what I do. If I am wounded, or even killed, it is by my own choice—I fight for you not because it is my sworn duty, but … because it is what I *wish* to do so.

"Your regret of using my skills dishonors and shames me. You no longer have faith in me; you no longer believe I am better than other men—that I will kill your enemies for you as I have always done before. I have failed you this time, so I will fail you again."

"But I—" Nathan's immediate gut reaction was to deny Billy's words, but then he snapped his mouth shut, suddenly realizing every word of it was true … *from Billy's perspective.* It was an epiphany for Nathan; it had never before occurred to him that his heartfelt compassion for another man might be viewed as a demeaning insult. It was an eye-opening revelation.

They sat in silence for another long moment, while Nathan fought down a very strong urge to apologize once again—this time for all the previous apologies! *No, that won't do at all,* he realized, slowly shaking his head.

He stood, turned to Billy and said, "You're absolutely right, scout—I stand corrected. It won't happen again." Without another word, he turned and strode off, leaving Billy sitting where he was.

ᔕᕮᑯᐯᔕᕮᑯᐯᔕᕮᑯᐯᔕᕮᑯᐯ

Evelyn sat at her desk reading the latest letter from Jubal, and as usual, suffering conflicting emotions over it. And once again, she debated telling Angeline and Jonathan, but then decided it was unnecessary—the only interesting item Jubal mentioned that had not already been in all the newspapers was just a rumor after all, and one Jubal himself misbelieved:

February 3, 1862
Winchester, Va.

Dear Evelyn,

I must apologize for the delay in writing you as I have been sick in bed for the last week and am finally feeling a little better. I am now able to eat and keep down my food, and have regained a little energy—at least enough to pick up a pen. But I must confess to feeling very low in general, having nothing to do with my recent illness.

After several hundred miles of marching, in the most horrible, freezing cold weather imaginable, in the end we did very little fighting, and accomplished nothing. As you can see by the address at the top of this letter, we are back where we started in Winchester. And though we successfully captured Romney during the course of our campaign, yesterday we witnessed General Loring lead his troops back into town, who'd been left behind in Romney by General Jackson. So after all that effort we have just given Romney back to the federals without even a shot fired!

But when I say we marched around and did very little fighting that doesn't mean men didn't suffer and die on the expedition—hundreds of our men have died since the start of the mission from the bitter cold and from the numerous deadly diseases that seem so eager to afflict men who are out of doors under these conditions. And of course, many others have lost fingers, toes, and whole limbs due to the dire coldness we were forced to endure.

And today, to add to our misery, a rumor has spread that General Jackson was so angry about General Loring's withdrawal from Romney that he has resigned from the Army! But though I believe the general is likely fuming mad over the whole thing, I don't believe he would just quit over it and leave us all, his loyal men, without a leader.

I pray all is well with you, and that you will find it in your heart to write me as soon as it is most convenient.

Your faithful friend,

Jubal Collins
2nd Lieutenant, 27th Virginia

ಬಡಚಿಚ್ಚಬಡಚಿಚ್ಚಬಡಚ್

Saturday February 15, 1862 – Richmond, Virginia:

"Oh, Evelyn, dear … there you are," Varina Davis said, smiling brightly. Evelyn noted how different Varina looked from the first time they'd met, when she was eight months pregnant, and clearly uncomfortable. Varina had slimmed back down and now moved with an easy grace.

"Come, I simply can't wait to introduce you to our guest of honor. She's one of my dearest long-time friends, and I'm sure the two of you will get along famously," Varina said, reaching out for Evelyn's arm.

Varina led Evelyn across the room, weaving her way between various groups of elegantly dressed women standing about sipping tea and chatting amiably. It was the very same room in the "Confederate White House" where Evelyn had been introduced to Varina the previous year. The day when Evelyn's attempt at spying on Confederate President Jefferson Davis had nearly gone disastrously wrong.

And today, as on that occasion, Angeline Hughes had arranged the whole event as a pretense to introduce Evelyn to another very special and important woman—important to their covert schemes …

"Lyd, darling … I'd like you to meet Miss Evelyn Hanson, the wonderful young lady I've been telling you about …

"Evelyn … please meet by dear friend, Lydia Johnston," Varina concluded the introduction, gesturing Evelyn forward.

Evelyn curtsied in the formal manner, and smiled brightly, "It is a pleasure and an honor to meet you, Miss Lydia. I have heard nothing but delightful things about you from Varina."

Lydia beamed. "The pleasure is all mine, Miss Evelyn. And … please, just call me Lydia; I'm sure we shall quickly become fast friends, even as Varina has said."

"Thank you, Lydia. And please, call me Evelyn. And … am I correct in understanding that your husband is the famous and gallant General Joe Johnston … in command of all the brave young soldiers even now protecting our beloved Richmond?"

Lydia smiled, and nodded, "Yes, dear. He is all *that* … fearless, heroic … a leader of men." Then she laughed, a bright, musical laugh that was very pleasant to Evelyn's ear, "to me he is just my Joseph … the man I love and who shares with me his heart and soul …" she gazed off out the window and sighed. "I miss him already. But happily, he is a very conscientious letter writer, for which I am most grateful."

Evelyn smiled. "He sounds like a wonderful man. I am very much looking forward to meeting him one day, whenever his duties allow him to visit Richmond," she said, while thinking, *General Johnston writes regular letters to his wife from the front lines — that might prove very interesting and informative …*

And then Evelyn suffered her inevitable twinge of guilt over her hidden agenda; she had immediately taken a liking to Lydia who, though nearly forty, had a pleasant, youthful manner which Evelyn found appealing. She was a good-looking woman, though not beautiful, with dark hair and eyes, a long straight nose, and good strong chin. Perhaps her most appealing feature, though, was a mouth that seemed to always have a mischievous half smile upon it.

And from what Evelyn had heard and could now plainly see, Lydia seemed a very warm and genuine person, despite her lofty station in society. In fact, Evelyn had learned from her briefing by Angeline that Lydia was the daughter of one of the wealthiest and most powerful families in the country. Her father, Louis McLane, had served in the House, the Senate, as Secretary of Treasury, and Secretary of State under President Andrew Jackson—a personal friend—and finally as Minister to England under President Polk.

And, important for Evelyn's schemes, Lydia had been raised as the closest thing to royalty one could get in the United States. In fact, when still a young child she had spent several years in England when her father was stationed there, where her family had been waited upon by a large household staff. It was said Lydia had even attended several birthday parties for Princess Victoria, now *Queen* Victoria.

So if anyone would be a good target for Evelyn's plot to plant a formally-trained servant as a spy in their household, surely it would be Lydia. The only problem Evelyn could see was that General Johnston, unlike Lydia's father, was *not* wealthy, being a career military officer. So very likely Lydia couldn't afford the type of servant Evelyn would be offering. But that was a minor concern, and Evelyn already had a plan to deal with that particular problem …

Because of Lydia's background, Evelyn and Angeline had decided to be more aggressive in their approach, thinking her likely more agreeable to the scheme than Varina, who was more ambivalent about such things. They considered Varina more of a long-term project in that regard, but one well worth working for the potential rewards. Evelyn decided to go to work on Lydia straight away, eager to see if she might take the bait.

"Lydia, I understand you've just recently arrived in Richmond … have you been able to find appropriate accommodations?"

"Oh, yes, so kind of you to ask, Evelyn. Thanks to Varina we have located a vacant house only a few blocks from here. Sadly, the owner, a colonel in our glorious southern army, gave his life to the cause at the battle of Manassas Junction last year. His wife has since moved back to live with her parents on their plantation … somewhere out to the west."

"That's good to hear—I mean about finding an available house—though it is sad about the family …"

"Yes … there's been a great deal of that sort of thing lately, I'm afraid. But let's not darken the happy mood with such talk … I am happy with our new home, for the most part, only …"

"What is it, Lydia?"

"I've … well, I'm a bit embarrassed to bring it up, but … with Joseph's military career, having to relocate frequently and often living in *Northern* cities … we've never owned any slaves. So, I'm finding with Joseph off to the war that running such a large house all by myself is a bit burdensome."

"Oh, yes … I would expect *so!*" Evelyn answered. She knew there was also the unspoken issue of the money it would cost to either buy a household slave or hire a freeman to do the work. Evelyn put on a thoughtful expression and said, "Lydia … perhaps we two could help each other in that regard …"

"Oh, how so, Evelyn?"

"Well, I don't know if Varina has told you the details of my little … *business venture* I started after I was forced to leave my mother's home?"

"No … not that I recall …"

Varina, who'd been listening in, just shrugged. Evelyn assumed it was a matter which held little interest for her, so she'd likely forgotten about it. Evelyn decided Angeline was right about Varina being a bit more of a challenge in that regard.

"Well, you see, it was shortly after a … *hmm*—well, let's just say the painful ending of what seemed a very promising courtship—my mother and I had a falling out. We disagreed about the type of men I should be seeing, and I'm afraid it turned a bit ugly." Evelyn felt oddly gratified that none of this was actually a lie. Her mother *had* been terribly upset to learn Evelyn was associating with certain men … *from the Underground Railroad!*

"That must have been very difficult and painful for you."

"Yes, it was, thank you … and with my Daddy's death a few years ago, I suddenly found myself with very little means of support. So I decided to draw upon some knowledge I had acquired concerning the proper, formal training of household servants, in the traditional manner of the European aristocracy. Fortunately, a friend of mine had a vacant house I could rent inexpensively, and so I began my little enterprise—training and supplying the very finest household servants to the most worthy families in Richmond. And I'm happy to say it has become quite successful. In fact, many of the women in this room are my happy customers, having acquired slaves who are now an indispensable part of their homes."

"How very impressive, Evelyn. I do so enjoy hearing stories of women doing great things beyond what might traditionally be expected of them. Good for you, dear. But … you said we might help each other …?"

"Yes, well … I was just remembering what Varina had told me of your family background, that you had spent time in England and had had servants there … do I assume correctly that you also have a great deal of knowledge in the formal manners expected of very high-end servants?"

"Well … yes, I suppose I do, though I never thought of it that way before."

"Oh, wonderful! You see, I presently find myself with several household servants who are *nearly* ready to send out on their own, but it is a lot of work on my part to put on those last finishing touches, if you understand what I mean."

"Yes … I can well imagine it …"

"So, it just now occurred to me … I might provide you with some helpful labor in the form of a very bright young woman I am currently working with, and in return you could finish up her formal training for me. It would be a great help to me, Lydia, if you'd be willing to do it."

Lydia looked thoughtful a moment, and said, "Oh … I don't know if I could accept—"

But Evelyn interrupted to sweeten the pot, not wanting to risk a rejection, "Lydia, before you say more, I must confess … it had occurred to me having such a prestigious family as yours for a client would be … *invaluable* to the reputation of my business. You would really be doing me a very great favor in that regard as well."

Lydia turned to Varina and smiled brightly, "Well, my dear, you certainly spoke truly when you said I would be happy to meet Evelyn." She turned back to Evelyn and said, "I would be happy to help, Evelyn. And that is a more than generous offer on your part. I must admit, I feel as if a great burden has been lifted from my shoulders. And I will be more than happy to do what I can to finish your young woman's training. Thank you, Evelyn."

"No, thank *you*, Lydia. You will be doing me a very great service, I assure you," Evelyn answered. *Yes, a very great service … much more than you know,* she thought and continued to smile.

🙢🙠🙢🙠🙢🙠🙢🙠🙢🙠🙢🙠

Several hours later, as the party was breaking up and the ladies were making their way out the formal front entrance, and down the broad steps that led to the gardens and a walkway out to Twelfth Street, Evelyn found a moment to have a quiet word with someone she'd wanted to speak with for some time—Varina's butler, and slave—a man named Hank.

"Hello, Hank," she said quietly, glancing over at him where he stood in a fine black suit at the edge of the doorway. His strong, handsome face and intense eyes would've marked him as a younger man had not the touch of gray at his temples betrayed him as middle aged. She graced him with a quick smile before turning away. He leaned forward, pretending to assist her with straightening her shawl.

"Hello again to you, Miss Evelyn," he answered quietly. And though he kept a straight face, she thought he smiled with his eyes.

"I have been thinking of you, Hank, and have not forgotten our little ... *agreement*." Hank had caught her going through Jefferson Davis's desk months ago on her first visit to the house. He'd agreed not to expose her for a spy if she agreed to help him escape to the North if and when the time came for him to seek his freedom. They'd seen each other since, of course, on several occasions when Evelyn had visited Varina, but they hadn't spoken since their first encounter.

"Likewise, Miss Evelyn," he answered, brushing the back of her shawl gently as if removing a bit of lint, before stepping away.

"Hank ... I have a favor to ask of you. It will cost you but little and may be of great help to our ... *mutual interest*."

He gave the slightest nod but said nothing, as she pretended to straighten the hair around her face and up under her bonnet.

"There may come a time when there will be a suggestion of bringing a highly skilled and trained domestic slave into Miss Varina's household. I want you to be supportive of the idea."

He raised an eyebrow at this and looked thoughtful for a moment. Again, he gave the slightest of nods before turning and stepping over to assist other ladies coming out at the door.

Evelyn smiled, then walked down the stairs and out to the street, where Angeline waited with her carriage.

༄ༀ༄ༀ༄ༀ༄ༀ༄ༀ༄ༀ༄ༀ

February 18, 1862 – Wheeling, Virginia:

"Sorry I'm late," Nathan said as he came up the outside steps of the Customs House, taking them two at a time, Harry the Dog bounding up behind him. "Did I miss anything important?"

Tom and Margaret were just coming out the door, and she crossed her arms and scowled at him. But Tom chuckled and said, "Nothing much ... just the final vote on the new constitution."

Nathan looked surprised for a moment, then nodded and said, "Oh, well ... as long as that's all it was!" he grinned, looked over at Margaret and shrugged apologetically.

45

"Nathan ... they finally brought it to a vote, and it passed ... without a single word concerning slavery!" she said, sounding exasperated.

"Ah ... I see. Well, that's disappointing ..."

"Disappointing? More like a disaster," she answered, continuing to frown.

"Hmm ... maybe ... but don't forget, Margaret, constitutions can be amended ... and most usually are."

She was thoughtful for a moment, then seemed to relax a bit, "True ..." Then she finally smiled, "All right, leave it to you, Nathan, to find the silver lining on the dark cloud."

He returned her grin, "You're welcome. I suppose John Carlile had the last say on the matter and carried the day? But were you able to persuade our other esteemed senator, Mr. Wiley, to argue for our side?"

"Yes, I did, and he did, but ... I'm afraid he's not a very persuasive speaker ... or man, for that matter. Everyone listened to him politely of course, but nobody's mind was changed, of that I'm certain," she answered.

"But it didn't *all* go against us," Tom reminded her.

"True ... they did ratify the public education article, and that's something to be proud of. I believe it may be the first of its kind in the nation, granting free universal public education to all school-age children—and expressly including black freemen children."

"Well, now that's something to celebrate, after all! Come on, let's go straight home and do so ... I believe there's a perfectly good bottle of whiskey and several cigars calling my name," Nathan said, and gestured for Margaret to descend the stairs.

⁕⁕⁕

Friday, March 14, 1862 – Wheeling, Virginia:

The Chambers' family dinner was winding down, and Nathan had pushed his chair back, feeling satisfied, when he remembered something he'd meant to ask Tom. "Hey, Tom ... didn't you say we received a letter from Captain Hawkins this afternoon?"

"Oh! Yes ... thank you for reminding me, sir," Tom answered, and reached into his vest pocket to retrieve it. "I have it right here ... shall I read it?"

"Yes please," he answered, and everyone paused to listen:

March 3, 1862
Paw Paw Tunnel, Va.

Dear Mr. Chambers,

I'm sure by the time you receive this letter you will have already heard the tragic news of the death of our beloved commander, Brigadier General Frederick Lander, who died yesterday after a prolonged illness. The entire command is in a state of shock and grief over it.

The general took ill after leading us on a successful attack against rebel guerillas and bushwhackers who'd gathered at Bloomery Gap, about fifteen miles south of here. He became so ill at one point he sent a telegram to the War Department asking to be relieved of his command so he could recover in hospital. I happened to be in his command tent when he received the reply from General McClellan denying his request. I couldn't believe it and am still feeling angered over it, but General Lander just shrugged his shoulders and went about his duty. Such a tragic, unnecessary loss of a truly great man. I don't know when I shall ever get over the pain of it.

And to catch you up on all the actions of the Seventh since I last wrote, I will start with our disappointing withdrawal, first from our very promising "reconnaissance" toward Winchester, followed by the demoralizing news that we were subsequently abandoning Romney to the rebels.

Before that bitter news we'd heard we would be going up against the rebels' so-called "Stonewall Brigade" that we'd heard so much bragging on, and I can tell you the entire Seventh was just itching to have a go at them. But

"*McClellan again!*" Nathan said angrily. "I'd already heard the terrible news about Lander, of course, but *this* ..." he growled, a dark frown creasing his brow.

"One more black mark in an ever-growing list against our good friend George B. McClellan," Tom said, nodding his agreement.

Miss Abbey shook her head sadly, "I can't believe he just let General Lander die like that ... it seems so ... unnecessary."

Nathan continued to scowl, "Apparently relieving Lander didn't fit with McClellan's plans, so he wouldn't approve it. The man truly only ever thinks of himself," he concluded, and then reached into his pocket, pulled out a cigar and began to chew on it, continuing to scowl.

"Well, at least there has been good news recently," Tom said, trying to lighten the mood, "I hear Stonewall Jackson has pulled back from Winchester, and Union General Banks has seized the town, so the rebel winter offensive has been a near complete failure. Perhaps we've finally seen the last of your old classmate Thomas Jackson in western Virginia."

Nathan was thoughtful for a moment, then said, "Hmm ... so it would appear ... but I wonder—" but if he had more thoughts on the matter, he kept them to himself.

"And what do you think about McClellan's monumental Army of the Potomac he's been building, sir?" Tom asked. "They say he has organized, equipped, and drilled one of the largest armies every assembled on the continent—well over 100,000 men!"

"Yes ... I will give credit where credit is due ... George does know how to build a fine-looking army," Nathan answered.

"But will he ever put it to good use, is the question," Tom said.

"Hmph ... I suspect if it was up to him the answer would be 'no'—he'll forever need one more artillery battery, one more cavalry company, one more infantry regiment, and on and on."

Tom smiled, and nodded his agreement.

But the two military men were surprised when it was Megs who spoke up to end the discussion, saying, "Well, the good news is, I don't reckon it's up to Mr. McClellan whether he do or he don't. I reckon at some point Mr. Lincoln is gonna lose his patience and put a boot to the general's backside."

Nathan turned to her and smiled, "Amen to that Megs. Amen to that!"

Chapter 3. A Web of Deception

"Oh! what a tangled web we weave
When first we practice to deceive!"
– Sir Walter Scott

Tuesday March 18, 1862 – Fort Monroe, Virginia:

Union Major General George B. McClellan leaned against the lighthouse railing gazing out across the waterway spread before him. His neatly cut dark hair streamed back in a steady sea breeze that'd forced him to remove and hold his crisp blue kepi hat, lest it be blown away.

"It's a glorious sight, General!" Brigadier General Fitz Porter said, leaning forward to join McClellan at the curved metal railing, holding his own hat on by the brim.

McClellan turned to him, smiled, and nodded. "Indeed it is, Fitz—a spectacular sight." He took a deep breath of the tangy air, then turned back toward the water—this time looking all the way to his far left, then slowly panning almost a complete circle to his right, taking in the full, magnificent vista—the vast waterway of Hampton Roads, one of the world's largest natural harbors, or "roadsteads," at its intersection with Chesapeake Bay off the Virginia Peninsula. Directly behind the lighthouse the massive stone walls of Union-held Fort Monroe loomed across a wide man-made moat.

And as spectacular as the busy waterway might be on a *normal* day, *this* day it had taken on a whole new dimension and significance. Hundreds of ships of all description and size filled the waterway, completely surrounding the tiny outcropping of land that hosted the fort. Stately three-masted ships of war, their sails billowing out, dazzling white in the bright sunlight, mixed with sailing ships that featured added steam engines, their telltale smokestacks protruding amidships. And more modern, mastless steamers, low-slung and bristling with guns along their sides, sailed next to even more modern, armor-plated vessels, sleek and deadly looking. And this vast fleet of warships was joined by dozens of commercial transports of varying shapes, sizes, and modes of propulsion—anything that could transport troops and materiel.

Two other generals, Brigadier General Randolph Marcy, McClellan's chief of staff—and father-in-law—and Brigadier General John Wool, commander of the U.S. Army Department of Virginia headquartered at Fort Monroe, were also on the lighthouse platform with McClellan and Porter. While Marcy was older than the first two generals by more than twenty years, General Wool was by far the senior member of the group at seventy-seven years of age. But Wool, unlike his contemporary, the recently retired Commanding General Winfield Scott, was neither obese nor in ill health; on the contrary, he was tall, lean and vigorous-looking, with the stern, forceful visage reminiscent of an eagle on the hunt.

Marcy stepped up behind McClellan and said, "I can't help thinking it's an odd-looking mix of the old and new, George. As if the ships of the sea are in the midst of a painful transition from sail to steam, and from wood to iron."

McClellan nodded, and said, "It makes me think of the awkward transition one suffers in his late teens; he is no longer a child, but not yet a man ..."

Marcy raised an eyebrow at this, but said nothing, thinking it was likely a very personal observation on the part of George McClellan, who'd been something of a child prodigy, famously enrolling at West Point at the tender age of fifteen.

Then Porter said, "Damn, I wish I could've been here to see that battle of the ironclads, *Monitor* and *Merrimack* ... this would've been a wonderful place to watch the show ..."

"*It was!*" General Wool said, joining the conversation for the first time.

This pronouncement made all three other generals turn toward him with interest.

"Of course, General Wool ... I'd forgotten you would've been here when it happened," Porter said.

"Yes … for much of the battle I stood on this very spot with my spyglass, watching the two ships hammer away at each other, neither seemingly able to penetrate the other's armor.

"It was … the dawning of a new era in the long history of war at sea. The Confederate ironclad *Merrimack* … now named *Virginia*, I understand … tore through our wooden sailing vessels like the proverbial hot knife through butter, until our own armored vessel *Monitor* finally arrived and came to their rescue.

"Yes, gentlemen … standing on this very spot just ten days ago I witnessed the very death-knell of wooden-hulled ships of war, now proven to be utterly obsolete."

McClellan nodded, a slight smile touching his lips, as he resisted a very strong urge to add, "… even as you clearly are, Wool," to the septuagenarian general.

Fitz Porter turned and gazed back at the tremendous fleet of ships filling every quay surrounding the fort, anchored offshore waiting their turn, or transporting their men and equipment to the beach via smaller, shallow-draft boats. Every square inch of shoreline was teeming with men, wagons, horses, and equipment being unloaded and brought ashore. "They're saying it's the greatest shipborne invasion force ever assembled in North America, and likely the world …" he said, awestruck.

But McClellan turned to Porter with a scowl, "Pray it shall be enough, General," he said, and snorted.

This statement seemed to greatly surprise General Wool, who gave McClellan a look of incredulity. "Whatever would prompt you to say such a thing, General McClellan?" he asked. "From the reports I've read you have arranged to bring to this peninsula more than 120,000 soldiers, tens of thousands of horses, several hundreds of cannons, and enough ammunition, food, and equipment to support same for several months, with more of everything readily supplied by sea as needed. Surely you don't think such a formidable force will prove insufficient to defeat the rebels and take Richmond?"

"General Wool, I don't need to tell you … no matter how many men you have, it may prove insufficient if the enemy has *more* men who are well-supplied and fortified in a defensible position."

"More men, General? How could you think ...? General, my own scouts tell me this peninsula is ripe for the taking, with woefully inadequate defensive fortifications and a serious shortage of soldiers and artillery. Did the War Department not pass along to you my most recent report on enemy troop strength positioned in front of us? If not, I will tell you ... we estimate the enemy at Yorktown has less than 15,000 men ... our best guess being 13,000, and no sign of imminent reinforcement arriving or major fortification being constructed across the peninsula."

"Yes, I have seen your report, General Wool. But that information is now nearly a fortnight old. Troops can be moved, artillery can be carted, fortifications can be built ... things can change."

Wool snorted, "I rode out myself not two days ago, accompanying our scouts to within eye view of Yorktown. And I could detect no discernable difference in the enemy's deployment from what I presented in my recent report to the secretary."

McClellan gave Wool a look filled with contempt, "Well, General, perhaps it could be your powers of observation are ... *not what they used to be*, shall we say?"

Wool's face turned red and twisted in anger. "You may be my superior officer — *for the moment* — General McClellan, but I'll not stand here and be insulted by *you* — or any other man, for that matter! I can outride, outdrink, and *outfight* any man here, and will be more than happy to *prove* it ... *sir!* I may have had a few more journeys around the sun than is typical, but I still have what it takes ... here," he said, pounding his fist against his heart. "Which I suspect is more than can be said for some *younger* men! Good day to you, *sir!*"

He turned and strode for the ladderway, departing without another word. McClellan turned to the other two generals, chuckled, and rolled his eyes. They smiled and nodded, turning back to the view of the incoming ships.

৪৩৪৩৫৫৩৪৩৪৫৫৩৪৩৪৫৫৩

Two days later McClellan met with generals Porter and Marcy in his command office in a building inside Fort Monroe. This time

McClellan did *not* invite General Wool—the two had not spoken since they'd had words up on the lighthouse, and McClellan was not inclined to be the first to reach out, nor was he in the mood to apologize.

And conspicuously absent against all tradition and protocol, McClellan's three corps commanders, Generals Sumner, Heintzelman, and Keyes were also excluded from the meeting. McClellan wasn't interested in their advice or input; when the time came, he would issue them their orders and expect them to obey—the men he needed to pass along those orders and get things organized were already in this room.

And if the two generals present were surprised a civilian was included in their strategy session, they didn't express it. The civilian, dressed in a fine, dark gray suit, was a large, imposing man who appeared to be in his mid-forties with dark but thinning hair and a thick, full beard.

"Gentlemen, I believe you have met Allan Pinkerton ..." McClellan began, "Mr. Pinkerton is tasked with providing us with more ... *accurate* ... enemy troop counts than what we've received to date. Frankly, gentlemen, I have no faith in General Wool's assessment—if not completely suffering from age-induced senility, he is very close. Nor do I believe the numbers supplied by Washington—*they* are not here, *we* are.

"Pinkerton, it is my belief, based on certain intelligence I have received, that even now General Johnston marches toward Yorktown with over 100,000 men under his command. At the same time General Beauregard is moving up from the Carolinas with 65,000 more. And key to the rebel strategy, General Jackson is even now marching south from the Shenandoah Valley with his five divisions—approximately 45,000 men and 200 artillery pieces, to catch us in a pincer.

"Gentlemen, these are the *realistic* numbers we are facing, and which Mr. Pinkerton is tasked with verifying—well over 200,000 men, well-equipped, I believe he will prove. And yet Washington insists we have more than enough men to take Richmond! Pray we may soon talk some sense into them, and that they will send us the reinforcements we so desperately need for the success of our current venture. In the meantime … let us move over to the map and discuss what we shall do for now … with what little men and materiel we *do* have."

Tuesday March 25, 1862 – Richmond, Virginia:

"Miss Eve … sorry to interrupt, but Miss Julia is here."

"Oh good; right on schedule. Thank you, Jacob," Evelyn said, setting down her pen and looking up from her desk where she'd been working through the mundane paperwork required to run her household and business. "Please, send her in … it will be a nice break from this … *tedium*," she said with a scowl that made the older white man chuckle. Jacob was her majordomo—the jack of all trades handyman who took care of everything, whether asked to or not: the type of man every business needed around, in Evelyn's opinion. Every day she was grateful that Jonathan had leant him out to her.

A minute later, Julia, an attractive, middle-aged black woman, entered the office, gave Evelyn a serious look, and curtsied in the formal manner. Evelyn scowled, raised an eyebrow, and then … laughed. Julia shared the laugh with her; the curtsy was part of Julia's act as a formal household slave for Lydia Johnston, wife of Confederate Major General Joseph Johnston. Julia was, in fact, a freeman educated in reading and writing by her altruistic former mistress who had used her for a nanny until her children were teens and then freed her. She was also a spy working for Evelyn on behalf of the Union war effort. Everything she knew about being a formal household servant had been taught her by Evelyn, and more recently by Lydia herself.

"Please have a seat, Julia. How have you been, my dear?"

But Julia surprised her by shaking her head and beaming brightly, "Oh no, Miss Eve … I can't sit just now—too excited to show you what I've brought you!" she said breathlessly, reaching up her sleeve and pulling out several tightly folded sheets of paper.

This pronouncement immediately brought Evelyn to her feet. She quickly moved around the desk as Julia unfolded the papers and spread them out on the surface.

"It's not the original, of course, though I was sorely tempted to just take it. But I remembered you telling me it was too risky — that it might be missed. So I waited until Miss Lydia was out of the house, and I copied it down, word for word on a new sheet of paper, just as you'd instructed."

"Good, good. Well done, Julia … you did the right thing …"

Julia smiled and nodded, then pointed down at the desk, "Read it! Read it, Miss Eve!" she said.

Evelyn leaned over and read:

> *March 21, 1862*
> *Rappahannock Station, Va.*
>
> *My dearest love, Lydia:*
>
> *I am always reluctant to trouble you with the details of military and political issues, but there are times when I feel I simply must unburden myself of my anxieties in that regard or I shall burst. And you are the only person whom I trust implicitly, and who I know will understand and appreciate the truth of what I am telling you through our long years of discussing such matters in depth.*
>
> *The present military situation concerning General McClellan's invasion of the Virginia peninsula along with the potential for additional Union armies attacking in coordination from the North, trouble me greatly. While long-standing military strategic doctrine, and even normal everyday common sense, dictates the defender who is vastly outnumbered should contract his lines of defense for mutual support, shortening of supply lines, and concentration of force, Jeff Davis and General Lee insist on doing entirely the opposite! They argue we should not give the Union an inch of our ground, contending that territory paid for in blood should not be so lightly given back to the enemy.*

While I appreciate the sentiment, of course, the logic is ludicrous, as you well know. Our present numbers simply do not allow us the luxury of such an over-extended line of defense. The enemy will simply push through and into our rear echelons at any point he chooses, and when that happens the rout is on, and all is lost.

To give you an idea how bad the situation is, while Davis and Lee force us to commit troops to defending the line of the Rappahannock River rather than pulling back closer to Richmond, say on the south bank of the Chickahominy, General Magruder, who is tasked with holding the line against McClellan on the peninsula at Yorktown and along the Warwick River, has only 11,000 men under his command against a Federal force estimated to be well over 100 thousand! Not to mention their abundance of artillery, ammunition, and supplies—and their advantage on the water, where their gunboats can bombard our troops almost at will whenever and wherever they wish.

Magruder is using his talents as an amateur thespian in an attempt to fool the Yankees into thinking he has more troops, more artillery, and better fortifications than he actually has – marching men around in circles, erecting cannons made of wood, and making all amounts of construction noise and dust pretending to erect fortifications that simply don't exist!

Now, rather than doing the sensible thing and pulling back Magruder and all available forces into a tight, impregnable ring surrounding Richmond proper, they talk of sending me out onto the peninsula to reinforce Magruder in his futile attempt to hold back the great tide the Union is marching against us! What hope we have of stemming that tide I can't imagine. I know you will tell no one of this, but my intention is to pull back and consolidate all our forces, even as I have argued, at the very first sign of a Union attack on Yorktown, which is simply indefensible.

And perhaps the most bitter pill in all of this, and the point which has caused the most heated debate among us, is the use of General Jackson and his armies. Rather than draw him back toward Richmond to lend his invaluable aid to its defense, they intend to send him on a fool's errand, randomly attacking in a general northerly direction down the Shenandoah Valley in hopes of frightening Lincoln into withdrawing armies from McClellan's offensive! It is a rash gamble which, in my opinion, will bear no fruit and will only deprive us of forces we desperately need in our darkest hour.

I must say once again, how sorry I am to trouble you with these burdens, but I have no one else to talk to, other than subordinates, which would be highly inappropriate of me.

You are, as always, my trusted confidant, and of course, the true love of my life.

Your devoted husband and servant of the heart,

Joseph.

Evelyn stood up and gazed wide-eyed at Julia, "Oh my dear God, Julia! You've done it … you've … you've found the *Holy Grail!*"

"The Holy *what?!*"

Evelyn grinned, and slowly shook her head, "Never mind … it's *wonderful* … fantastic even. Why, Julia, do you realize … this information—in General McClellan's hands—will very likely win the war?!"

৪৩৪৩৫৪৫৪৩৪৩৪৫৪৩৪৫৪৩৪৩৪৫৪৩

"But Jonathan, I don't understand," Evelyn said, setting down her cup of tea after taking a sip and deciding it still needed to cool a bit. "Why not just send the information to your contacts in the Union War Department, and be done with it? They can forward the information to General McClellan and … and … well, then he will very likely take Richmond within mere days, destroying the better part of the Confederate Army in the process."

Jonathan stood, gave Angeline a look, then began pacing the room before answering. Finally he turned back toward Evelyn and said, "A month ago I would've agreed with you, and done exactly that. But … we've received some troubling information from our sources since then …"

"What sort of information?"

"That Secretary of War Stanton and General McClellan are at odds over strategy. Specifically, that the secretary insists McClellan has more than enough men and munitions to launch a decisive offensive against Richmond, while McClellan insists he is still outnumbered and needs a large influx of additional reinforcements to guarantee success. Of course, the former viewpoint would lend credence to the idea of an aggressive, fast-moving assault, while the latter would indicate the need for a more cautious approach to prevent a potential disaster. It is not clear which side of the debate Lincoln falls on, but given what I know about politicians, I suspect he would prefer a more aggressive timeline."

"Well … then wouldn't our new information, in the form of General Johnston's letter to his wife, help to decide the debate in the secretary's favor? Convince General McClellan he truly has nothing to fear from the enemy?" Evelyn asked.

"It's a reasonable assumption, and I agree it will likely be the case … *if* the information is presented to him properly," Jonathan said.

"Properly? What do you mean?"

Angeline answered this time. "We fear … if the information comes to McClellan via the War Department, or even the White House, he will simply dismiss it out of hand as a thinly veiled attempt to get him to move more quickly, against his better judgment. It may appear … a little *too* convenient that the secretary just *happened* to miraculously acquire the specific and vital piece of information he needed to decide the debate in his favor."

"Ah … I see what you mean. Then how can we get around that?" Evelyn asked.

"I have some thoughts," Angeline answered. "First, it is clear we must deliver this information into General McClellan's own hands ourselves, using our own agents and not anyone connected with the Union government."

"Yes … agreed. Then what? Why would he believe our people any more than he would believe his own government?"

"We must … convince the general of our honesty, integrity, and sincerity. We must provide *proof* that we are who we say we are and that we are only motivated to provide him with truthful intelligence."

Evelyn looked thoughtful, "Yes … like we did with Miss Abbey when Mr. Chambers was lost in the woods … a *testimonial*, say, from someone he trusts?"

"Yes, exactly."

"But Angeline … who could possibly vouch for us here in Richmond?" Evelyn asked, and immediately thought of Nathan, remembering he and McClellan had been classmates at West Point. But she quickly dismissed the idea—Nathan was too far away, and currently out of reach with the war heating up.

Angeline tilted her head and smiled, "I … have an idea, but it will take some arranging … I'll not say more until I've made a few inquiries."

"All right, that's fair," Evelyn said.

They were quiet and thoughtful for several moments, then Evelyn announced, "*I* should be the one to deliver the message to General McClellan."

"*What?!* Oh, certainly *not*, Evelyn," Jonathan answered, sitting up in his chair. "It is *far* too dangerous. It's very likely there will be actual warfare going on in the areas that must be traversed."

"And what of it? Is a man more bulletproof than a woman? I have already participated in dangerous and risky operations. I don't see how this is any different," Evelyn answered.

"But Evelyn … sneaking into Jefferson Davis' office is one thing, but … crossing belligerent, heavily defended lines in the middle of a battle is … something else entirely …" Jonathan said, becoming a little red in the face.

"Don't forget, dear … the incident with the confederate agents …" Angeline interjected, "Evelyn has proven herself quite resourceful … even in dire and violent situations."

Jonathan looked over at her, mouth agape. "I … I assumed you'd side with me on this one, Ang … I …" he looked down and shook his head slowly.

"Look, Jonathan … there are a number of advantages to sending a woman," Evelyn said. "First, she is less likely to be suspected of espionage, so can more easily evade suspicion. And then, if caught, a man would be hanged for spying, while a woman will only be imprisoned, so it's a lesser risk."

"Yes, yes … I know all that, but …" he looked up at her, and she could see his eyes were slightly watery, and it touched her. He gazed up at the ceiling for a long moment, before looking back at her.

"I … never had a daughter you see," he continued in a softer tone, "four sons, but no daughters, though I always wished for one …" he looked over at Angeline, who smiled and nodded.

"Anyway … Angeline and I have … well, we've come to think of you as the daughter we never had, Evelyn … you are … everything we would have wished for in that regard. I … I just don't want to lose you," he concluded in almost a whisper, his voice betraying strong emotions such as Evelyn had not heard from him before.

She wiped back a tear, and answered, "I am touched … truly, Jonathan … Angeline. I have become so very fond of you as well, and am now closer to you than to my own mother, as you well know.

"But … you must allow me to do what I *must* do, regardless of the risk. Even as my mother has been forced to do," she concluded. But in her mind she added, *And even as dear Nathan has been forced to do!*

☙❧☙☙❧☙❧❧☙❧☙❧☙❧☙☙❧❧

Two days after her meeting with the Hughes, Evelyn received a cryptic message from Angeline, delivered by one of her regular couriers. The note said to come the next day at a certain time to a specific address in Richmond and stated that she should not tell anyone where she was going and should make sure to arrive and depart "unobserved."

The following day, she left several hours ahead of the specified time so that she could stop off and visit her longtime friend Belinda, whom she hadn't seen in several weeks.

Belinda's home was a modest, two-story house in downtown Richmond, not far from Evelyn's mother Harriet's house. Belinda shared the home, of course, with her newlywed husband Oliver, when he wasn't away to the war, as he was at present.

As she entered the foyer, Evelyn could see that her friend was clearly upset. "What is it, dear one?" Evelyn asked.

"I received a letter from Ollie today and I …" she began to tear up, and couldn't continue, but handed the letter over to Evelyn to read.

Evelyn quickly read through the short letter and looked up. "Oh my … General Joseph Johnston is ordered to the peninsula to stop General McClellan's invasion. And Ollie is one of General Johnston's staff officers … which means …"

"Yes … my Ollie will be in the very most dangerous place to be in the whole entire war!" she said, and began sobbing uncontrollably.

Evelyn stepped up and wrapped her arms around her friend. Then she too began to cry, suddenly wracked with guilt over what she was about to do—betray General Johnston to the Union Army … and Ollie with him!

৪৩৫৫৫৪৩৫৫৪৩৫৫

When Evelyn arrived at the address from Angeline's note, she wasn't particularly surprised when a well-dressed black maid greeted her at the door of the upper-class home with a curtsy—introducing herself as Mary.

Mary led Evelyn to a sitting room, where Angeline rose to her feet and greeted her warmly before introducing her to their hostess, a woman in her mid-forties named Elizabeth Van Lew. Elizabeth had dark hair tied up in a bun on the back of her head, a thin face, but a ready smile and bright, sparkling eyes. Evelyn took an instant liking to Elizabeth.

But now that introductions had been made, and small talk exchanged, Evelyn began to wonder why all the secrecy. After all, it was perfectly normal for either she or Angeline—or both—to have tea with another upper-class woman in the middle of the day! But she was confident Angeline would explain it all in good time, so she focused on getting to know Elizabeth a little better and forcibly kept her curiosity in check.

"Evelyn, I have told Elizabeth about our little ... *endeavors* ... and your recent, wonderful success in that regard."

Evelyn raised an eyebrow at this, but said, "So ... I take it we are all ... on the same side in the present conflict?"

Elizabeth laughed, "If you are asking if I am a sworn abolitionist, violently opposed to the Slave Power and the secession and everything it stands for, a devoted supporter of the Union cause, and a willing aid to its soldiers ..." she laughed again, "the answer is clearly, 'yes.'"

Evelyn looked at Angeline, who smiled brightly, nodded her head and crossed her arms in a self-satisfied gesture. Evelyn returned the smile and slowly shook her head. "I take it, Elizabeth, you have made no secret as to where your loyalties lie?"

Elizabeth chuckled again, "Yes, you could safely say that, Evelyn. I have been an outspoken critic of the slavers, both before and after the secession, and an unashamed and vocal proponent of the Union cause."

"A ... different approach to supporting the same cause," Angeline said, still smiling.

Elizabeth returned the smile and nodded, "Yes, it would seem so, Angeline. Though it's not my way, clearly ... I have to say I'm impressed with how well you've kept the secret of your loyalties. I had no idea of it until we spoke yesterday ... assumed you and your husband were the very picture of a Slave Power family."

"That's the idea," Angeline said with a more serious look.

"Oh ... and in case you were wondering, Evelyn," Elizabeth said, "Mary, who greeted you at the door, along with two other servants in this house, are paid freemen, *not* slaves—freed by my own hand when I inherited my father's house and business a few years back. That too is no secret ... unlike with Angeline's 'employees.'"

"I'm very happy to hear it, Elizabeth," Evelyn responded sincerely.

"Evelyn, I have been thinking of involving Elizabeth in our activities for some time," Angeline said, "but the right opportunity hadn't presented itself until now."

Evelyn looked at her with curiosity, but said nothing, allowing Angeline to continue her explanation.

"The other night when we were discussing how to gain a testimonial that might put us in good standing with General McClellan, I thought of Elizabeth."

Elizabeth nodded in acknowledgment.

"You see ... Elizabeth has become a bit of a fixture at Libby Prison," she continued.

"Where they hold the Union prisoners of war?" Evelyn asked.

"Yes, that's right," Elizabeth answered, "I believe in putting my money where my mouth is, so to speak, and have been going there regularly to give whatever aid and comfort I may to the Union soldiers held there. The money, by the way, is to bribe the guards into allowing me to continue doing it ..."

"And one of those Union prisoners of war happens to be a West Point graduate who was at the academy during the same time as McClellan," Angeline explained, "so the two were most certainly well-acquainted."

"His name is Colonel Augustus Adams," Elizabeth added, "he was captured at the Manassas battle."

"Ah ... now it's starting to make sense ... and do you think this Colonel Adams will help us by writing a testimonial, Elizabeth?" Evelyn asked.

"Of course he will," she answered with a grin, "aside from the fact he's a good, loyal Union officer ... I bring him home-baked pie once a week!"

"So everything is now in place, Jonathan?" Evelyn asked, as she slipped the neatly folded testimonial up her sleeve, then took another sip of tea.

"Yes ... expecting that Miss Elizabeth would come through with the Colonel's letter as promised, we've gone ahead and arranged for a fishing boat to take you down the James to Hampton Roads where the Union Navy patrols. You'll start out at night, the day after tomorrow. One of the blockading Union vessels should intercept you, and then ... well, then you must just talk them into taking you to General McClellan."

Then he smiled for the first time during their discussion, "And I have no doubt about your ability to succeed with *that* part of the mission, my dear!"

"Yes ... I can imagine I will likely have some good success convincing the Union sailors to ... *assist* me," she said, and chuckled. But then she thought, *Maybe I'm getting a little too good at this.* Then she had another thought and asked, "Jonathan ... do you trust this fisherman?"

"No ... certainly *not*," he answered and frowned. "Ironically, my shipping company owns dozens of boats, but none I can use for this purpose—they'd be too obvious and raise too much suspicion with the Union Navy controlling the riverways. No, I don't know this fisherman, and I have a hard time trusting someone who's willing to break the law for money, but ..." he shrugged, "what can I do? I can't exactly put an advert in the newspaper."

"True ... we'll just have to ... hope for the best, I suppose," she answered.

Angeline nodded her agreement, but gave Evelyn a concerned look as she took another sip of tea.

Jonathan stood and walked across the room to the large desk there. He reached around the left side, and Evelyn heard a click. She was not surprised when he came back with something in his hand—she knew of the secret compartment in that part of the desk from long experience, and had even used it herself on a few occasions.

He returned to his seat and handed a small wooden box across to her.

She took it and asked, "What's this?"

"A gift … something that may prove useful on your journey, and … will help me sleep at night while you're gone," he said with a rueful grin.

She raised an eyebrow in curiosity, then opened the lid of the box. Inside was a tiny revolver, small enough to be hidden if covered by a single hand. It had a walnut handle, smooth cylinder, and octagonal barrel a little over three inches long. It had no trigger guard over the trigger, aiding in its small profile. She bounced it in her hand, impressed with its very slight weight.

She looked up and smiled, "Very nice little revolver, Jonathan … thank you. I expect this will be very easy to carry and conceal."

"Exactly what I was thinking," he said. "So I took it to the saddle maker and had him fashion a simple, glove-soft leather holster that you can strap to your forearm, though you'll likely need to cut out a seam in your sleeve to get at it," he said, handing across the holster to her. She slid the pistol into it, then held it up against her left arm, handle toward her wrist.

"Yes … yes, I think that will work very nicely," she said. "Thank you, Jonathan."

"Oh … but you haven't seen the best part yet," he said, handing her another even smaller box, this one made of cardboard.

"What's this?" she asked.

"Open it … go on," he prompted, clearly excited for her to see whatever it was. Angeline shook her head and rolled her eyes.

Evelyn opened the small box and saw it contained a whole lot of tiny brass cylinders, each less than an inch long and no bigger around than a pencil. Each cylinder was flat on one end, and round on the other. The round end appeared to be fashioned of lead rather than brass.

"What is this?" she asked, holding one up and gazing at it closely.

"That, my dear, is the future," he answered, "a fully-integrated bullet cartridge."

"Bullet cartridge? But … how does it work?" she asked, wide-eyed.

"Well, you see, the gunpowder is contained inside the brass cylinder, and the flat end has a percussion cap built into it. The round end, of course, is the lead bullet. Here … let me show you how to load it … it's really quite ingenious," he said, the proceeded to press the tiny latch at the base of the barrel, allowing it to pivot upward exposing the cylinder, which he then removed.

"You insert the cartridges from the back, like so," he inserted one to demonstrate. "And then, once you've fired all seven shots, you take the cylinder back out again, and use this pin that rides under the barrel, to push the empty brass tubes out so you can put new ones in."

"Oh! How very clever. That will certainly make loading—and reloading—much simpler, quicker, and less messy," she said, genuinely impressed.

"Yes indeed, but there's another huge advantage to the integrated cartridge: it's practically waterproof, so you can leave the pistol loaded for days and never worry about the powder getting wet and fouling."

"I've never even *heard* of such a thing before. How ever did you come by it?"

"Oh, I had to smuggle it in from Boston—there are none to be had in the South. It's patented by a new company called Smith and Wesson and only comes in that small .22 caliber bullet you see there. Perfect for your purposes, but not yet potent enough for battlefield use, I'm afraid. But I'm sure one day soon they'll come out with a larger caliber version. Anyway, it'll make me sleep better at night knowing you have a little extra protection."

"And speaking of protection," Angeline said with a smile, "I too have a parting gift for you, my dear."

Then Angeline gave Evelyn a beautifully made Italian stiletto, the blade less than six inches long, as thin as her little finger, and razor sharp—another deadly weapon, if used properly.

The stiletto, like the pistol, was intended to be carried hidden; it came with a shiny, black enameled sheath with leather straps for securing it around the thigh. A secret slit inside a pocket would allow the wearer quick and easy access in need. Angeline explained she had acquired it years ago when she and Jonathan had visited Italy, but she had never had a good use for it until now.

Evelyn thanked Angeline for this gift as well, though she wasn't sure how she felt about going around with such deadly weapons strapped to her body. *Perhaps one can get used to it*, she thought, *the same as anything else …*

ℰ◯ℰ◯ℭ◯ℰ◯ℰ◯ℭ◯ℭ◯ℰ◯ℰ◯ℭ◯ℭ

Though Angeline had offered to send a carriage for her use, Evelyn had declined, choosing to walk instead. Her house was in the neighborhood of Richmond called Church Hill, which was only a half-dozen or so blocks from the wharves on the James River where the fishing boat awaited her. It would be an easy walk, downhill all the way.

And though it was a warm evening, she wore a long cape with the hood over her head to help disguise her features, not wanting to be recognized or to attract unnecessary attention. It would also help that the sun had just set, and it would soon be dark.

They'd decided Evelyn should set out at night for several reasons, all having to do with secrecy, with the main one being the new Confederate fortification seven miles downriver at a place called Drewry's Bluff. The Confederate Army had announced that there would be no civilian boats allowed downriver from Richmond due to Union naval activity on the river, and the gun emplacement at Drewry's Bluff would actively enforce that ban. And though the announcement was couched in terms of "for your own good and safety," Jonathan's sources had informed him that the government was mostly concerned about Union spies in Richmond, and wanted to stop all non-military travelers from leaving the city, especially if they were headed in the direction of the Union forces. When he'd told Evelyn this news, he'd smiled ruefully, chuckled and said, "How scandalous! Union spies in Richmond?! Who would've ever imagined such a thing?!" to which Angeline rolled her eyes, and Evelyn laughed.

So the plan was to slip the small fishing boat out at night, with its sails furled, and let it drift quietly down the river. It was a moonless night, so they hoped to slide past the fort in the dark without being noticed.

As was typical with Jonathan and Angeline, they'd tried to plan the mission as thoroughly as possible, but Evelyn felt anxious knowing there was only so much one could do before just pressing ahead and hoping for the best.

And after only two blocks, she began to believe her anxieties were *not* so ill-founded; a man in a dark suit was now following her, a half-block or so behind. She turned left at the next corner rather than continuing in a straight line toward the waterfront, to test if he was truly tailing her, or if it was just coincidental. To her relief when she came to the next intersection and quickly glanced back there was no one in sight behind her. She turned down the street to her right and continued toward the James.

She continued along this street for two more blocks, then turned right again to resume her original course. There was a tall hedgerow lining the street on her right side preventing her from seeing around the corner until she made the turn.

She stopped in startlement. The man in the dark suit stood in front of her, facing her direction, and blocking the path.

"*Oh!*" she said, "You startled me, sir!" but even as she spoke, she slipped her right hand into the slit in her left sleeve, gripping the handle of her tiny pistol.

"Sorry miss," he said, then paused a moment, gazing at her before he continued, "I was just wondering … what a fine lady like you would be doing out here alone at night …"

And though it was too dark to make out the man's features, there was something familiar about the voice, though she couldn't quite place it.

"Do I … *know* you, sir?"

He chuckled. "Could be," he said, then reached into his jacket. She flinched and nearly unholstered the pistol. But then he pulled out a cigar and a match and she relaxed a little but still kept a grip on the pistol. He struck the match and held it up to light the cigar. In its glow she saw a familiar face, and let out a sigh of relief.

"*Joseph!* Oh *my* … it's you!"

"Yes, it's me," he said, and smiled.

"Well, you gave me a bit of a fright there … what are you doing here, anyway? And why are you dressed like that? I've never seen you attired as anything but a common street beggar."

"I was … I was sent on a mission by the Employer and I … I saw a young woman walking alone in the dark and was concerned and … curious …"

"Uh huh …" she said, suddenly feeling skeptical. "And I suppose, your … *mission* … just happens to take you down to the waterfront?"

"Well … yes, as a matter of fact, it does …" he answered, but she thought she detected a smile at the corners of his eyes.

Jonathan! she thought, as a scowl creased her brow. *He sent Joseph to watch over me—despite all my arguments and justifications as to why I should go alone, the incorrigible man just smiled, agreed with me, and then … did entirely the opposite!*

But then it occurred to her Jonathan's only motive would've been concern for her safety, so she decided that was hardly something she could be angry about or hold against him.

"All right then, since you're here and we seem to be going in the same direction, we may as well walk together."

He smiled. "Agreed. Shall we?" he said, gesturing ahead with a slight bow.

A few blocks later they reached the waterfront, and started walking down the wood-planked pier toward the place where her vessel should be. But she was dismayed to see soldiers marching along the quayside watching the boats; apparently the army was serious about enforcing the announced sailing ban.

They walked casually along, arm in arm, as if they were nothing more than a couple out for an evening stroll by the river, reconnoitering the situation. But though the common soldiers paid them little mind, Evelyn noticed a man in a uniform, with sergeant's stripes on his sleeves, appeared to be eyeing Joseph with suspicion. When they came nearer, he broke away from the group of soldiers he'd been talking to and headed in their direction, a determined look on his face.

Evelyn had a bad feeling, so she paused, turned to Joseph and embraced him, leaning up to give him a quick kiss on the lips. If he was surprised, he had the presence of mind not to show it, and they stayed in their embrace until Joseph looked down at her and nodded, which she took to mean all was clear. She returned the nod, turned back in the direction they'd been headed, and they resumed their walk. The sergeant, apparently satisfied, had returned to the group of soldiers and was once again engaged in conversation.

As they reached the designated slip, they could see a small, wooden fishing boat there, somewhere around thirty-five to forty feet in length, and ten or twelve wide, with a single mast and a small cabin amidships. A barefoot, dirty-looking, middle-aged sailor sat on a stool by the railing, smoking a pipe. He eyed them as they approached, and Evelyn gave him the pre-arranged signal—a tug on her right ear followed immediately by adjusting the brim of her hat. The man nodded and gave her the return sign—removing his hat, wiping his brow, then putting it back again. But then he pointedly nodded and glanced back toward the soldiers. His meaning was clear: as long as the soldiers watched, they'd not be able to launch. Then he did an odd thing, and it took Evelyn a moment to catch his meaning; he lifted a coil of rope for a moment, then set it back down by his feet. Then she realized it was the only rope tied to the pier holding the vessel in place, and now she understood it wasn't tied to the boat. So all the sailor had to do was let go of the rope, shove off, and they would drift away down the river.

But if they tried it now, they'd be an easy target for the soldiers' rifles, despite the darkness. They would have to be several hundred yards away before they'd be lost to sight from the wharf.

As they turned and continued their stroll, Evelyn wracked her brain for a solution to this conundrum, but could come up with none. There was simply no other form of transportation that could even get her past the belligerent forces now swarming the narrow peninsula, let alone in a timely fashion. She must get aboard a boat of some kind, but as long as the soldiers were guarding the waterfront, *that* was next to impossible. And it was unlikely the Confederate Army would relent in their watchful duty as long as the Union Army remained on the offensive.

But Joseph leaned down and said in a low voice, "I have a plan to get you aboard that boat… but it will be a bit risky."

"I'm listening …" she said, noncommittally.

"I mean to cause a distraction by picking a fight with that large, serious-looking sergeant. While I have their attention, you will slip back to the boat and shove off with the fisherman. Hopefully by the time they notice your absence, the boat will be out of sight in the darkness."

"No! I don't like it, Joseph. You'll be seriously outnumbered and could get hurt. And very likely will end up thrown in jail … or worse."

He chuckled, "It wouldn't be the first time for any of those things, Miss Eve … unless you have a better idea …"

She shook her head.

"All right then, it's settled. Let's turn back toward that group of soldiers, and as soon as I have their undivided attention … you must slip away in the distraction. And Evelyn …" he said, surprising her by using her real name for the first time that evening, "Godspeed to you and … whatever you hear … don't turn back."

She saw the sincere, concerned look in his eyes, and could feel her own eyes beginning to water, "Thank you, Joseph," she whispered, "I shall not forget …"

He nodded and gave her a tight smile, but though he tried to exude confidence, she also saw trepidation there. She had great respect and admiration for Joseph; he was a man who took great personal risk on a daily basis for the sake of their cause. But the man was only human, after all, and knew he was likely to get hurt. She prayed it would not be too badly …

They turned and walked back in the direction from which they'd come, this time angling such that they'd pass close by the group of soldiers they'd seen before. When they were within a few yards of the group, Joseph surprised her by suddenly laughing out loud, as if Evelyn had just told a hilarious joke.

Several of the soldiers turned to look at him, including the burly sergeant they'd nearly had an encounter with earlier.

"Hey … what are you looking at, mister?" Joseph said, stopping to point at the sergeant, suddenly sounding highly offended.

But the sergeant just scowled and folded his arms across his chest, "I … don't know what you're talkin' about, buddy …" he answered.

"What I'm talking about is … I don't appreciate how you were looking at my wife just now …" Joseph said, taking another step toward the sergeant. Evelyn noted Joseph had slightly slurred his speech this time, sounding as if he'd had too much liquor to drink earlier.

"I wasn't looking at your wife … hadn't even noticed her … was just lookin' 'cause you was makin' such a racket."

"Oh … so *now* you claim my wife isn't worth looking at, eh? Is that it? You go from ogling her to insulting her by saying she's not good enough for you? What kind of a man talks about another man's wife that way?" Joseph answered, becoming red in the face and almost shouting, taking another step forward.

Evelyn noticed the soldiers nearest Joseph had stepped back, and were now glancing back and forth between this apparently drunken, obnoxious gentleman and their sergeant, waiting to see what would happen.

Snap out of it, Evelyn … stop being a spectator and do your part, she scolded herself, and started slowly inching backward.

"You've had too much o' the sauce old man … best go home and sleep it off 'fore ya go'n get yourself hurt," the sergeant said, the scowl now turning into a dark frown.

"The only one's gonna get hurt here … is *you!*" Joseph said, and punched the sergeant hard under the chin. The blow caught him by surprise and he staggered back and might have fallen had not two of his privates caught and steadied him. Two other soldiers immediately gripped Joseph from behind, holding him fast.

Evelyn had had to surpass a gasp when Joseph had unexpectedly punched the sergeant, but this time she remembered to do her part, and continued easing back, away from the crowd. She adopted a frightened expression such that if any of the soldiers happened to glance her way, they'd just assume she was backing away in fear of the fight. Which actually wasn't too far from the truth, now that she thought about it.

The sergeant regained his footing, shook off the privates who'd been holding him up, and said, "Let him go … we'll settle this like men …" This brought smiles to the soldiers who immediately formed a circle around the two belligerents as if they'd practiced the maneuver.

The sergeant stepped up and took a swing at Joseph who blocked the blow neatly and counter-punched, again knocking the sergeant back. But this time he was ready, and immediately bounced back, landing a hard blow to Joseph's midsection that made him gasp. This elicited a whoop of pleasure and excitement from the men gathered around; now the fight was on!

Evelyn quickly checked to make sure no one was looking her way, then turned and ran for the boat. As she ran, she heard shouts, curses, and blows being landed, followed by grunts of pain, and had to force down tears that were threatening to flow. She resisted a very strong urge to look back, knowing if she did Joseph's sacrifice might prove to be in vain.

When she neared the boat, the fisherman saw her and stood. She waved at him to start shoving off. When she reached the boat, she grabbed the railing and shoved, then vaulted over and landed with both feet under her on the deck. Afterward when she thought about it, she was surprised she hadn't gotten tangled in her skirts and fallen on her face!

Her momentum gave the boat a good start, and the fisherman added to it by pushing against the pier with a long pole. The boat slowly eased away from the dock as the sounds of the fight continued to echo down the quayside.

In minutes they were well out in the midst of the wide stream, now lost from view in the darkness. And the sounds of conflict soon faded away until they were replaced entirely by the soft sloughing of the water against the hull of the boat. Evelyn stood by the railing and watched as the lights of Richmond grew smaller and fainter behind them, a single tear making a glistening track down her cheek as they rounded a bend in the river and the city was completely lost from view.

❧❧❧❧❧❧❧❧❧

The fisherman, whose name was Cyrus, turned out to be surly and uncommunicative, which suited Evelyn just fine; she was in no mood for conversation anyway. He did offer her his cabin to sleep in, but she declined for now—she was far too wound up to even think about sleep, despite the lateness of the hour.

Cyrus told her she may as well relax, as nothing of interest would happen for the first two hours or so until they reached Drewry's Bluff. He knew this part of the river well, and could navigate it with confidence in almost complete darkness, which was a fair description of the conditions at the moment.

At Drewry's Bluff they would have to pass their one major obstacle: the Confederate fortress there with its gun emplacements, positioned to stop river traffic from moving in either direction. But Cyrus was confident in the dead of night, with the sails furled and the navigation lamps out, they'd be almost invisible to any lookouts on the bluff, and would just float on past unnoticed. So Evelyn felt little concern and tried to relax as he'd suggested.

When they were within a mile of the bluff, Cyrus told her to get inside or behind the cabin on the port side of the boat so she'd not be seen by anyone looking through a spyglass up on the bluff, if they happened to have installed some kind of light, such as was used on a lighthouse. He would likewise hide behind the wooden

75

sides of the ship until they were past. That way, even if the boat was spotted, there was a good chance they'd assume it was just a derelict that'd broken free of its moorings and was adrift down the river. To aid in that impression, he intended to free the tiller and allow the boat to spin however it would with the currents and eddies of the stream.

Evelyn did as she was bid, and hid on the outside of the cabin behind its port side wall, and peered out as the bluff loomed up out of the darkness on the starboard side. When they came to the place where the slope began to rise, Cyrus let loose of the wheel that controlled the tiller, and assumed his own hiding place behind the solid wood siding on the starboard side of the boat up under the railing. Sure enough, the little boat began to turn slowly and lazily to port. But the water was wide and smooth in this part of the river, with a slow but steady flow, so there was no concern. As the vessel turned and Evelyn began to lose the cover provided by the cabin wall, she too hunkered down behind the ship's side rails to stay out of view from the hillside now looming above. She could see the lights of the fort high overhead, but could make out few details.

It seemed as if Cyrus' simple plan was going to work; they'd drifted past the center of the hilltop fortress with no discernable reaction from its occupants.

Evelyn let out a sigh of relief, only just then realizing she'd been holding her breath from the tension. She started to rise when the boat hit hard against something and lurched suddenly to starboard, banging her against the bulkhead of the cabin. The boat shuddered hard and there was a loud squealing sound of wood on wood, and a sound of rushing water, sloshing under and around the ends of the boat and rocking it violently.

"Damn it!" Cyrus shouted, and was up on his feet rushing forward and scooping up the long pole he'd previously used to cast off the dock. "They've sunk a ship in the channel to block the way and we've struck her! Quick, bear a hand or we'll flounder!"

Evelyn got to her feet, staggering to keep her balance as the boat rocked and shuddered, squeezed between the wood of the half-submerged vessel and the rushing waters of the river, now piling up behind the suddenly stationary boat, turned sideways to the flow. Evelyn fell hard to the deck as she tried to make it across to the starboard railing. She regained her feet, gripped the railing, and made her way along it to where Cyrus stood, leaning out over the railing, the pole wedged against something dark rising up out of the water on that side.

"Take ahold and pull!" he shouted, nodding with his head toward the upper end of the pole above his own hands. But Evelyn wasn't tall enough to reach, so she threw caution to the wind, climbed on top of the solid wood siding, leaning her shins against the railing for balance, grabbed the pole with both hands and pulled, pulled, pulled, putting all her weight into it.

She felt the boat bouncing and shuddering and feared it would soon splinter into pieces, but she kept straining against the immovable wood of the pole as if her life depended on it.

And if their situation wasn't desperate enough, she could now hear shouting from above, and then a loud *pop* in the distance, followed by another, and then several more. Men in the fort had taken notice and were now shooting at them with rifles! She squealed, and flinched, but managed to hang on as something hit hard against the cabin wall just feet away, sending deadly wood splinters flying across the vessel. She wondered how long before they were targeted with the artillery.

"Pull!" Cyrus shouted, and she renewed her efforts, but the wood of the pole was still entirely unyielding. She pulled harder, and then … suddenly it gave way with a loud *squawk*, and the boat was free, bouncing and lurching sickeningly, but then leveling out and once again drifting with the river's flow. Cyrus ran back to the wheel, straightened her out, then ducked to the floor as more bullets struck the woodwork. Even as Cyrus had been moving toward the wheel the regain control of the boat, Evelyn scrambled around to the front of the cabin and ducked down to the floor, putting the structure between herself and the rifles of the fort.

Then, just as quickly as the noise and terror had struck, it was gone again, and the boat resumed its quiet, lazy, gentle drift down the river as the sparkling lights of the fort faded into the distance.

It'd been a long, frightening, stressful night followed by a long, hot morning since she'd left her house in Richmond, and now in the early afternoon, with the sun beating down on her, Evelyn was starting to feel the effects. She leaned back against the bulkhead of the small fishing boat next to the door to the cabin. Soon her head began to nod, despite repeated attempts to shake herself into wakefulness.

Something startled her awake. She looked up, and Cyrus was standing in front of her, only a few feet away.

"Uh, beggin' your pardon, miss ... not meanin' to disturb you or nothin', but there's something I needed to speak with you about concernin' our present course," he said, and took a step closer.

"Yes? What is it?"

Cyrus's hands shot out and grabbed her arms, pinning them to her sides. A wicked looking leer showed his green teeth. "Was thinkin' I might just take my payment *early*. Ain't had me a sweet little tart like you in quite a spell."

She struggled, trying to break free of his grasp. But though he wasn't a large man, she could feel he was immeasurably stronger than she. Wrestling against him would be in vain. So, she relaxed and allowed him to push her back against the cabin bulkhead.

He leaned his face in close to hers, "That's better, missy. Why fight it? It'll only cause more trouble ... and more *pain.*" He pressed forward, as if to kiss her. His breath was foul, and he gazed at her with an intense, lustful fire in his eyes.

She closed her eyes, and seemed to relax even more, slightly parting her lips as if to receive his kiss.

"*Mmmm ...*" he responded, pushing in closer. But when he pressed his body full up against hers, her right knee shot up hard into his groin.

"*Ooooph!*" he grunted, and stepped back, hunched over, hands covering his aching manhood.

She stepped forward and punched him hard in the face with her right fist, throwing all her weight into the blow. He staggered backward.

"My Daddy wanted a boy. He taught me how to fight!" she sneered.

"You *bitch!* Owww ... *shit*, that hurt ... *Goddamned whore* ... you'll regret that," he growled, still grimacing in pain, clutching his groin and rubbing the side of his face, but taking a step back toward her.

But when he looked up, he stopped, suddenly staring down the barrel of her small Smith & Wesson revolver. She cocked the hammer with a *click!*

"He also taught me how to shoot," she hissed.

Cyrus flinched, "Now miss ... just put that thing away before someone gets hurt ..."

"The only one who's going to get *hurt* is *you!*"

"Now missy ... be reasonable. Ain't no need for that. I was just ... *playin'* is all ... didn't mean nothin' by it. No harm done."

She poked the gun barrel toward him, "Shut up, you lying filth! *Not ... another ... word!*

"You have *no idea* who you're dealing with! I've killed much better men than *you* and thought little of it. I may yet put a bullet in you just for the pleasure of spilling your guts! Or perhaps *several* bullets, starting down low and working my way up," she aimed the gun at his still tender crotch. He flinched again, attempting to cover his delicate regions with his hands.

She glared at him, her anger barely contained. She was already tired, stressed, and afraid. His attack had been the last straw. An image of Nathan staring down Walters at the wedding back at Mountain Meadows, his face a dark storm cloud and his trigger finger twitching, flashed through her mind. She smiled at the thought.

"If I didn't need you to sail this boat, I'd shoot you right now, and toss you to the fishes! But don't think I won't still do it; I'll steer this *tub* myself if I have to!"

He cowered and slowly raised his hands in surrender, no longer meeting eyes with her.

"Get back to your station and pray I don't change my mind about letting you live!"

"Yes, missus … uh, *ma'am*," he said, before snapping his mouth shut with a grimace, remembering she'd threatened to shoot him if he talked. He moved back to the ship's wheel where he stared down at his feet and seemed to be muttering to himself.

"And don't even *think* about taking me anywhere other than where I wish to go!"

He nodded emphatically but didn't speak or look up.

Evelyn silently let out a deep breath, and tried to relax, but couldn't stop shaking. She lowered the hammer on the Smith & Wesson and slipped it back into its hiding place up her left sleeve. She resisted the urge to rub her painful knuckles where they'd connected with the man's face. It was the inevitable downside of throwing a punch—she could never understand why men liked fighting so much when it was often so very painful, even for the winner!

After a few moments, she felt the anger and stress draining away. And she was surprised she was no longer shaking but now felt sharp and alert. She was determined he would *not* get the jump on her again, even if she had to stay awake all night.

But after a few hours, as she fought to keep her eyes open against the gentle rocking of the small boat, floating slowly down the smooth waters of the James in the waning daylight, Evelyn began to understand the truth of the old saying, "the spirit is willing, but the flesh is weak." She shook her head, and thought, *It's from the Bible, isn't it? … Luke, I think … or maybe Matthew … Nathan would know … oh Nathan … my dear sweet love …* And then … there he was, his handsome face smiling down at her … She jerked awake, nearly falling over. *This won't do. I must get some rest!*

So she turned and entered the small cabin, closed the door, and threw the bolt closed. She moved over to the small cot at the far side of the room and examined the wrinkled and disheveled bedding. It looked foul, and smelled of sweat and … a hint of dead fish, maybe? *Well, any port in a storm … isn't that what the sailors say, after all?*

She shrugged, and decided she was past caring about the typical niceties of civilization. She lay down on top of the bedding, saying a quick prayer that she'd not acquire any fleas or lice from the experience. Thankfully she was so tired, she was soon in a deep, dreamless sleep.

In the deep hours of the night, she awoke. Something had pried her from a heavy slumber. But at first she was confused and befuddled, her head uncooperative and thick with sleep. She laid there a moment, trying to get her bearings and think of what it might have been that had penetrated through to her subconscious mind.

She listened a moment, but heard nothing beyond the soft flowing of the river past the side of the boat. Then it hit her: the boat was no longer moving. If it were, it would be floating along *with* the water and she'd hear soft lapping of waves as she'd heard all the previous day. She took a deep breath and relaxed. *Cyrus has dropped the anchor for the night is all,* she decided, and rolled over, trying her best to ignore the stale smell of the bedding under her.

But even as she had nearly regained her previous blissful state of slumber, she heard a loud, metallic clang out toward the back of the boat. It sounded like something large and heavy had hit the deck. She held her breath and listened. For a few moments there was nothing, then suddenly she heard more clanging and banging and a shout that sounded like Cyrus.

She bolted upright on the cot and shook her head to clear away the sleep. *Something is amiss … surely we are boarded by the enemy!*

She stood and pulled the pistol from the holster on her left sleeve, immediately cocking the hammer. Whoever they were, she was determined they'd not get her without a fight!

She stepped up to the cabin door and threw back the bolt, then opened the door and stepped out with the pistol held in front, expecting to encounter a chaos of action. But instead she saw … *nothing.* The deck was dark and silent, and there was no movement.

"Cyrus?" she asked the darkness. But there was no answer.

Chapter 4. When Truth Is a Lie

"What people believe
prevails over the truth."
– Sophocles

Tuesday April 1, 1862 – On the James River, Virginia:

Evelyn stepped forward into the darkness of the boat deck, straining to see anything at all in the near total blackness, the only illumination being the navigation lamps at the bow and stern.

Something struck her hard on her right forearm, a stinging blow that made her lose her grip on the pistol, which went clattering across the decking.

Strong arms seized her from behind, pinning her arms back against a hard, muscular body. At first, she assumed it was whoever had boarded the ship and overwhelmed Cyrus. But then she heard a familiar voice … and smelled a familiar rancid breath.

"Ha! Got you this time missy! And no pistol to keep me off this time. How you like them apples, eh?! *Ha!*"

Evelyn struggled to free her arms, and tried kicking backward, but he was clearly more prepared for her tricks this time, and simply gripped her harder and more painfully.

He laughed at her frantic efforts, fruitless against his immeasurably stronger physique. He was a fisherman, spending his days wrestling heavily laden nets full of fish, while she did almost nothing of a physical nature on a regular basis.

"No, no … none o' your tricks this time, missy. No kicking me in the balls, that's for sure … which reminds me … I owe you one for that," he said. He let loose of her right arm, and punched her hard in the lower back on her right side.

She gasped from the shocking pain of it, fighting not to pass out as sparks swirled in her vision. But even in her darkest moment of agony and fear, a tiny spark of fighting spirit said, *Thank you, God … just the break I needed …*

Her freed right hand slipped into the pocket of her skirts, gripped the smooth steel handle of the stiletto, and pulled it free—even as she had practiced a hundred times before.

She sucked in a deep breath, reversed her grip on the handle, and thrust backward with all her strength. She felt the back of her fist impact against Cyrus' stomach with a thud. He grunted, then gasped. She yanked the blade free.

His grip on her was gone as he staggered back. "You … you Goddamned *whore* … what have you done?! You've … you've stuck me! Ahhhh … *Goddamn it!* Shit … that hurts!"

He gripped at the place on his side where the stiletto had poked him and grimaced in pain. But though the wound was painful, and quite possibly fatal in the long run, it was not immediately mortal.

Cyrus looked up at her and grimaced. And even as he grasped the wound with his right hand, he reached behind his back with his left and pulled out a rough, wood-handled knife of the type fishermen used to gut fish. "I was just gonna have a little fun with you, but *now* … I'm gonna *kill* you, *bitch!*"

But before he could step toward her, she lunged forward, plunging the stiletto up to the cross guard into the center of his chest. She jerked the blade back out again. It made a sucking noise exiting his chest. A gush of dark liquid followed.

"Ugh …" he gasped, staggering forward, dropping his knife to the deck. He clutched in vain at the hole pumping spurts of blood from his chest.

"Dead men don't kill the living," she said and stepped back out of his reach.

He stumbled a few steps, then leaned partway over the railing, clutching at the ropes that ran along the sides of the boat.

Evelyn stood where she was, staring at Cyrus' back, watching his last sputtering breaths until his chest stopped moving and he collapsed against the side of the boat. His body hung limply on the railing—a dark pool of blood spreading out around his bare feet.

It was then she realized she was shaking uncontrollably and couldn't stop. She let the stiletto slip from her grasp and fall clattering to the decking, then sat down right where she was. She wrapped her arms around her knees, pulled them up under her chin, and cried.

ഇരുജാക്രജാജ്രയുള്ള

A short time later Evelyn jerked awake, realizing she had nodded off where she sat on the deck, nearly toppling over.

She sat up straight, rubbed her eyes, and gazed over at Cyrus, still hanging on the railing. She sighed heavily, stood, and walked over to the body.

Get ahold of yourself, Evelyn, she scolded herself, *the Union Navy controls these waters; at first light they'll come to investigate a boat anchored alone on the river and it won't do to have them find things like this ... they'll never let me near General McClellan if they think I'm a crazed murderess.*

She shuddered at the thought of touching the dead body and looked away. Then she noticed the trail of blood starting back toward the cabin where she'd initially stabbed him leading to where he hung on the railing. Then she looked down at herself and realized her clothes were badly stained—spots, splatters, and smears of a dark, thick liquid, now crusty and nearly black. *No, that definitely won't do,* she thought.

She turned back toward the body and considered what to do. *I suppose, being a good Christian, I should say a prayer for his soul,* she thought. But then she shrugged, knelt down, grabbed him around the ankles just above his bare feet, and lifted. *But I'm not feeling very good or Christian just now,* she decided.

She struggled with the weight, finally managing to get the ankles raised to where they rested on her shoulders, one on each side. Then she stood, raised her arms, and heaved with all her strength. For a moment the body hung there, and she thought she might collapse from the strain. But then she felt it; the body was slowly starting to slide forward. And after a long moment, which seemed like an eternity, it suddenly went with a rush that nearly toppled her overboard with it.

The body splashed into the murky green water, but to her dismay, it quickly surfaced again, floating face down, arms stretched out to the sides. In the lamplight, she could see a dark stain spreading out around the body as it drifted away with the river's current.

Next, she went looking for a bucket and mop. And though it was still pitch black out, the boat wasn't very big and there was just enough light from the navigation lamps to find what she was looking for. After a few minutes of mopping, she realized the job would be difficult even in daylight, as the mop seemed to just smear the blood around. But then she remembered how disgusting the boat had been when she'd arrived — fish blood and entrails everywhere — until she'd complained and Cyrus had half-heartedly thrown a few buckets of water on the worst parts. She shrugged, set the mop down, and tossed the bucket of water at the blood trail. *It will have to do*, she thought.

Then she stripped off her top and her skirts, stuck a heavy lead fishing weight in the middle, tied it into a bundle, and threw it into the river. Unlike the body, the clothing quickly sunk out of sight.

She went back into the cabin and pulled spare clothes from her bag and dressed again. Then she stepped back out, retrieved her weapons from the deck where they lay, and returned them to their hiding places, after wiping the stiletto blade clean.

She stepped to the door, took one last look out, then closed and locked it before returning to the bed and laying down. And though she was exhausted, it was a long time before she could find sleep.

ঙ৵৲৹ঙ৵৲৹ঙ৵৲৹ঙ৵৲৹ঙ৵৲৹

A sudden noise startled Evelyn awake — a man was calling out in a loud voice. She noticed it was now daylight; light streamed in from the small portholes on each side of the cabin, and from under the door.

Then she heard the sound again, this time more clearly.

"Halloo the boat … we hail from the warship U.S.S. *Galena*. Prepare to be boarded in the name of the United States Navy," the voice called out, this time from only a few dozen yards away, by the sound.

She stood and stepped to the door, unlocking it and pulling it open.

She gazed out and saw a Union Naval officer standing in the prow of a small rowboat being oared by two sailors. Two marines stood in the back of the boat, rifles in their hands.

She waved to them and smiled, making sure they knew she was friendly and not any kind of threat. The young officer waved back, but maintained a stern visage.

When the rowboat reached the side the officer leaned forward, reached across and quickly looped a rope around the railing, tying it down smartly. One of the sailors, who'd pulled up his oar, did likewise in the back of the rowboat so it was now tied alongside the larger vessel. The officer then said, "Permission to come aboard, ma'am?" and though he still didn't smile, he now had a friendlier tone, she noticed.

"Certainly officer, and welcome … I've been expecting you."

He raised an eyebrow at this, but didn't answer and immediately clambered up over the railing as easily as she would sit in a chair for tea. The two marines followed, while the sailors stayed in the rowboat.

"Good morning, miss," he said as he stepped up to her and made a slight bow and tipped his hat, "I am Ensign Withers of the U.S.S. *Galena*, presently on patrol in these waters."

"Pleased to meet you, Ensign," she answered and smiled, giving him a slight curtsy, "I'm Eve Smith."

"A pleasure, Miss Smith," he answered, in what sounded like a New England accent to Evelyn's ear. He was young and fair-haired, a handsome fellow, she thought, with a neatly trimmed beard.

"But … where are the sailors, ma'am? Surely you are not sailing this ship alone?"

"Well … unfortunately at the moment it seems I am … or would be if it hadn't been for your timely and fortuitous arrival."

"I … don't understand …" the ensign answered with a frown.

"Well … yesterday I chartered this vessel in Richmond to carry me here, and since there was to be no fishing to speak of, the owner of this vessel dismissed his crew and opted to sail the vessel by himself," she explained. So far, she'd told the simple truth, but next would come the big lie she'd come up with to explain Cyrus' absence.

"Our journey was uneventful, but shortly after we anchored at this spot the man brought out a bottle filled with some sort of liquor and began drinking. It quickly became apparent the man was a drunkard, so I went into the cabin and locked the door. As the evening wore on, I heard him staggering about the ship, singing loudly and offkey. He tried to coax me out of the cabin, but I refused. After a time, I heard a loud noise, like something hitting hard on the wood of the boat, and then a loud splash.

"I called out for him, but there was no answer. So I cautiously opened the door and peered out, but could see no sign of him. I then searched the boat and confirmed he was no longer aboard. I can't imagine where he went, unless he was angry with me and decided to abandon me by swimming to shore ..."

"Not likely," the ensign answered, "sounds to me like he fell in his inebriation, hit his head, and then went over the side."

"Oh! My goodness! Do you really think so, Ensign? The poor man ..."

"Look, here, sir," one of the marines said, pointing at the deck, "blood drops."

The ensign stepped over and glanced down. Evelyn winced — clearly she'd missed some spots in the darkness. She was about to spin a tale of Cyrus catching a large fish and gutting it, but the ensign relieved her of that burden, when he said, "Yep ... I'd say that confirms our theory ... hit his head, was staggering around drunk and bleeding, slipped and fell overboard."

"Seems so, sir," the marine agreed.

"And here's where he fell," the other marine said, leaning out over the side and pointing to where a streak of blood ran down the wood planking on the side of the boat.

Evelyn turned away, "Oh ... this is most upsetting ... I don't think I can look."

"It's all right miss, we'll not make you look ... but ... you still haven't explained why you're here—why you hired a boat to come here in the first place ... and from *Richmond,* of all places!"

Evelyn met eyes with him and gave him a serious look, "That I can only tell you in private, Ensign ..."

He raised an eyebrow at this, then turned to the marines and said, "Return to the tender, men. I will join you shortly."

"Sir!" they said, and each snapped a salute before clambering back over the railing and onto the smaller boat.

"Please, Ensign Withers, come with me into the cabin ... I need to collect my things and we can talk while I do."

He nodded and followed her into the cabin, where she closed the door behind them.

He said nothing, but stood looking at her with a curious expression, clearly baffled as to what this was all about.

"Ensign ... I may not look the part, but I have been actively engaging in military espionage in Richmond on behalf of the Union."

As expected, this pronouncement was met with a shocked look from the young officer.

"You're ... you're saying you're a spy?"

"Yes ... that's exactly what I'm saying, Ensign ... and a very good one, it turns out. In fact, I am currently in possession of information that is absolutely vital to the success of General McClellan's present campaign. As you can well imagine, it is essential I meet with him at the earliest possible moment."

The wide-eyed officer whistled and scratched his head up under his hat, "That's ... that's one heck of a tale, miss — certainly not anything I'd have ever expected from looking at you."

"I understand *that*, Ensign, but it is, in fact, true. You must take me to the general immediately."

"Well, as for that, ma'am ... it's not within the purview of my rank and duties to go directly to see the commanding general, let alone take someone else to him. The commodore will have to order it."

"The commodore?"

"Yes, ma'am. Commodore John Rodgers, presently in command of the James River Squadron and captain of the *Galena*. He can send you to the general, if he has a mind. I will take you to him straightaway. If you'll just gather your things, we can be on our way."

"Thank you, Ensign."

Commodore Rodgers had greeted her cordially after she boarded the very impressive-looking ironclad steamship, guns bristling from gunports along its sides. And like the ensign, he had believed her story almost immediately. It occurred to her the tale was just odd enough that nobody would make up such a thing—and surely someone pretending to be a spy would look and act more ... *spy-like*, which was definitely *not* how Evelyn appeared, despite her casual attire.

So now, three hours after the Union rowboat had first arrived at the fishing boat, Evelyn sat in a small office inside Fort Monroe, staring out the window at the fort's thick concrete walls, waiting to meet with General McClellan. She now felt confident he would also take her at her word, and all would be well.

She'd been sitting in the small room, accompanied once again by Ensign Withers of the *Galena*, for only a few minutes when a gentleman entered the room. He was a large, serious looking man with a thick brown beard and intense blue eyes. He was neatly dressed in a fine gray suit rather than a military uniform, which surprised her.

She stood to greet him, and he bowed slightly. "Good morning, Miss Smith ... I am Allan Pinkerton," he said, "I currently head up the Union Intelligence Service on behalf of the military."

"Oh! Well met then, sir; you are clearly the man I need to meet with ... in addition to the commanding general, of course."

"So it would seem, Miss Smith. I understand based on the written communique from Commodore Rodgers you have been actively engaged in certain ... *clandestine* activities on our behalf?"

Evelyn nodded and smiled, "Let us speak plainly, sir ... I am currently serving as a spy in Richmond on behalf of the Union. And I represent an extended espionage ring that has been active since even before hostilities broke out—I believe certain persons in your own War Department are well aware of our efforts. I have come here because I have information vital to the success of the current Union campaign."

Pinkerton raised an eyebrow at this, then glanced from her over to Ensign Withers.

Evelyn took his meaning, looked over at the ensign and smiled, "In order to gain an audience with the general it was necessary to confide in the ensign and his captain. We must assume at this point the two of them will exercise the very utmost in discretion concerning this matter."

The young ensign turned red in the face, and nodded emphatically, "Yes, certainly ... of course, Miss Smith ... Mr. Pinkerton ... I swear on my life and on my honor as a naval officer and a gentleman that I will never repeat a word of whatever may be said in my presence concerning this matter."

Pinkerton gazed at him a moment, then nodded, "Very good, Ensign. But you may return to your ship now. I thank you for your assistance, but we will take charge of Miss Smith from here on."

Withers glanced at Evelyn for confirmation, and she nodded and smiled, "Thank you, Ensign ... for all your help."

"Never mention it, Miss Smith," he said as he stood, and tipped his hat to her. "And thank *you* for all you have done on behalf of the country ... It is ... a thing most admirable. Godspeed to you, ma'am."

After the ensign departed, Pinkerton surprised her by taking a seat opposite her in the small room rather than taking her immediately to see General McClellan. He quizzed her for the next hour or so, asking her to tell him everything she intended to impart to the general, and prodding her with detailed questions at various points. The only queries she refused to answer were concerning the names of people involved in Jonathan's spy ring, though she noticed when she used the name "The Employer" Pinkerton raised an eyebrow, as if he had at least heard the term, and he asked no specific questions about it.

When he seemed satisfied, he left, telling her he would return shortly. Though she was eager to speak with the general, she supposed he was a very busy man having over a hundred thousand men under his command to organize. She couldn't imagine the awesome responsibility that entailed, so was willing to forgive him for keeping her waiting.

But when the door to the room reopened it was neither Pinkerton nor McClellan who stepped in, but rather a burly young Union sergeant with a thick black beard and a serious expression. He nodded and said, "Miss Smith, the general will see you now. Please follow me …" he gestured toward the hallway with a slight bow.

"Thank you, Sergeant," she said, gracing him with a bright smile.

He nodded, but said nothing in return, nor did he return her smile. *Not exactly warm and friendly*, she decided, but shrugged it off; likely the man was just not the outgoing sort—or was unused to dealing with women.

But if Pinkerton's greeting had been businesslike, and the sergeant's cold and stiff, General McClellan's by contrast was warm, friendly, and enthusiastic.

When she entered his office he rose from his seat, smiled brightly, and stepped around the desk greet her. "Miss Smith … George McClellan, your humble servant, ma'am," he said bowing, then taking her hand and lightly kissing the back of it in the formal, European manner.

She returned his smile with one of her own, "A pleasure and an honor, sir," she replied with a curtsy. She decided George McClellan was every bit as handsome in person as he appeared in photographs she'd seen of him: neatly trimmed brown hair and matching mustache, and dark intense eyes. He also had an admirable physique: lean but barrel-chested like a man of great personal strength. But she was surprised how diminutive he was—an inch or two shorter than herself. A sudden image of Nathan, towering over her, flashed through her mind and she smiled.

"The pleasure is all mine, Miss Smith," he responded, "please, have a seat. My apologies for keeping you waiting—hazards of the duty, you know."

"Think nothing of it, General ... I appreciate what an important responsibility you have," she said, as she sat.

McClellan nodded and smiled, then pulled his chair out in front of the desk and set it in front of her. "May we offer you something ... tea perhaps?"

"Oh ... yes, that would be lovely, General," she said, as she took a seat next to the general's desk. "I have had a long, hot morning of it already."

"So I understand ... *Sergeant!*" he called out toward the doorway. In a moment the serious, bearded sergeant stepped into the doorframe.

"Sir?"

"Andrew ... would you please be so kind as to fetch us a fresh pot of tea? And perhaps some of those sweet biscuits we had earlier in the morning, if any are left? There's a good fellow ..."

"Sir!" the sergeant responded, immediately pivoting and exiting the room.

McClellan took his seat, looked over at Evelyn and smiled, "A fine, efficient young fellow, but not overly ... *effusive*, shall we say?"

Evelyn returned the smile and nodded, "I'd noticed something of the sort ..."

McClellan chuckled, and nodded his head. "So ... Miss Smith ... *Eve*, was it?"

"Oh, yes ... certainly, General, please call me Eve ..."

"Ah, excellent—*Eve*, then. Eve ... I understand you have some very important information for us that you've apparently gained through some very daring and effective clandestine activity ... *spying*, might be the proper word for it, I suppose?"

"Yes ... *spying* is exactly what it was, General. And yes, I do have some very important information for you, as I've already imparted to Mr. Pinkerton."

"Ah ... speaking of, there he is now. I've asked him to join us that we three might discuss the details of what you wish to impart to us."

Evelyn began to rise as Pinkerton re-entered the room, but he waved her off, indicating she should remain seated.

"Sorry, General ... I was called away for a moment on ... another matter."

"All is well, Allan; never mention it," McClellan responded affably, gesturing toward another open chair a few feet from where Evelyn sat. Pinkerton took the proffered seat.

At that moment the sergeant re-entered with the tea and treats. Evelyn noted the sergeant had brought three teacups rather than two. She was also surprised by the quality of the tea service—a finely engraved silver tray and tea pot, and richly decorated China teacups. A set that would feel right at home in Angeline's library, she decided—certainly not what she expected at the headquarters of a general actively engaged in a major military campaign. She briefly wondered if McClellan had brought this finery with him, or if it was something that'd already been at the fort when he arrived. But then she shook off these thoughts as immaterial.

After the tea was served out and the sergeant departed, closing the door behind him, Evelyn was surprised it was Pinkerton who initiated the discussion.

"Please, Miss Smith, repeat for the general the events and information you shared with me earlier today ... I apologize for making you reiterate the details, but I think it important the general hear it in your own words ..."

"No apologies necessary, Mr. Pinkerton. I am more than happy to tell my tale in full to the general ... it was, in fact, my wish to do so."

Pinkerton nodded, and then gestured for her to proceed.

For the next half-hour Evelyn spelled out the details of her successful spying activity that'd resulted in the acquisition of the critical details concerning the dearth of available Confederate troops defending Richmond—obtained from General Johnston's letter to Lydia.

During her narrative, McClellan stood and started pacing about the room, a serious look knitting his brow for the first time since Evelyn had seen him.

She reached into her sleeve and pulled out a neatly folded sheet of paper, handing it across to the general. Pinkerton raised an eyebrow—she'd not shared this with him earlier—but he said nothing.

"What's this?" McClellan asked as he unfolded the paper.

"This is an exact copy of General Johnston's letter to his wife, as transcribed by my freeman spy planted in his household. In it you will see confirmation of the information I have just given you."

"A copy? *Not* the original?" McClellan asked with a frown.

"General … if my lady had taken the original it may have been missed … it was too great a risk. So she took out pen and ink and copied it verbatim onto a new sheet of paper."

"Hmm … too bad," McClellan said, "Mr. Pinkerton has men back at the War Department who might have compared the writing to various documents written out by Joe Johnston when he was stationed there before the war. That could've verified the veracity of the information."

"Yes, it is unfortunate … I understand that. And I appreciate it is your duty to verify the information I have given you as authentic, and I take no offense from it. And for that reason, I have gone to the additional effort of obtaining a signed letter from a Union officer of high repute and your personal acquaintance who will vouch for my loyalty to the Union cause. This letter you can send to the War Department for verification, even as you have described," she said, and handed him across another sheet of paper. He read through both letters, then handed them to Pinkerton, who quickly did the same.

"Colonel, Augustus Adams?" Pinkerton asked, after reading the signature on the second letter.

"In my class at West Point, '46," McClellan answered, "captured by the enemy at Bull Run. Still held at Libby Prison in Richmond, awaiting prisoner exchange."

"Ah … yes, very good, sir. I'll have this sent off immediately by courier for verification of his writing. The Academy should still have samples, if not the War Department."

"Yes … please do so at your earliest convenience," McClellan said, but now appeared thoughtful, distracted even, as if struggling to digest all the information he'd just received. He continued to pace the floor, now staring at his boots as he did so.

An awkward silence fell on the room as McClellan continued to pace. Evelyn began to feel anxious … fearing perhaps McClellan was still unconvinced of her veracity. So she decided to sweeten the pot. "General … there is one more way you may verify my personal reputation, integrity, and loyalty …"

He stopped pacing and gazed over at her, "Oh, what would that be, Eve?"

"Yes, well … before the war … I was *very* well acquainted with one of your old West Point classmates, who is now living in the North and working on behalf of the Union, as I understand it. You'll be able to communicate directly with him about me, if you wish. I believe he will vouch for my good reputation, integrity, and loyalty to the Union."

"Ah! Very good, Eve. And who would that be?"

"Nathaniel Chambers."

"*Oh …*"

❦❧

"Well, Pinkerton?" McClellan asked, after Evelyn had been dismissed from the room.

"This seems like *very* good news, General … good beyond our wildest hopes. And it serves to confirm General Wool's original assessment—that the enemy's strength is so depleted and scattered that we might sweep aside his defenses in one bold thrust … Yes, it seems like … unbelievably good news."

"Hmm … yes … *unbelievable* being the operative word …" McClellan answered with a smirk.

"Oh? Then you are inclined to misbelieve the young lady? She seemed … most sincere to me …"

McClellan leaned back in his chair and put is boots up on the desk. "Think about it, Pinkerton … why would they send a woman like *that* to see me? Did they think she could use her obvious feminine charms to befuddle me?"

"I … never thought of that … I'd be inclined to think the opposite, General. If *I* was the enemy, I'd send someone who seemed more ... *obvious*. A slight, sneaky-looking fellow, for example."

"Well, that's the difference between you and I, Allan ... your thinking is more conventional, while I'm more open to other ideas ..."

"Ah ... if you say so, General. But ... what of the letter from Colonel Adams? Shall we not at least validate its authenticity before deciding about the young lady?"

"And what would *that* prove, pray? Even if it *is* authentic, the man is being held prisoner by the rebels, subjected to who knows what torture and depravation. A man in that situation would likely write anything he was told to by his captors. And how did she just happen to get hold of a letter, written out by a man held under lock and key by the enemy ... answer me that?"

"It's ... a reasonable question, now that you mention it ... perhaps we should bring her back and ask her ..."

McClellan waved off the suggestion, "If we do, she'll likely just have a prepared, fabricated story for that as well."

"All right, assuming you're right about her ... why would the enemy go to all the trouble of sending her with this *particular* information? What does it gain them to tell us they have insufficient defenses to hold us back? I would think they would want to convince us of just the opposite to make us hesitant to attack."

"Ah! There you go again, Allan! You see ... that's what they *want* us to believe, when in fact they have us badly outnumbered, even as I have said all along. They want to lull us into complacency—so that I won't ask for the additional reinforcements and equipage from Washington that I so desperately need. And so that I'll throw caution to the wind and rush headlong into a deadly trap, annihilating my army! And this talk of Jackson attacking north—ha! I would be willing to wager he is already moving south, ready to supply the hammer for Joe Johnston's anvil, should we be foolish enough to take the bait."

Pinkerton scratched his beard thoughtfully, nodded and said, "Hmm ... could be ... could be. But then, what about this

Chambers fellow, your other classmate … shouldn't you at least talk with him about her?"

McClellan scoffed, "Chambers?! I've never liked the man, even back at the academy—an arrogant know-it-all, thinks he's a better soldier than anyone else just because General Scott pinned a gold medal on him down in Mexico."

Pinkerton nodded, but said nothing.

Then McClellan leaned forward, and spoke in a quiet, confidential tone, "Just between you and me, Allan, I wouldn't be surprised if Chambers is secretly working for the enemy … he is a *Virginian*, after all!"

"Oh! Do you really think so?"

McClellan shrugged, "Why else would he refuse to enlist and fight, instead ingratiating himself with various high-level Union government officials?"

"Hmm … does seems suspicious, now that you say it that way. I'll have my people start looking into him straight away. But if it turns out he's *not* a rebel agent …?"

McClellan snorted, "For all I know Chambers is an agent of the Lincoln administration, and Miss Smith was sent here to try to prod me into precipitous action against my better judgment, as Lincoln is so often wont to do. And that's nearly as bad as a Confederate agent in my book—maybe worse, as it's more insidious and difficult to counter."

McClellan then chuckled, "Well, at least I can thank our friend Eve for one thing …"

"Oh? And what would that be, General?"

"For helping make my decision on what to do about Yorktown. I was considering launching an all-out assault to see if we might punch through their lines and flank the force defending it … but now I know that would be a disaster. No doubt they have an overwhelming force positioned for just such an event, ready to counter-attack, cut our force in two, and crush us piecemeal. No … I have decided, I shall dig in, lay siege to Yorktown, and bombard it into submission."

"But, sir … that could take … oh, I don't know … weeks, maybe."

"More likely a month, Mr. Pinkerton … but in the end when we are victorious, the rebels are defeated, and my army is still intact, it shall have been worth the wait."

Pinkerton nodded, but again chose not to comment. After a long silence he asked, "So … what do you wish to do about this … *Miss Eve Smith*, General?"

McClellan gazed at the ceiling for a long moment, then looked back at Pinkerton with a frown, and said, "Have her arrested as an enemy spy … and throw her into the deepest, darkest prison you can find."

❦❦❦❦❦❦❦❦❦

To Evelyn's surprise, General McClellan didn't ask to speak with her again, but sent a serious-looking, middle-aged Union captain to escort her from the fort. He led her back out to the same long wooden pier where she'd arrived earlier in the day. There was once again a small rowboat there, this time with a different officer and sailors. She was slightly surprised that there were two armed marine guards for her escort duty, even as there'd been when they'd boarded the unknown fishing boat in the morning. *Perhaps it's just standard procedure in a war zone*, she thought with a shrug.

But then the captain turned to her and said, "I'll just take your bag now ma'am."

"Oh, thank you, Captain," she answered with a smile, but he returned the smile with a severe look, which surprised her.

He handed the carpet bag across to the ensign manning the boat, then reached behind his back and brought out something metallic that jingled. At first she couldn't tell what the object was. But then he held the thing out, and she saw it was a set of wrist shackles such as slaves or prisoners wore.

"*What?!*" she looked up at his face, and her heart sank—the look in his eyes was deadly serious.

"Miss Eve Smith, you are under arrest for espionage against the United States government and its armed forces. Please extend your wrists that I might restrain you—I would prefer not to use force on you, ma'am."

"But I ..." she said, her mouth dropping open in shock. She glanced over at the seamen, but they only returned curious looks—though one of the sailors looked down at his feet and seemed embarrassed when she made eye contact with him.

She slowly extended her wrists and the captain slid the shackles on and locked them with a key. When he was fastening the one on her left arm, his knuckles brushed against the pistol holster hidden there, and he looked up at her with a raised eyebrow. He felt the outline of it, then opened the concealed flap on her sleeve and pulled out the pistol from its holster. He gave her a hard look, which she returned evenly. He then felt of her right forearm, but finding nothing there, he handed the pistol over to the ensign, who appeared startled, but stuffed it into her carpet bag. Evelyn felt some relief the captain had not discovered the stiletto strapped to her right thigh. At least she retained that, should it be needed.

The captain then took her by the arm and helped her into the boat, where she took a seat. As she watched the fort slip away behind them to the rhythmic sound of oars dipping and rising, she slowly shook her head, wondering what could possibly have gone so terribly wrong.

Chapter 5. Prison Break

"You cannot escape the
responsibility of tomorrow
by evading it today."
*– **Abraham Lincoln***

Tuesday April 15, 1862 – Washington, D.C.:

The Old Capitol Prison was drafty and either too hot or too cold, depending on the weather, but Evelyn imagined as prisons went, this was probably about as nice as they ever got. Though the original door to her room had been replaced by one of welded iron bars with a lock that only opened with a key from the outside, her room did have a window overlooking the prison yard below. She was only on the second floor, so it might have been possible to escape out the window, except for the iron bars they had installed on the inside, which also prevented the window from being opened, making it stuffy and overly warm whenever the sun shone in.

And though the room wasn't large, it held two double bunk beds, though she was currently the only occupant. She couldn't decide if this was because the upper floor reserved for women was currently only sparsely populated or because they didn't want the evil spy having too much undue influence on the other prisoners.

She was not the only woman in the prison, but she was the only woman *spy* in the prison, and didn't know if there had ever been any others. Likely they didn't know quite what to do with her, proven by the fact that they'd allowed her to change into her prison clothes in privacy—all the guards being men—which had allowed her to retain the stiletto, still strapped to her thigh. She wasn't sure how long she'd be able to continue hiding that fact from the guards, but for now it gave her a slight sense of security.

The building itself had a storied past, originally serving as the temporary U.S. capitol building while the real Capitol Building was being rebuilt, after being burned by the British during the War of 1812. Over the years it had also served as a private school, and even a large boarding house. When the Civil War broke out, it was converted for use as a prison—mostly for inmates the government didn't know what else to do with, such as spies, blockade runners, and Union officers awaiting court martial for various offenses. And it was one of the few places they held female prisoners, mostly prisoners of war—women captured while fighting alongside men in various Confederate formations.

Evelyn spent the majority of her days either up in the mess hall during meals, out in the prison yard if weather allowed, or if not, in the large common hall, originally used as the meeting place for congress. Unless they were being punished for some rule violation or other prison offense, the inmates were generally only locked in their rooms at night. All in all, it was not a terrible existence, just tedious and monotonous.

And each day increased her growing anxiety over what was happening out in the wider world. Though the guards were happy to share news about the war—who'd won which battle and so on—of the specific people and activities Evelyn was most concerned about she, of course, could receive no news at all. Though regular prisoners of war were allowed to write and receive letters—postage due, of course, with no guarantee of delivery—Evelyn, being accused of spying, was not allowed the privilege. She assumed it was for fear she would continue to disseminate vital military secrets, though what that might be inside this prison, she couldn't fathom. So she worried constantly over those she cared about, only calming herself for short spells through sheer force of will.

Fortunately the guards were generally respectful and courteous, especially toward the women, which she greatly appreciated. It'd been a source of some anxiety before her arrival, but she'd only suffered one uncomfortable incident in that regard since she'd been there. One night, an hour or so after being locked in her cell, the door unexpectedly re-opened and a guard stepped in, holding a finger to his mouth in a shushing gesture. She felt no fear, since the door was completely open to the outside hallway, other than the iron bars preventing escape. If she screamed it would be heard all throughout the second floor. She knew this for certain, because she often had trouble sleeping when other inmates were talking loudly, even on the far end of the long central hallway.

But when the guard, a young man who'd been wounded and had a limp, offered to arrange for preferential treatment—better food, special treats, outings beyond the prison yard—in exchange for certain "sexual favors," she glared at him and answered flatly, "The last man who tried to take advantage of me is floating face down in the Chesapeake Bay, likely feeding the sharks attracted by all the blood spewing from his stab wounds." The guard's face turned pale, and without another word, he backed out of the cell, locking the door behind him.

But for the most part she got along fine with the guards, especially the officer of the guard, Sergeant Murphy. He was the senior member of the guard staff—somewhere around forty years old Evelyn guessed—and walked somewhat stiffly due to some sort of injury. He'd apparently been placed in command of the prison guards while recuperating. Though serious and often stern seeming, he was always polite and often betrayed a kindly smile, nod, or tip of the hat. Evelyn took an immediate liking to him; something about him reminded her of her father.

With every able-bodied young man needed for the fighting, prison guards were hard to come by. She even heard a rumor that the facility next door, Carroll Prison, had a female guard who'd dressed as a man and joined a New York regiment, adopting a man's name. Once they'd discovered her secret, not knowing what else to do with her, they'd sent her to be a prison guard, still wearing her Union uniform, and still being addressed by her adopted masculine name. Apparently with men in such short supply, the prison was happy to overlook the fact that this willing and able-bodied young man was actually a woman.

One day, after she'd been there several weeks, Evelyn's dull prison routine was disrupted by the arrival of another woman who'd been pretending to be a man—this one serving as a Confederate soldier in a Virginia regiment. Jane Perkins was about the same age as Evelyn, and though not as tall, was thick and muscular looking. She had a masculine face, so Evelyn could easily imagine her being mistaken for a man—likely all the way until she was examined by some unfortunate Army surgeon, who likely suffered a terrible shock at the revelation.

Jane's arrival was like a stone thrown into a quiet pool, sending ripples out in every direction—and not in a pleasant way. Loud, crude, and antagonistic toward the prison rules, Jane made it clear from the start she was still ready to fight, despite no longer being in uniform or on a battlefield.

The guards became more tense and short-tempered, not used to being confronted, cursed at, and berated regarding the most trivial prison procedures. On one occasion, an unlucky carpenter found himself on the receiving end of Jane's wrath. While making some repairs near the door to the prison yard, his hammering apparently annoyed her. She stepped up to him, grabbed his hammer and his box of tools, and flung them down the steps to the courtyard below. When he stood up to confront her, she grabbed hold of him and threw him down the stairs as well.

An angry Sergeant Murphy stepped up to her and said, "Now Jane, that's just about enough out of you! I'll be escorting you to your room now, where you can cool off for the rest of the day."

But she was having none of it, firing back, "I'll not go anywhere with a mother-humping son of a bitch like you. You can just go to hell."

"We'll see about that," he said, taking hold of her arm, intending to drag her off by brute force if need be.

But she jerked her arm away and punched him hard in the nose. He grappled with her, and in the struggle, they tripped, and both fell to the floor, where they continued to wrestle until two guards rushed up and pinned Jane down. The officer of the guard then slapped iron shackles around her wrists and the two guards dragged her to her feet, still cursing and spitting. They hauled her off to her room where she yelled and screamed until the guards came back and tossed a bucket of cold water on her through the bars of her door. Then they threatened to stuff a wool sock—used and very dirty—in her mouth if she didn't quiet down. That seemed to finally do the job, as they heard no more from her until morning.

But if Jane Perkins was hard on the guards in general, she seemed to take particular pleasure in tormenting Evelyn any chance she got. Jane quickly became the de-facto leader of the twenty-some women who'd taken up arms with the rebel army, and almost immediately turned them against Evelyn, though previously there had been no issues between her and the other inmates.

When Evelyn walked past, Jane would call out, "Oh, lookie here, ladies … it's the *spy princess*. Careful, princess … when you fuck the guards you might break a nail!" to which the others would laugh and hoot, adding their own sarcastic, derisive remarks.

Evelyn's immediate thought was, *Thank God the other prisoners believe I was caught working for the Confederate side. If this is how they treat someone supposedly on their side, imagine how they'd treat me if they knew the truth!* And at first, she just ignored the noise and walked past, figuring the bully would soon tire of the sport if it provoked no reaction.

But as the days wore into weeks, Evelyn sadly concluded Jane was *not* going to relent, and if anything was only going to get worse. In fact, it had gone from teasing and name calling—Jane's new favorite was to call Evelyn "the whore princess"—to pushing, tripping, and hard bumping when walking down the hall, or out in the prison yard. And it was no longer just Jane; lately some of the others had begun to join in.

The guards did what they could, them naturally liking Evelyn and likewise having a very strong dislike of Jane. But they weren't always around, and couldn't be expected to watch over Evelyn every hour of the day. Nor could they do much about the verbal abuse. No, Evelyn concluded, if something was to be done, she'd have to do it herself. But what?

Then one day as she was leaving the mess hall, she heard the familiar harangue, "Had a nice lunch, whore? Or would you have rather sucked one of the guards for your supper?" It was the same old stale garbage, but Evelyn was exasperated with it, and this time something inside her snapped.

Evelyn wheeled around, glared at Jane, and said, "You know, Jane … you sure are an expert on whoring. Seems to me the only way one acquires such intimate knowledge is through *long, hard* experience. As for sucking the guards … I'm sure they'd much prefer a highly skilled professional, such as yourself, to a complete novice like me."

Jane's jaw dropped open at the unexpected retort, which provoked peals of laughter, and hoots of derision from the women sitting around her. Evelyn turned on her heels and strode briskly out of the room. She didn't slow down until she was out in the yard, walking across the grass. She was still fuming when she reached the far wall of the yard. For a moment she just stared at the whitewashed boards, wallowing in frustration, pain, and anger at the mind-numbing, thoroughly helpless situation she currently found herself in.

She took a deep breath, then turned around. It was only just in time. The first thing she saw as Jane's angry face, beet red, coming toward her, only feet away. And the next thing she saw was a fist coming right at her face. She ducked.

Jane slammed her fist into the sturdy fence with a loud *crunch*. She immediately bent over, clutching at her mangled right hand with her left, groaning in pain. Evelyn swung her fist at the side of Jane's face, putting all her weight into it, even as her Daddy had taught her, and as she had done many times fighting the boys in her neighborhood growing up. Jane collapsed to the ground, moaning and clutching at an eye that was already red and swelling, while still gingerly dangling a right hand that likely had suffered broken bones.

Evelyn resisted the urge to rub her throbbing, almost numb right hand. *Damn, that woman has a hard head*, she thought and grimaced.

Evelyn glared at the other women, a half dozen or so, who'd followed along to enjoy the show. She still held her hands balled up into fists, and her legs bent slightly and balanced, ready to move and to fight. She briefly considered reaching for the stiletto to force them back, but thought better of it; if she pulled it out now the guards would seize it and it'd be lost to her. Better to take a beating …

But the women either backed away wide-eyed, or held out their hands to show they weren't interested in a fight. One even smiled and nodded.

Evelyn relaxed her fists, then walked straight through them as they parted to make way. She didn't stop until she'd re-entered the building, never looking back.

She assumed there'd be more trouble from Jane once she'd recovered, but the next day Evelyn learned Jane had been transferred to a prison called Fitchburg, which was said to specialize in housing especially troublesome, uncooperative prisoners. Apparently, the guards had also had enough of Jane Perkins.

ଞ୬ଧୠ୬ଔଔଞ୬ଧୠ୬ଔଔଞ୬ଧୠ୬ଔଔ

After the incident with Jane, Evelyn became obsessed with the idea of escape. In the first few weeks of her incarceration, she'd been certain someone in the government would realize the mistake they'd made and come free her. Either that, or else surely Jonathan's contacts in the War Department would soon come to her aid … *wouldn't they?*

But now, as a month had come and gone with no end in sight, she decided she would have to take matters into her own hands. She'd not spend the entire war in prison, doing nothing, while those she loved were out there—somewhere—risking their lives for their country. What if she were released after years of confinement only to discover that the war was over and everyone she cared about was already dead? It was unthinkable. She had to *do* something.

She started observing, thinking, and planning. While inside the building she carefully watched the routines of the guards— how many were on duty at a time, where they were stationed, what routes they walked, the hours when they were changed, and so on. Which guards were attentive and which were not. And she

106

familiarized herself with every door—where it led to, when it was closed, locked, and guarded—and, when it wasn't.

When out in the yard, she took stock of every detail—how sturdy the outer fence was and how tall, in which places buildings either intersected with it or approached it closely. Were there any windows without bars in upper stories near the outer wall? She noted any loose or weak-seeming boards, and any places where there was soft dirt underneath that might be dug out.

The prison "yard" was actually made up of three distinct sections: west, south, and east, with the main prison building occupying the north end of the facility.

The west yard was a small, square, entirely enclosed area forty feet across on the west side of the prison abutting First Street, which ran north to south and was the street of the main prison entrance just to the north of the yard outer wall. The male and female inmates took turns either being in this yard, or out in the other two yards to keep them separated. Evelyn quickly discarded any notion of launching her escape from this small yard, as the thirteen-foot-high fence—the same that encompassed the entire prison grounds—wrapped around the whole enclosure with no breaks, and no access from any buildings other than a single door into the main brick prison building. All the windows facing this yard were heavily barred.

The south and east yards were larger and more open, connected by a broad, brick-paved walkway along the north side of the yards. The south yard included a gate—though it was always locked, and she'd only seen it opened to bring in supplies when all of the inmates were kept inside the building. On the other side of the gate was an alleyway connecting First Street in the front of the prison with Second Street in the back. Tall bushes lined the alleyway on the prison side; she knew this because the tops could be seen just above the outer fence.

The south and east yards were separated by a long, rectangular, single-story building containing the kitchen, a guardhouse, and the laundry. This building eventually became the focal point of all her attention, planning, and scheming. On top of this one-story structure, they had built a flat deck with a wooden railing that ran the entire breadth and width of the building. The deck had an outside staircase leading up to it on the west side, accessible from the south yard. Two or more guards regularly patrolled this deck, as they could monitor both the south and east yards from there, as well as anyone leaving or entering any of the buildings around those yards. And, on top of the deck, near the northeast corner, they'd built a small hut to provide the guards with a place to get out of the weather, if need be.

This building immediately piqued Evelyn's interest because the narrow south end of the deck came to within only a few feet of the south wall and was even with the top of it. If one could just get up on that deck and jump to the top of the wall …

She again paid careful attention to the routine of the guards, this time out in the yard—where they positioned themselves when stationary, and where they went when they moved. Where they walked, how closely they watched the prisoners, and how they reacted when there was a disturbance.

She tried to memorize every detail she could throughout the day, and then back in her cell at night she'd try to piece together an escape plan.

She remembered the many lessons her father had taught her about how to solve a seemingly impossible problem with a relatively simple solution. She thought of young Julius Caesar tracking down the pirates who'd kidnapped him and held him for ransom by simply counting the number of inlets leading to their hideout. The memory of her Daddy telling that tale, gesturing broadly and speaking with great excitement and enthusiasm, still brought a smile to her face after all these years.

This was really just another puzzle—the intersection of the guards and their activities with the physical structure of the prison and its grounds. All she had to do was find the points where those intersections were weakest and most vulnerable. After a little more than a week, she had pieced together the beginnings of a plan that seemed plausible. She drilled down on the details, continuing to refine them, leaving nothing to chance.

She then turned her thoughts to what would come next: what would happen once she was clear of the prison grounds.

All prisoners had to forgo the clothes they came in with and don drab, gray, cotton clothes that were all the same, except for size. The women's garb consisted of a dumpy-looking, simple dress, gathered at the waist and hanging limply to just above the shoes. The top half of the one-piece outfit unbuttoned in front with a row of simple, gray buttons. Straight, three-quarter length sleeves that hung loosely about the arms completed the incredibly dull ensemble.

They were also given a simple bonnet to help keep off the sun and the cold. It too was gray, though of a darker shade than the dress. They were each given a scarf—gray, of course—to keep them warm in the cooler weather—a simple triangle of rough wool so itchy that Evelyn could hardly stand to pull up too close to her neck, even on the most frigid days.

Evelyn smiled ruefully when she thought of how unhappy she'd been as a young lady having to wear her mother's old hand-me-down dresses to formal events, thinking them hideously old-fashioned and embarrassing. Those gowns were magnificent and queenly compared to how she was now clothed, she thought. *Imagine what the fine ladies of Richmond would say if they saw me dressed like this!* she considered, slowly shaking her head.

But being too unfashionably ugly to wear in public was not the main issue; the prison clothes would be a dead giveaway. Anyone in the surrounding neighborhoods would immediately recognize her as an inmate if she were out walking around in that attire. What could be done about that? Dying the clothes some bright color, or altering their appearance to make them appear more fashionable somehow?

She was mulling over the clothing conundrum while walking to the mess hall, and wasn't paying close attention to where she was going; she nearly bumped into one of the other women. She immediately apologized, embarrassed for her lapse. But the woman, who was named Cordelia, just smiled, and said, "No harm done, Eve; think nothing of it."

Evelyn had spoken with her on occasion, as Cordelia was a fellow Virginian, one of the women who'd dressed as a man to fight for one of the Virginia regiments.

… She'd … dressed as a man …

Evelyn's eyes widened, and she resisted the urge to slap herself on the forehead. *Of course! The answer has been all around me every day, everywhere I go, and I've been too distracted to think of it — this prison is filled with women who'd disguised themselves as men in order to fight!*

She broke into a bright grin, and said, "Thank you so much, Cordelia, darling!" with such enthusiasm, Cordelia left with a puzzled look, wondering why Eve had been so pleased about being forgiven for such a minor offense.

But Evelyn was now so excited she wolfed down her dinner, hardly noticing what she was eating, eager to sit in her cell and think. *How to dress like a man …*

Evelyn had now determined the place and the timing of her escape, and how she'd slip away unnoticed after, though she still had to work out many of the details.

The final piece of the puzzle was what to do about the guards. Clearly, she would need a distraction of some kind … but what? This one seemed easier than the others, however, and came to her quickly—likely because she herself had been a party to just such a distraction when she'd ducked Jane's punch, and then beat her down to the ground out in the yard. She remembered how quickly the guards had arrived to make sure there was no further trouble. *Hmm …*

She decided the clothing problem was the thing that would take the longest to physically solve, so she set to work on that task immediately. First, she considered somehow stealing men's clothing. But the guards' uniforms would be too obvious, and also might be noticed if one went missing. Besides, there was nowhere in her room to hide anything, except under the sheets of the bed, which would be the first place someone would look if they were suspicious.

Then she thought of the male prisoners. They also wore drab, gray clothing, but pants instead of a dress, and a loose fitting, long-sleeved shirt. Their clothing would also be recognized in the neighborhood, but perhaps she could alter them just enough …

But the male and female inmates where kept separated at all times—for obvious reasons—with different mealtimes, different prison yard times, and segregation by floor and hallway. Attempted cross fraternization between the sexes was severely punished, with the women spending up to a week locked in their cells—with only a bedpan to relieve themselves—and the men forced to endure a public flogging. She shuddered at the thought.

Getting into and out of one of the male inmate areas unobserved while stealing a set of clothes would be nearly as difficult as the escape itself, so she soon discarded the idea.

It came down to fashioning something herself. The women prisoners were each given two dresses, so one could be laundered while the other was being worn. And they were given a needle and small length of thread as they were expected to make their own repairs as needed. The women took turns working the laundry; Evelyn traded shifts with one of the ladies so she could get there sooner. As the women working the laundry also delivered the clean clothes at the end of the day, it was simple for Evelyn to sneak an extra dress in under her own clean dress. If the miscount of dresses was noticed at all, which seemed unlikely, they'd figure someone had just forgotten to turn in her dress for laundering that week.

She had no scissors, but the stiletto was razor sharp, and after a little practice she found it cut the cloth beautifully. To ensure she had enough thread she carefully undid the existing seams, rather than cutting them, so she could re-use the original thread.

Every night for the next week, after she was locked in her cell for the night, she brought out the needle, thread, and the extra dress, and began her alterations.

And every meal, if it included anything at all capable of putting a stain in fabric, she'd smuggle a portion out in her hand, or inside her mouth.

❧❧❧❧❧❧❧❧❧

When she was down to just the final finishing touches on her "new wardrobe" it was time to plan the distraction she would need to execute her plan. Though she typically dined alone, this

111

day during the noon meal she stepped over and sat at the table with the POWs who'd served in various Virginia regiments—a half-dozen women, all in their twenties or early thirties, who tended to spend their free time together.

The women from Virginia sat at their own table for meals. North Carolina was the only other state with enough women, at five, to have their own table. Various other states were represented by a smattering of women—too few to form any large groups.

Ever since the incident with Jane Perkins the women POWs in general treated her more respectfully, and those from her own state even acknowledged her standing as a fellow Virginian.

Even so, she noted startled looks when she set her plate down and sat in an open chair at their table.

"Good afternoon, ladies ..." she said.

"Hello, Eve. Good afternoon," Cordelia answered, which was echoed by several of the others, along with polite nods and smiles.

They all ate in silence for a few minutes, until Evelyn set down her fork, looked around to make sure no guards were nearby, and that no one at any nearby table might be listening. "Ladies ... I need your help," she announced.

Once again it was Cordelia who answered, "What do you need help *with*, Eve?"

"I need y'all's help ... to *escape*."

This statement was met with stunned looks and silence. Finally, one of the others, a slender, young woman from Arlington named Sue asked, "So ... you're gonna take us with you when you go?"

Evelyn looked around the table, and met eyes with each woman before answering. She knew she'd earned their respect, and even a little fear, due to her new-found dangerous reputation, and she meant to use it to her advantage. "No," she answered flatly.

"No?" Cordelia asked, "if you'll not take us with you, why should we risk punishment by helping you escape?"

"Because y'all are prisoners of war. As such you are eligible for exchange for Union soldiers being held in the South. Why risk the dangers of escape when you'll be freed anyway in a few weeks?"

"True ... but what about you? Won't they exchange you, too?"

She gave them another hard look. "I'm *not* a POW, I'm a *spy*. If I was a man, they'd have already hanged me. Since I'm a woman they will likely first torture me to get any information they can, and then lock me up either here or somewhere else, for the remainder of the war."

This was met with nods, and serious looks, but no one could argue against what she'd just said. But Sue finally said, "You still haven't said what's in it for us ... why should we risk punishment to help you?"

"Look ... it's not just about helping me ... y'all have no reason to help me as a *person* ... we're not exactly kin or even close friends—though we *are* fellow Virginians, which should count for something. But this is about more than just me ... this is about winning the war."

"Winning the war? How does you escaping help win the war any more than any of us being freed or escaping?" Sue asked.

Evelyn was thoughtful a moment, then said, "Let me ask you this, Sue: on a good day, in the heat of battle—assuming your rifle didn't foul, and you never ran out of ammunition or powder, how many Yankees you reckon you could kill in a day?"

Sue looked around at the others, shrugged and said, "Oh ... I dunno ... maybe five or six ... Why?"

"Alright ... let's say six ... and there are six of you. So in ten days of hard battle, if none of you was wounded or killed, you'd kill three hundred and sixty of the enemy. That's a whole lot of Yankee soldiers!"

There were smiles and nods at this.

"So ... if General McClellan's army of ... hmm ... a hundred and twenty thousand or so ... were suddenly deprived of three hundred and sixty of its best fighting men ... what you figure would happen then?"

Now they were no longer smiling. This time Cordelia answered, "Not a damned thing, I reckon."

Evelyn smiled and nodded. "And what would you say if I told you … at the time I was arrested, I held in my own two hands information so secret and vital it could've changed the outcome of a major, critical campaign, and possibly the entire war?"

She let this sink in a moment before continuing.

"Of course, I can't share with you what that information was, or how I acquired it, or even who it was for," Evelyn said cryptically. The statement about the vital intelligence was entirely true, but since she was assumed to be working for the Confederate side, she was not about to tell them that her information was intended for the benefit of General McClellan and the Union Army!

"But since I was caught and arrested, the intelligence I carried is no longer of use … time has marched on; I'll not lie to you and say I need to get free so I can finish *that* mission. I'm telling you this because it is an example of how important my work is. While y'all have been brave and admirable, shouldering a rifle, and marching against the enemy, in the end each of you is only one soldier in a great sea of other soldiers. You alone can't change the course of a battle, or a campaign, or a war …" she paused and gave the group another meaningful look, *"but I can."*

ꙮꙮꙮꙮꙮꙮꙮꙮꙮ

The next day Evelyn was once again in the mess hall finishing up her lunch, but this time she was back to sitting alone. As she rose from the table, she made brief eye contact with Cordelia, sitting at the usual Virginian table one over. Cordelia returned the look with a nod. It was the pre-arranged signal to begin the operation.

Evelyn washed, dried, and put away her dishes, then casually strolled out to the prison yard. Once outside, she turned to the right and walked over to the east wall of the south yard and leaned up against its fence where the westering afternoon sun had created a narrow strip of shade. The shade was not just a reasonable excuse for lounging around in that area; today she was wearing two layers of clothing, and was beginning to sweat and feel uncomfortably hot just walking around in the sunshine of a warm spring day.

She'd not picked this spot for its shade, but rather because it afforded her a view of everything she needed to see for her particular purposes. From this specific vantage point, she could see all the way along the brick walkway clear to the northeast corner of the east yard. She could also monitor the stairway leading up to the guard hut and observe any guards patrolling up on the deck.

She fought to quell a growing sense of anxiety as the moment of truth approached. Everything would have to go like clockwork, or the scheme would fail.

She said a quick prayer that nobody would get seriously injured during the "distraction" she'd orchestrated, which she immediately realized was more than a little ironic, considering there was a war on and these were, in fact, her avowed enemies. She couldn't risk trying to persuade one of the other state groups of women to join her plot for fear word would get out to the guards, so the fight the Virginians were about to pick with the North Carolinians would be a *real* one!

She resisted the urge to pace, in her growing unease, and was grateful she didn't have a pocket watch as she'd be too tempted to check it every half minute or so.

Then she finally heard the sound she'd been waiting for …

"Get out of my way, *bitch!*"

Evelyn looked over and saw Cordelia stride right through the gathering of North Carolinian women, shoving one of them to the side before walking over to join her group of Virginians in the far northeast corner of the yard. The women from North Carolina took up the challenge, as expected, and approached the Virginians as a group. The two sides faced off, and after some additional loud name calling, pushing and shoving soon turned into punching, kicking, biting, and pulling of hair.

As entertaining as this was, given the extremely monotonous and mundane nature of prison life, Evelyn pulled her eyes away in order to focus on the actions of the guards. As expected, the guard patrolling the east yard was the first on the scene, while the other guards, one in the south yard, and four up on the deck platform, watched attentively.

The east yard guard stepped up to the group, blew his whistle, and yelled at the women to separate and stop fighting. But as planned, one of the Virginians grabbed him, and pulled him into the melee, where two others immediately jumped on top of him, pinning him to the ground.

This new and unexpected threat triggered the reaction Evelyn had been waiting for: the south yard guard immediately ran in that direction, along with most of the women he'd been watching—they were just eager to see some good entertainment! The south guard had abandoned his post, leaving behind only a small handful of women who declined to join in the fun, including Evelyn. She suspected if anyone noticed her reticence, they'd think little of it, as she had a reputation of staying aloof from the various inter-state group rivalries. *Two guards down ... four to go,* she thought, watching to see what the ones up on the guard deck would do.

At first, these four just shouted and blew whistles. But after a moment, three turned and raced for the stairwell, hustling down to the south yard, then sprinting toward its opening into the east yard. She noticed one of these was Sergeant Murphy. She knew her window of opportunity was quickly closing, as the sergeant was quite competent and forceful, and would likely put an end to the disturbance in short order.

But there was still one guard up on the platform, and she saw him glance back her way, as if taking stock of what was going on in the rest of the prison, as was his duty. She waited anxiously, watching as he slowly turned back toward where the fight was still raging. Evelyn decided to at least move closer to the stairs, in case this last guard decided to join the fray. But as she reached the point where she would lose sight of him if she went any farther, she stopped ... and waited. Then she saw him move behind the guard hut, out of sight on the very northeast corner of the deck.

She felt frozen in place, standing in the middle of the yard, agonizing over what to do, even as the sounds of the fight began to die down.

She took a deep breath and plunged ahead, risking all. She raced to the bottom of the stairs and quickly climbed to the top. When she reached the point where her head would be visible from where the guard was standing, she slowed and peered up cautiously. There he stood, just twenty feet away, but he was still looking in the other direction, down toward the fight. She hurried the rest of the way to the top of the stairs and turned to her right, quickly putting the guard hut between herself and the guard. She hurried along the deck toward the south end, resisting the urge to run and doing her best to deaden her footfalls. She prayed the guard wouldn't step back to take a look at the south yard and catch sight of her out the corner of his eye.

After what seemed an eternity she reached the south end of the deck, and quickly scrambled over the railing, glancing back toward the hut. Still no guard … she turned toward the outer prison wall, a thirteen-foot high, whitewashed wooden fence. This was the part of the plan that was the most dangerous, and where she was most likely to fail; she'd have to jump a little over three feet from the outer edge of the deck to the thin top of the fence without toppling over it—she could only imagine what would happen if she fell to the hard gravel of the alleyway from thirteen feet up! But there was now nothing to do but leap, and so she pulled her skirts up with her hands, and jumped. She landed well, but for a moment teetered on the edge, overbalancing and nearly falling backward back into the prison yard. But she regained her balance and stayed atop the narrow wall.

She turned toward the prison, knelt down, grasped the top of the fence, and lowered her body down the outside of it, until she was gripping the top edge with only her fingertips. She said a quick prayer that she'd not break an ankle or worse, and let go.

Even dangling down her full height, it was a terribly high, six-foot drop. She hit hard, but thankfully a bush had partially broken her fall. Once she was back on her feet, a quick onceover proved she hadn't suffered anything beyond a great shock, bumps, bruises, and scrapes.

With no time to waste, not knowing if she been observed or missed, she quickly moved to the next phase of her plan.

Scrambling deeper in behind the thick row of bushes up against the outside of the prison fence, she found a spot where she could not easily be seen from the alley. She quickly stripped off her dress, rolled it up into a bundle, and shoved it under a bush.

Next, she removed her shoes and socks. These she hid in a place she could identify and easily find later; she couldn't imagine walking barefoot all the way to her final destination, but the shoes were feminine in style, and would be a dead giveaway. Better to go barefoot, as many vagrants were known to do, and retrieve the shoes later.

Under the dress she was already wearing the rough, baggy shirt and trousers she'd fashioned from the dress she'd stolen. Though they'd been made from the same material, the pants were no longer gray, but a dark, dirty brown. This she'd painstakingly accomplished by slowly staining the fabric a few inches at a time via various foods she smuggled from the mess hall. She pulled a hat out that'd been tucked inside the shirt against her skin. The hat had been fashioned by combining the wide brim from her bonnet with the thick wool from the shawl. She tucked her hair up inside the hat and pulled it down snugly over her ears. She'd purposely made it tight enough to prevent the hair from falling loose, as she had nothing to pin it up with.

The last thing needed to complete the outfit was dirt, and plenty of it; she scooped handfuls from around and under the bushes, immediately rubbing in on her face, hands, feet, and shirt. When she figured it had been enough, she did more. *The dirtier the better*, she told herself, thinking how horrified her Momma would be!

When she was finally satisfied with her new look, she crept to the edge of the bushes. So far, nobody was in sight, so she stepped out onto the gravel of the roadway. But instead of dashing off down the alleyway, making good her escape, she did a thing that seemed entirely incongruous: she walked slowly to the far side of the alley, put her back to the brick wall of the building there, and sat, pulling the brim of her hat down over her eyes, trying her best to look relaxed.

In less than two minutes, the prison gate opened and five guards came rushing out, including Sergeant Murphy. Two privates turned left and came her way, while the other three men headed in the opposite direction toward First Street. The two privates immediately trotted straight toward her, and for a moment she feared she'd been discovered. They stopped in front of her, but she kept her eyes down, the brim of her hat covering her face.

Then one of the privates said, "Hey buddy, you seen a young woman come by here a few minutes ago, likely running fast?" For a moment she felt panicked; if she spoke, they'd know she wasn't a man. But then without looking up she slowly held out a dirty, shaky hand—trying to imagine how an old derelict might look and behave—and pointed off down the alley.

"Much obliged," the private said, and the two of them hurried on. She waited a few more minutes, then stood and walked out toward the street. She tried to move slowly and slightly hunched over as if old and somewhat feeble. She'd considered walking with a slight limp, but given she'd just dropped from a high wall, she feared that might raise suspicion and give her away, so she'd thought better of it. She soon reached the street, encountering no one. She took a quick glance to her right, back toward the front door of the prison, to see if she could spot the other three guards, but there was nobody in sight. She turned to her left and started down the street, away from the prison and toward freedom.

Evelyn continued to walk slowly, keeping her head down to help conceal her face. After a few steps she heard a man approaching and couldn't resist a quick glance. But when she looked up, their eyes met, and her heart sank. There was an instant look of recognition in the man's eyes; it was Sergeant Murphy staring straight at her, wide-eyed.

They both stopped and for a moment neither one spoke. Finally, Sergeant Murphy tipped his hat and said, "Miss Eve …"

"Sergeant ..."

And though she felt a crushing weight of despair—abject failure just as she seemed so close to success—she couldn't help noticing Murphy had an odd, inscrutable look on his face, not at all the angry, stern visage she had expected. Then he shocked her by what he said next ...

"So ... what happens now, Miss Eve? Will you try to kill me in order to make your escape?"

Then for the first time since she'd begun her escape attempt, she remembered the stiletto, still in its sheath strapped to her right thigh. Other than being used to cut cloth for sewing her masculine clothes, it had played no role in her escape plans. Until now ... all she had to do was reach into the false pocket she'd sewn into her pants, and then ... *Am I willing to kill this good man in order to escape?* she asked herself. And the emphatic answer came back, *No! No, never! Never in life. I'd rather die myself!*

"I ... I would *never*," she answered, "I would never even *harm* you. What makes you even *say* such a thing, Sergeant Murphy?"

"When they brought you here, they warned us you were not what you appeared—not to take you lightly ... that you were a very dangerous and deadly spy. There was even a rumor going around that you'd murdered a man down on the Virginia Peninsula just before they arrested you. I didn't believe it after being around you for a bit; you always being such the polite, kindly, and perfectly behaved young lady.

"But then I saw what you did to that awful Jane Perkins ... the woman nearly took my head off when I tried to restrain her a few weeks ago, but you gave her a beat down like it was mere child's play. I ain't never seen the like before ..."

"I ... I just got lucky with her is all ..."

"Hmm ... no, I don't think so. Not after what you just pulled off today. I don't know even a single *man* who could've done what you did just now ... planning it all out, then carrying it off with great courage, skill, and timing. And if I hadn't happened to look up just at the right moment and seen you jumping from the guardhouse railing onto the top of the fence, you'd likely have gotten clean away. When I saw it … I was so amazed, I was sore tempted to just let you go."

"You could've, you know …"

He breathed a deep sigh, "You know it's my duty to bring you back, Miss Eve, despite my personal liking of you. And besides … you *are* an enemy spy, after all."

But then it was Murphy's turn to be shocked, when Evelyn teared up in her dismay and frustration, choking out her next words between sobs. "It's true … I am a spy, Sergeant Murphy. Dangerous? *Deadly?!* I don't know …" She shook her head. "I suppose if you're trying to hurt me, or someone I love … I *do* know how to fight …

"But Sergeant … though it's true I'm a spy, I'm a *Union* spy! The man I love fights for the Union and I hate slavery. I help slaves escape Virginia through the Underground Railroad. I've risked my freedom and my very life this past year down in Richmond gathering Confederate military information for the Union War Department! In fact, just before I was arrested, I provided General McClellan with information vital to his Peninsula Campaign—information that could've ensured a Union victory!"

"*What?!* Then why are you here, Miss Eve? Why have they arrested you, if you're on *our* side?"

"I … I don't know. I've asked myself that same question a thousand times since my arrest. Something went wrong … for some reason General McClellan distrusted me … something I did … or something I said … made him doubt me, made him doubt my information.

"From what I've heard from the guards, McClellan's campaign has *not* gone well, and clearly he has not acted on the information I provided him. He must've thought I was a Confederate agent sent to mislead him with false information—to lead him into a trap—so he ignored it and had me arrested. He could've won a great victory if he'd used the information I gave him—maybe even won the war … But by ignoring it …"

"He may very well bring defeat on himself and all of us …" Sergeant Murphy concluded, nodding his head sadly and looking thoughtful. He looked up and met eyes with her, "I believe you, Miss Eve. But it's still my duty to take you back …"

"But Sergeant … isn't it your *first* duty as a soldier to try to win the war? And isn't it more likely the Union might win if I'm back in Richmond finding out vital military information, rather than wasting away in this prison?"

"True … but …"

"Sergeant … I would not ask you to do something that would compromise your position, or even possibly get you hanged for aiding a spy … but if you just walk past now, you could say you never saw me … only an old man in a hat that you asked about the runaway prisoner. No one could prove otherwise. And it'd only be a *small* lie … maybe to help win a *great* war …"

He gazed up at the sky a moment, then looked back down at her and sighed. "I suppose I—"

"*Ah, Sergeant!* There you are! I've been looking all over for you," a voice shouted out; both Evelyn and Murphy flinched at the sound.

One of the privates came trotting up, stopped and put his hands on his knees, panting. "I done ran all the way down the next block and back, and I ain't seen any—" he stopped in mid-sentence as he gazed at Evelyn's face and made recognition.

"Miss Eve! Sergeant, you found her …"

"Yes … I've found her," he answered. But the young private thought his sergeant's expression odd—not elated or victorious as one might expect under the circumstances … more like … *sad*, maybe?

The private looked at Evelyn and said, "You led us quite a good chase, Miss Eve. That was mighty clever of you, dressing up like a man and all. I figured you'd done got clean away. If it wasn't for the Sergeant here …"

She met eyes with Murphy, and he gave her a serious look. But when the private reached behind his back and brought forth a set of iron shackles to put around her wrists, the sergeant stopped him. "That won't be necessary," he said. "Miss Eve … if you give us your word of honor you'll not try to run off again—at least not today—then we'll forgo the usual rules on the matter."

The private seemed surprised at his sergeant's sudden softness, but looked over at Evelyn for her answer.

She reached up with her sleeve and wiped away the remains of her tears before nodding, "Of course, Sergeant; you have my word."

"Thank you, Miss Eve. Shall we?" he said, gesturing back toward the prison doors.

◦◦◦◦◦◦◦◦◦◦◦◦

Friday, April 25, 1862 – Thibodaux, Louisiana:

"Addie! Addie, where are you?" Edouard shouted as he closed the front door of the house and removed his hat. But only the silence of an empty house answered him, so he strode down the hallway, first glancing into her room, and then the nursery. *Nobody.*

Hmm, think Edouard—where would she have gone with the boy on such a pleasant day as this one? Oh! Out back on the swing! Of course! He slapped his forehead in mock reproach for not thinking of it before and simply walking around the outside of the house to the backyard in the first place. He hurried down the hall toward the backdoor, eager to share the news he'd just heard in town.

"Addie!" he called out as he opened the back door and stepped onto the back porch.

"Over here, Uncle," she called back, waving at him from precisely the spot he'd expected to find her, sitting on the swing in the far corner of the yard under the shade of an ancient, massive willow tree.

When he reached the swing he saw the little boy, crawling around in the grass only a few yards away, poking with a stick—looking for bugs and worms, apparently. He was just beginning to take a few tentative steps, but definitely still more comfortable down on the ground.

"Addie … I am simply about to burst …" Edouard said as he sat down beside her. Then suddenly he felt as if it might be true—he'd been in such a rush to get home that he was fairly out of

123

breath, and was frustrated with himself that he had to pause a moment to catch it.

Adilida smiled and patted him gently on the shoulder, "Why Uncle … you've worked yourself up into a frenzy! You must rest a moment and then tell me what has happened to excite you so."

He smiled, and squeezed her hand, then took a couple of deep breaths, before blurting out, "They're here, Addie! They're finally here!"

"They? Who …?"

"The Union … the warships … they've broken through! The entire Union fleet is anchored in the river at New Orleans!"

"*Oh!* Oh, my goodness, Uncle!" she shouted, jumping to her feet and bouncing up and down in her excitement, then pulling Edouard up and bouncing him as well.

He laughed and shook his head, as tears of joy streamed down her face. "*Oh!*" she said again, and this time stepped over to scoop up the boy, kissing him on both cheeks and cooing, "Oh my sweetheart, my lovely little boy … we are finally going to go see your Daddy!" The boy gazed at her with a puzzled expression, but grinned brightly, happily reflecting the joyful look on his momma's face.

She hugged him and danced around the grass for several minutes until he was giggling hysterically. Edouard sat back on the bench and watched, thoroughly enjoying and embracing the happy moment they'd been waiting so long for.

After a few more minutes she set the boy back down and calmed herself enough to sit and ask her uncle for the whole story.

"It has been all the talk in town today, Addie, which is why I have come home early—I simply couldn't wait any longer to tell you. They say sometime late last night there was a tremendous ship battle down at the forts guarding the mouth of the river. The northern warships finally broke the boom chain that had been blocking the river, and they ran the gauntlet between the two Confederate forts with cannons blazing on both sides. Ah … I wish I could've seen it … one can only imagine the fire, smoke, and awesome noise of it …" he shook his head, and gazed off into the distance, as if trying to picture it in his mind.

"And ... then *what*, Uncle?"

"Then the Confederate fleet, which had been stationed upstream of the forts, launched their counterattack—a dozen or more gunboats, some even the new frightful modern ships they call 'ironclads.' But they proved no match for the northerners, and the Confederate fleet was utterly destroyed, to the very last vessel!"

Adilida gasped, putting her hand to her mouth as her eyes teared up, "Oh ... oh *my* ... I can't even imagine it ... all those dear, brave young men ..."

"Yes, yes ... war is a great tragic tale, no matter which side wins. But, if we must have a tragedy, how much better to have it fall upon the other side!" he said and smiled broadly. She shook her head, but she'd always found his jolly face infectious, and couldn't help smiling back.

"So ... now the Union ships are anchored in the river, bristling with guns, filling the entire waterway in front of the city," he continued.

"Then ... will there be a battle, Uncle? Will the Confederate Army fight, do you think?"

"It appears not. From what I have heard, they have already abandoned the city, heading north and away from the river so as to be out of reach of the Union Navy's guns. No, Addie, it seems like it has finally, really happened; the war is over, at least for us."

"Oh thank God, Uncle ... thank God! I feel like I've just been let out of prison! Meaning no offense ..."

"None taken, dear one ... None taken."

⊱⊰⊱⊰⊱⊰⊱⊰⊱⊰⊱⊰

Three days later, Edouard and Adilida stood in the square next to city hall in New Orleans, the little boy held tightly in Adilida's arms. They'd traveled there in Edouard's coach the day before—against his better judgment—as Adilida was becoming frustrated with the lack of any news about a Union takeover, and could no longer sit still, insisting on going there to see what was happening for herself.

From the stories they'd heard, the mayor had refused the Union Navy commander's demand that he surrender the city, and the townsfolk had also shown a stubborn willingness to resist, tearing down an American flag someone had raised above one of the government buildings. All this despite the Confederate Army's complete abandonment of the city.

And now that they were here in person, they could see and feel for themselves the hostile, anti-Union mood of the large crowd gathered in front of the city hall.

They'd been enjoying lunch at a sidewalk café table when they suddenly saw large groups of people hurrying down the street as if something momentous was happening. So, they'd jumped up and followed along.

And now they knew what it was all about: the Union Navy's commander, a tall, handsome, determined-looking middle-aged man, had come himself, leading 250 armed men. They'd marched through the streets of the city, intending to raise the Stars and Stripes above city hall, officially claiming the city on behalf of the Union—surrender or no.

But though they were well armed, and seemingly disciplined and well led, Adilida felt a growing sense of dread and anxiety. This small group of soldiers stood facing a massive sea of disorganized humanity, several thousand strong, which now surrounded them and stood between them and city hall. And the crowd was in an angry, belligerent mood. She could see many of the young men carried sticks, bottles, or rocks. She would not be surprised if some were secretly armed with pistols, as well, though no firearms were visible that she could see.

The Union officer stepped forward and said in a loud, commanding voice, "I am Captain David Farragut of the United States Navy, Flag Officer for the Western Gulf Fleet. We have bombarded your forts and destroyed your fleet. Your own army has evacuated the city and abandoned you.

"Like it or not, we are now in command of this city, and we mean to claim it in the name of the Union. I wish for no further violence, but I will not be gainsaid from my duty. Please stand aside immediately, or I shall have no choice but to use force."

But the crowd did *not* disperse, and there were angry shouts directed at the soldiers, and even a few random projectiles thrown. To Adilida's eye, it appeared things were about to get very ugly. She shared a fearful look with Edouard.

And then to her dismay, the Union officer shouted a command, and the armed men of his company quickly started moving. At first she couldn't tell what they were about, but then in a moment they were still again, and she knew.

The soldiers had formed a square, with men facing outward in all four directions toward the hostile crowd surrounding them, just a few dozen yards away. The soldiers' square now consisted of two rows of men, the first row having taken a knee, so that now the row behind could fire over them.

There was a sudden silence, and Adilida could feel a sharp tension and bitter fear in the air. Some people were moving back, slipping out of the crowd, anxious to get away. But the bulk of the people remained, especially the angry-looking young men.

Then the officer shouted, "Present ... *arms!*" and all the soldiers simultaneously snapped their rifles forward, bayonets bristling outward.

Edouard grabbed Adilida by the arm, "We must get out of here, Addie!" She glanced around and saw many more people streaming away, desperate to escape the deadly guns.

But too many remained—it would be a terrible slaughter. But the soldiers were badly outnumbered, and likely would also be killed. And the fighting would go on ... and the war would continue ... and she would *never* get to see Thomas ...

"No! NO!" she shouted, and almost without thinking she was running toward the soldiers, out in the gap between the two belligerent groups of men. She stopped and turned toward the crowd in front of city hall. "NO! This must STOP!" she screamed, and she held her young child up for all to see.

"This fighting must *stop* ... for our children ... for our families ... will you have the Union Navy bomb our town? Destroy our homes? Kill our families? For *what?!* For WHAT?! The battle is already lost ... the Union has won ... let them raise their flag … Go home to your families … kiss your babies … let them live …"

She turned from side to side as she shouted, showing her young son to the crowd so all could see exactly what was at stake. But as she turned her foot caught against a stone, a missile that'd earlier been thrown at the soldiers, and she lost her balance and fell. Her only thought in that instant was the safety of the baby, so she hit hard on her back holding the boy above her against her breast. For a moment her eyesight swam, she felt dizzy, and did not know what was happening.

And then she looked up and saw a stern looking man in a blue uniform and hat with gold braiding and buttons standing over her, looking down at her. He offered her his hand, and raised her to her feet, still clutching the baby to her breast.

"I am Captain Farragut … that was as boldly and bravely done as anything I've seen in a long lifetime of fighting, miss."

She nodded to him, but could think of no words to say. She didn't feel bold or brave, but rather sheepish and … slightly foolish. She couldn't think of what had come over her to do such a thing—whatever it was, it wasn't bravery, of that she was sure. Desperation and fear were closer to the mark.

But when she gazed about, she noticed she was now within the square of the soldiers—it had moved forward to surround her, now having reached the steps of city hall and taken charge of it, the crowd having parted to let them through.

Then she looked around for Edouard and spotted him, talking animatedly with one of the soldiers, who was holding him back with a rifle held out sideways.

"Oh, Captain … will you please ask your soldiers to let my uncle through? I'm sure he is terribly worried for me."

"Oh, most certainly, dear lady," he responded with a bow and a tip of his hat. And a few moments later Edouard was there by her side, helping to steady her, as she still felt a little light-headed and wobbly.

"Uncle … please … will you take me home now?"

"Of course, of course, my dear one. We will leave first thing in the morning; we will be in Thibodaux by nightfall."

But she shook her head and smiled, "No, not to Thibodaux, Uncle … take me to my *real* home. The home where my heart dwells … take me home to *West Virginia!*"

Thursday May 15, 1862 – Wheeling, Virginia:

"What's the news today, Tom?" Nathan asked, then took another drag on his cigar. He and Tom were enjoying their regular after-dinner ritual of whiskey and cigars on the tiny back patio that served as their "veranda" at Belle Meade Farm. Being proper gentlemen, they'd waited until the ladies had retired for the evening to light up.

Tom picked up the newspaper sitting on the table next to him, unfolded it, and gazed a moment at the headlines. "Says here that Stonewall Jackson's northward march was finally stopped at Franklin, Virginia by forces of Union Major General Fremont. That occurred after Jackson had defeated a sizeable federal force of Fremont's further south at McDowell four days earlier."

Nathan snorted derisively, "Stopped by *Fremont?* More like Jackson got tired of chasing him as he ran away with his tail between his legs!"

Tom chuckled and shook his head.

"Makes one wonder what things would look like right now if Rosecrans hadn't been sacked by McClellan and was still in command of the Western Virginia theatre," Nathan continued with a scowl. "If Rosecrans had all the divisions currently under Fremont and General Banks, I promise you Jackson would be on the run—steadily pushed back toward Richmond, rather than on the offensive moving north."

Tom nodded, but had nothing to add; he and Nathan were in complete agreement concerning the relative merits of General Rosecrans, who was currently languishing in some back office in the war department, versus the Union generals now in the field.

"But what I was really asking about, Tom, was news of Adilida. I saw you received a letter from her this morning, and I assumed it was a follow-up on the good news of the Union's capture of New Orleans ..."

"Oh! Yes ... yes, indeed. Sorry, sir, I should have shared that earlier, even with the ladies. Guess I've been ... a bit tight-lipped today ... trying to get used to the whole idea, I suppose."

Nathan nodded. He had a pretty good idea that Tom was feeling a bit of anxiety and more than a little trepidation now that Adilida's arrival was becoming ever more likely. Tom had never had a serious love interest before, and the idea of suddenly having a woman in his life fulltime was a little overwhelming.

"Well, of course, it's none of my business if you don't wish to speak on it. Just curious is all ..."

"Oh, no ... of course it *is* your business ... having strangers coming to your home ... I was intending to speak with you about it, only ... I hadn't made up my own mind yet," Tom said.

"Made up your mind about *what*, Tom?"

"Well, in her letter she says that Uncle Edouard has decided to accompany her and to relocate to the north permanently. So ... he is going to try to sell his house and business before coming. That will delay their journey a bit, no doubt, while he is making those arrangements. But it implies two new people coming to Belle Meade, and it's not fair to ask you to just take them in, like you have everyone else who's come along," they shared a rueful grin.

"The farmhouse isn't nearly as large as the Big House at Mountain Meadows," Tom continued. "We're already completely full, as far as bedrooms are concerned. So, I was pondering finding them a house somewhere nearby. And then ... depending on how things play out ... I may end up joining them there."

"Nonsense, Tom! Let them stay here ... the more the merrier. Right now, everyone has their own room, but we can have people bunk up. I can move in with you and Edouard can have my room. Then Adilida can share Margaret's room with her—from what you've described of her, I can see the two of them getting along brilliantly, like sisters."

Tom nodded, "Yes ... that could work ..."

Then Nathan grinned, and leaned over to give Tom a good-natured slap on the back, "And if things ... *'play out,'* as you say ...

then we can rearrange things again to be more suitable to that scenario!"

Tom blushed, but returned Nathan's grin.

"Thanks for being so understanding and accommodating, sir. You have greatly relieved my mind."

"Never mention it, Tom. I'm happy to see this great big Chambers extended family keep on growing. With Megs and Margaret, the soldiers, and all the freemen ... it's practically an army already!"

Tom laughed.

Nathan took another sip of whiskey and another puff on his cigar, then leaned forward with a more serious expression.

"Now ... getting back to General Jackson and his present depredations in the Shenandoah Valley ... I've been pondering the idea of killing two birds with one stone, so to speak," Nathan said.

"Oh, how so, sir?"

"Tom ... it is becoming more and more obvious that my old classmate Thomas Jackson is more than capable of out-thinking, out-maneuvering, and out-fighting the Union generals he's coming up against. And I have little faith in their ability to keep a close watch on him and to keep him contained. So, I have a mind to keep tabs on him myself."

"I see ... and the *second* bird?"

"I'm sure you've noticed ... though Billy appears to have healed in the *physical* sense, he seems very low, to me—listless and uninterested in what's going on either here or in the wider world ..."

"Ah ... I'm beginning to get the picture ... you are thinking to send him out on a mission ... to scout out what General Jackson is up to, and report back to you on a regular basis ... via the telegraph service, I suppose—that would be the quickest."

"Yes, precisely. Unless you think it's still too soon to send him out again ..."

"No, sir ... I think it's *exactly* what he needs. And I suppose you'll be asking Stan to go along with him?"

"Of course, though the *asking* part is really only a formality with him!"

They clinked their glasses and took another sip.

❧❧❧❧❧❧❧❧❧

The next afternoon Billy and Stan once again rode heavily laden horses up the drive, and led a spare horse whose pack saddle was bulging with supplies. As they reached the main road and turned their horses north toward Wheeling, Stan took a deep breath and let it out with a satisfied sound, "Ah … feels good to be finally *doing* something again, eh, Billy?"

Billy turned to him and grinned, the first genuine warm expression Stan had seen from him in months. "Yes, Stan … it feels like … like we have just broken out of prison."

Chapter 6. Roads to Harpers Ferry

"I have lately returned from Harpers Ferry,
to which place I was suddenly called,
on the 17th instant, by causes
the most disturbing and destructive
to the peace and safety of this State."
– Virginia Governor Henry Wise,
after John Brown's
failed raid on Harpers Ferry

Friday May 23, 1862 – Washington, D.C.:

Evelyn was in the middle of the third day of her two-week-long punishment for attempting to escape. The punishment, ordered by the warden, was that she must remained locked in her room twenty-four hours a day, with meals brought in, and chamber pot provided for her other necessities. But Sergeant Murphy had exercised his discretion in vetoing the chamber pot idea, instead allowing her escorted trips to the toilet. He said the chamber pot was messy, smelly, and ultimately "undignified for a proper lady such as yourself," for which she was greatly appreciative.

She was now almost obsessed with the idea that Murphy had believed her when she told him she was on the Union side. And she was almost certain he would've let her go right then, if the private hadn't come rushing up when he did. It gave her hope that once her lockdown punishment was over, she could convince Murphy to reach out to Nathan that he might use his War Department connections to intervene on her behalf. The more she thought about this, the more confident she began to feel about it.

Then she chuckled to herself, envisioning Nathan storming into the prison himself, along with all his men, weapons drawn, demanding her immediate release. It was just the kind of thing he would do.

She was ruminating on these thoughts and finishing up her lunch, a bland soup of carrots and potatoes along with some unidentifiable type of meat, when the barred door to her room was opened by one of the guards.

"I'm not quite finished yet, but if you'll give me but a moment …" she said.

"Never mind that, Miss Eve; I'm not here to collect your dishes this time. The Sergeant says you're wanted in the guardroom, post haste. So … I suppose you'll have to finish it up later."

"Oh … all right," she answered, standing up from her bed and setting the half-finished bowl on the wooden tray sitting on the floor next to the bed. "But never mind about the food … it isn't that good anyway," she said, giving the guard a half smile, which he readily returned and nodded.

She walked a few paces in front of the guard, as was customary when being escorted, down the hall to her right, and then down the stairs to the first floor where the inside guard room was located. She wondered if the warden had decided to lay on additional punishment for her escape. Though she liked Sergeant Murphy and most of the guards, she had no good feelings for the warden. He was a quiet, mousey-looking older man, who gazed at her unsmiling over thick spectacles. He gave her a creepy feeling, like he was constantly sizing her up for his bed. Then she had to suppress a chuckle as a wicked little thought came to mind, *given the rumors going around, he's probably too afraid of me to ever try anything. Probably thinks I'll murder him in his sleep. And he might be right, come to think of it.*

But when she arrived at the guard room, she was surprised that it wasn't the warden waiting for her with the sergeant, but another man, a Union Army major, by his uniform. And this man immediately gave her a very bad feeling—if anything, worse than the warden. This man looked at her not as a man sizing up a sexual conquest, but more like a cat sizing up the meal he was going to make of the pet canary—after first mangling it painfully.

The major appeared to be in his mid-forties, with a hint of gray at his temples and in his neatly trimmed beard. He was attractive, but in a severe way, and she shuddered at the evil look he gave her as she entered the room. She quickly glanced over at Sergeant Murphy seeking to gain some comfort from his kindly face. But if anything, the concerned look he gave her made her even more anxious.

The major glanced down at a sheet of paper he held in his hand and said, "So ... Miss Eve *Smith*, is it?" he snorted derisively, "Not your *real* name I assume ... not especially creative ..."

She shrugged, trying to appear calm, "Would you prefer I made up another? It is of no difference to me."

He smiled, "No ... that won't be necessary, Miss Eve. We will find out your *real* name soon enough. At the War Department we have men ... hmm ... who are especially good at extracting the truth from those who are ... how shall we say? *Hesitant? Reluctant? Recalcitrant?* At any rate, I have a *particular* man in mind who is very skilled at ... *convincing* people ... to tell him anything he wishes to know ..."

He gave her such a vile leer as to leave little doubt the man he was speaking of was himself. Once again, she had to resist the urge to shudder and look away, determined to look him in the eye and show no fear.

But then Sergeant Murphy, who was becoming red in the face, said, "Listen here, Major ... I'll not sit idly by and allow you, or anyone else, to harm this proper lady ..."

"Proper lady?! I see no proper lady here, only a despicable spy—lying, whoring, and murdering ... all to destroy our great country in the name of some ridiculous and outdated concept that should've been cleansed from the earth decades ago."

Sergeant Murphy stood to his feet, "Now you look here, sir; I'll not have you speak to this lady in that manner, and I'm certainly not allowing you to take her away to do ... *God knows what* to her ..."

"Oh? Is that so, Sergeant? And how is it you think to stop me? I am, after all, your superior officer, not to mention I have a signed transfer order here, authorizing me to remove this prisoner and take her away with me ..."

"Oh, but I *can* stop you, sir! You see, this isn't the proper form ... this is the *old* form. We stopped using this one ... oh, six months ago. Look here," he pointed to the sheet of paper in front of him on the desk, as the major leaned over for a look, "there's supposed to be a countersignature of the duty officer certifying the orders. This form's got no countersignature, therefore I can't release the prisoner to you … *sir*." Murphy sat back in his chair, folding his arms, but not quite looking smug.

The major scowled, "Sergeant … did you happen to notice who specifically signed this document?"

Murphy leaned forward and examined the signature on the order, "Um … looks like … *Edwin … Stanton*. Uh … would that be *Secretary of War* Edwin Stanton?"

"Yes … and I'm sure the secretary will be so happy to hear that, due to his inadvertently grabbing the *old* form to secure this prisoner, he'll not be able to have her interrogated today as he has himself ordered. Allow me to write down your name and regiment number that I may pass it along to his honor that he might … *properly thank you* for doing your duty so thoroughly … *private*." The major gave Murphy a wicked looking half smile, and the veiled threat of a demotion was not lost on him.

But Murphy proved himself no coward, and now his dander was up. He glared at the major, and said, "It's Murphy … spelled M U R P H Y … Sergeant Major Patrick Murphy, Twelfth New York Volunteer Regi—"

But Evelyn placed her hand on Murphy's arm and said, "No, Sergeant. I thank you for your concern, but I will not have you punished on my behalf, and to no benefit."

She met eyes with Murphy for a long moment, and finally he sighed, and nodded.

"I will go with this man—and willingly," she continued. "At least then I will finally have my say. We must have faith, Sergeant Murphy, that all will turn out for the best. To paraphrase our Lord the Christ, '*They* shall learn the truth, and the truth shall set *me* free.'"

But the major scoffed, "Oh, we'll learn the truth all right. As for the other part … I'd not be so sure about *that* if I were you …"

ᔰᑑᑐᙯᙰᘯᔰᑑᑐᙯᙰᘯᔰᑑᑐᙯᙰᘯ

The major, whose name was Cooper, put iron shackles on her wrists before escorting her out the front door of the prison to a waiting coach. He carried a pistol in a holster at his waist, but said, "I assume I can keep my sidearm holstered—that you'll not attempt to resist?"

She nodded, "Yes, Major. I am more than ready to get to … wherever we are going."

"Good. The more you cooperate the easier it will go for you," he said. And though he'd not warmed up any, he seemed to have lost some of his earlier cruel edge. It made her wonder how much of that had been for the sergeant's benefit. *Men*, she thought.

And though she was still filled with much trepidation, she could take solace in the fact she was finally out of prison … at least for the moment.

At first, Evelyn paid little attention to their route, but after a few minutes she realized they weren't going in the direction she'd expected. Though she'd never lived in the city, she had visited once as a young girl, and had studied maps of the nation's capital with great excitement and enthusiasm both before and after that visit. One could easily see the Capitol Building just a block away to the west of the Old Capitol Prison, and she knew the War Department building was sited right next to the White House. They should have headed west and circled around the north side of the Capitol grounds, then turned right onto Pennsylvania Avenue, to the northwest. But instead, they were traveling due north on First Street. *That's odd*, she thought.

"Where are we going, Major?"

She half expected him to snap back that it was none of her concern, but instead he answered her question with a question, "Where do you think we are going?"

"I … I assumed we were going to the War Department, but it's not in this direction …"

"You are quite observant and clever, just as I have been informed, Miss Eve. Or should I say, Miss Evelyn Hanson?"

"Oh! So you *do* know my real name, after all."

"Yes … I know that … and many other things about you."

"I suppose that's a good thing, as I have nothing to hide. So ... where did you say we were going?"

"I didn't. But you will know soon enough. Then *all* your questions will be answered."

She couldn't puzzle out what it meant, but apparently he was right about not waiting long: a few blocks later the carriage turned right, into an alleyway off First Street, and then came to a stop behind a large house.

"Ah ... this is our stop," the major announced with a grin. She didn't like the look of that grin, and couldn't understand why he was taking her to this house. Was it a place where they took prisoners to be interrogated? Away from the eyes, and more important, the *ears* of the regular Army officers at the War Department? Or could it be something more nefarious? Perhaps the major's personal hideaway where he took female prisoners so he could have his way with them?

She had little choice but to comply—for the moment, anyway—at least until she knew what this was all about ... for good or ill. She still had the stiletto, and was confident she could pull it from its sheath on her thigh if need be, though that would be a risky thing against a man armed with a pistol.

Two men came out, one white and one black, to secure the horses. The black man came around and assisted her down from the carriage. The heavy iron shackles on her wrists made the whole maneuver awkward, so she was grateful for the help.

Major Cooper led her in through the back door, down a hallway, then into a larger room like a library or sitting room. She noticed he carried a green canvas bag with leather handles, which she recognized as her own, the one she was carrying when she was arrested in Virginia.

He set the bag down on a side table, reached into his jacket pocket and pulled out something small and shiny. "Hold out your wrists, please," he said.

She complied, and he used a small key to unlock the shackles, tossing them casually into a chair to one side of the room. She rubbed at her wrists, grateful to have the annoying weight removed.

"Thank you," she said.

He pointed to a chair in the corner which had something in the seat. "I will leave you alone for a moment so you may change into those clothes. I trust they will fit and I'm sure you'll be happy to rid yourself of that deplorable prison garb and change into something a bit more ... *fashionable*. I shall return momentarily."

She nodded, but said nothing as he exited the room.

But she did not immediately move toward the pile of clothes, instead going directly to the side table and her travel bag. She dug through it quickly and was almost shocked to find the small Smith & Wesson revolver was still there! Apparently, the Major hadn't bothered to search the bag before carrying it away from the prison, foolishly assuming it only contained clothing and other personal effects.

She checked the pistol's cylinder and was once again surprised to see it was still loaded. So, her bag had sat all that time in some storage place in the prison guardhouse with a loaded pistol in it! She shook her head slowly in disbelief. She had to assume — it being such an unusually modern weapon — the guards had never seen anything like it before, and didn't know how to unload it. They probably decided it was best to just leave it alone, and so they had. And that had proved to be her great good fortune. Her confidence soared; now she truly *was* a dangerous spy, even as Sergeant Murphy had said.

Approximately ten minutes later, there was a soft knock on the door, and Major Cooper reentered. She was surprised to see he was no longer wearing his Army uniform. Instead, he wore the dark suit of a gentleman, such as a government official might wear in Washington City.

And the major was surprised to find a loaded pistol pointed at his face as he stepped into the room.

His eyes widened and he slowly raised his hands, "Th ... th ... that won't be necessary, Miss Evelyn, I assure you ..."

"I'll be the judge of that," she answered, with a scowl. "Now ... I *will* have my questions answered ... what is this place, and what am I doing here?"

"I will happily answer all your questions, Miss Evelyn, but first … may I sit … please?"

She nodded and waved him toward a chair with the pistol. He moved cautiously toward it, keeping his hands raised, and his eyes on her.

"Perhaps before I answer your other questions, Miss Evelyn, it might help matters if I tell you my name … my *real* name."

"Yes?"

"My name is Nigel Hughes … you may recognize the name … I believe you know my cousin, *Jonathan* Hughes, though I should not utter that name again in this city. From here on I must refer to him only as … *the Employer*."

Her mouth dropped open and she lowered the pistol, slowly letting down the hammer. "Hughes …? Then you're … you're …"

"Yes, I'm from the Boston side of the family, and I have come to Washington to break you out of that prison. And *that*, my dear lady, is *exactly* what I have just done!" he said and beamed. It was the very same smile Jonathan displayed when he felt proud of himself, further proof that he and Nigel were closely related. And this time the smile was of the genuine, warm kind, and there was no evil in it.

"Then … Nigel, you are also one of Jonathan's spies?" she asked.

"Oh, no! Certainly not! I'm only a bookkeeper at the family shipping business. No, no, heavens no. Doing the things *you* do would scare the life out of me! I could never do it."

"But then … what you did today …?"

"Oh, *that*. Well yes … what did you think of my performance?"

"It was … very convincing. You had me truly afraid of you — that you were the very worst sort of villain."

He smiled brightly, "Good, good. Then I haven't lost it!"

"I … I don't understand … you say you're not a spy, but you dressed as a Union officer, and helped me escape from a prison. If you're not a spy, then …?"

"I'm an *actor*, my dear. Or at least I want to be … more of an amateur really, at this stage … oh, that was a pun … actor, stage …" he chuckled.

She smiled, "So, you're only an actor?"

"Well, I'm not sure I like the use of the term *only* … but, yes. Once Jonathan had figured out where you were, and had hatched his scheme to get you out, he contacted me. He asked if I thought I could play the part of a ruthless Union officer from the War Department. Of course, I jumped at the chance to play such a challenging role! Almost overdid it there with your sergeant, though, I fear. If you hadn't intervened when he discovered the paperwork we'd forged was the *old* form, I'm not sure what I'd have done. He was a stout fellow, more than ready to call my bluff."

She smiled, and shook her head, feeling the tension drain from her body as her fears dissipated.

"Yes, the sergeant's a good man. And yes, it was truly a masterful performance, Nigel, I must say. You played the heartless villain perfectly."

"Thank you, my dear."

"*No!* Thank *you*, Nigel, for being so brilliant and brave, risking all to break me out of prison!"

❧❦❧❦❧❦❧❦❧❦

"Come, Miss Evelyn … you really must get changed now, and once you're finished, the maid will help you with your hair."

"Help with my hair? This seems an odd time to worry over my hair …"

"She has a very good hair dye; it will turn your hair black. But never fear, it will wash out in a few weeks."

"Oh! Do you really think that's necessary?"

Nigel smiled and reached up to his ear, grabbed hold of a corner of his beard and pulled. The beard began to peel off, followed by the mustache, until he appeared completely clean shaven. Then he rubbed his hair at his temples, and the gray she'd noticed earlier seemed to flake off, leaving him looking at least ten years younger. His appearance was no longer anything like the frightful, older Union officer he had seemed only a few minutes earlier. He now appeared as he truly was: a handsome, clean-cut young gentleman in his early thirties.

"We can't be too careful, Miss Evelyn. Once they discover there *is* no major in the War Department named Cooper, they will be looking for a middle-aged man with a beard and a beautiful woman with long, blonde hair …"

"You're not going to ask me to cut it?! It has taken years to grow it to this length."

"No … that won't be necessary. Once it's dyed the maid will pin it up in a bun … no one will be able to tell its length."

"Oh, all right then. But … where are we going? To your family in Boston?"

He smiled, "As much as I would enjoy keeping you near me … I fear you would not long enjoy being stuck in Boston. No, not to Boston, but … we *do* have a train to catch, if you'll just get changed."

Now that he'd switched out of his "major" role, Evelyn noticed Nigel was becoming flirtatious, and was clearly attracted to her. She thought again of Jubal, and shuddered. She'd thoughtlessly used his attraction against him, and had since come to regret it. She would have to be careful with Nigel, not to mislead or hurt him, as she already owed him her freedom.

☙☙☙☙☙☙☙

It was only a few blocks to the main B&O station, but despite the noisy carriage ride, Evelyn couldn't hold back the flood of questions that'd been burning in her mind for the last month and more.

"Nigel, please tell me … whatever happened to Joseph on the night we parted in Richmond? I've been so worried about him, and I prayed for him every day that I was incarcerated."

"*Joseph?* I … I don't recall hearing anything about a man by that name. Why, who is he?"

"He's one of Jonathan's men. He helped me sneak out of Richmond by picking a fight with some soldiers who were guarding the docks. I have been so worried he may have been badly injured … or worse …"

Nigel looked thoughtful for a moment, then shook his head, "I'm sorry, my dear … I don't recall hearing anything about him. Perhaps we should take that as a *good* sign …?"

She nodded, but looked down at her feet for a long moment. Finally she sighed, wiped her eyes, and looked back up.

"Nigel … why didn't Jonathan arrange to get me out sooner? He is always talking about his many contacts in the Union War Department … why didn't they just send a *real* major to get me out and set me free? Why all the subterfuge, even now, when the fact is I'm really on the Union side?"

Nigel nodded, and said, "I can see why it would feel that way from your perspective … but the problem was, Jonathan didn't know where you were. Nobody did. Nobody except General McClellan and his trusted men, of course."

"What?! You mean the general sent me to prison without the knowledge of the War Department?! That seems … *bizarre,* at a minimum."

"Yes … I agree with you, and so does Jonathan. Though I haven't spoken with him in person, of course, I understand your disappearance was … well, extremely upsetting to him and to Angeline—to say the least. They dropped everything they were working on and redirected all their people toward finding you. At the beginning they feared the worst, especially after the fishing boat that had transported you went missing … and then its captain was found washed up on shore with stab wounds. It took a long time to discover that you had in fact made it safely into General McClellan's camp."

Evelyn groaned, "Yes … I can see how they would've assumed the worst. But I really had no means to communicate with them that whole time. I thought … wrongly it now seems … that the general would accept my information at face value and then assist me in returning to Richmond straight away. Clearly something went wrong … instead, they escorted me straight to prison in Washington, accusing me of being a spy for the rebels."

"Well, I am not privy to the details, but you know Jonathan … somehow he found out where you were. But then … he didn't know who he could trust. Obviously General McClellan was no longer completely cooperating with the War Department. There have even been rumors of a rift between him and Secretary of War Stanton, and possibly even with the president! But McClellan has allies in the War Department, who obviously report things directly to him. And there have also been rumors of Confederate spies inside the Department. Jonathan just couldn't risk exposing you to the enemy, so he decided to ... 'keep it in the family,' as it were. And so ... you were stuck with being rescued by an actor."

"I wouldn't call it 'stuck,' Nigel. You have carried off your part quite heroically."

"Thank you for saying so, my dear. It is greatly appreciated."

ༀༀༀༀༀༀༀༀༀༀ

Evelyn and Nigel boarded a northbound train at the Washington B&O Station. Nigel carried forged papers proving he was a mid-level federal government official on important business of the Lincoln administration, and he was being accompanied by his wife as it was to be an extended posting. The conductor gave the paperwork only a cursory glance and waved them aboard.

"Where are we going, anyway, Nigel?" Evelyn asked. She'd been so happy to be free, and so curious about what her allies had been doing to secure her escape, that she hadn't thought much about their route back to Richmond. Now it occurred to her they were heading north toward Baltimore ... in exactly the opposite direction as Richmond.

"Ah ... it's a good question. It turns out there's a war on, which is making travel a bit ... *tricky*," he said, with a grin.

She rolled her eyes, "You don't say ..."

"Yes, well ... hmm ... anyway, all the direct routes are cut— sea, rail, road—there's just no way to get to Richmond from here right now, unless you have a very large army at your disposal ... and apparently that is proving insufficient at the moment, at least for General McClellan." He chuckled at his own humor, and shook his head.

"Yes, yes ... then *what?*"

"Well, ironically, the easiest way to get to eastern Virginia right now, is from western Virginia."

"Oh?" Evelyn started to have an odd, tingling feeling about where this was headed ... *Nathan lives in western Virginia ...*

"Of course, I would've had no idea about any of this, but Jonathan ... well, he's been the head of the family ever since father died ... definitely the one the rest of us look to for making the difficult and important decisions. Anyway, he has figured out how to get you back to Richmond, though it does seem a bit roundabout.

"We will first take this train to Baltimore, where we'll spend the night in a boarding house owned by the company. Then in the morning we'll board another train headed west through northern Virginia, taking it all the way to its terminus at Wheeling."

At the name "Wheeling" Evelyn's heart skipped a beat. *Nathan's new farm is in Wheeling!*

"And then ... Jonathan has arranged for a small boat to take us down the Ohio River to the mouth of the Kanawha River. There we will take a steamboat upstream as far as it's navigable, after which we'll hire a carriage, or obtain horses, and work our way up the Kanawha Valley. The valley is currently held by Union forces all the way to Greenbrier County, where the Confederates still hold sway. The only really tricky part of the journey will be when we have to cross over into enemy territory somewhere around ... hmm ... what was the name of the little town there?"

"Lewisburg?" Evelyn suggested. *Mountain Meadows Farm ... Nathan's old home, sits just down the road from Lewisburg!*

"Yes, that was it. Once we've gained the Confederate side, we should have no trouble passing on over into eastern Virginia. Though when I say, 'us,' I actually mean *you* ... in Lewisburg I am to hand you off to another of Jonathan's men who'll take you the rest of the way, so that I may return to Boston and not risk being apprehended by the enemy. I'm not privy to what your route will be from that point, though I suspect it may also prove roundabout in order to avoid any active warfare."

"Thank you, Nigel. And you're right ... that does sound very convoluted ... I hope it will all work out," she said, but her mind was already wandering down another path, which asked her, *how will I ever leave Wheeling if* he *is there?*

"Hopefully we'll be able to get aboard a westbound train in Baltimore; there are rumors of a possible battle brewing out west, and the army may be packing every available train full with troops."

"Oh? Where out west?"

"Harpers Ferry."

ঙⅅঙⅬⅭⅫঙⅅঙⅬⅭⅫঙⅅঙⅬⅭⅫ

Friday May 23, 1862 – Wheeling, Virginia:

"Good morning, your honor. Have you a moment?" Nathan said, standing in the doorway to Governor Pierpont's modest office, Harry the Dog next to him, gazing in at the governor, his tongue hanging out to one side as usual. It was just after sunrise and the governor hadn't yet finished his first morning cup of coffee, but he was never surprised to see Nathan in this early; such was his habit.

"Good morning, Nathan," Pierpont responded, "I would have a free moment, if it weren't for this tremendous stack of damned requisition papers I've got to sign. Can't get a loaf of bread out to our troops without sixteen signatures, seems like!"

Nathan snorted a short laugh, "Yep … welcome to the Army, Francis."

"Come on in, Nathan … have a seat. I'm always happy to postpone doing paperwork," Pierpont said, with a rueful look.

"Thank you, but I'm not here to sit … I've brought a map I'd like you to have a look at with me, if you would," Nathan answered, stepping over to the governor's side table, and unrolling the map.

The governor stood, came around the desk to the side table, then gazed down at the map. "Shenandoah Valley?" he asked.

"Yes … I've been gathering together all the scouting reports, dispatches, and even newspaper articles concerning General Jackson's moves in his current campaign. I even sent some of my own men out to the valley to see what they could discover."

146

"Oh? And since you are not yet a general in the army, what is your purpose for doing all this extra work, or haven't I given you enough to do yet?"

Nathan scowled at him, but chose to ignore the last question; they both knew well Nathan and his men had been asked to do multiple overlapping jobs at once on behalf of both the Restored Government and the new West Virginia government to be, and rarely was there a moment they weren't involved in some activity in that regard.

"I know my old schoolmate Thomas Jackson probably as well as anyone on the Union side at this point, so I think I have a pretty good idea how he thinks when it comes to executing a campaign. I thought if I looked through all the information available, I might be able to discern what he means to do next, and possibly even his overall strategy for the offensive."

"Yes ... seems reasonable ... and were you able to come up with a plausible theory, Nathan?"

"I have, your honor, and to be honest, it frightens me. That's why I'm here: to discuss my thinking with you and then for the two of us to figure out what, if anything, we can do about it."

"Oh, dear! If something frightens *you* ... well, it's got to be pretty ominous."

"I fear so. Look at this, Francis," Nathan said, pointing to a spot on the map. "Jackson's last known position was here ... up the main section of the valley at Harrisonburg. He'd pulled back to that position after besting General Fremont's forces at McDowell ... here."

Pierpont nodded.

"But the dispatches I've seen from General Fremont's scouts have reported no movement whatsoever from Jackson since just after the engagement at McDowell two weeks ago."

"Yes ... So?"

"So, the one constant with Jackson is change. He doesn't believe in sitting still for long, especially when he's on the offensive. And he knows he's ultimately outnumbered by the overall Union forces in the area, but that they are currently not in position to attack him with combined strength. However, if he stays put for too long his enemies can close with him and put him at a disadvantage. So …"

"So he has to keep moving. But if Fremont reports Jackson is staying still …"

"Yes, your honor, it's most likely a ruse—that Jackson has left enough men in camp with instructions to march around, make a lot of noise, light fires at night, and so forth to convince the Union scouts he is still there. Meanwhile he has marched the bulk of his army out quietly at night unobserved."

"It's a good theory, Nathan, but—"

"It *was* a theory your honor, but not anymore."

"Oh?"

"I sent my men Billy and Stan over to have a look—see if Jackson's army is really there, or just a group of play actors. I just received a telegram from them saying Jackson is *not* there, even as I had feared. They are now following after him, but Jackson has a considerable head start on them, so it will likely take days to hear any definitive news concerning the rebel army's whereabouts."

"So then … we wait?"

"No. If we wait, it could be too late."

"Too late for what, Nathan?"

"Too late to save our nation's capital!" Nathan answered with a grim look.

After a moment's shocked silence, Pierpont said, "Please explain to me why you think Jackson is a threat to Washington from … well, *wherever he is* in the Shenandoah Valley?"

"Look at the map, Francis … General Fremont is here, at Franklin—too far out to the west at the moment to have any effect on events that may be unfolding in the valley.

"And General Banks' main force is here, at Strasburg."

"All right … but that would seem to put Banks, at least, between Jackson and Washington. And if I'm not mistaken, he has a *very* sizable force—certainly more than a match for Jackson."

"It would be, if Jackson were to attack him head-on. But it's not what *I* would do, and I don't think it's what Jackson will do."

"What would *you* do, then?"

"I would attack here, at Front Royal, a dozen or so miles to the east. Banks has only a small garrison stationed there, no match for Jackson's main force."

"*Front Royal?* Hmm … Front … Royal … why is the name of that town bringing something to mind …?" Pierpont said, scratching the whiskers on his chin and gazing up at the ceiling for a moment. "*Oh no* … Nathan, I saw a dispatch from the War Department yesterday, complaining they'd suddenly lost communication with Front Royal, asking if we knew anything about it. They feared the telegraph line had been cut by the rebels! You don't suppose …"

Nathan nodded, "I suspect it means an attack is either imminent, or already underway. But look here … there's a main road from Front Royal straight to Winchester, General Banks' supply base. Worst-case scenario, Jackson rolls through Front Royal, moves on Winchester, and flanks General Banks in the process, either routing him or driving him off to regroup. Now … your honor, trace a line from Winchester to the nearest bridge across the Potomac into Maryland … here, and you have a wide-open road straight to—"

"*Washington!* Now you have *me* frightened, Nathan. But surely the capital is well defended? There must be … several divisions at the least, positioned for just such an eventuality."

"Normally there would be … but from what I understand, McClellan has not only moved the vast Army of the Potomac to the Virginia Peninsula for his invasion, he has also dragged along with him pretty much every able-bodied Union soldier available. The capital has been nearly depleted of its defenders. The closest army would be that of General McDowell, who even now is marching south through Virginia to meet up with McClellan and join his offensive. I have not been able to discern exactly where McDowell is at the moment; the War Department hasn't been especially forthcoming about that detail."

"All right … assuming for the moment McDowell is out of the fight, what's left? Are there no Union forces at all between Winchester and Washington?"

"Only here," Nathan pointed to a spot on the map where the closest bridge to Winchester crossed the Potomac at the confluence with the Shenandoah River, "at Harpers Ferry. The so-called 'Railroad Brigade' commanded by a Colonel Miles. The brigade is currently headquartered there, but spread out all along the rail line to guard the B&O from rebel guerillas. There are less than a thousand soldiers at present in Harpers Ferry itself. And despite being such a strategically important crossroads, the town has no fortifications and no permanent garrison or artillery emplacements."

"*Oh my God* … what should we do then? What *can* we do?"

"We must do everything we can to prevent a catastrophe, your honor. Firstly, *you* must fire off a telegram to the War Department, warning them of the danger, and beseeching them to send every man they have who can carry a rifle out to Harpers Ferry, as soon as can be arranged. And plenty of heavy artillery!"

"All right, I can do that. But what will *you* be doing?"

"I'll be on the next train to Harpers Ferry."

ЖѲЖѲСЯСͰЖѲЖѲСЯСͰЖѲЖѲСЯСͰ

"Where the hell you boys been?" Jim asked, with a scowl as Jamie and Georgie stepped into the bunkhouse, looking glum and disheveled. "We been lookin' high and low, but nobody knew where you'd got to. And … what the *hell* happened to you sorry sum-bitches?" He asked, noticing for the first time that Georgie was sporting an eye that was red and half swollen shut, and Jamie had a split lip and blood splattered all down the front of his shirt. Georgie just grumbled something unintelligible before flopping down on his bed and putting his hands over his face.

Jamie said, "We were havin' ourselves a fight, if you can imagine that, Sergeant Jim."

"With each other? What's wrong with you two numbskulls anyhow?"

"No, no … not with *each other*, Sarge … not this time, anyway … no, it was some local yokels all dressed in blue with brass buttons, itchin' for to pick a fight with us."

150

"Hmm ... musta been some awful tough bastards by the look o' you two," Jim answered with a grin, unable to resist getting in a little dig.

But then Jamie also grinned for the first time, showing blood on his teeth, "Not hardly, Sarge ... there was five o' them, you see ... and ... you ain't seen how sorry they're lookin' just now. Like a blind cobbler's thumb, I'm telling you. I figure even their dear mommas won't know them after how they're lookin'."

"Ah ... well, that sounds a might better, I'll warrant," Jim said. "But ... what was the fight about anyway?"

"The usual ..." Jamie said, and plopped down on the bed next to Georgie.

"Hmph!" Jim snorted, "I've had a bellyful of them hotheaded young toughs thinkin' they're somethin' keen just 'cause they've put on an Army uniform. Like we weren't out in Texas all them years fighting Indians in them blue suits before them fellas was weaned from their momma's tits!" he turned to spit for emphasis, then realized he was indoors and thought better of it.

"True, sir ... but sometimes a man tires o' explainin' the thing for the umpteenth time, and decides to just knock someone's teeth out instead," Jamie answered with a shrug.

"Damned nuisance, all right. But happily the Captain says they's a big battle brewin' over to Harpers Ferry, and we're all invited to the party. So get off your sore bums and get your gear together!"

This news made Georgie sit straight up on the bunk, "Well ... 'bout damned time! Finally some *good* news around here!"

❦❧❦❧❦❧❦❧❦❧❦❧

Tony sat on a wooden bench in the old toolshed that'd become the classroom for the freemen children who were being taught reading and writing by Mr. William and Miss Margaret. It was also the unofficial meeting place of Tony's close group of freemen friends, Big George, Ned, Henry, Cobb, and Phinney, who'd become especially close after fighting during the breakout from Mountain Meadows—a friendship that'd been further cemented with their clandestine attack on their murderous neighbor Ward and his cronies a few months back.

But the usual humorous, manly banter was conspicuously absent this morning, replaced by a self-conscious, nervous quietness, resulting from the odd nature of their "summons" to this meeting.

They'd been out in the fields working when the white foreman Zeke came striding out and told them the Captain wanted to speak with them right away—that they should drop their rakes where they were and come to the "classroom" immediately. So, here they were, waiting anxiously—but so far, no Captain.

Tony met eyes with Big George and said, "What you reckon it's about George?"

But he just shrugged his broad shoulders, and said, "Got no idea, Tony ... ain't even heard the whiff o' any rumors this mornin'" Then George looked over to the others, "Anyone heard anything?"

But they all were just as puzzled, and either shook their heads or shrugged. Then Ned scowled, and said, "As usual, the weeds ain't said nothin'," which made Tony snort a short laugh.

They didn't have long to wait. At that moment the Captain came in and immediately took a seat facing the group, his large hound plopping down heavily next to him.

"Good morning, men, and thanks for coming so promptly," he said.

They greeted him in kind, and Tony resisted the urge to ask him what it was about, knowing he would get to it soon enough. But he also thought the Captain looked anxious about something and seemed somewhat distracted and in a hurry.

"I'll get right to it, men. Firstly, I still haven't had any news about getting y'all into the fight for the Union, though you can believe me when I tell you I've promoted the idea to anyone who'll listen—generals, War Department officers, government officials, politicians ... even newspaper men. And ... I think it likely I'll have a chance to speak with the president himself later in the year when I go with some others to speak with him about the new state. Then I mean to talk to him directly about that very issue … and other urgent related matters. But sadly, that's a discussion for another day …

"The reason you find me so impatient and rushed is that there is a potential battle brewing out east of here at a place along the Potomac River called Harpers Ferry, where the railroad crosses by a bridge. But as of now the Union forces are woefully inadequate to stand against the rebel forces threatening. I mean to go there and do whatever I can to help organize the defense of the town. I will take my experienced Texas soldiers with me to assist in that effort, but sadly I can't take y'all—for the reason I just stated, but also because I still fear our old enemy Elijah Walters may once again try to take advantage of my absence and that of my other men. I really need you freemen armed and ready, standing guard day and night here at the farm while I'm gone."

Tony, not waiting for the others, said, "We're your men, Captain; you ain't got to worry none on that. We know we can't go out an' fight in the war yet, but we sure as hell can shoot ol' Walters if he come onto this-here farm."

The others nodded, and Big George added, "Amen to that, Tony!"

Nathan smiled, and nodded. "Thank you, gentlemen. I knew I could count on you. And I think you can consider it a testament to my complete faith in you that I am entrusting you with the safety of my own Momma, Megs, and my sister Margaret; that is a thing I don't take lightly, as you can well imagine."

"Yes, Captain," George said, "and we'll not let you down, sir."

"I know you won't, and I thank you. Now … there is one more matter I wish to discuss with you men. It's related to the first topic—that of y'all not yet being able to fight …

"I've been thinking about this a lot and …" he looked over at Henry and held his eye in a meaningful way, then continued, "like *other* decisions I might not have considered years ago, I believe this one is the *right* thing to do, though it may not be, strictly speaking, the *'proper'* thing to do." Henry smiled and nodded, acknowledging that the Captain had earlier compromised his own sacred honor and principles in order to forge Henry's manumission papers, making him a freeman.

Nathan looked back at the group and said, "I wish I could take y'all along to the battle. But since I can't, I'd at least like to take one of you along to serve as a witness for the other freemen—a witness to this crucial battle, since you're the ones most affected by the eventual outcome.

"Though, I am obliged to warn you: if the battle goes badly, some of us, or all of us there may be killed, though I know you men are no stranger to that. God knows you proved your courage many times over on the way here from Mountain Meadows and after. Anyway, I will leave now that you may discuss it amongst yourselves, whether or not you wish to send someone, and if so, who it will be."

But Big George looked around at the others, who immediately nodded, then he turned to Nathan and said, "You ain't got to go, Captain, 'cause we got nothin' to discuss. We agree with you on it."

"Excellent, and thank you kindly," Nathan answered, "but you should at least discuss who should go to represent you."

But George shook his head, and Tony was in agreement; obviously Big George should be the one to go. But George surprised Tony by grabbing him by the shirtsleeve and saying, "It's gotta be Tony … he's our leader and by rights ought to be our witness to the big ol' gun fight."

Tony was shocked, and turned to George to object, but Ned said, "He's right, Tony. It gots to be you. You're our man …"

Nathan nodded, and said, "Good. It's settled then. Tony, pack your things, we leave within the hour." He stood and headed out the door, a smile touching the corner of his eyes; it was *exactly* the outcome he'd hoped for.

છତઉચ૪ઉ૪ૐছତઉচ૪ઉ૪ૐছତઉচ૪ઉ૪ૐ

William knocked softly on the door to Margaret's bedroom. He still felt uncomfortable coming into the farmhouse uninvited, though the logical part of his mind knew that nobody minded him doing so and he was welcome anytime. But today he had another reason to feel anxious: he was not looking forward to saying what he had come to say to Margaret.

154

In a moment the door opened, and Margaret smiled brightly when she saw it was him. "William! What a pleasant supri —" she stopped mid-sentence when she saw the look on his face, "What's wrong?" she asked, her expression darkening in an instant.

William took a deep breath and answered, "The Captain says there's a big battle coming on out to the east of here, at Harpers Ferry, and all of us men are needed."

"Oh," she said, turning away, walking back toward her bed and sitting down.

William stood in the doorway feeling awkward. She'd not exactly invited him in, and yet ... he felt there was more that needed to be said.

"May I ... come in?" he finally asked.

"Yes, come ... come," she answered, but not in a friendly way to William's ear.

He came and sat in a chair across from the bed.

"I'm sorry there's such short notice about it," he said, "but I only heard of it a few minutes ago when the Captain returned from town —" he began, trying his best to soften the blow.

"It's not about the warning, William, it's about ..." but she turned her head and gazed out the window, leaving the sentence unfinished.

William could think of several things he *might* say at that moment, but none of them seemed worth the breath they would take, so he waited for her to say what she would.

Finally, she turned and looked him hard in the eye, "Why *must* you go, William?"

"Oh ... well, the Captain says the garrison there is inexperienced and outmanned and needs our help setting up a proper defense and —"

"William ... I don't mean why must *Nathan* and the others go ... I mean why must *you* go? I ... I am *afraid*, William ..." she said, dropping off into almost a whisper. And he knew it was true ... The fear gripping her was palpable.

"I ... I must go because there will be fighting, Margaret ... men will be hurt — wounded badly, suffering great pain and fear. I must help them ... I must do what I can ..."

But she just shook her head slowly as he spoke, tears beginning to stream down her face, and he knew he was not getting through to her …

"The army has other surgeons, William … It's a war … there will always be men killed and wounded … You can't stop it, William … you can't save them all …" she said, in a voice choked with emotion.

"Maybe so, Margaret, and in the larger war in general I might be inclined to agree with you, but … this is the *Captain*, Margaret … and the men I care about most in the world—my closest friends and brothers in arms—if they're going, I must be there with them, to fight at their sides, and to succor them if, God forbid, they fall wounded," he answered. He felt his own strong emotions welling at the thought of potentially withholding his care from his friends in their hour of need.

"William … almost every night I wake up in a cold sweat from a nightmare of Walters … he's … he's looming over me … gloating as I'm held, helpless in front of him … and I can't move and …" she wrapped her arms around herself and shook, her eyes wide with fear.

William came over, sat next to her on the bed, and tried to put his arm around her. But she pulled away suddenly and stood, walking over to the window and gazing out. "If you must go, William, then you'd best do so …" she said in a cold, far away voice.

He sat there a moment more, but could think of nothing to say. He rose, and left the room, slowly closing the door behind him.

☙❧☙❧☙❧☙❧☙❧☙❧

"Yes, I *know*, William," Nathan said, as he shoved clothes into a pack up in his bedroom in the farmhouse, "she's afraid. And rightly so; I'm afraid too. Afraid for her, afraid for Megs and Momma … afraid for the country. But we men must do what we must do and trust to our friends to do their part to help us. There is nothing else we can do."

William nodded, but could think of nothing to say to that. He knew it was true, and he also knew Nathan felt as badly and as guilty about leaving as he did, so there was no use trying to make him feel any worse.

"I have complete faith in the freemen, William. And if it helps, I was already planning on asking Henry to serve as Margaret's personal bodyguard wherever she goes, here on the farm and also into town, with one of my pretty little Colts in his pocket. As you know, he's a very clever and tough man—quite courageous—and … he owes her a great deal. I think if anyone other than you or I will be motivated to protect her, it's him."

"True … thank you, Captain. That does make me feel … *somewhat* better. Margaret, on the other hand …"

"Margaret is stronger than she believes, William. In the end she will chin-up and do her part … and let us do ours."

"Yes, sir. I expect you're right. So why do I feel so awful about the whole thing?"

Nathan turned to him, patted him on the shoulder, and said, "Because you're a good man, William."

ᙁᘜᙓᙏᙎᙅᙓᙁᘜᙓᙏᙎᙅᙎᙅᙁᘜᙎᙏᙎᙅᙎᙅ

"Rosa … you heard the news?" Tony said, coming to a stop in front of her out in the field of beans she was hoeing. He put his hands on his knees, and gasped for breath, looking up into her eyes.

"What is it, Tony? What's happened?!" she said, suddenly feeling concerned. It wasn't like Tony to get all excited and worked up, and he'd never run out to see her before. "Is there some kinda trouble?"

"No … no," he said, trying to catch his breath, "sorry … I had to run … 'cause I'm leaving in a couple o' minutes …"

"Leaving? Leaving for where, Tony?"

"I don't know … someplace I ain't never heard of called Harpers Ferry. Captain says they's a big old battle comin' there and we's gonna go out and fight them damned slavers."

"Fight? They's finally gonna let the freemen fight?"

"No … not exactly … the others ain't goin'. Just me."

"You? Why you, Tony? Tell me what's going on … I don't understand …"

"Captain and the white soldiers is goin' to this battle, and he asked for one of us to go along as witness for the other freemen, since it's really our fight in the end. And the other fellas picked me. Big George even said I was their *leader* ... can you believe it?!" he grinned at her; even now the memory of it gave him a warm, proud feeling.

But Rosa's reaction was not so enthusiastic. "Oh ... that was *nice* of him ... that means you get to go get shot at ... and the others get to stay home, all safe?"

Tony frowned, "It ain't like that ..."

"Then what is it like, Tony?" she asked, a tear now trickling down one cheek.

But with a sudden epiphany, for the first time ever Tony understood what she was thinking and feeling. So instead of his usual not knowing what to do or say, or worse, saying exactly the wrong thing—this time he stepped up to her, put his arms around her, and said, "I'm sorry, Rosa. I know this-here's hard on you."

She wrapped her arms around him and squeezed, harder than he knew she could.

When she let go and stepped back, she smiled through her tears and said, "You keep your head down, Tony ... don't go bein' no hero now, y'hear?"

He smiled back, and said, "Don't you worry none, Rosa, darlin'. I done promised to jump the broom with you ... and no power on earth ... nor in *hell* ... gonna keep me from *that!*"

She snorted a short laugh, shook her head, rolled her eyes, and wiped away the tears. "You go on now ... don't keep the Captain waitin' ..."

He leaned in and kissed her, "Goodbye for now, Rosa," he said, turned, and ran off toward the farmhouse.

☙❧☙❧☙❧

Saturday May 24, 1862 – Washington, D.C.:

Secretary of War Edwin Stanton sat at his desk in the War Department, absently scratching his chin up under his full beard while poring over the various documents laid out before him. He sighed heavily and pushed back his chair, intending to fetch his assistant, Lieutenant Gray, so he could dictate another urgent message to the president.

But at that moment he heard the door open and looked up to see Lieutenant Gray standing in the doorway. Oddly, the young lieutenant was standing stiffly at attention, despite Stanton's longstanding orders to the contrary, having little patience for the protocol and etiquette of the military when he was trying to get work done.

He was about to remind the young man of same, when the lieutenant said, "Mr. Secretary ... the President, sir," and snapped a salute.

Abraham Lincoln entered the room, then turned to the young man and said, "Please, Lieutenant ... be at your ease, and as you were."

"Thank you, Mr. President," the lieutenant answered, and assumed the formal, "at ease position" with feet slightly apart, hands neatly behind the back, head erect, and eyes staring straight ahead. Lincoln looked at him a moment, slowly shook his head, and smiled before turning to Stanton.

"Edwin ..."

"Mr. President ... sorry for the lack of a reception, but nobody told me you were coming ..."

The president entered the room, removed his tall, black "stovepipe" hat, and set it on a side table as he sat down heavily into a chair in front of Stanton's desk. "That's because they didn't know I was coming ... I didn't even know it myself until a few minutes ago. I felt the need of a little fresh air, and to stretch these long legs ... so I decided to take a stroll around the grounds outside the White House. And as I was walking, I looked up and saw the War Department across the lawn, which of course, made me think of you. And that got me to thinking about what you may have heard today of events in the war that you've not had time to pass along."

"Well, your timing is impeccable, Mr. President, as I was just getting up from my desk to send you a message. And yes, I have heard news this morning ... disturbing news, I'm afraid."

"Oh?"

"It appears as if Jackson has now overrun Front Royal, Virginia, though communications are spotty and conflicting. Likely the enemy has either cut the telegraph lines, or is using them to send false information."

"Front Royal? But that's ... much farther north and to the east than Jackson was reported to be, isn't it?"

"Yes, sir. General Fremont's latest report said Jackson was still in the main part of the valley, further west near Harrisonburg ... well, step over here, sir, if you would, and we'll just have a look on the map ..."

Stanton gestured toward the far wall, where a large map of the Shenandoah Valley covered much of the left side of the wall. Lincoln noted the right side contained an equally large map of the Virginia Peninsula where McClellan's Army of the Potomac was currently engaged.

"Harrisonburg is ... here, Mr. President."

"Yes ... and Front Royal is ... way over here," Lincoln said, pointing to a spot on the map well up the wall and to the right of where Stanton was pointing.

"Clearly Jackson continues to confuse and evade our forces with his maneuvering ..." Stanton said.

"Hmm ... apparently so," Lincoln answered, gazing out beyond where his finger marked the small town of Front Royal. "Then ... what's next? Where's Banks with his main force?"

"Well, he was in Strasburg ... here, about twelve miles west of Front Royal, but I doubt he's still there, sir."

"Oh? He's attacking Jackson at Front Royal then?"

"No ... he'd risk being cutoff and surrounded if he were to lose the engagement. Likely he's retreating toward Winchester."

"Winchester ... hmm ... all right, I see it ... just north of both Jackson and Banks' forces ... what? ... maybe thirty miles?"

"Yes ... looks to be about thirty from Front Royal ... but only ... twenty-some from Strasburg."

"Ah, so Banks should get there first, don't you think?" Lincoln asked, beginning to understand Stanton's concern, a knot starting to form in his already sensitive stomach.

"I fear it won't matter, sir. Even if Banks wins the race, which is debatable given Jackson's reputation for moving his troops around at great speed, he'll not get there in time to dig in or fortify his position. And the reports we are managing to get don't sound good; it's already a panicked and uncoordinated retreat, from the sounds of it."

"And if Banks is routed at Winchester ..." Lincoln said, his mouth dropping open as his finger traced a line from Winchester to Washington City. "Where's General Fremont?"

"Here, sir ... at Franklin, Virginia ... a hundred miles to the southwest of Winchester. You recall he had a run-in with Jackson at the town of McDowell earlier this month, and was forced to pull back to Franklin."

"A hundred miles southwest? *Damn* ... Jackson seems to be everywhere at once, and yet ... nowhere you expect him to be."

Stanton nodded, but said nothing.

"And how far south on his trek to Richmond has General McDowell gotten by now?"

"Currently at Fredericksburg ... let's see, looks like about ... eighty miles, more or less, southeast of Winchester."

"So ... he's also out of position to aid Banks. But at least McDowell is only fifty some miles from Washington?"

"Yes, Mr. President ... but promised to General McClellan for his Peninsula Campaign ..."

"We've talked about this before ..." the president shot back, "we promised McDowell's force after assurances from McClellan that he'd left sufficient manpower in place to defend Washington, which we have since discovered was *not* the case ..."

"True, sir ..."

The two men gazed at the map in silence for several minutes until the president finally asked, "What forces do we have, then, between Winchester and the capital?"

"Only a small force here, at Harpers Ferry. It's not much more than a small garrison, with only about 1,000 men and no artillery. It's commanded by a ... Colonel Dixon Miles."

"So ..." Lincoln said, continuing to gaze at the map, "what you're telling me, Mr. Secretary, is that if General Banks is routed and either run off or destroyed at Winchester, there are only a thousand Union soldiers with nothing but their own rifles standing between General Jackson's entire army of two full divisions, and this very building?"

"Essentially … *yes*, Mr. President."

ಬಿಐಚ಼ಬಿಐಚ಼ಬಿಐಚ

For the next hour, the president and the secretary of war discussed how to ensure the safety of the capital. They could agree on only one thing: that General McDowell's march south to join up with McClellan must be halted immediately, and he must prepare to send at least half his force north toward the capital in all haste, should it be needed. Stanton wrote out a telegram to McDowell with his new orders on the spot, and had it sent before they continued with their discussion.

"Mr. President, I think our best strategy is to pull everything we've got back to the capital. Concentrate our forces to give ourselves the best chance of success in the defense. Evacuate Harpers Ferry and order the brigade there to pull back to Washington, or possibly to engage the enemy in a fighting retreat to slow him.

"At the same time," Stanton continued, "have General McDowell return with his full army immediately, rather than waiting for events. And in case he can't get here timely, send orders for every regiment on the eastern seaboard, fully trained and equipped or not, to move to the capital as soon as feasible, either by rail or by forced march. We'll set up a perimeter with as much heavy artillery as we can muster, and dig in. Surely even Jackson would not be so bold as to attack such a stout, well-supplied, and concentrated defense?"

But Lincoln didn't immediately respond, continuing to gaze at the map. After a moment he turned, walked slowly back to his chair and sat. Stanton followed him and sat back at his desk.

"Edwin … if there's any chance at all that General McDowell's army could make the difference between success and failure in McClellan's offensive against Richmond, then I am loath to recall him unless it's absolutely necessary. I feel like McClellan has a good chance of winning the war right here and now, if we just give him the resources and support he needs."

Stanton nodded noncommittally as if not fully convinced. But he knew the president well enough by now not to interrupt, and to allow him to elucidate his thoughts.

"As for pulling back and concentrating our forces here at Washington ... I think the answer must be *no* ... Imagine if Jackson were to come close enough to shell the White House or the Capitol Building ... Even if he failed to capture the city, the damage to the morale of the nation could very well be irreparable.

"No, if he can't be defeated, he must at least be held off, well out in the field. And it seems to me from looking at the map, and from all we've discussed, the place to do it is at Harpers Ferry, before he can cross the Potomac.

"No, Mr. Secretary ... if Winchester falls, which now seems likely to me, Harpers Ferry must be held at all cost. Now the question becomes, *how?*"

Stanton nodded his head, conceding the argument, then turned and gazed across the room at the map again. "We would need a division there at the least, with a general in command, I should think," he said.

But Lincoln gave him a wry smile and said, "If you know of a division lying around somewhere unused, Mr. Secretary, this would be a very good time to disclose it."

Stanton scowled. "I don't even have a proper field general 'lying around' to assign at the moment, let alone a division, as you well know," he replied.

"What about Rosecrans? Isn't he here in this very building, after having been replaced out west by General Fremont?"

Stanton snorted derisively, "Rosecrans? The man is incorrigible. All he wants to do is disagree and argue with everything I do and say. I fear his removal was *one* thing General McClellan was right about. No, Mr. President ... I've no faith in General Rosecrans' willingness to take orders from me, so if you wish me to run this operation ..."

"Now, now, Edwin ... no need to get your whiskers in a lather ... I was only *asking*, and now you've answered. Who then?"

"That's the problem, Mr. President ... all our other experienced field generals are currently ... well, *out in the field*, as they should be. Although ..." he stopped and looked thoughtful. "I did receive a *very interesting* telegram yesterday afternoon. It's from Governor Pierpont of the Restored Government of Virginia. I didn't know quite what to make of it last night, but now ..."

"What's it about? Does the governor have a general he can loan us?"

"Not exactly, but ... well, *here*," he rummaged through the papers on the top of his desk and found what he was looking for: a small sheet of yellowish paper, and a file folder. He handed the slip of paper across to Lincoln. "Here it is ... see what you think ..."

Governor's Office – Commonwealth of Virginia
Wheeling, Virginia, May 23, 1862

The Hon. E.M. Stanton
Secretary of War

Mr. Secretary:
Reports have reached this office of a most disturbing nature concerning present campaign of Jackson's army. We fear General Banks' force is in danger of being swept aside or circumvented, leaving only a skeleton force at Harpers Ferry to prevent a march on the nation's capital. I am sending a very experienced man, Nathaniel Chambers, to do what he can to help organize the defense of said post, but beseech you to send a suitable force with artillery to reinforce the garrison there as quickly as may

"Hmm … seems like the governor is more on top of this matter than we've been …" Lincoln said.

"Yes, but he's not trying to run a war …" Stanton snapped back.

"All right, Edwin … I meant no criticism by it, just impressed with Governor Pierpont is all. And … who is this *Chambers* fellow anyway? What do we know of him?"

"I asked that same question myself after I read the telegram yesterday … seems all the career soldiers are *very* familiar with him, especially the Mexican War veterans and the West Pointers. Here's the report my people gave me …"

He handed Lincoln the file folder. The president scanned through it for a few minutes, then looked up and said, "Mr. Secretary, please tell me why this fellow isn't out leading our troops in the field? Is he suffering some injury or illness?"

"Not that I'm aware of, sir … my understanding is he has been instrumental in helping to organize the restored government out there in Wheeling, and more recently that of the potential new state; also leading the fight against the guerilla rebel forces and putting down other lawlessness out in western Virginia."

"Hmm … don't suppose there's enough time to get him commissioned and back in uniform? Regardless, him being there could be of great help, with our lack of experienced field generals just at the moment."

"Agreed, sir. With his help out there, I was just thinking what we really could use is someone with the organizational and logistical skills to quickly build up the manpower and resources we need to defend the town."

"You mean … like a quartermaster or something?"

"Exactly what I was thinking, Mr. President. I have in mind Brigadier General Rufus Saxton, currently serving in the quartermaster's office just downstairs. He seems a very competent and capable fellow. And agreeable ..."

Stanton continued, now thinking aloud, "I figure we have at least two or three days before Jackson arrives to mount an attack ... we'll give Saxton the command, send him out to Harpers Ferry, and then let him reconnoiter the situation out there. He can tell us what he needs to hold the town ... perhaps with the help and advice of Mr. Chambers. We'll suspend all rail traffic on the B&O line between Baltimore and Harpers Ferry, and start sending Saxton every man with a rifle and a uniform we can find along the entire eastern seaboard, as quickly as we can do it. Along with any artillery, munitions, and equipment he may require."

"All right ... that sounds as good a plan as any. Please make it so, Mr. Stanton ... and then keep me informed."

"That I will Mr. President. I'll send for General Saxton immediately, sir, and put him on the next train out to Harpers Ferry."

"Good man," Lincoln said with a thin smile. Then he stood, replaced his hat, and patted Stanton on the shoulder before turning and walking out the door, a concerned look knitting his brow.

𝕭𝕴𝕹𝕮𝕽𝕮𝕭𝕴𝕹𝕮𝕽𝕮𝕭𝕴𝕹𝕮𝕽𝕮

"Lieutenant, Collins ... enjoying yourself?" Bob Hill asked as he pulled open the canvas flap on the back of the captured Union supply wagon and looked inside. There he found Jubal sitting on a pile of rations, along with two privates. All three were busily stuffing bread into their mouths from a loaf they were sharing around—clearly enjoying themselves after living on short rations for nearly a month of hard marching for Stonewall Jackson.

"Mmmph ... hmmph ..." Jubal said with a grin, trying to answer with his mouth full. Finally he swallowed, and said, "Come on in, Captain ... there's plenty more."

"Yes, so I can see. And a hundred more wagons just like this one, bless the Lord," Bob answered, reaching in and grabbing a loaf of bread from a large burlap sack and immediately taking a large bite.

166

"Or maybe you should thank Union General Banks for his kindly donation," Jubal added with a smirk.

"I'm not sure he'd appreciate the sentiment," Captain Hill said with a chuckle.

The Stonewall Brigade's sudden, unexpected abundance was thanks to an entire supply train abandoned by General Banks' Corps after they were flanked and nearly cutoff and destroyed by General Jackson's army. In their desperation to escape the rout, Banks' soldiers had abandoned everything—tents, wagons, food, ammunition, and artillery. It was a magnificent bounty such as the rebels had not seen in several months of fighting.

"When you've eaten your fill, stuff your packs before the quartermasters get ahold of this stuff and we never see it again," Captain Hill said. "But don't get too comfortable … we march again within the hour."

"March again?" one of the privates asked. "Ain't we just whipped every Yankee in the valley? That's what I heard some o' the others sayin'. What's left to march to, Cap?"

"Harpers Ferry," Captain Hill answered.

"But, Captain," Jubal put in, "what's there at Harpers Ferry? I heard it ain't even got a garrison."

"You heard right, Jubal … but they've got a bridge over there that crosses the Potomac."

This made Jubal sit up and suddenly become more interested, "And … why would we be wantin' to cross that bridge over to the North side, Captain Hill?"

"Because … on the other side of that bridge is a clear road, unguarded, straight to Washington City!" the captain said, and grinned broadly.

"*Holy Jesus …*" one of the privates said, dropping his chunk of bread from his open mouth.

જીલ્સ⦂ભ⦂ભ⦂⦂

"Gentlemen … I know this is a bitter pill," Lieutenant Colonel Kelley said to the grim group of Seventh *Loyal* Virginia Regiment officers, including Captain James Hawkins. "But those're our orders … straight from the War Department, as I understand it. I heard both General McDowell and General Shields were none too happy about it either, not that it helps ..."

"But sir," Hawkins finally spoke up, no longer able to contain himself, "our men just got here to Fredericksburg after marching more than a hundred miles at speed so we could join General McClellan's campaign against Richmond. A large number of our men have no shoes for having worn them out or chucked them along the way due to blisters from the long, forced hike. Now you're telling us we've go to tell them to turn around and march straight back to where we come from?!"

There was general agreement and grumbling in support of this sentiment, but the Colonel held up his hand for silence.

"Look, men ... I understand, and I agree ... but orders are orders. And besides, what good will it do if we take Richmond, only to have the enemy take Washington behind us. Even now Stonewall Jackson threatens the capital after routing General Banks' army. We've got to hot-foot it back there to cut him off."

"Hot-foot it to where?" one of the officers asked, "back to Front Royal?"

"At least ... or if necessary, all the way to Harpers Ferry," the colonel answered grimly.

🙰🙰🙰🙰🙰🙰🙰🙰🙰

Nigel had been right about the train traffic west on the B&O from Baltimore. The Army had commandeered all rail traffic, and civilians were being turned away, along with regular freight trains.

But Nigel was undeterred. They approached the conductor of one of the trains and Nigel immediately put on his very best haughty, frosty, self-important government official act, flashing his forged Lincoln administration paperwork. But when the conductor remained unmoved, having been given explicit instructions on the matter, Nigel was forced to slip a $20 gold coin into his hand, with the promise of another upon their arrival at Wheeling. But the conductor said he could only guarantee getting as far as Harpers Ferry, as he had no specific instruction on where to go after that. Nigel had reluctantly agreed, and he and Evelyn had squeezed aboard.

When she thanked Nigel for his extravagance on her behalf, he smiled and answered, "Oh, never fear, my dear; Jonathan said to spare no expense getting you home to Richmond, so he'll happily reimburse me when the time comes."

It was standing room only, full to the gills with wide-eyed young soldiers and their rifles, many without proper uniforms or even shoes. But being a beautiful young lady has its perquisites, and Evelyn soon accepted one of a dozen immediate offers of a seat; and of course Nigel was allowed to sit next to her. So they enjoyed their ride in relative comfort, despite the close quarters. And once the train got moving, the breeze coming in through the open windows cooled the car and helped dissipate the smell of so many sweaty young men.

As the train rolled along, Evelyn confided in Nigel about her angst concerning passing through Wheeling. She couldn't imagine going through that town, knowing Nathan was there, without seeing him. But once there, in his new home, back together with him for the first time in over a year, she wasn't sure she'd have the willpower to leave him again and return to Richmond. Once she started talking, she realized how easy he was to talk to—a kindly, empathetic listener, more so than anyone she'd been around since leaving Nathan at Mountain Meadows. She ended up pouring her heart out to him, much more so than she'd intended, including the painful, "who am I" incident after the "Big Wedding." It occurred to her he was the first human being to hear the full story from her own lips. She noticed some of the young soldiers standing or sitting nearby seemed to be listening as well, so she refrained from talking about anything to do with her current "occupation" or her involvement with the Hughes. Otherwise, she didn't care if the young soldiers heard her tale; it actually felt good to finally let it all out. And as she let it out, she thought she detected some teary eyes and empathetic nods amongst the young soldiers.

When she was finished, she asked Nigel about his home in Boston, and he proceeded to regale her with humorous tales of the shipping business and the northern branch of the Hughes family. She so enjoyed their talk that the miles quickly flew by, and she was caught by surprise when they rolled in to a tunnel and the conductor announced they would soon be crossing over the Potomac to their stop at Harpers Ferry.

When the train came to a stop at the Harpers Ferry station, the soldiers politely allowed her and Nigel to depart first. But by the time Nigel paid the conductor and they'd secured their luggage, the platform was flooded with hundreds of troops, crates of ammunition, and piles of supplies such that they could scarcely move. The conductor told them to check back in a few hours to see if he was continuing on or if some other train would be heading out to Wheeling. He said he thought it likely they'd load up a train with civilians to get them out of harm's way in advance of the coming battle.

As it was mid-afternoon and they'd had no lunch, they decided to walk into town to see if they might find something to eat before—they hoped—catching an evening train westbound for Wheeling. Nigel took her by the arm and began weaving his way through the crush of soldiers on the platform.

ஜௐௐௐ

As their eastbound train from Wheeling came to a stop, Nathan leaned out the window and saw there was already a westbound train stopped at the station. He was gratified to see Union soldiers peering out the windows and exiting the passenger cars in a steady stream.

He sat back down, turned to Tom, and grinned, "Looks like Francis got through to them and we may not all be killed after all." He reached in his pocket and grabbed a cigar, sticking it in his teeth unlit.

Tom snorted a chuckle, "Always good to hear one will get to live another day … But maybe the Army figured this one out on their own …"

"Could be," Nathan answered, still grinning, "there's a first time for everything, I suppose."

Tom rolled his eyes and smiled.

Nathan turned around and addressed Jim, who was sitting behind them. "Jim … with all these soldiers and their officers arriving, Tom and I will head straight for the inn to make sure they don't give away our rooms. You and the men go ahead and secure the horses and baggage."

"Yes, sir. We'll get 'er done," Jim answered good naturedly.

"Come on, Tom … let's see if we can squeeze our way through this crowd."

Chapter 7. A Rapturous Meeting

*"There are no
accidental meetings
between souls."*
- Anonymous

Saturday May 24, 1862 – Harpers Ferry, Virginia:

As Nathan, Tom, and Harry the Dog stepped down from the train, the station at Harpers Ferry was already full to overflowing with thousands of soldiers unloading from the train Nathan had seen arriving from the east. And wagons were already lining up along the tracks to unload the huge burden of supplies they'd brought with them—food, fodder, ammunition, and all the various sundries required to put an army into the field. All were being offloaded as quickly as humanly possible.

Noticeable by its absence however, to Nathan's eyes, was any heavy artillery—the one thing most desperately needed if they were to have any hope of holding off Stonewall Jackson. All he saw were a handful of small howitzers, of the type that could be pulled by a single horse—only good for short-range skirmishing.

But though the press of arriving manpower was gratifying, it made for a difficult passage through the heavy throng, as the men from Nathan's eastbound train were trying to cross through the arriving troops to get into town, while the newly arrived soldiers were generally moving in the opposite direction out toward the defensive lines to the west. It made for a confusing weave of bodies, which Nathan and Tom had to work their way through.

When he was about halfway across the platform Nathan noticed a young gentleman in a suit working his way in their direction—most likely either a government or B&O official. A woman walked next to him, clutching his arm—his wife, Nathan assumed. He couldn't make out her face as she wore a stylish hat and was looking down at the moment. But he noted a long strand of black hair that'd apparently come undone from whatever held the rest of it up under her hat.

As they came closer, Nathan nodded at the man, who tipped his hat and smiled — as they were the only "civilians" on the platform, the polite greeting seemed only natural.

As the couple stepped up to Nathan and Tom and began to pass by, the woman glanced up and met eyes with Nathan for the merest fraction of a second …

Nathan took one more step then stopped dead — his breath catching, his eyes wide with shock. He spun around even as Evelyn leapt into his arms, throwing her arms around him and burying her face between his neck and shoulder.

"*Evelyn!* Oh my dear God … *Evelyn! I … don't believe it!* Is it really *you?!*" he gasped in a voice choked with emotion; he thought his heart would burst.

But she had not yet found her voice, and just nodded, continuing to hold on tight. She was now sobbing and Nathan felt the sweet wetness of her tears flowing down the side of his neck — and he thought it the most glorious feeling on earth. And then he realized his own tears were streaming down his face to merge with hers.

After a moment she leaned back, still held in his strong arms, her feet dangling off the ground. The young soldiers, sensing something very special was happening, parted around them as they passed by, smiling, nodding and whispering to one another.

Evelyn grasped the sides of Nathan's face in both hands and gazed into his eyes for a long moment — a serious, intense look on her face.

"Oh *Nathan … my love* … are you really here … after all this time?!" she finally said, her voice barely more than a whisper. Then, not waiting for a reply, she leaned in and kissed him, long and hard on the mouth. He returned the kiss eagerly, as a man stranded in a desert, dying of thirst, will drink from a deep, cool pool of water.

Tom, who'd not noticed Nathan stop until he'd gone several more steps, turned to see what was happening. He immediately saw Nathan embracing a woman, such as he'd never seen his captain do before. In a flash of intuition, he knew she must be Evelyn, though this woman had dark hair, incongruously—but gauging Nathan's reaction, Tom knew it could be no other.

He stepped up to the gentleman in the suit who held a puzzled expression and a hesitant smile, watching Nathan and Evelyn embracing. Tom had seen the man accompanying the woman who he could now see was definitely Evelyn, so he stepped up to him and extended his hand, "Tom Clark …"

"Nigel Hu—*uh* … that is … *Smith*. Nigel *Smith*," the man said, taking Tom's proffered hand in his and exchanging a firm handshake.

"Good to meet you, Mr. *Smith*," Tom said.

"I take it they … *know* each other," Nigel finally said, looking a bit sheepish, as if he suddenly didn't know what to do with himself.

Tom chuckled, "Yes … you *could* say that, Mr. Smith."

Then Tom put two and two together: Evelyn worked for the *Employer*, and the Employer's men often used the pseudonym "Smith."

"I assume, sir, you are affiliated with … *the Employer?*" Tom asked.

The man looked startled for a moment, then nodded and smiled, "Why, yes, Mr. Clark … but *how* …?" and then he too made the connection. "*Oh* … wait … this must be Nathan Chambers and that would make you … *that* Mr. Clark."

Tom nodded and smiled, and Nigel said, "Well then … well met, Mr. Clark … well met, indeed."

"Likewise, Mr. Smith. Likewise."

☙❧☙❧☙❧☙❧☙❧☙❧

Introductions were quickly made, and Evelyn gave a brief explanation of who Nigel was, and what he'd done on her behalf. Nathan thanked Nigel profusely for his role in Evelyn's rescue, then Tom, knowing Nathan would need some time alone with Evelyn, invited Nigel to accompany him to the inn where they could find some supper.

Nathan and Evelyn walked up a street leading away from the busy downtown area. It rose gradually above the river level until they located a pleasant, sloping field overhung by several large trees overlooking the Potomac. On the far side of the river rose the imposing cliffs of Maryland Heights.

Harry the Dog lay down and immediately rolled onto his back to give himself a good scratching in the soft grass. Nathan and Evelyn sat in silence for a moment, first taking in the view, and then turning to gaze into each other's eyes, hands clasped together.

Finally, Nathan spoke. "You have no idea how I've dreamed of this moment—of seeing you again in person, of holding you, and looking into your beautiful blue eyes."

She smiled and laughed softly, "Oh ... I think I *do*, Nathan. I have dreamed of your eyes every night since we were last together ... your image has never changed ... never faded."

He leaned in and kissed her again, this time softly, gently ... They lingered for a long moment, neither one wanting to break the wonderful spell of this long-anticipated moment.

But when they again pulled apart, he took her in fully with his eyes—the shape of her face, the perfect lines of her nose, her soft warm lips, the smooth skin of her neck, leading to her lovely bustline ... over which flowed her long, wavy black hair ... *black?*

"Evelyn ... I've just been wondering ..."

"Yes?"

"Um ... I don't want to seem rude, but ... what happened to your hair?"

She gazed at him a moment with a straight face, and said, "Whatever do you mean, Nathan?"

He could feel a blush coming on ... he didn't want to insult her, but ...

Then she smiled ... and giggled. He returned the smile, knowing he'd just been teased. He should've remembered it was one of her favorite tricks.

She tilted her head, and pulled loose the pins holding her long hair up under her hat, letting it cascade down to its full length. Just as he'd remembered it, long flowing curls, but this time instead of a wonderful dark gold color, her hair was entirely black.

"Don't you like it?" she asked with a smile, and a twinkle in her eye, as she fluffed the hair with her hand.

"Well … actually … *no*," he answered, returning her bright smile with one of his own.

She threw back her head … and laughed—the first good, honest laugh she'd had since she couldn't remember when. He laughed along with her, for the sheer joy of seeing her so amused.

Once she caught her breath again, she said, "It was Nigel's idea—part of his escape plan. He thought they'd be scouring the countryside for a blonde woman and this would be the perfect disguise. It was a reasonable idea, but likely unnecessary. With everyone at the War Department busy with—oh, I don't know … *the war*, maybe?—I highly doubt they've even yet noticed I'm gone."

He smiled, "Well, I suppose it may grow on me …"

"Don't worry, Nigel says it'll be gone in a few weeks and then I'll be the old me again."

Nathan smiled, but then turned thoughtful, "And then … which *you* will that be, I wonder …"

Her look turned more serious, and she said, "Yes … I *know* I have a lot of explaining to do … I have not exactly earned your faith and trust the last two times we were together."

He nodded, but said, "Well … if you never say another word about it, but greet me as you did here today, I shall be entirely satisfied."

She smiled, "Oh … *that* was a glorious moment! One I will never forget as long as I live. Seeing you unexpectedly in the middle of that crowd, I thought my heart was going to burst through my chest. I couldn't believe it! Never in my wildest dreams did I imagine you'd be here today."

"Me?! What about you? As far as I knew you were still in Richmond, with two large, belligerent armies surrounding it. I can't wait to hear how it is you're here, and why the Employer had to rescue you from … of all places … a *Union* prison!"

She smiled and shook her head, "And I thought I might see you in Wheeling, but I never imagined you'd be in Harpers Ferry. And yet … here you are!"

They gazed in each other's eyes another moment, then couldn't resist another long kiss.

ℤℤℤ

"Speaking of … why *are* you here, anyway, Nathan? What's going on here? Nigel said he'd heard rumors of an impending battle somewhere around here, and when we saw all the soldiers getting off with all their equipment, it seemed to me we might get caught up in one."

"Yes … there's likely going to be one right here in the next few days. My old classmate Thomas Jackson is up to more of his antics. Seems like he and his men might just roll through here on their way to Washington City for a talk with Mr. Lincoln."

"You mean General Jackson, the so-called stone wall? His winter campaign didn't end up amounting to much … do you really think he'll do better this time?"

"He already has … word is he's re-taken Winchester, and General Banks' army is falling back in disarray. The fear is Banks' defeat will turn into a rout that will carry Jackson well into the North."

"But what of General Fremont? Surely he will intervene … or General McDowell?" she answered, "I understand he is now in charge of a sizeable force somewhere in the area of the capital."

Nathan was impressed with her knowledge of the disposition of the belligerent armies … on both sides of the divide.

"Fremont's a hundred miles out to the west of Jackson's force, though I expect he's already on the move … and McDowell is well on his way to Richmond to link up with McClellan, though I'm not sure precisely where he is just now."

"*Oh!* Then Harpers Ferry is—"

"Yes, basically the only thing right now standing between General Jackson and a march straight down Pennsylvania Avenue to the Capitol Building …"

"Well … then Harpers Ferry *must* be held, clearly."

"And *that* answers your original question … why I'm here. Governor Pierpont sent me to see what I could do to help organize the defense … in case Washington was otherwise occupied. Happily, it looks as though Mr. Jackson has gotten their attention, and they're sending out the troops as quickly as they can load them up on rail cars. Thank God for the good old B&O Railroad, otherwise it'd be impossible to get them all here in time.

"Anyway, as usual, I'm just here to do whatever I can to help the Union cause. The bigger question is … why in the world are *you* here, Evelyn? Please … I beg of you … tell me what's been going on with you. I've been so worried about you ever since we met in Richmond, when it became clear you were involved in activities that were … well, *dangerous* at the least. Clearly there's quite a story behind all you've been doing."

"And I've been dying to hear of all your adventures, Nathan … starting with what happened that horrible day when you were attacked on the streets of Richmond …"

"Oh … well … I had assumed you knew all about that from your … *association* … with the Employer …" he answered.

"True … but only the general outline … none of the actual details. Oh, Nathan … when I heard you'd been attacked and injured … or *worse* … that day in Richmond, I was so terribly frightened. I've been dying to hear what actually happened …"

She sighed, "But … I supposed it's only fair I tell my tale first, since you know almost nothing of it. Then you can satisfy my curiosity about the details of your escape from Richmond, and then your heroic breakout from the siege of Mountain Meadows."

He nodded his agreement, and she began her tale, starting with her rescue of the runaway slave Violet on the streets of Richmond.

When she began to describe the events leading to their awkward meeting at the ball, he suddenly interrupted her, exclaiming, "That *damned* note!"

"Note?" she asked.

"Yes … you remember … the note you handed me when we parted and I left the ball … the night you were being escorted by … by that *other* man."

"Oh … yes, of course. *That* note."

"Yes, *that* note. I have only read it a thousand, thousand times, and have kept it on my person nearly every day since. It's now so worn and tattered one can practically see through it. I've finally had to leave it in a desk drawer at home for fear it would crumble into dust.

"And yet, after all this time … never once have I understood what it means; *'Trust not your eyes, but rather your heart.'*"

"But Nathan, I thought it would be so unmistakably clear. Your *eyes* would see me with another man … but your *heart* would know I still loved *you*. Could you not *tell?* I was sure by the way I looked at you and the way I spoke everyone in the room would know I was in love with you."

"I thought I felt *something* … but you were with another man … I felt so confused and unsure …"

"Oh, Nathan! Did you not think to ask someone *else* what it meant … Miss Abbey, perhaps?"

"Well … I discussed it with Tom, but …"

"Tom?!" she shook her head and scowled, "He's a *man*. He would likely be just as confused as you. But any *woman* worth her salt would've known *exactly* what it meant!"

"Yes … I can see that now. I should've asked a *woman* what it meant …"

"Oh … I'm *so* sorry I put you through that. You have no idea how much I agonized over it beforehand, and how much I wanted to jump into your arms, embrace you, and kiss you that night. But … well, as you now know … I had already committed to the cause … even before *you* did, I believe. The people I was involved with were already sure there would be a war and were positioning me to help the Union side. If I showed you any affection it would give me away and spoil all our efforts. It pained me so to treat you that way, which is why I wrote the note … so you'd know it was only a ruse. Please forgive me, my dearest. And please believe I had no interest in that despicable *Stevens* … and have never loved any other man but you!"

He leaned in and gently kissed her again, then said, "There is nothing to forgive, dear one … you have done nothing wrong, and everything right. It was only my lack of good sense—as you say, not thinking to ask a woman the meaning of the note—that made the whole matter an issue."

"Thank you for being so understanding about it," she said, and returned his kiss with one of her own. They lingered for a long moment, until she pushed back and said, "you are making me breathless once again, Mr. Chambers, even as you were wont to do back at Mountain Meadows!"

He grinned and nodded.

"But if we keep this up, I shall never finish my tale, and then I'll never get to hear yours."

"Very well … please do continue, my dear," he answered.

For the next hour Nathan said almost nothing, listening with amazement to Evelyn's tale. She left nothing out, save the names of the Hughes, all the way up to her ill-fated journey by boat down the James. She decided there was no need to tell Nathan about what happened *that* day … she knew it would upset him terribly, and besides … she wasn't ready to talk about *that* yet with anyone, not even Nathan. She hadn't yet reconciled her own feelings about the incident—the embarrassment, the shame, and the guilt—but more than that, she wasn't sure she wanted Nathan to carry an image of her as a woman capable of murdering a man with a knife, dumping his body unceremoniously into the river, then calmly cleaning up the blood after. She was fairly certain it wasn't the picture most men wanted to have of the woman they loved.

She described only accepting the fisherman's earlier offer of his cabin, and locking herself in for the night. Then being awakened by the sound of Union sailors hailing the boat. It was true as far as it went, but she did feel a slight twinge of guilt for once again not sharing with Nathan those critical "unsaid things" that'd been an issue at the very start of their relationship, long ago, in what now seemed the most idyllic times she'd ever spent—being with him back at Mountain Meadows.

When she described her meeting with General McClellan, Nathan sat up and a dark scowl knit his brow.

Then when she talked about how he'd had her arrested and sent to a prison in Washington City, apparently ignoring her critical information, Nathan startled her with the vehemence of his reaction. "Damn him, I'll kill the scoundrel!" he snarled, pounding his fist into the dirt. "He's gone too far this time … it's one thing going after me … but now *you?!* He'll not get away with it this time, I swear it! Throw *you* into prison?! This demands an answer!"

Evelyn was wide-eyed at such a strong reaction from Nathan, despite his admitted temper.

"But Nathan …. I don't understand," she said, "When I heard you'd been classmates back at West Point, and fought in the Mexican War together, I assumed … Oh! I see … *not* the best of friends I'm now guessing …"

"You could say that. We fought at the Academy—schoolyard stuff back then, but now it's turned into all out warfare," he answered, continuing to frown angrily.

He described to her his dealings with McClellan at Rich Mountain and later with General Rosecrans back in Washington at the War Department, concluding with his unadulterated opinion of McClellan as a general, and as a man.

"Nathan … this is *very* upsetting news … from what we've come to understand in Richmond, General McClellan is considered the Union's most formidable general. After all I went through to get him that intelligence … this is a *most* bitter pill."

"Yes, it's a great misfortune for our cause that he has convinced the Lincoln administration that he is capable of something he clearly is not," he said.

He was quiet and thoughtful for a moment; his expression softened. He turned to her and said, "But … my dear *Evelyn!* I just have to say … *oh my God!* I could not be more impressed with you and all that you've done. I have always said there is something very extraordinary and special about you, and that there's nothing you can't accomplish if you set your mind to it … and yet, you still continue to surprise and amaze me with the things you do. I am just … *awestruck.* But please … do continue your tale— though I don't much fancy hearing about you being thrown into a prison."

She smiled, "Thank you for the kind words, Nathan. I can't tell you how much that means coming from *you*. I … never really knew what you would think of me … of the things I was doing."

"Dear God, Evelyn! The way you shot those murderous, scoundrel rebel agents, then completely took charge after … that was magnificent! None of my experienced fighting men could've done better."

"Thank you, dear one. I'm so happy you don't … think *ill* of me," she said, and suffered another tiny bout of guilt over not telling him about the *other* incident … the one on the boat. *Maybe later …*

❧❧❧❧❧❧❧❧❧

When Evelyn finished her tale, up to the point of their meeting at the train station, it was Nathan's turn. As she knew the overall story, he instead focused on filling in various interesting details, such as Tom and Joseph's heroics, along with Georgie and William, in getting them safely out of Richmond. And Harry the Dog's part in rescuing them in the woods.

When he told her about freeing the slaves, and how Megs was intentionally kept for last, Evelyn burst into happy tears, saying, "Oh … I do love her so!" to which Nathan readily agreed.

Then he told her of the courageous heroism of the freemen in the battle against the secessionist militia, and their desperate battles all along the road on their way north. He was about to tell her the story of Margaret and her escape with Henry, when Evelyn distracted him by kissing him softly on the neck as he talked.

He looked over at her, and she smiled. "Don't stop Nathan …" she said, then kissed him in the same spot again.

He snorted a short laugh, then turned and kissed her softly on the cheek. She turned her face toward his mouth and softly kissed his lower lip, then switched to the upper one, smiling as his mustache tickled her.

He sighed and reached across, gently taking the back of her head in his hand to pull her kisses in closer, taking her mouth full onto his. She reached out and wrapped her arms around his neck,

182

even as he leaned back onto the grass with her now laying against his chest.

She gazed into his eyes again for a long moment, then said, "You are such a … wonderful, strong, heroic man … I just can't—" but she said nothing further for a long time as she leaned down and pressed her lips to his. He could see her face was flushed, and now she pressed the full length of her body against his where he lay. He could feel himself becoming aroused by her closeness, but she did not pull away.

She was the most beautiful, desirable woman he'd ever known, and he wanted nothing more than to be with her in the most intimate way possible … and his body was urging him onward, saying, *Why … not … now?*

But he remembered the first time this had nearly happened at the top of his Grandaddy's hill, and how it had not yet been the right time. And he knew in his heart—and in his mind—the same was true this time. He knew he had one thing he must do first. He interrupted the kiss, gently rolled her off him. They now lay side by side on the grass, almost nose to nose as they gazed into each other's eyes. His right hand rested on her waist, and her left softly stroked his upper arm.

"Evelyn … you have no idea how I've dreamed of being with you … I mean … together as a man and woman … well, *you know* …" he said, and sighed.

She smiled, and nodded, but still hadn't caught her breath enough to speak.

"But I promised myself if there ever was a *next time*, I'd not lose my control like I nearly did the *first time* … at least not until—"

She raised an eyebrow questioningly.

"Not until I had a chance to ask you a question. And the last two times I tried to ask it … well, let's just say *circumstances* prevented me from doing so."

"Yes? What is it you wish to ask, dear?" she said, raising up on one elbow, but still laying on her side in the grass.

He surprised her by standing up and offering her both his hands to assist her to stand, which she accepted. They now stood facing each other, holding hands, and he must've found her puzzled look amusing, as he suddenly smiled brightly.

Then he surprised her again by going down on one knee, while still holding her hands. He gazed up into her eyes for a moment, then said, "Evelyn Hanson ... I love you as I have never loved another woman, with my very heart and soul, and I want us to be together ... *always*. Will you marry me and be my wife to the end of our days ... and beyond?"

The question she had so dreaded to hear back when they were first together at Mountain Meadows now seemed so simple and natural, she just laughed and said, "Of course, Nathan. I love you too ... with all my heart. And I've always believed I would marry you one day ... once I was ready ..."

He embraced her and they kissed once again.

When they separated, his face was alight with a joy, "You've just made me the happiest man alive, Evelyn."

She returned his happy smile, and said, "It's like a dream, Nathan. From the moment I first saw you back at Mountain Meadows I knew we were meant to be together—like the angels set out to make the very best match ever on earth. And now —"

But Harry the Dog, for reasons known only to him, chose that moment to stand, stretch, yawn loudly, and shake the grass from his fur, sending a small dust cloud floating away on the gentle breeze.

Evelyn laughed, turned and spoke to him, in the sweet musical voice parents often use with small children, "Oh ... Harry, you're just *so* cute ..."

And to Nathan's amazement, Harry turned his head, gazed at Evelyn, and wagged his tail.

"Wait! *What?!* Do that again, Evelyn ..."

"Do what? Oh, that. *Harry* ... you are *such* a good boy ... such a big, *beautiful* boy," she said once again in a sing-song voice, and this time she reached out and scratched him between the ears.

Harry opened his mouth, hung his great tongue out the side, and again wagged his tail, ever so slightly, gazing at Evelyn the entire time.

Nathan slowly shook his head, as Evelyn looked back at him in puzzlement, "What is it, dear?" she asked.

"He's never wagged his tail before … not for me, not for anybody. Not until just now for you. Of all the oddities …"

But Evelyn giggled, "Maybe it's not so odd … could be he thinks of you as his Daddy, and now that he knows I will be his Momma … well, you know how boys *do* love their mothers!"

Nathan snorted a laugh, "Perhaps you've got something there," he said, continuing to gaze at this gigantic, ferocious hound who had suddenly turned puppyish with Evelyn.

"You are a wonder, Evelyn, and you continue to amaze me."

She leaned forward, capturing his lips again, and they lingered there for another long, passionate kiss. This time Harry the Dog watched them with curiosity, tilting his head as he did so.

"Evelyn, let's make the dream a reality. I have a room reserved in a boarding house just up the hill from the main part of town … you can stay there with me tonight and tomorrow morning catch the train out to Wheeling, and when I return, we can be married straight away."

Nathan was surprised to see her frown at this, but thought he knew why, "I … presume you'd planned on leaving here tonight continuing on to Wheeling. But don't worry, darling … there's no chance of Jackson arriving for two or three more days, and I'm certain they will continue evacuating the civilians by train during that time."

But he could tell something he'd said displeased her.

"Nathan … if I stay here tonight with you and we … *make love* … how will I ever be able to leave you again?"

"Why would you want to do that? I thought we just agreed we'd be married. I … I assumed you would stay in Wheeling, and I'd come meet you there directly after the battle …"

But Nathan had a sudden sinking feeling that the more he talked, the worse he was making the situation, for reasons he was at a total loss to comprehend.

"And then … assuming you survive this battle and *do* come home … what then would you envision for me? Staying in Wheeling on your new farm with Miss Abbey?"

"Well, yes ... of course. It's not as nice as Mountain Meadows, I'll grant you, but it's really quite a pleasant place, and the people of Wheeling are the nicest I've ever been around, and —" But he cut himself off, her deepening scowl making him realize whatever hole he had stepped into was only getting deeper.

"What is it, Evelyn? What's bothering you? What have I said to upset you?"

"Nathan ... you are asking me to give up everything I've been doing ... all that I can *still* do for the runaway slaves and for the war effort ..."

"Well ... that wasn't my intent, but ... I suppose you'd not be able to do those things from Wheeling ... But Evelyn, don't you think you've done your part already? Risked your freedom and likely your very life to obtain information that quite likely could've won the war, if only McClellan hadn't been such an incompetent ass! It's as impressive a feat as any I've ever heard any *man* do, let alone any *woman*. Don't you think you've already done enough? Isn't it time someone else took over the risky job you've been doing?"

But she continued to frown, and was beginning to get red in the face. "Nathan ... you've freed over a hundred human beings from slavery, and then rescued them along with the rest of your household from men who would imprison or harm them. You helped to win an important battle at Rich Mountain, and are preparing to take part in another. And you've helped organize a new state for the Union while doing vital service recruiting and training its new regiments — a task you could continue doing from Wheeling. Are you ready to stay home now on your farm and live with me, regardless of what happens in the wider war?" She asked the question in a tone that said she already knew the answer.

"No ... but ... I ..."

"Nathan ... there are people counting on me back in Richmond."

"The Employer?" Nathan asked, now feeling a little heat himself, "has your service to him become more important to you now than being with me? I thought you just agreed to marry me?"

"No … I mean, yes …" she sighed, then took a deep breath. "Can't you see, Nathan? I can't just *quit* now. I need to finish what I've started."

"But the marriage …"

"I said I would marry you, but when I said it, I assumed—after everything I'd just told you—that you would understand it would have to wait until …"

"Until the war's over?! That could take years. It's been hard enough to wait *this* long … I'm not sure I could stand it."

"It's been hard on me, too, Nathan. But, *no* … maybe it won't take until the war's over, maybe just … a while longer. Until some of the plans I've been working on come to fruition …"

He groaned and looked away.

"Nathan … please don't turn away from me …"

He turned back toward her, but she could see his frustration was threatening to turn into anger.

"Nathan, you feel you have to do your part … for the country, to free the slaves, to stand by your men … how is what I'm wanting to do any different?"

"It *is* different, Evelyn … my whole adult life has led up to this moment. I believe that God has led me to this very moment in time that I might do something monumental that will make a *real* difference …"

She frowned at him a moment before answering, "And the fact you're a *man* and expected to do these sorts of things, and I'm a *woman*, and not expected to, has nothing to do with it?"

He looked up as if considering the question, but didn't immediately answer, so she continued.

"Nathan … you realize I could make the very same arguments … that God has prepared me for this very moment in time, to do something 'monumental,' as you just said. Only I've been preparing my *entire* life, starting with the fact my Daddy wished for a boy, and though he loved me dearly—of that I have no doubt—he quenched his desire to raise a boy by teaching me all the things he'd learned growing up: riding, hunting, fishing, and fighting, for starters … but he also taught me how to think analytically, to solve difficult problems using the power of my mind, and how to debate deep philosophical questions."

Nathan nodded, but held his tongue.

"And then there was my Momma; after Daddy died, she took charge of my training, not just teaching me how to dress, talk, and act like a proper Southern lady, but—most important for my current activities—how to play a role ... to convince people I am something I'm not, and to do it so well they never suspect otherwise.

"Even as West Point and the soldiering you've done since have trained you for fighting this war, so has my upbringing trained me for *my* part in it."

She felt a hint of pride for finally putting into words the various thoughts she'd been mulling over concerning why she was doing what she was doing, and why she seemed to be so very good at it. She hadn't put those ideas into a cohesive whole until this very moment. But the look on Nathan's face dampened her enthusiasm—he clearly wasn't hearing it.

"Evelyn ... I appreciate you are extremely smart, clever, and capable ... but it's still not the same; with me it feels like ... like it's my destiny, to lead men into battle in a great war for a righteous cause ..."

"And how are you so sure it's not my destiny to extract the enemy's secret plans, so men like you can win the important battles?"

"Maybe ... maybe so, but I don't think I could stand the thought of you going back into harm's way ... never knowing if something might go terribly wrong and I'd never see you again ..." he said, almost pleading.

But Evelyn now felt her anger rising. "And how do you think it will feel to me, waiting at home for you as you ride into battle, not knowing if you'll be terribly wounded or even killed?" she shot back.

"But that's been, for better or worse, the role of women since the beginning of time. You are the strongest woman I know ... if those other women could handle it—"

"Maybe I'm not like other women—not willing to sit at home and do nothing."

"It's not *nothing*, Evelyn; it's giving the man a place to come home to, a reason to keep living when things are at their worst. Giving him the reassurance that all is well back home so he can continue doing what he has to do," he argued, beginning to sound more heated.

"Don't you think that's a bit selfish?" she answered, crossing her arms and sitting up straight.

"I don't see how … the man is the one out risking life and limb. It doesn't seem too much to ask that his wife mind the house while he's gone."

She resisted the urge to blurt out how she'd already risked life and limb on that fishing boat in the James, and had had to murder the fisherman to save herself. Though it would've felt satisfying to say it, she knew it would not serve her argument.

But she realized she was not getting through to him. "I … I thought you appreciated all I've been doing … I thought you would understand …" she said, her frustration turning into a growing sense of sadness.

They sat in silence for a long, awkward moment, the previous joyful feelings evaporated.

She stood, wiped her eyes and said, "I think I should go now. I … must return to Richmond, and I think … I think it would be for the best if I left today …"

He looked up at her with a frown, still sitting on the grass. "Yes … perhaps you should," he finally answered.

Evelyn turned and strode off down the hill, back toward the train station.

Nathan continued to sit, gazing off at the river. He reached down, picked up a stone, and hurled it with all his strength, down toward the water. He groaned, then put his head in his hands, sighed heavily, and closed his eyes as dark despair washed over him.

☙❧☙❧☙❧

Nathan stood gazing across the platform at the train whose engine was heating up, preparing for its westbound journey — great puffs of steam curling skyward from its stack. A dark frown knit his brow as Tom strode up.

"Sir … uh … not meaning to pry, but … where is Miss Evelyn? I expected to find the two of you together."

"Leaving …" he said in a hollow voice, never looking at Tom nor taking his eyes from the train.

Tom was shocked to see tears running down the sides of his face. "I … I've just ruined everything Tom … I've … driven her away … I …"

Then he turned and stared intently at Tom. "I can't lose her again, Tom. I just can't! I've got to get on that train."

He took a step forward, but Tom jumped in front of him, placed both his hands on Nathan's chest and physically held him up.

"Sir … you can't. You can't leave now."

"What?! What are you doing, Tom?! Get out of my way. I must go to her … *I must go with her!*"

"No, sir … there's a battle coming and your men are here …"

Tom could see he wasn't getting through, so he did the one thing that always seemed to register when nothing else would: he called his Captain by his given name.

"*Nathan* … look at me!" he said, even as Nathan tried to push him aside so he could get to the train. Nathan paused, and looked Tom in the eye.

"*What—?*" Nathan said, seeming confused or disoriented.

"Nathan … you've brought your men here to fight a battle. If you abandon them now and then one of us — or even all of us — gets killed in the fighting, how will that make you *feel*, sir?"

Nathan stopped shoving and stared at Tom a moment, then a look of horror came over his face, "*Oh!* I'd … I'd …" He turned and gazed at the train, now starting to slowly roll away from the station, "*Damn it!*

"And damn *you*, Tom!" he said, his voice choked with emotion. He sunk down on the wood of the platform and sat, burying his face in his hands.

Tom sat down next to him.

"I'm such a damned fool, Tom ... I've just sent her away ... I've just ruined my chance at ever again having true love and happiness in this life," he said, and then said no more for a long time.

ঙ৵ঙঀৎৠৣঙ৵ঙঀৎৠৣঙ৵ঙঀৎৠৣ

Nigel felt a tight knot in the pit of his stomach as he sat next to Evelyn, this time on a train bound for Wheeling. Something had gone terribly wrong in her reunion with Mr. Chambers, but so far she'd been unwilling to say anything, and had been snappish when he'd tried to inquire. But his growing anxiety forced him to press the matter.

"Evelyn ... please ... I know something went wrong ... please just tell me ... I'm a good listener, if nothing else ..."

She turned to him, smiled, and patted him on the arm. He could see tears welling up. "You're a good man, Nigel," she said. And for a long moment he thought he would get nothing more out of her.

But then she turned back to him and said, "I've been a terrible fool, Nigel ... I may have just ruined my life ... destroyed all hope of happiness. I know the things I said were right, and I'm doing what I have to do ... but I shouldn't have left in anger. I should have stayed, and talked it out with him, made him understand—" she looked up at the ceiling and then gazed around the interior of the passenger car as if seeing it for the first time, or suddenly realizing where she was. This time there were no soldiers, and the car was almost empty as it carried only a few of the remaining civilians getting out of town while there was still time before the battle.

"I shouldn't be here, Nigel ... I shouldn't be on this train. I should be with him ... I should—"

He could see her eyes were widening, and she was becoming almost frantic, as if a panic was taking hold over her.

"Shall I stop the train, Evelyn?" Nigel asked. "I can pull the emergency brake line and they will stop it for you. You and I can still walk back to the station; it is not too far yet."

"Yes!" she said, "Yes! Stop the train, Nigel. I must get off!"

He nodded, and rose from his seat. But when he tried to move out into the aisle, he found he couldn't move for something pulling on this sleeve. He looked down and saw Evelyn had ahold of his arm with a firm grip. She was slowly shaking her head. He sat back down next to her.

"No …" she whispered. "Thank you, Nigel … but no … I *must* return to Richmond. If I turn back now, how will I ever work up the courage to leave him again?" she said, and then covered her face with her hands.

But after a moment she stood, and said, "I must get some air. Please, let me by, Nigel."

"Yes, certainly, my dear. Shall I come with you?"

"No … thank you, Nigel, but I … I wish to be alone for a moment."

"Of course … certainly … I understand. I noticed this car was built to be the last on the train; there is a small platform outside at the back with a nice, firm railing. You can stand there safely and get some air."

"Thank you," she said as she stood and moved to the back of the train and out the door to the aft platform.

She stood for a moment, gazing back at the town now fading from view.

"*NATHAN!!!!*" she screamed as the town disappeared around a bend in the tracks, "Oh, Nathan … my love … what have I done …?" she whispered, her voice suddenly failing. She slowly sank to the floor of the platform, where she wrapped her arms around her knees, leaned her head forward, and wept bitter tears.

CHAPTER 8. THE EVIL THAT MEN DO

"The evil that men do lives
after them, the good is oft
interred with their bones."
*- **William Shakespeare***

Monday May 26, 1862 – Wheeling, Virginia:

Henry had been standing to the side of the entrance to the Customs House for six or seven hours now, watching people come and go. The same as he'd done yesterday, and the day before.

Before he'd left for Harpers Ferry with Tony and the old soldiers, the Captain had asked Henry to take on a special assignment of critical importance: to guard Miss Margaret's life both on the farm and whenever she traveled to town, which she did regularly for the constitutional convention. On those trips Cobb would also go along as the driver, giving her a little extra protection if needed. Of course, Henry had agreed without hesitation. The Captain had thanked him, and then handed him a small Colt revolver such as he carried himself, and said, "Just in case … keep it hidden and only bring it out if it's a matter of life or death. Cobb also carries one in his pocket. Have him show you how to load and shoot it."

Then the Captain had impressed upon him the seriousness of his bodyguard duties: that Miss Margaret's very life was in danger from Walters. Henry didn't complain nor shirk his duties, but carefully watched everyone going into the building for any familiar faces—that is, any white men who'd worked for Walters—or of course, Walters himself, or anyone at all who appeared to be armed and dangerous looking. But so far, he'd seen no one suspicious.

It would've been easier had he been allowed to accompany Miss Margaret into the meeting hall, but black freemen were not allowed in, despite this supposedly being an "enlightened

Northern" town. It helped lessen the sting of that fact knowing how much it galled Miss Margaret and the Captain. At least those two were always firmly on their side, of that he was certain.

The main challenge was staying alert despite the monotony. That and avoiding the harassment of young white men who didn't especially like blacks. Some of the freemen had been surprised by the lack of warmth in the reception they'd received in the North, but Henry hadn't. White men, even in the North, weren't quite ready to see black men as their equal, and most weren't happy about the idea of fighting, and possibly being wounded or even dying to free them. They'd much rather think they were fighting to "save the Union" or some such. But Henry was philosophical about it, believing it didn't much matter *why* they fought as long as they did.

But this day, as it turned out, he was unable to avoid the hard truth that some white Union soldiers resented the fact a part of the reason they were fighting was because of slavery.

As he stood there watching the door, three young white men, dressed in the uniforms of Union privates were walking down the street when they stopped in front of him. "Hey, *you* ... darkie. Come down here and shine our boots. Reckon if we gots to go get ourselves shot at on account o' your kind, it's the least you can do for us."

Henry, not wanting to start anything, smiled and said, "Oh yes sir, I would sir, 'cept I ain't got no boot polish nor any rags to buff 'em with."

"That's okay, just lick 'em off with your tongue," one said, and laughed. The others laughed too.

But though Henry was willing to go out of his way to avoid a fight with these fellows, there were some things he just wouldn't do. He just looked at them and shrugged, but said nothing.

"Hey, whatcha doin' hangin' around by this doorway anyhow, darkie?" one asked.

"Just a waitin' on my mistress," Henry said.

"Well, we don't like the ugly look o' you standin' there," another one said, "go stand across the road where ya won't bother nobody," he said.

But though Henry wouldn't abandon his post guarding Miss Margaret under any circumstances, he still tried not to offend the young men, responding, "Much as I'd like to do as y'all says, masters, my mistress done told me to stand right here 'til she comes out, so that's exactly what I'm fixin' to do." He gave them a friendly smile, hoping to keep things peaceable.

"Listen here, darkie; we said to move on over t'other side o' the road. So you gotta do as we say. Lookie here," the one on the right said, pointing to the single private's stripe on his blue sleeve, "this here says we're Union soldiers, which means you gotta do as we says."

"Sorry fellas," Henry said, still trying to be friendly and non-confrontational, "but my mistress said to stay here—"

Then with no warning the one on the left, who was dark-haired and a bit thick in the middle, stepped up and punched Henry hard in the stomach. The unexpected attack caught Henry by surprise, and he doubled over in pain, even as another man struck him on the head with a fist. He covered his head with his hands as they proceeded to pummel him with fists and then kick him with their boots. The blows came so hard and fast he feared he might pass out.

He briefly considered pulling out the small Colt revolver the Captain had lent him, but decided it was better to just take the beating; the Captain had said only to use the pistol in the gravest emergency to save Miss Margaret's life. This beating, though painful and potentially dangerous, didn't rise to that level in his mind.

But then the pounding eased up and he heard shouts, curses, and scuffling, as the three men suddenly backed off. He looked up and saw Cobb on the back of one of the men, his left arm wrapped around the fellow's neck as he punched him in the side of the head with his right. The other two were circling around, trying to get a swing at Cobb as he yelled, cursed, and punched like a mad man. Henry jumped up and launched himself at one of the two, hitting him mid-section and taking him tumbling to the ground. There they grappled and punched at each other. But despite their determination and ferocity, Henry and Cobb were outnumbered by the three strong young men, and soon were getting the worst of it.

And then Miss Margaret arrived. She stepped out of the Customs House and saw a crowd gathered around the steps watching an intense fight taking place to the side of the entrance to the building. Another glance showed her that two of the combatants were hers—Henry and Cobb—and that they were outnumbered and taking a serious beating.

She felt a welling of righteous wrath. Looking around for some kind of weapon, she saw a white man—apparently a coach driver—standing in the crowd with a buggy whip in his hand. She reached over and snatched it from him.

"Hey!" he said and frowned at her.

But she answered, "I need to borrow this a moment," and the look on her face left no room for discussion, so he just shrugged. She pushed her way through the crowd, stepped up behind the nearest of the white soldiers and lashed him across the back with the whip as hard as she could.

"Ow! *Goddamn it!*" he exclaimed, letting off from punching Henry to wheel around toward her. As he took a step toward her, she whipped him across the face, sending him ducking to the ground. Then she stepped over and lashed the second man, who was on top of Cobb, giving him three hard whacks—*snap, snap, snap!* He groveled on the ground moaning, covering his head with his hands.

She stepped up the third man, but he'd seen what'd happened to the others and backed away, holding up his hands.

"Don't hit me with that thing, miss! Why're you doin' that anyhow?" he asked.

The fight had stopped. All eyes were on her, including those of Henry and Cobb, both of whom sat up to stare at her.

But she was fiery mad, and didn't care what anyone thought about it. "How *dare* you attack my men!" she shouted. "Who do you think you are?! You're a disgrace to that uniform you wear!" she screamed at them.

"Who're you to tell us what to do, *bitch?*" the first man said, rubbing at the whip welt on his face, "Fact is, we don't much care to go out and get ourselves kilt on account o' a bunch o' ungrateful black slaves!"

She waggled the whip at him, causing him to flinch again, "You'll do your *duty* … as men … or I'll *whip* you again," she said. "And if you won't listen to me, I'm sure Mr. Chambers will have plenty to say about it when he returns!"

At the mention of Nathan's name, the three soldiers suddenly seemed concerned.

"Captain *Nathaniel* Chambers, ma'am? What's he got to do with this-here business?"

"These're his men, that's what. And I'm his sister!" she snapped, still fired up.

Apparently, Nathan's name carried weight. The three soldiers stood up, remove their hats, and apologized to her and then to Henry and Cobb.

"Sorry, ma'am. We didn't mean no offense. Just … havin' a bit o' fun; blowin' off a little steam is all, you know … Not meanin' no offense to any o' Mr. Chambers folks," the one who'd thrown the first punch said.

"This is the sort of *fun* that got us into this war in the first place," she answered, still steamed, but beginning to calm down a little. "It's this kind of festering evil that brought our country to its present dire circumstances. Give *that* some thought as you are praying Mr. Chambers doesn't hear of this incident."

"Yes, ma'am. Sorry, ma'am. Sorry fellas," they said to Henry and Cobb, suddenly contrite and ashamed—at least to all appearances.

But Henry thought it likely had more to do with their fear of the Captain—or the wrath of Miss Margaret—than any sudden, honorable feelings toward the freemen.

Margaret walked over to the man from whom she'd taken the buggy whip and handed it back to him. "Sorry for my rudeness earlier, and thank you kindly for the use of this," she said, in a voice that was now quiet, and slightly shaky.

But the man grinned brightly and tipped his hat to her, "Oh, never mention it, ma'am. It was well worth it to watch the show you just put on!"

She returned his smile, but shook her head and rolled her eyes, *Perhaps not my finest moment*, she decided.

And now that the adrenaline was subsiding, Margaret suddenly felt a bit wobbly and unsure of her footing. Henry noticed and stepped up to take her gently by the arm, "It happens even to me sometimes, Miss Margaret … after gettin' all fired up mad … get to havin' the shakes so bad afterward I can hardly stand myself."

"Thank you, Henry."

"No … thank *you*, Miss Margaret. Here I was charged with protectin' you and you ends up savin' my sorry hide," he grinned brightly.

She smiled back at him, and patted his arm, "Well, we do have a history of looking out for one another, don't we, Henry?"

He laughed, "That we do, Miss Margaret … that we do!"

But as Henry, Cobb, and Miss Margaret returned to the carriage and boarded for the ride back to Belle Meade, none of them noticed a scruffy-looking man in dirty, well-worn clothes who'd watched the fight and its aftermath with great interest. He'd then saddled up and followed them as they departed.

ജ്ഞാജ്ഞാൽഞ്ഞാൽഞ്ഞാൽ

The stranger kept well back on the ride home, such that the carriage's occupants never even noticed him. But he never let them out of his sight.

They encountered no other travelers on the road save another carriage, heading toward town. It was driven by a well-dressed black man, and its occupants were a handsome, well-groomed young gentleman, and a startlingly good-looking, dark-haired lady. The stranger caught her eye as they passed, so he grinned at her and tipped his hat. But she turned away quickly, not acknowledging the gesture. *Snobby bitch!* he groused.

After the carriage he'd been following turned off the road to the right, onto the drive leading to Belle Meade, the rider made a strong mental note of the location, and then continued on for a few more miles before turning off to the left.

Now that he knew the location of the Chambers' farm, he had another place he wished to investigate; he'd heard rumor of an abandoned farm, the next one just past the Chambers' place. The rumor was the fellow had gotten into a dispute with Chambers who'd then sent his men out to murder the poor fellow along with all his friends.

When he arrived and went inside, what he observed seemed to confirm the rumors; the place hadn't been lived in for quite some time, and clearly had been suddenly—and violently—vacated. Foul, dirty dishes were still piled in the sink and dirty glasses were on the kitchen table, along with a scattered deck of cards. Most telling, though, were the large bloodstains on the floor and splattered on the walls around the table.

He slowly shook his head. *That Chambers is one mean son-of-a-bitch*, he decided, then turned and walked back out the door. He saddled up and rode back toward Wheeling, passing back by the drive leading to Belle Meade Farm, and continuing on until he was a half-mile or so from town. There he took a side trail off to the right that wound off into the woods for another three-quarters of a mile to a small clearing. Several tents were pitched around the meadow, and a campfire was still smoldering from earlier in the day when it'd been chilly.

He walked over to the second tent, the largest of the group, pulled back the tent flap and stepped inside.

"Found them," he said to a large, somber-looking man seated at a small table inside.

"Good. And the other, abandoned place?"

"Yep ... it's there too, just as the rumors said."

The seated man grunted in acknowledgment.

"I've also confirmed that Chambers and his Texans are out of town. Left for Harpers Ferry on the train two days ago; some battle or other is said to be brewing over there."

The seated man had a thoughtful expression, slowly nodding his head. Then he looked up and said, "Pack up this place. We'll sleep under a *real* roof tonight; that abandoned farm will seem like a palace after months sleeping in a tent. And then ... we'll pay Chambers' new farm a visit ..."

He stood and grabbed his jacket from the back of a vacant chair to the right side of the table. He struggled a moment to put the jacket on, the process made more awkward than it should've been due to a missing left hand.

꧁꧂꧁꧂꧁꧂꧁꧂꧁꧂꧁꧂

Though he was in no mood for it, Nathan felt obligated to seek out Colonel Miles, who was currently the officer in command at Harpers Ferry, to offer his services after handing across the letter of introduction from Governor Pierpont. And though Miles was receptive to the notion, he informed Nathan that a brigadier general named Rufus Saxton would be arriving from Washington by train in the morning to take command, and likely whatever arrangements they might agree on today would be countermanded by the general come the morrow.

Nathan thanked him and departed, finally making his way to the inn, as he'd intended to do before unexpectedly running into Evelyn in the morning. At the memory of *that* meeting an aching knot formed in the pit of his stomach.

He and Tom had a late dinner together at the inn, the rest of the men having gone out to see if there was anything to see or do around the town. Harry the Dog also left them, going outside to find a good spot to take a nap. Nathan was in a surly mood, and only picked at his food, saying very little. After dinner they sat for a time smoking cigars and drinking whiskey, and Tom didn't press him to engage in any conversation.

Finally Tom announced he was tired and ready to retire for the evening. But he politely offered to continue keeping Nathan company, so he'd not be alone.

"I thank you for the consideration, Tom, but I know I'm pretty damned poor company at the moment. It's probably for the best I just be alone with my thoughts … such as they are."

They said their goodnights and Tom went off to his room and bed.

Nathan continued to sit and drink whiskey until he knew he'd had way more than was good for him; the room was beginning to move of its own volition, and people walking about or conversing had become slightly blurred and indistinct. But he no longer cared, welcoming the pleasant numbing sensation it was bringing to his painful, swirling thoughts.

And then a sudden noise out toward the entrance to the inn cut through his fog and brought him out of his reverie—a young woman's voice, sounding frustrated and disappointed, though he couldn't make out the words. A moment later she entered, an attractive young lady in her early twenties, with dark hair and a lean, pretty face. She was dressed nicely, as an upper-class lady would be, but in casual traveling clothes rather than anything formal.

She gazed quickly around the room until her eyes met Nathan's. She lingered on that eye contact a moment before smiling slightly and immediately walking in his direction. She untied a lacey bonnet and removed it from her head as she walked.

When she reached the table, he stood and made a slight bow, resisting the urge to keep a hand on the table to steady himself. She smiled again, and gesturing toward the chair opposite him said, "May I?"

"Oh … yes, certainly, miss. Please, do join me, if you wish."

"Thank you, sir. My name is Belle … Belle Boyd," she said, extending a hand covered in a thin, white glove. He took her hand and kissed it in the formal manner.

"Nathan … Nathan Chambers, ma'am. Very good to meet you, Miss Belle. Please … be seated."

"Thank you," she said, settling into the offered chair.

"I … couldn't help overhearing some sort of … *concern?* Out in the lobby … Is there aught amiss, ma'am?" he asked.

"Oh … well … nothing to concern yourself about, sir. It's just that … well, you see … I have only just arrived in Harpers Ferry after being forced to flee my home just south of here for fear of the advancing rebel army. Beastly men … unclean … unshaven, and many bare-footed, if you can believe it! I could only imagine what such men would do if they were to come upon a young woman alone and undefended in her home. So I rode here as fast as I could, hoping there were some good, loyal Union soldiers in Harpers Ferry who might offer a lady some protection."

"That was wise, I suspect. It's never a good place for civilians to be, when armies are preparing to meet in battle."

"Thank you for saying so, sir. But, alas … I have been all over town, and this is the last place I've checked. But it seems all the rooms for rent are taken."

"Well … a large troop train arrived earlier, so I suspect the officers have snapped up every available room in town for the foreseeable future. It's possible some private homes may open up for boarding tomorrow …"

"Oh! Well, it's at least reassuring to hear that several hundred soldiers have arrived to help protect us."

"A few thousand, more like …" he corrected her.

"Oh! Even better."

"And … don't worry about your room. You can have mine; I'll bunk up with one of my men. Fortunately, we had already rented out several rooms before the train arrived."

"Well … that is *most* gallant of you, Mr. Chambers … but I wouldn't want to inconvenience you …"

"Not at all, Miss Belle, not at all. It's the least a gentleman can do …"

"Well, I must say … in the space of mere moments you have eased all my fears and concerns, Mr. Chambers," she said, smiling brightly.

"Please, call me Nathan," he said, "… and think nothing of it, Miss Belle."

"Well, then, Nathan … you must call me just *Belle*, as we are now fast friends."

"Belle, then …" he responded, and returned her smile.

"But Nathan … now you really *must* indulge my growing curiosity … you speak as a man very knowledgeable in military matters, and in fact when I saw you from the doorway you struck me as a man of military bearing … and yet …"

"Yes, I know … no uniform. I get that a lot …" he said with a rueful grin. "And no, you are not mistaken … I *am* a military man, just not in uniform at the moment."

"Oh … I see. Now, there *has* to be an interesting tale behind this seeming contradiction …"

He smiled, and started to take another sip of whiskey, before realizing his near rudeness and setting down the glass.

"I'm sorry … I haven't offered you any refreshment, Belle. Will you join me in a drink? Or are you hungry after your travels? Likely the kitchen can still come up with something …"

"Oh … well … perhaps just a splash of warm brandy … to take the chill off the evening."

"Certainly," he answered, and waved down the innkeeper, who immediately came and took the order.

"Getting back to your inquiry, yes, I'm a military officer and veteran of long service. But currently I'm serving as a … hmm … military advisor to the new governor of Virginia in Wheeling. Recruiting and training new regiments, organizing efforts against enemy guerilla actions, and so on. Each time I try to step away from those duties and don a blue uniform it seems something serious comes along to prevent it."

"Well, well … military advisor to the governor … that's very impressive, Nathan. Even more so than just a low ranking general … like the one's with only one star on their uniform … how do you call them?"

"Brigadier … they're called a *brigadier* general, as they are expected to command a *brigade*-sized force."

"Oh! I never knew that … thank you."

"Never mention it."

"Anyway, I would think the military advisor to a governor would be a very important and prestigious position, yes?"

He shrugged, and this time went ahead and took another swallow of whiskey as she had been served her brandy while they talked.

"Maybe so, but still … for an old army veteran like me, the call to be out in the field, engaging in battle, is a hard one to resist."

She shook her head and said, "It's certainly a manly concept, and hard for a lady to comprehend. I'd never in life want to be anywhere *near* a battle!" She smiled brightly again, and he decided she had a pretty smile. "And … is that why you're here, Nathan? To join in a battle, despite being out of uniform?"

"Maybe … if needed. I came here to help organize a defense against General Jackson. But it sounds like a Union brigadier general will be arriving in the morning to take charge, so … we'll see what he has to say about it."

"Oh! How interesting … a general is arriving in the morning? Bringing an army with him, I suppose?"

Nathan looked at her, and shrugged, "I haven't heard. Possibly … hopefully," he added, "and artillery."

"Artillery? Isn't that those large, loud guns … *cannons*, I believe they're called?"

"Yes, those are the ones. Harpers Ferry has only a few small cannons, but will need a good number of larger guns if the Union hopes to hold off General Jackson."

"Well then, let's hope the new general brings them along, these arti … what was it again?"

"Artillery."

"Yes, the *artillery*," she said with a chuckle, shaking her head. "I'm sorry, Nathan … these military terms make my head spin. It's not something a lady is taught to know anything about, I fear."

"Quite understandable, Belle. No reason you should need to know anything about it."

After another hour of small talk, which mostly consisted of Belle quizzing Nathan about various aspects of Harpers Ferry—its general layout, how he expected Jackson to approach it, how he would hypothetically defend against such an approach, etc.—and several more drinks, he found himself about to nod off in his chair, so offered to show her to her room so he could go bunk up with Tom and get some desperately needed sleep.

When he got up to escort her, he felt wobbly, and the room spun disconcertingly. He realized sometime since her arrival he'd gone from having had a bit too much whiskey to being completely drunk. The rational part of his mind felt ashamed, knowing he'd likely been slurring his speech while speaking to the young lady.

But he shrugged it off, and somehow managed to guide her to his room. He fumbled with the key, but finally unlocked the door, and ushered her inside.

"I'll just grab … hmm …" he gazed around the room, but everything looked fuzzy and indistinct in the dim light of the lamp burning on a side table. He spotted the pack containing his clothes, leaning against the headboard of the bed, and grabbed it, "… a few items I'll need in the morning, otherwise the room is yours."

But when he approached the door, he was surprised to find it closed and Belle standing in front of it.

She stepped up to him, smiled and said, "You don't have to go …"

But in his whiskey-muddled mind he didn't at first take her meaning. "Oh, I'm afraid I'm more than talked out for the night, and must get some shut-eye, Belle," he said.

But she stepped up closer, gazing into his eyes for a long moment, before saying, "We needn't talk any more, Nathan …"

Then she leaned up against him, reaching up to kiss him softly on the lips. Her soft, warm body felt good pressed against his, and her warm, moist lips were making his head spin. He reached down and grasped a handful of her long curly, dark hair, letting the pack slip to the floor. *Dark hair … why does Evelyn have dark hair? Oh, yes, I remember … she'd dyed it dark to escape the prison … oh, Evelyn … I've missed you so,* he said, not sure if he'd spoken aloud. He leaned into the kiss, pulling her closer in to him.

Then he leaned back from the kiss to gaze into her lovely blue eyes … but her eyes were now brown … *how did that happen? You can dye hair … but not eyes …* then with a shock he pulled away. *This isn't Evelyn …* he realized. And then he remembered who she was … Belle. He stepped back, rubbing his forehead, trying to clear away the fog.

"I'm sorry, Belle … I … didn't mean to do that …"

But she pressed forward again, "It's all right, Nathan … you've done nothing wrong … we're both adults here …"

He shook his head, "No … I'm … I'm betrothed to another … or at least—"

But Belle just chuckled, "She'll never know, Nathan ... she's not here, but *I am* ..." then she leaned up to kiss him again.

This time he pulled away, and said, "No ... I can't do this, Belle ... I ..."

But she leaned forward and put her hand against his crotch, rubbing slowly up and down, feeling his growing manhood through his clothes. She laughed, "It feels like you can ..."

He grabbed her hand and moved it away, then held her by the wrists as he moved to the door, opened it and stepped out into the hall.

"I'm sorry, Belle, but I ... just ... can't."

She stood in the doorway, a pouty look on her face as he turned and strode off down the hallway, trying to remember which room Tom was in.

He managed to find Tom's door, but when he reached up to knock, he realized how late it was—likely well past midnight—and was also feeling embarrassed about his state of inebriation, so he thought better of it. He shrugged; it was a mild night out after a warm, sunny day. He'd slept outdoors in much worse. So he went out the back door, down the outside stairs, and stepped out onto the lawn unsteadily, looking around for a likely patch of grass to lay down on. He gazed up at a dazzling display of stars overhead on a moonless, cloudless night. But his head was too muddled to entirely appreciate the view.

Then a sudden thought hit him and he smiled, put his fingers to his mouth, and made a loud whistle. A few seconds later the silhouette of a large four-legged shape came trotting up out of the darkness.

☙❧☙❧☙❧☙❧☙❧☙❧

After a good long cry and an even longer nap, Evelyn had the rest of the long, overnight train ride to Wheeling to think over what had just happened in Harpers Ferry.

And now that her initial emotions had been spent, her anger toward Nathan was beginning to subside. She knew in her heart that he had reacted out of fear, and that he really was a fair and open-minded man. Would he eventually come around to her way of thinking? She prayed it would be so.

But another question now haunted her … they'd agreed to be married, but then they'd fought and had never discussed it further. She couldn't decide if she should assume they were still engaged, or that it was now called off.

These lingering doubts helped her make up her mind about the next decision she'd been mulling over: whether or not to visit Miss Abbey and Megs in Wheeling, to see if they could help answer those questions—and so she could begin making amends with them.

❧❧❧❧❧❧❧❧❧

Monday May 26, 1862 – Wheeling, Virginia:

When the carriage pulled to a stop in front of the farmhouse, Evelyn was a little surprised at the contrast between this old, slightly shabby, and much smaller house and the grand Big House back at Mountain Meadows, despite Nathan's warning to that effect. She couldn't help asking the driver, "Are you *certain* this is the Chambers' place?"

The driver, a middle-aged black freeman who'd been hired along with the carriage from a gentleman in Wheeling, laughed and said, "Oh, yes ma'am, this here's Belle Meade Farm, all right. Though I don't know Mr. Chambers personally, of course, everyone o' my particular … *complexion*, you might say … knows o' this place. We call it 'Freeman Town' amongst ourselves, on account o' all of Mr. Chambers' former slaves who's livin' here now. See there," he waved his hand out to his right, away from the house.

Evelyn looked and saw row upon row of white tents, perfectly aligned on sturdy wooden platforms, stretching out across the pasture next to the farmhouse. *Of course! The tents made of the sailcloth Jonathan sent to Nathan as a gift!* she remembered.

Evelyn and Nigel had arrived in Wheeling the previous day after riding the train all night. They'd found a room in a boarding house, and she'd spent a long, restless day fretting about whether or not to go through with her visit to Nathan's new farm and face the likely rancor of its inhabitants.

She debated with herself about backing out of her meeting. No one had seen her yet, so it wasn't too late. She feared the reception she would receive from the farm's inhabitants; the last time she'd seen any of them had been the day she'd suddenly left Mountain Meadows without explanation, leaving Nathan bewildered and heartbroken. And the former residents of Mountain Meadows, both black and white, had been fiercely loyal to Nathan even back then; they had even more reason to be now.

She looked over at Nigel, who nodded and smiled encouragingly. He knew she was feeling reticent about the encounter, but he had agreed it was the proper thing for her to do and might be a help in her relationship with Nathan.

And then, before she could change her mind, the front door opened, and a woman stepped out. Miss Abbey looked just the same as Evelyn remembered—tall and thin, with a lovely face that seemed to defy her age—though she now dressed more casually than she had at Mountain Meadows. Abbey shaded her eyes with her hand and gazed into the carriage to see who her visitors might be.

It struck Evelyn as odd that no grooms had met the carriage, and that Miss Abbey was answering her own door. But then she remembered, there were no longer any slaves to do things for her. Likely she now had to do a lot of things she'd never had to do before!

After gazing for a moment, Miss Abbey's face lit up, "*Evelyn?!* Is that *you*, my dear? And with black hair?!" she asked, and Evelyn instantly knew she'd been anxious for naught, and that her greeting would be a warm and kindly one after all.

"Hello, Miss Abbey," Evelyn answered, "it's so wonderful to see you again!"

"Oh my goodness gracious, *Evelyn!* You have no idea how happy I am that you're here. *Megs!* Megs, come outside, my dear! There's someone you'll want to see."

Not waiting for Megs' arrival, Miss Abbey came down the steps to the driveway even as the driver was helping Evelyn down from the carriage. As she stepped out onto the gravel Abbey embraced her warmly, and kissed her on both cheeks. Evelyn returned the hug and kisses with heartfelt affection. She had loved Miss Abbey from the moment they'd first met, and it had stung bitterly to feel she had let her down and likely ruined their friendship. She felt a sudden welling of joy such as she hadn't expected to feel at this meeting.

And then Megs came out of the house and saw Evelyn. She too beamed brightly, and laughed out loud, "Why, Miss Evelyn, as I live and breathe!" She rushed down the steps, and she too embraced and kissed Evelyn, which was also returned with enthusiasm.

By this time Nigel had come around from the far side of the carriage, and introduced himself. "Hello, Miss Abbey ... hello Miss Megs ... my name is Nigel Smith. It's a pleasure to finally meet you two ... I've already heard so much about you from Miss Evelyn."

"Mr. Smith, a pleasure," Abbey said, with a slight bow and a curtsy. Megs likewise greeted Nigel and curtsied.

"*Smith* ... hmm ..." Megs said, a thoughtful expression suddenly creasing her brow, "any relation to the Mr. Smith who was sent by the Employer at the time of the Captain's escape from Richmond?"

"Yes ... very likely," Nigel answered with a grin.

"Thought so," Megs responded, "you Smiths seem to have a rather large family."

Nigel chuckled, "Yes, I suppose you could say so ..."

"Well, please, Evelyn, Mr. Smith ... come inside and get out of the sun. The place isn't much, Evelyn, compared to what we had before, but it's beginning to feel more like home every day. We've even started a new flower garden." She looked over at Megs and the two of them shared a warm smile.

"Well, it is quite a pretty setting, Miss Abbey," Evelyn answered, trying to come up with something complimentary to say. But when she reached the top of the stairs, and gazed out at the view, she saw the Ohio River, sparkling in the sunlight, not far off through the trees, "Oh! I can see the river from here … how lovely!"

Abbey smiled, "Thank you, dear. That's one feature we *didn't* have back at Mountain Meadows."

Once they'd been seated, and the guests had declined the offer of refreshments, Abbey said, "Evelyn … I'm so sorry to have to disappoint you, dear, but Nathan is out of town at the moment … and we don't know precisely when he'll return."

Evelyn smiled, and answered, "Oh, never worry, Miss Abbey … I came here *specifically* to see you and Megs—to see if we might rekindle our friendship."

But then she couldn't help giggling at Miss Abbey's puzzled look, and Megs' frown.

"Sorry … I couldn't resist … you see, I already met Nathan."

"You *did?!*" Miss Abbey gasped.

"Where? … *How?*" Megs said.

"We met in Harpers Ferry, by pure accident … or perhaps divine providence … Anyway, I was just getting off a westbound train when he was getting off one coming in from the east. We bumped into each other crossing the train platform."

"Oh! How wonderfully fortuitous," Abbey said, "that must've been quite a shock."

Evelyn smiled and gazed up at the ceiling for a moment as tears began to well in her eyes. "It was … it was *just … wonderful!* One of the happiest moments of my life … If I live to be a hundred, I shall *never* forget it …" she answered, in a quiet voice, as if lost for a moment in the memory. Abbey and Megs smiled.

Then Megs said, "Now you've got to tell it from the start … beginning with how it is your beautiful golden hair has turned black as coal!" she tugged at her own hair and snorted a quick laugh, "Like mine *used* to be, 'fore it started gettin' all this gray!" Evelyn chuckled and nodded.

"Very well, but I will start the day *after* leaving Mountain Meadows … *the* day I left I won't willingly relive for any reason," she said with a frown. The other women nodded their understanding, but said nothing.

"But first, before I tell my overly-long tale … It is only fair to tell you … I believe Nathan and I are now engaged to be married!" she announced, as tears once again filled her eyes.

Abbey jumped up from her seat, and came over to embrace and kiss her once again. "Oh, Evelyn! You don't know how I've prayed for this moment … how I've prayed for the two of you to finally come together as I knew you should."

But Megs stayed in her seat, and held a puzzled expression, "But, Miss Evelyn … why did you just now say you *believe* you are engaged … don't you *know?!*"

Evelyn shook her head sadly … "That is the *other* reason I'm here … to get advice from you two ladies. You are not only two of the wisest women I know, you are also the two women in the world who know Nathan best; and right now I desperately need your counsel.

"But please … allow me to tell my full tale and then I beg you to grant me the favor of your opinions and advice on it."

"Very well, dear … please, tell us your tale," Abbey answered, settling back into her chair.

"First, though I trust everyone in this household implicitly, I must tell you, so that it's clear … many of the things I'm about to tell you are secrets which must not be repeated."

Both Abbey and Megs nodded their understanding, assuming she was referring to her various clandestine activities with the mysterious Employer.

Evelyn proceeded to tell them the very same tale she'd told Nathan the day before on the grass at Harpers Ferry. Though Nigel knew much of the story already, there were many parts he'd never heard before, and he nodded appreciatively at several key points.

She paused in her tale at the point just before their train arrived at Harpers Ferry.

"I have told you everything up to this point so you will understand what I have been involved in, and … well, maybe you'll understand why I did and said what I did when I met Nathan …"

Abbey slowly shook her head as if searching for the right words, "Evelyn … I … I am just *amazed!* I've never even *heard* of a woman doing the things you've just recounted. I am just *in awe*, Evelyn, truly."

"I ain't never heard of a *real* woman doing even half them things you just described," Megs said, nodding her head.

"Very gracious of you to say," Evelyn answered humbly. "Now I wish to tell you what happened at Harpers Ferry," she said. Though she intended to tell the tale in a matter-of-fact manner, by the time she reached the end she was so choked with emotion she could scarcely finish, and Miss Abbey had to offer her a handkerchief to wipe away her tears.

She turned to the two women and asked the question that'd been burning in her mind since she'd left Nathan standing at the railroad station in Harpers Ferry, "So … was I in the wrong, do you think? Should I have relented and agreed to stay home and tend to the farm while he goes off and fights the war?"

Miss Abbey looked thoughtful, and didn't immediately answer, but Megs was not so hesitant, "No, Evelyn, you weren't wrong; you done *right, girl!* Good *gosh* … you make me proud to be a woman! All them things you done … practically would've won the war all by yourself if a *man* hadn't been too stupid to follow the wise advice you gave him!"

"Thank you, Megs … that means a lot to me, coming from you …"

But Miss Abbey hadn't yet spoken, and seemed to still be contemplating the question, so the other two ladies turned to her, waiting for her answer.

"I think …" she started then paused again. Evelyn found herself holding her breath, so she willed herself to relax.

"I think Nathan is a proud, stubborn man … and Lord knows he has a temper when he thinks he's in the right!" She shook her head and smiled.

"But he's also a kindly and reasonable man, and there's one thing I know for certain …"

"What's that, Miss Abbey?" Evelyn asked.

"He loves you like nothing else in this world, Evelyn. I have seen it in his eyes when he speaks of you. I suspect the reason he was so upset with you is he loves you so, and aches to be with you. He doesn't know if he can wait for months or even years longer. And he is deathly afraid something bad will happen to you and doesn't know if he can bear the pain of that."

Evelyn smiled and nodded—Miss Abbey had just confirmed what she herself had been thinking and praying for. She had to wipe back tears once again.

"But don't you worry, dear," Miss Abbey said, "he *can* wait for you, and he *will*. He's a good man, and he'll come to realize you're doing what's right—doing what you *must* do, and that he's only being fearful and selfish."

Evelyn now sobbed openly, covering her face with the hankie.

Miss Abbey reached out and patted her gently on the back, "Never you fear, my dear; Nathan will come around. In fact, I would bet he's already feeling badly about what happened and wishes he could take back his angry words. I will go so far as to say I predict he is already penning a letter of apology to you and—God willing, and if the postal service is actually functioning—it'll be waiting for you when you arrive back in Richmond."

Evelyn snuffled a few more times, then thanked Miss Abbey for making her feel better, but Megs scowled and said, "And if he hasn't yet penned that letter, I'll whup his backside as I used to when he was an ornery little boy!" which made Evelyn smile.

❧❧❧❧❧❧❧❧❧

Before she departed Belle Meade, Evelyn wanted to walk the farm and visit with the freemen she had known back when they were slaves at Mountain Meadows. After how Miss Abbey and Megs had treated her, she was no longer surprised she was greeted warmly by everyone she encountered.

She was especially touched by the enthusiastic greeting from Rosa, who smiled so brightly Evelyn couldn't resist giving her a warm embrace when they parted.

She was saddened, however, that Cobb wasn't home, having driven the carriage into Wheeling on some sort of business. She

213

did speak to Cobb's wife, Hetty, who assured her Cobb still spoke of her fondly, and still bragged about being her best dance student. She said Cobb would be terribly disappointed to have missed her visit.

The visit to Wheeling and Nathan's farm, which Evelyn had been so dreading, had turned into such an uplifting and enjoyable visit that the time seemed to fly by, and soon it was time for her and Nigel to depart. When she walked toward the open carriage door, she suffered a sudden strong temptation to change her plans and stay here after all, awaiting Nathan's return.

But she took a deep breath, sighed heavily, and stepped up into the coach, sadly waving goodbye to everyone who'd turned out to see her off. She wondered if she would ever see them again, a thought that added to the melancholy she was now suffering.

The ride back to town was uneventful, and they only passed two sets of fellow travelers, the first being a fine-looking coach heading in the opposite direction. Evelyn couldn't see the driver, and didn't recognize the thin, dark-haired young lady riding within, nor the older black man sitting across from her.

Unknown to her, Cobb, who was the driver of that other carriage, also never noticed Evelyn, but tipped his hat and smiled at her freeman driver, whom he had spoken to several times before at the Customs House.

The only other traveler they saw was a lone rider, also going in the opposite direction a short distance behind the carriage. A lean man, he wore dirty, worn clothes and was unshaven. When they met eyes he smiled, and Evelyn thought it an evil look, so instinctively turned away, giving in to a sudden urge to reach over with her right hand and feel the bulge of the small pistol in its holster up her left sleeve.

It was a full moon on a warm, still evening and Margaret was feeling restless and anxious. It was after her usual bedtime, but she wasn't feeling at all sleepy. Adding to her general discomfort, her bedroom seemed hot and stuffy after a day of full sun beating down on the house. She decided to take a stroll in the moonlight—perhaps down to the bench by the river. It was a place that held pleasant memories for her; it was there William had first kissed her.

William, she thought, *please keep yourself safe and return to me soon.*

She knew her unrelenting anxiety stemmed from several different sources, but worry about William was at the center of it. Adding to that, she felt badly about how they'd parted, and now prayed she would have a chance to make amends with him.

And she'd spent several hours fuming over the unexpected visit earlier in the day by Evelyn, which Margaret had missed, being in Wheeling all day at the convention.

From what Miss Abbey had told her after she got home, it seemed that Evelyn had once again played with Nathan's emotions, this time by first agreeing to marry him, and then refusing to come *live* with him! *What kind of a wife does that?!* she wondered. *The woman is shameless, the way she plays with his emotions. Poor Nathan … he's so competent and capable in every other way, but seems helpless—childlike even—before this emotionally ruthless woman! Oooo … how I despise her! If only I'd been here …*

But there were also the concerns about the course of the Constitutional Convention, the war in general, and then—ever and always, looming like a dark cloud of dread on the horizon—the fear of Walters.

She had no trouble making her way down the trail through the woods to the river, as the bright moonlight provided just enough illumination. And she knew from previous visits that they'd made the path smooth and level, so there was little fear of tripping or falling in the darkness.

But as she reached the little clearing by the riverbank and looked out at the sturdy old bench—a permanent fixture there—she was surprised to see someone already sitting there. From the size and general outline, she decided it was one of the black women.

"Hello ..." Margaret said as she approached the bench, not wanting to frighten or startle whoever it was by suddenly appearing beside them.

The woman turned around and looked, "Oh! Hello, Miss Margaret."

From the voice and the outline of her face in the moonlight, Margaret recognized the woman and said, "Hello, Rosa. Sorry ... I didn't mean to disturb or startle you ... I didn't think anyone would be out here at this hour."

"Oh, it's all right, Miss Margaret. I was just enjoying the sight of the river. It's so pretty, how it sparkles in the moonlight. Please, come sit with me, if you wish."

"Thank you, dear. Very kind of you to share."

Rosa slid down a bit and Margaret took a seat to her right on the bench. For several moments they said nothing, just gazed out at the rippling waters of the Ohio as it rolled silently past.

But after a moment Rosa sighed.

Margaret turned to her and said, "Can't sleep either?"

"No, ma'am. I feel ... sorta restless, I guess. Worried, maybe ..."

"Hmm ... I'm thinking you and I may be worrying over the same things ..." Margaret answered.

Rosa looked at her and they met eyes, "Yes, I 'spect so, ma'am. Worryin' 'bout the Captain and his men ... out fightin' them wicked slavers."

"Yes ... I'm worried about Nathan and the others for certain," Margaret said, "but also ... I'm worried for one *special* man among them ... one who has become dear to me. Am I right in thinking you're feeling something of the same ... for *Tony*, isn't it?"

Rosa smiled, "How'd you know *that*, Miss Margaret?"

Margaret chuckled, "My dear, there are very few secrets for very long on this farm ... I've seen the two of you together ... how you *look* at each other."

"You mean ... the same way you and Mr. William look at each other?" Rosa answered, with a mischievous half smile.

"Yes ... as I said, there are very few secrets on this farm," Margaret answered with a smile of her own.

They were quiet again for a few moments, when Rosa asked, "How do they do it, I wonder?"

"How does *who* do *what?*" Margaret asked.

"The wives … the women … when there's a war on … and the men are off fighting. How do they survive it? How do they go on living their lives without bein' frozen with fear? It's only been a couple days and already I feel like I can't sit still—like my skin is crawlin' with bugs or something."

"I know what you mean …" Margaret said, nodding. "I wish I knew the answer … I surely wish I knew."

After a moment she turned and faced Rosa again, "Maybe you and I can help each other get through it … you know, be friends … and have someone to talk to who will understand what you're feeling, at least."

Rosa seemed surprised, but nodded, "Yes … yes, Miss Margaret … I think I would like that … thank you."

Margaret held out her hands and clasped Rosa's. "It's agreed then. And since we're now friends, you must call me just Margaret from now on."

"Oh … okay … *Margaret*," Rosa said, and smiled brightly. But Margaret could see a hint of tears forming in her eyes.

ഇൻഇൻഇൻഇൻഇൻഇൻഇൻ

An hour later Margaret was finally feeling more relaxed, like she might be able to finally get some sleep. After their decision to become friends, she and Rosa had spent the next half hour talking about their budding relationships—how they'd started, how things were feeling at present, and where they might be going. They were surprised at how much they had in common, how much their experiences were similar.

Margaret felt very thankful to now have another young woman to talk to about these things. Miss Abbey was always willing to talk, of course, but her own marriage had been anything but romantic, so it was hard for her to relate. And Megs, wise as she was about most things, had never been romantically involved with anyone by her own admission, so she was of little help in that regard.

Margaret sighed deeply, attempting to release the last remnants of her anxiety and relax before heading off to bed. She stood and took one last look at the river before turning and heading back toward the house. Rosa, who'd been out longer and had begun to feel chilled, had already gone to bed a few minutes earlier.

She was feeling very pleased about her potential new friendship, thinking happy thoughts and paying little attention to anything around her as she stepped out from the woods.

She took a single step and gasped, but no sound came out; someone had grabbed her from behind, immediately slapping a large, firm hand across her mouth, preventing her from screaming. Another iron-strong arm gripped her around the midsection as she squirmed and punched ineffectually with her fists and tried to kick with her feet.

But the man leaned his head in next to her ear, snorted a quick laugh and said, "Gotcha! Don't fight now, or I'll have t'hurt ya." She could feel his hot breath on her neck, and smell its foul stench.

He squeezed her hard around the middle, until she ceased resisting. She realized he wasn't bluffing about hurting her if she continued to fight. He lifted her feet from the ground and carried her across the drive toward one of the outbuildings. But instead of entering the barn as she'd feared, he walked past the door and continued around to the side.

Then Margaret saw a sight that made her heart stop and sent the cold chill of fear through her body like a jolt of lightning. Five men were there, sitting on horses. Four of these were men she didn't know: hard-looking men, well-armed with rifles in their hands, and pistols at their hips—the very picture of outlaws or rebel bushwhackers. But it was not these men who caused her such trepidation; the man in the center of the line she knew all too well: her evil, maniacal husband—*Elijah Walters!*

He gazed down at her with the chilling, bland expression she still saw in her worst nightmares. She also noticed he was now missing his left hand, and shuddered, remembering Big Stan describing having "winged" him. One more reason Walters had to hate her and Nathan.

"Hello, Mrs. Walters," he said mildly, leaning forward in his saddle.

Though the man holding her had freed her mouth, Margaret said nothing. She felt incapable of speech, fearing she might faint from sheer terror. She knew she was now a dead woman; in Walters' hands her life was forfeit, though likely before her death she'd be forced to suffer unimaginable, unbearable pain.

"What? … Not happy to see your husband, after such a long … hmm … *unhappy?* … separation?

"What's this …? Nothing to say to the man you betrayed … then cheated on, with that shameless whoremonger and abolitionist Chambers?" he sat back in his saddle and gazed at her a moment. "Good of you to be out wandering around alone … saved me the trouble of looking for you."

Then he spoke to the man holding her, saying, "Put her on the spare horse and tie her on. I'll enjoy dealing with her later."

The man farthest to Margaret's left kicked his horse forward, and she could see he was leading a horse with an empty saddle. One of the other men also held a riderless horse; she assumed it belonged to the man who was holding her.

Then Walters spoke to all his men, "Once she's secured, we'll attack the house. Remember, the older blonde lady is *mine*. Use the other women as you see fit, then kill them all."

A deafening noise like an explosion punished Margaret's ears. Then inexplicably, she fell backwards. She glanced up and saw the man who'd been leading the spare horse had a gaping red hole where his nose had been. She hit hard on her back, nearly knocking out her breath. But the man holding her had broken her fall; she'd landed on his chest. More gunshots sounded, echoing loudly off the farm's outbuildings.

Then strong hands gripped her wrists and yanked her to her feet. She was immediately thrown over a man's shoulder. He turned and ran away from the riders. She glanced down at the man who had been holding her where he lay on the ground. He stared back lifelessly, his throat slashed open. Blood pumped out, streaming down his neck.

Other gunshots exploded, quickly followed by a cacophony of shouts, screams, horses squealing, and multiple *more* gunshots—both thunderous rifle shots, and more staccato pistol shots.

But Margaret was carried quickly around the corner of the barn and on across the driveway, toward the house and away from the fighting. The man carrying her was moving at great speed despite her weight on his shoulder. And then a familiar voice reassured her, "Don't you worry none, Miss Margaret, I've got you now and am gettin' you outta here!" *Oh, thank God, I'm saved,* she thought, *it's Henry!*

When they got to the corner of the farmhouse, he set her down on the grass, and turned to look around the corner of the house back toward where the fighting was. He pulled a revolver from his pocket and cocked the hammer. "You all right, Miss Margaret?"

"Yes … I think so … thanks to you."

"Not just me, ma'am. All the men of the Watch … and Rosa."

"Rosa?"

"It was her who spotted some suspicious men on the farm and fetched us. She also warned me you were alone down by the river … so I come a' runnin'," he grinned at her, then went back to watching back across the roadway. Margaret felt a growing sense of relief, knowing Henry would guard her with his life.

The gunfire had now stopped, but they heard a sudden rush of horses, further back among the outbuildings. And then they saw three riders come out onto the drive and gallop off into the darkness.

And then the quiet stillness of the night returned as quickly as it had been interrupted. The front door of the house came open and Miss Abbey and Megs stepped out cautiously. Margaret was surprised to see each of the women carried a small revolver in her hand—and each looked like they knew what to do with it!

But Henry called out to them, "Stay back inside, Miss Abbey, Megs. Let our men handle the fightin'. Wait 'til they say it's safe for y'all to come out."

Abbey looked over toward the sound of his voice, "Henry? Is that you? Where's Margaret? She's not in the house!"

"I'm here, Momma … and I'm fine … thanks to Henry."

"Oh! Thank God, Margaret! I was so frightened when I couldn't find you. We feared the worst."

"It very nearly *was* the worst," Henry answered, and met eyes with Margaret, who nodded, mouthing the words, *thank you.* Henry pulled a knife from his belt and wiped blood off the blade on the grass before putting it back, "You're more than welcome, Miss Margaret."

And then Big George stepped out from the corner of the barn and shouted, "All's well now. They's all gone … or dead, so y'all can come on out. But Phinney's been hurt … *bad* …"

Margaret felt dread in the pit of her stomach at those words.

Then Big George and several of the other men of the Watch turned and started trotting off down the driveway, rifles in hand, presumably to keep an eye out and make sure the riders did not return. But they'd only gone a few steps when one of them stopped and turned around. In the darkness Margaret couldn't make out who it was. The man said, "Hey, Henry … you over there?"

Henry answered, even as he and Margaret were already up on the drive, moving toward the barn to check on Phinney, "Yeah, Ned … I'm here."

"Miss Margaret all right?" Ned asked.

Margaret was almost as shocked by this question as by anything else that'd just happened. Ned had never even said "hello" to her, though she'd tried to engage him on several occasions. "I'm fine, Ned. Thank you kindly for your concern," she answered.

Then Henry added, "Yep, not a scratch on her."

Ned nodded, and said, "Well … they's a pretty good scratch 'cross the throat o' the fella that done grabbed her," and he snorted a laugh, before turning and running after the others.

Henry and Margaret exchanged a look, and Henry shrugged, "He *did* like that story about you whippin' on them soldiers that was fightin' with me'n Cobb …"

ଅଓଅଠଇଓଅଓଅଠଇଓଅଓଅଠଇଓ

Margaret was disappointed but not surprised to find Walters was *not* among the three dead invaders. And then all such concerns were quickly swept away over concern for Phinney. He lay on the ground, clutching at his right upper arm, grimacing—clearly in great pain.

Those gathered around felt William's absence keenly; he always knew what to do in these situations, calmly taking charge and efficiently tending the wounded with great skill and compassion. And in a sudden flash of empathy, Margaret realized how selfish and wrong she'd been, trying to guilt William into staying home to protect her; in a real battle there would be dozens if not hundreds of soldiers wounded as badly as Phinney, or worse, and they'd be totally dependent upon William to ease their suffering and more than likely to save their lives.

Then she realized that even Nathan and some of the other soldiers from Texas had had enough experience with battle wounds that they likely would've known what to do in this situation. But none of them were here now, and nobody who *was* here had any idea what to do. They hovered over Phinney, asking how he was feeling, asking what they could do for him, and generally being useless and ineffectual.

Margaret decided she had better take charge or nobody would. She'd never done anything like this before, but she'd read a lot, mostly out of intellectual curiosity, including a few books on anatomy and the treatment of serious wounds.

"Quickly … he must have a tourniquet above the wound to stop the bleeding. Cobb, tear off a strip of shirt from one of the dead men … about so big. And then we'll need a stick … a sturdy stick, not too thick and a foot or so long." Men scrambled to obey her orders.

"Megs, please fetch him water … he will need to replenish the liquids he's lost from the bleeding … he'll be suffering a terrible thirst shortly." Megs gave a quick nod, then trotted off to get water as ordered.

A moment later, Cobb came back with the piece of shirt she'd asked for and one of the men brought a stick that would serve. She looked at Phinney and said, "Sorry, this may hurt."

He nodded, and she quickly threaded the cloth under his arm and up through the armpit above the wound. Then she tied off the cloth and threaded the stick through, twisting until it was tight enough to stop the bleeding. "Cobb ... sorry, I also need a short piece of rope or strong string to tie it off ..."

"Yes, ma'am," he said, and turned back toward the dead men to search for what she'd asked. "Not finding anything, Miss Margaret ..." he said, frantically searching among the bodies. "Might've had some in their saddle bags, but their horses done spooked and it'll take time to round 'em up. There's rope over in the toolshed, though ..."

"Never mind, just tear off another strip of cloth, smaller than the first ..."

He was back in an instant, handing her the requested strip of cloth. It was dirty and bloodstained, but she twisted it up until it approximated a length of rope, then slid it under the tourniquet, wrapped it around one end of the stick and tied it off.

"Now, Phinney ... the bleeding is stopped, so ... can you move your hand please, and I'll have a look at the wound?"

He shook his head, a look of fear in his eyes.

"Please, Phinney ... I must see what we can do to patch the wound ... I have to see the damage ..."

They met eyes for a long moment, then he finally nodded, and slowly released his grip and moved his hand away. To Margaret's relief, the tourniquet held, and there was only a slow oozing of blood. But when she looked at the wound, she had to stifle a gasp and suppress a strong desire to look away ... or even to *run* away ... or to vomit ... or pass out.

But she did none of those things, forcing herself to examine the gory wound. Clearly he'd been hit with a large caliber bullet, likely from a rifle. It'd punched through the bicep and straight through the humerus bone, completely shattering it, before creating a jagged, gaping exit wound out the back. The arm below the break now hung at a sickening, unnatural angle, such as no sound arm ever could.

She knew with a cold certainty that Phinney was going to lose the arm. But she hadn't the heart to tell him, nor the knowledge and skills needed to take it off. *Damn it, William! Why do you have to be gone now?!* She prayed Phinney would live long enough for William to return, so he could remove the ruined arm properly.

She looked up at Cobb, and they exchanged a serious look. But she said, "We must splint it … I'll need … uh … two more sticks … both a little larger than that first one. And more cloth to tie it together … hmm … and the cleanest strips of cloth you can find to pack into the wound. Oh, and then a larger piece of cloth to fashion a sling."

While the men were gathering these items, Megs arrived with the water and lifted Phinney's head so he could drink. He drank greedily at first, but after a moment he coughed, and shook his head, so Megs pulled the water away. "Thanks …" he said in a weak, raspy voice.

Margaret noticed Miss Abbey stood a few yards back, wringing her hands, a look of fear and shock on her face. *She needs a task*, Margaret thought. "Momma … have we any whiskey?"

"Oh! Yes, of course … I will go fetch a bottle," she said, and rushed off to perform her assigned duty.

In a few moments the men had gathered what Margaret had asked for and she set to work. Again she warned Phinney it would likely hurt a bit, and again he nodded his assent. She placed the sticks from a point just below the tourniquet down to his elbow, one on each side of the arm, and then used the cloth wraps to tie the sticks together, slowly straightening the arm out to its proper angle as she did. Phinney grit his teeth and quietly whimpered, but said nothing.

She fashioned a sling from the largest piece of cloth, wrapping it around the lower part of the arm and tying it up around Phinney's neck so he'd be able to walk once he was feeling up to it.

And just as she was finishing the last knot, Miss Abbey arrived with a bottle of whiskey and a glass.

"Thank you, Momma. Please pour him a drink. Phinney, the whiskey will help take some of the edge off the pain. Drink as much as you can stomach, but not so much as to make yourself sick or pass out."

Then she looked around and saw a large crowd had gathered out in the drive—all the freemen had come out to see what was happening, but they stayed back respectfully, allowing Phinney to be tended.

While Phinney was drinking, Margaret had another thought, "Megs ... do we still have the stretcher they carried Nathan in when he was unconscious during his escape from Richmond?"

"Well, yes ... I believe we do. I think the Captain kept it ... just in case."

"Well, we now have the *case*. I—" but as Margaret stood, the world began to spin.

Henry stepped up to support her. "Come now, Miss Margaret ... you done all you can do for Phinney ... you've been through a terrible shock and need to rest. Come with me now." She nodded her agreement, but turned to Miss Abbey and said, "Momma ... when Megs returns with the stretcher, have the men lift Phinney onto it and carry him into a bed in the house."

Abbey nodded, and Margaret walked slowly toward the house supported by Henry on her left side. But she was surprised to feel another arm grip her on the right side and looked over to see Rosa's smiling face.

"I seen what you just done for Phinney, Margaret, and ... well, all's I can say is, I'm right proud to call you my friend. It's plain to see why the Captain wanted you for a sister."

But Margaret found her voice was suddenly choked up, and she could say nothing in return, so she just nodded and smiled. Then Rosa's lovely face became blurry and indistinct as tears flooded Margaret's eyes.

Chapter 9. Backs Against a Stonewall

"The President of the United States of America,
in the name of Congress,
takes pleasure in presenting the Medal of Honor to
Brigadier General Rufus Saxton, Jr., United States Army,
for extraordinary heroism on May 26 - 30, 1862,
while serving with U.S. Volunteers,
in action at Harpers Ferry, West Virginia,
for distinguished gallantry
and good conduct in the defense."
– Citation, Congressional Medal of Honor

Sunday May 25, 1862 – Harpers Ferry, Virginia:

Nathan felt something tugging at one of his boots. In his mostly asleep, muddled state of mind, he tried kicking at the thing, hoping it'd relent and let him go back to sleep. But then the thing talked and said, "Sir ... is that you under there?"

The voice sounded familiar somehow, and in a moment it came to him, "Ungh ... good morning, Tom."

"Ah, it *is* you, sir! Good morning. But ... what're you doing under that bush, if you don't mind my asking?"

Nathan rolled over onto all fours, scrambled out onto the grass, and sat, gazing up at Tom with bleary eyes. There was another rustling in the bushes, and Harry the Dog came scrambling out. He plopped down on the grass next to Nathan with a grunt.

"We got a bit cold, I guess," Nathan finally answered.

Tom snorted a laugh, "Well, that answers the under-the-bush part of it, but ... why were you sleeping outside? I've been looking all over for you after I found your room empty."

"Oh ... well, a young lady showed up at the bar after you went to bed and I let her use my room as all the others were taken.

226

Didn't want to wake you and it was a mild night, so I just decided to sleep out under the stars with Harry."

"Ah. Very gallant and considerate of you, sir. And … how're you feeling today?"

Nathan looked up at Tom and rolled his eyes, "If you're referring to the copious amounts of whiskey I consumed last night … the answer is my head feels like Big Stan used it for a punching bag. But I'll live."

Tom chuckled. "Well, looks like your room is available once again, if you'd like to sleep it off in more comfort."

"No … but thank you, Tom. I've always believed a hard day's work with a pounding head and a queasy stomach was a proper and just punishment for being stupid enough to imbibe too much liquor the night before. I shall take my punishment like a man, thank you very much."

Tom chuckled, and said, "Well, they're serving up breakfast in the common room even now, so perhaps we can at least help settle that queasy stomach."

Nathan nodded and held out his hand, "Lead on, my good man." Tom grabbed his hand and pulled him up onto his feet.

ಬಜಿ)(ಜಿ ಬಜಿ)(ಜಿ ಬಜಿ)(ಜಿ

Since Nathan hadn't ended up bringing along any spare clothes due to his awkward, unexpected encounter with Belle, he and Tom stopped off at his room so he could change before they headed to the common room for breakfast. Tom agreed it was a good idea considering Nathan had slept all night under a bush next to a very large, dirty hound; he looked a little rumpled, to say the least.

But as he was changing his shirt, Nathan noticed something on the side table that caught his attention. His leather saddle bag lay there where he'd left it, but the strap was unbuckled. *Odd*, Nathan thought, *I never opened it after arriving … so why is it open now?*

He walked over and lifted the flap, looking inside. The papers he'd brought were still inside, so he shrugged, and started to re-buckle the strap. But then a thought struck him and he stopped. He reached inside and pulled out the stack of papers, setting them down on the table. He flipped through a few pages and stopped … his eyes widened. They were in the wrong order …

He turned to Tom, who was sitting on the bed waiting, reading a newspaper he'd brought from Wheeling.

"Tom … do you recall that newspaper story you were telling me about yesterday … you know the one … about a brazen female spy working for Stonewall Jackson?"

"Oh … yes, of course. It said … oh, well it's right here in this paper, actually … give me a second," he said, flipping through the pages, scanning for the article.

"Ah … here it is:"

> *War Department officials report that rebel General Thomas "Stonewall" Jackson has been employing a bold female spy by the name of Maria Isabella Boyd, known as "Belle." Miss Boyd is said to be an attractive, young woman in her early twenties, who adopts the aspect of a "damsel in distress" arriving alone at a Union outpost or garrison targeted for imminent action by Jackson. Boyd then shamelessly seduces Union officers into showing her their force deployments, defenses, etc. Then she sneaks away and rides like the wind back to Jackson's camp to report this vital information to him for exploitation in the coming action. Union Intelligence Service chief, Allan Pinkerton, has employed a number of special agents to track down the brazen spy, but so far she has escaped capture and continues to pose an espionage threat to Union forces in the field.*

Nathan groaned, slapping his hand to his forehead, "Son of a *bitch!*"

"What is it, sir?!" Tom asked.

"Tom … last night I very nearly slept with the enemy!"

ↂↇↂↇↂↇↂↇ

As Nathan entered the common room, he noted Belle was there, as he'd expected—this time sitting and chatting amiably with a handsome, well-groomed man in a Union Army major's uniform. Nathan shook his head, *Already picking out her next target ...*

He stepped up behind her, followed closely by Tom, Harry the Dog, a Union Army lieutenant, and two privates with rifles on their shoulders.

The major, who was facing them, looked up with a startled expression, causing Belle to turn and look.

"Oh! Good morning, Nathan!" she said, smiling brightly.

But now that he was sober and knew what she was about, her charms of last night fell decidedly flat in the bright light of day.

"I think *not*, Miss Belle," he answered in a flat tone.

The major frowned, and stood. "What is the meaning of this intrusion, sir?!" he asked, his face turning red.

Nathan gave him a hard look. "Major ... you *don't* want to be here just now ... it will *not* go well for your reputation. I suggest you take a walk ..."

The major looked startled at this reply, and stood gazing at Nathan, as if struggling for what to say.

The lieutenant then stepped forward, and said, "He's right, sir. It would be best if you just ... leave now ... *sir*."

The major gazed at the lieutenant a moment, then back at Nathan who continued to scowl. Finally he looked down at Belle, who was now staring down at the table and no longer smiling. The major's eyes widened with sudden comprehension. He scooped up his hat, plopped it on his head, nodded toward Belle, and said, "Ma'am," before striding past Nathan and out the front door.

"Maria Isabella Boyd," Nathan began in a formal tone, "you are under arrest for espionage against the government of the United States and its armed forces."

But if he had expected Belle to go quietly and meekly into custody, he was soon disabused of the notion.

She stood, and moved up in front of him, ignoring Tom and the soldiers. She reached out and straightened Nathan's collar in a seductive manner, once again smiling, "I would've thought after last night's ... *pleasures* ... you would've forgiven my little indiscretions. After all ... what possible threat can one helpless young lady be to such big, strong men as y'all?"

He shook his head, but said, "Your efforts were entirely wasted and in vain, Belle. My papers contained nothing useful for your purposes, and all my talk of defending the town last night was only hypothetical—nothing General Jackson wouldn't already know—and likely the new Union general will decide to do something entirely different."

But she smiled coyly, "Oh, I wouldn't say *all* my efforts last night were wasted, Nathan, dear. You *are* a very big, handsome man ..." then she laughed, "big in *several* interesting ways ..." she added shamelessly.

Nathan could feel his face turning red.

"And ... who is *Evelyn?*" she asked, startling him.

"Evelyn? What do you know of her?" he asked.

"Oh, well ... in the ... hmm ... *heat of battle,* as you soldiers might say ... you called me by her name. Your betrothed?"

Nathan glared at her but could think of nothing to say. The woman had no right to bring Evelyn's good name into this shameful display.

Belle smiled wickedly, sensing she'd hit a nerve, "She's a lucky lady ..." she said.

But Nathan thought about how he'd treated Evelyn the day before—with anger and lack of empathy—and how he'd gotten drunk afterward, then ended up kissing Belle, though more or less accidentally. He shrugged and said, "Given my recent behavior ... I'm not so sure about that ..."

Belle laughed.

"Lieutenant ... take her away," Nathan said.

The lieutenant stepped up, holding out a pair of wrist shackles. "If you will, miss ..." he said.

She gave Nathan one last, leering look, then held out her wrists as the lieutenant closed and locked the shackles, then led her away.

"Tom ... please accompany them to the colonel's office and tell him the whole story. Make sure he doesn't believe any lies she may attempt to tell him to try and gain her freedom."

"Yes, sir," he said, and turned to follow the soldiers.

⬥⬥⬥⬥⬥⬥⬥⬥⬥⬥⬥⬥⬥

After Tom and the soldiers departed with Belle, Nathan sat down at the same table Belle and the major had just vacated, intending to order breakfast—hoping to finally settle his stomach. Harry crawled under the table, lay down, and was soon twitching and snuffling in his sleep.

Nathan pulled out a cigar and lit up, but he resisted the urge to call for more whiskey to take the edge off his aching head.

After a few minutes of sitting, Nathan looked and was surprised to see a man standing next to his table looking down at him. He was about Nathan's age and showing a few days' growth of beard at the moment. A neat gray suit and matching bowler hat marked him for a gentleman, though the jacket showed signs of recent travel.

The man smiled, nodded, and said, "Mr. Chambers … may I?" gesturing toward an empty chair opposite Nathan.

Nathan waved his hand toward the chair, and the man sat. He removed his hat and set it in the seat of the empty chair to his right.

"Will you kindly join me as I break the fast, sir?" Nathan offered politely.

"Oh, yes, that would be splendid, thank you. I've spent a long hard night of travel and have only arrived early this morning. Fortunately, in time to witness … the *interesting* events that just recently transpired here."

Nathan grimaced at the thought of the embarrassing public display Belle had chosen to instigate. He looked over toward the bar, caught the proprietor's eye, and gestured for service. The proprietor nodded and went to fetch cups and the coffee pot.

"You have me at a disadvantage, sir …"

"Yes … we've never met, Mr. Chambers, though I *have* seen you before from a distance. I was … in and around the Capitol in Richmond many times during the recent unhappy events surrounding the secession."

"Hmm ... I've a good memory for faces, but I don't recall seeing *yours* there, sir."

The man smiled, "Ah. Then I was doing my job. You see, I was there in an ... *unofficial capacity* ... shall we say?"

Nathan raised an eyebrow at this, but resisted the urge to dig, instead taking another pull on the cigar, allowing the man to continue.

"Anyway, I wanted to congratulate you on discovering the rebel spy and having her arrested, and to thank you for it. I've been trying to bring Maria Isabella Boyd to ground for several months now. But despite the brazen use of her own name, and lack of any disguises, she has proven herself surprisingly elusive."

"Oh! Then you work for the War Department? For Mr. Pinkerton?"

"No ... not exactly; though my *Employer* is in collusion with the Union government."

"Ah! The mysterious Employer again! Considering I've never met the man, don't know his name, nor even what he looks like, it's amazing how many dealings I've had with him."

"Yes, he does seem to have taken a ... *particular* interest in you, Mr. Chambers."

"That's an understatement. I sometimes feel he's my own personal guardian angel."

The man smiled, "I believe he would humbly reply he had been somewhat derelict in that regard in the recent past, especially considering the near-tragic events in downtown Richmond prior to your departure from same."

"Well, nobody's perfect, and all's well that ends well. I'm certainly thankful for all his help since. The gift of the sailcloth for tents was especially timely."

"He will be pleased to hear it; I shall pass that along when next we meet."

"Thank you, Mr. ..."

"Smith. Though you may call me ... *Isaiah*. Of course—"

"Let me guess: it's *not* your real name ..."

Isaiah smiled, "You catch on quickly, Mr. Chambers. You would make a good spy."

"Oh, I very much doubt *that*, Isaiah. God knows I'm not subtle enough for such work!"

"But I submit you are a quick learner, sir. Speaking of ... it was a good piece of work today putting a stop to that ... *trollop* ... and her disreputable activities."

"*Trollop*, you say? Yes, I suppose so ... though I'm hardly in a position to judge in that regard. In John chapter eight our Lord says, '*He that is without sin among you, let him first cast a stone at her.*' I can assure you, sir; I dare not even *touch* that stone, let alone cast it!"

Isaiah smiled, "Well, as you say, 'nobody's perfect,' Mr. Chambers."

But Nathan scowled, "Suffice to say, this was *not* my proudest hour, Isaiah. I am ... ashamed of my behavior last night and am feeling most repentant this morning, not to mention a pounding head from too much whiskey."

Isaiah chuckled, "Fear not, sir; most of us have suffered similar lapses in judgment, and yet have come out the other side no worse for the wear. And when it comes right down to it, there can be no doubt who's side you're on, sir; I speak of God and his angels."

"Yes ... I'm always on *their* side, but sometimes I wonder if I deserve to have them on *my* side," Nathan answered, but he finally cracked a slight smile and took a sip of coffee that'd just been poured out by the proprietor.

"I don't believe our Lord demands perfection, Mr. Chambers. Undying loyalty—mixed with the occasional bout of humble repentance—is usually sufficient, I find."

Nathan nodded, "My man Tom has said much the same thing on occasion, whenever I've indulged in a bout of self-pity or doubt." He smiled, and idly reached down to scratch Harry between the ears.

"Mr. Chambers ..."

"Please, do call me Nathan, since we have established we are on the same 'team,' so to speak."

Isaiah smiled, "You honor me, sir. Nathan then ... the other reason I came to speak with you is of a more *urgent* nature."

"Oh?"

"Yes ... the presence of Belle Boyd in the city at this time is telling. As you are aware she is known to be working closely with C.S.A. General Thomas Jackson, whom the newspapers have been referring to as 'Stonewall'—though I think 'Lightning' might be a better appellation, given the way he moves his troops around from place to place at great speed.

"Her *modus operandi* has been to precede Jackson's assaults with her spying activities."

"Yes, so I've heard ... and that confirms Jackson now has his eye on Harpers Ferry."

"More than that, Nathan ... I believe an attack is imminent. Possibly within mere hours!"

☙❧☙❧☙❧☙❧☙❧

Since they'd had no news from Billy and Stan for several days, Nathan sought out Georgie and Jamie then sent them out with orders to find their missing comrades if they could, and then to scout Jackson's army, shadowing them and sending reports back on their position when possible.

It was early afternoon when he finally had time to meet the new Union commander, Brigadier General Rufus Saxton, who'd arrived mid-morning on the train. He prayed Saxton would turn out to be another capable soldier like Rosecrans, and not an incompetent strutting rooster like McClellan.

☙❧☙❧☙❧☙❧☙❧

"Thank you for bringing the information about Jackson's spy to me, Chambers, and for your offer of assistance," General Saxton said, sitting across from Nathan in the kitchen of a small house the Army had requisitioned for his headquarters.

Saxton was a bit older than Nathan, balding, with a full beard, pleasant round face that seemed to smile easily, and a quiet, reserved demeanor. Nathan took an immediate liking to him, despite a seeming lack of forcefulness. *Perhaps he just needs a little drawing out*, he decided.

"Of course, we've feared Jackson would move on Harpers Ferry—that's why Washington sent me out here, after all," the

234

general continued. "We've already had frightening reports and wild rumors of Jackson's imminent arrival, but your news seems to confirm the worst …

"By the way, the Secretary of War told me to expect you, Chambers, and gave me a briefing on your … *ahem* … impressive record. He instructed me to … 'utilize your expertise however I deemed appropriate.'"

"Happy to hear it, General. Please let me assure you I have no intention of undermining you. I'm only here to help in any way you might need or desire."

"I appreciate that, Chambers. Though … seeing the report of your previous service Secretary Stanton showed me, I don't quite understand your present circumstances …"

"It's complicated, General. For now, just assume I'm a well-informed civilian advisor, and leave it at that."

"Very well, Mr. Chambers. And to make sure we are clear … I am *not* a field commander by experience; I am a quartermaster, good at organizing and logistics, but battles … that's a whole other matter."

"Well, then perhaps we can consider our knowledge … *complementary*. At any rate, I want to make sure you know I have no delusions of grandeur here. You are the commanding general, and I'm just your advisor."

"Very well then. Thank you, Mr. Chambers. I—" Saxton stopped in mid-sentence as the telegraph began clicking on the other side of the room. He looked over to where the telegraph operator, a lieutenant, sat at the kitchen table scribbling down the letters the machine's noises dictated. Saxton walked over and stood behind the operator, gazing down as the young man neatly wrote out the letters on a sheet of paper with a pen. Nathan joined him, and took a look as well, but there was not yet enough of a message to make any sense of it. Then he noticed a stack of telegrams neatly piled to the side of the operator. Saxton saw his look and said, "We have a direct line to the War Department and have been keeping the line humming ever since my arrival this morning."

Nathan leaned over and picked up the pile of telegrams, "May I?" he asked.

"Certainly, Mr. Chambers. These should be all the messages to and from the War Department, in chronological order, since this morning. It'll be a quick way to get you up to speed on what we know ..."

Nathan started with the message on the bottom, which was the first Saxton had sent shortly after his arrival in the morning:

Harpers Ferry, May 25, 1862—9:45 a.m.

Hon. E. M. Stanton, Secretary of War:

I arrived here at 9:15 a.m. The telegraph messages this morning say that General Banks is retreating from Winchester. I do not think the information altogether reliable. It may be the enemy have got possession of the telegraph.

R. SAXTON,
Brigadier-General.

✦✦✦✦

Harpers Ferry, May 25, 1862—10:05 a.m.

Hon. E. M. Stanton, Secretary of War:

Heavy firing was heard near Winchester this morning. To obtain reliable information is difficult. Cavalry for scouting purpose is very much needed. If the whole movement of the enemy is not a feint in force, there is a possibility they may move on this place.

R. SAXTON,
Brigadier-General.

✦✦✦✦

Harpers Ferry, May 25, 1862 — 10:20 a.m.

Hon. E. M. Stanton, Secretary of War:

In case we are attacked two light batteries and two eight-inch howitzers would be of great service to command the river and bridge. There is no artillery here. The facilities for obtaining accurate information are so limited, and so many rumors are in circulation, I cannot realize yet the immediate danger here.

R. SAXTON,
Brigadier-General.

✦✦✦✦

War Department, May 25, 1862 — 10:40 a.m.

General Saxton, Harpers Ferry:

I have ordered General Dix to send you artillery from Baltimore. I will send some from here tonight. Call upon General Dix, as well as upon me for anything you want.

EDWIN M. STANTON,
Secretary of War.

✦✦✦✦

Harpers Ferry, May 25, 1862 — 11:20 a.m.

Hon. E. M. Stanton, Secretary of War:

Stragglers have come in from Winchester and report that General Banks attacked the rebels this morning in front of Winchester and was driven back into the town. General Banks' army is disorganized and in full retreat on Martinsburg. They report that 15,000 men are moving down upon Harpers Ferry. I think the rebel force has a large amount of artillery. It was this which defeated General Banks. We have no artillery here yet. Have 2,500 men. Is it better, if we are attacked, to risk an engagement on this side of the river, with the river in our rear, or

*retreat to the other side and guard the bridge? We feel the
want of artillery severely.*

R. SAXTON,
Brigadier-General.

Nathan looked up just as Saxton was finishing reading the
latest message which he then handed across:

War Department, May 25, 1862 — 12:00 p.m.

Brigadier-General Saxton, Harpers Ferry:
*You will have before morning a large force of artillery
with officers and artillerymen. Hold firm and keep calm.
Assistant Sec. of War Peter Watson is on the road with a
train of artillery from here besides that from Baltimore.*

EDWIN M. STANTON,
Secretary of War.

Saxton immediately dictated his response to the lieutenant,
who tapped it out on the machine:

Harpers Ferry, May 25, 1862 — 12:10 p.m.

Hon. E. M. Stanton, Secretary of War:
*If the artillery arrives in time, so that we can command
the bridge, etc., we can hold it with less disaster. The want
of artillery and manpower of only 2,500 men, is the only
thing that would make me think of withdrawing to the
other side.*

R. SAXTON,
Brigadier-General.

"General ..." Nathan began, wanting to tread lightly, "before
I came to see you, I saw thousands of newly arrived troops
debarking from the train, along with what appeared to be several
batteries of light artillery ..."
"Yes? And ...?"
"And ... you've just now told the Secretary of War you have
only 2,500 men and *no* artillery ... do you think that's wise?"

Saxton smiled, "You forget, Chambers ... I'm an old quartermaster ... I know how these things work. You always tell them you have less than you have and that you need more than you need. Then when they give you the small fraction of what you've asked for, all is well."

Nathan slowly shook his head, "I hear what you're saying, and believe me, I'm very familiar with the concept having served out in Texas. And normally I'd agree with you, but it seems like the secretary and the president are determined to give you whatever you require, and whatever they can, to make sure you can defend this station."

Saxton frowned, "Though I have somewhat exaggerated the numbers, I have not overstated the desperation of our situation, Mr. Chambers ... from all accounts Jackson has somewhere between fifteen and twenty thousand soldiers marching upon this command, with artillery numbering somewhere in the neighborhood of fifty. I fear the worst, even if the secretary does come through with everything I ask. I assume we have no more than a day or two before Jackson comes beating down our door. Time to withdraw our forces to safer ground up in the hills above the town, over on Maryland Heights across the Potomac, perhaps. We can burn the bridge and then try to keep him from crossing the river."

"Withdraw, General?"

"Despite our growing numbers, our troops are terribly inexperienced, and we have no fortifications. General Jackson has a reputation for chewing up poorly organized defenses. And though I do now have a handful of small carriage howitzers, what I really need is a battery or two of large, long-range artillery to have any hope of keeping him at bay.

"Of course, Washington has promised to rush me the artillery I've asked for. But so far, I've received nothing but telegrams! I fear even if it arrives in time, which is questionable, it shall still be insufficient to hold the town."

Nathan was quiet for a moment, gazing at the general, who seemed to have trouble maintaining eye contact. Brigadier General Rufus Saxton was only a few years older than Nathan, but he looked ten years older from the amount of gray in his thick mustache and the lack of hair on his head. Though older, he'd graduated West Point *after* Nathan and had missed serving in the Mexican War, so did not have that experience to draw upon.

As was his usual habit when mulling over a problem, Nathan reached into his pocket and pulled out a cigar. He idly stuck it unlit between his teeth and chewed on it while reaching down and stroking Harry's ears.

"General … do you want to be known as the commander who fled in the face of the enemy? Ran for the hills in fear? Or would you rather to be known as the man who finally put a stop to the *mighty* 'Stonewall' Jackson and his rampage through the Shenandoah Valley?"

General Saxton scowled, "Well, the latter of course, Chambers! But I'm not a *fool*. I'd rather risk tarnishing my reputation and live to fight another day than stay here and be annihilated by the enemy."

"General, what I've seen here in Harpers Ferry is disheartening, but not hopeless. There's still time to get things put into proper shape, and time for more troops and equipment to arrive. The B&O main line runs directly to Baltimore from here, and another trunk line from there to Washington. I'm sure the Army has cleared all traffic to rush you your reinforcements and artillery.

"If Jackson doesn't want to risk fording one of the rivers under fire, he's clearly got to come from the west. And you've got several hills to the west to serve as redoubts, with good fallback points. If you put a battalion or two on those heights across the rivers, to avoid the enemy raining artillery shells on you, this town makes an ideal defensive position on its narrow peninsula.

"I already have several men out scouting Jackson's army. I expect them to report back his position soon, and then shadow him until he's in position to launch his attack. We'll have a pretty good idea when and where he's going to attack, his numbers, artillery, etc., well ahead of time. We'll know where to place our artillery to the best effect, and where to dig in the strongest defense against him. And … he doesn't yet know *we* know for sure he's coming; that alone gives us another advantage."

"Well, I have to admit, you're making me feel more hopeful, Chambers."

"It's not just hopeful, General," Nathan grinned, "we're going whip his sorry rebel ass this time. And hand it to him on a platter!"

Saxton returned the smile and shook his head. "I admire your confidence, sir."

"We have every reason to be, General! I'm confident when the time comes, we'll have the artillery we need. And we'll have enough men, well-armed and provisioned, to hold off an army twice the size of Jackson's. Combine all that with a good, defensible position.

"And … we have *you* to lead us, Rufus! The Union needs to put a stop to Jackson in the Shenandoah, right here, right now, or his next stop will be Washington. And I believe you're just the man to do it, sir!"

"Thank you for saying so, Nathan. Though right now I don't feel like much of a leader."

"Nonsense! I mean what I say, General. You're a West Pointer! You couldn't have graduated that prestigious academy if you didn't have *greatness* in you. Now is your hour, sir; let your light shine forth for the world to see!"

Saxton smiled and nodded, and Nathan thought he sat straighter, and had a determined look in his eye for the first time since they'd met.

"Besides, General … you have one *more* thing *Stonewall* Jackson doesn't have and won't suspect."

The general raised an eyebrow questioningly, "Oh? What's that?"

"You have *me!*" Nathan said, with serious, intense look. "Thomas Jackson and I were classmates at West Point and fought together in Mexico. There has always been a good deal of mutual respect between us. He knows my capabilities, even as I know his. If he knew I was here … I believe it would cause him some concern."

Saxton nodded—based on what he knew of Nathan from the secretary's report, he believed this was not mere braggadocio.

Both men looked over as the telegraph came noisily to life again. Saxton read the message, and suddenly had a serious, concerned look. He handed it across to Nathan. This message, unlike the others, did *not* come from the secretary of war; this one came from the president:

> *War Department, May 25, 1862—12:23 p.m.*
>
> *General Saxton, Harpers Ferry:*
> *As you have but 2,500 men at Harpers Ferry, where are the rest which we have sent forward? Have any of them been cut off?*
>
> *A. LINCOLN.*

Saxton frowned, thought a moment, then dictated his response to the president:

> *Harpers Ferry, May 25, 1862—12:36 p.m.*
>
> *His Excellency the President:*
> *All the troops which were in this vicinity are here. None of the troops which have arrived since I came here have been cut off. The whole force here does not amount to over 2,500 men. I am anxiously looking for artillery.*
>
> *R. SAXTON,*
> *Brigadier-General.*

Nathan scowled, but Saxton shrugged his shoulders, and said, "Let's see what happens." They didn't have long to wait for the answer, as the machine almost immediately began clicking again:

> *War Department, May 25, 1862—12:47 p.m.*
>
> *General Saxton, Harpers Ferry:*
> *The 2,500 reported by you seems small to me. I feared some had got to General Banks and been cut off with him. Please tell me the exact number you now have in hand.*
>
> *A. LINCOLN.*

Saxton gave Nathan a wan smile, and said, "Please do resist the urge to say, 'I told you so,' Mr. Chambers …"

Nathan snorted a laugh. "Don't worry, General … I've already got my man Tom Clark out making a survey of our troop numbers, their equipment, and state of readiness. Mr. Clark is also an old quartermaster, and very efficient at his duties. I expect he'll have a detailed report to us in a few hours."

"Oh … thank you, Mr. Chambers … thank you very kindly indeed."

છ૭ઝ૦ચ૭ૹ૭ઝ૦ચ૭ૹ૭ઝ૦ચ૭

It was a contrite and humbled commanding general who dictated the following message some four hours later:

Harpers Ferry, May 25, 1862 — 4:46 p.m.

His Excellency the President:
I have had as careful an estimate made of the force here as is possible at present. It amounts to 6,700 men. Many more are on the way. A portion of the artillery has arrived, including one light battery. No signs of the enemy yet.

R. SAXTON,
Brigadier-General.

છ૭ઝ૦ચ૭ૹ૭ઝ૦ચ૭ૹ૭ઝ૦ચ૭

Nathan and General Saxton decided the first order of business was a tour of the lines and current troop dispositions. They were accompanied by Saxton's personal staff and Colonel Miles, who knew the most about the current situation in Harpers Ferry, having just relinquished command of the town. Nathan's remaining men, Tom, Jim, William, Tony, and Zeke joined them, along with Harry the Dog, and Nathan made introductions all around.

Surprisingly, General Saxton was most interested in Tony, having never had much of an opportunity to interact with a black freeman, and never having met one who was a freed slave.

"Let me ask you, Tony," the general said, "do I assume correctly that you were one of the freemen who helped Mr.

243

Chambers fight his way out of eastern Virginia, devastating a battalion of rebel militia on the way?"

Nathan was as surprised by this question as Tony was. He had no idea *that* story had spread as far as Washington. Saxton sensed his startlement, and turned to say, "Such was in the report Secretary Stanton showed me ..."

Nathan raised an eyebrow, but nodded saying nothing, turning to Tony to let him answer the general's question.

"Yes, sir, General," Tony said, "Me'n the other fellas was taught to load and shoot rifles by Captain Chambers and his men ... and how to make a bayonet charge. And I reckon that's just what we did. Them rebs was none too happy 'bout it neither."

Saxton turned to Nathan, "*Bayonets?!*" he said.

Nathan grinned, but just shrugged.

"Impressive ..." Saxton said, turning back toward Tony. "So, now that the war is on in earnest ... what is it you and your fellow freemen wish to do, Tony?"

Tony looked over at Nathan, who nodded, then back at the general, "We just want to fight, sir. We want the chance to fight them rebel slavers, and show 'em we're men ..."

Saxton nodded, looking thoughtful. Then he smiled, reached out and patted Tony on the shoulder. "Good man," he said, "I pray you shall soon get your wish. And when I return to Washington, I shall speak with the secretary about that very thing ..."

"Thank you, sir," Tony answered.

☙❧☙❧☙❧☙❧☙❧

Monday May 26, 1862 – Harpers Ferry, Virginia:

"Good morning, Mr. Chambers," General Saxton said as Nathan entered the kitchen that served as Saxton's headquarters office.

"Good morning, General. Any news?"

"Well, I suppose the good news is we are still here ... and General Jackson is *not* ..." he smiled ruefully.

Nathan snorted a short laugh, "One can be grateful for that, I suppose."

"Come ... please have a seat ... I have just been mulling over something I wish to discuss with you. Coffee?"

"Please," Nathan answered, and happily accepted a steaming hot cup delivered almost immediately by Lieutenant Allen, who also took shifts manning the telegraph machine.

"Nathan ... I've been looking over your Mr. Clark's very excellent detailed report on the recently arrived troops, and I'm seeing a very troubling trend ... a serious dearth of officers. It seems with the great rush to get me troops there are many formations that are woefully lacking in that regard.

"This one is especially troubling: the 102nd New York Infantry Regiment is missing its colonel, lieutenant colonel, major, quartermaster, and commissary officers—all out on furlough!"

"Hmm ... yes, I can see where that'd be a problem, all right."

"Yes, and not one I can readily remedy. I was wondering if *you* might be able to suggest ... at least a *temporary* solution ...?"

Nathan met eyes with the general for a long moment, then nodded, "Yes ... I might at that, General ..." he said, and absentmindedly reached into his pocket for a cigar to chew on while mulling over the general's request.

"To answer your unspoken question, Rufus ... I am one hundred percent certain that the veterans I brought with me from Texas would make excellent officers. They each have the knowledge, confidence, and temperament for the job at just about any rank save possibly that of general.

"But I'm personally not able to enlist yet for various ... *complicated* reasons ... and my men have expressed to me on several occasions a desire to wait and enlist when I do, so that we may serve together as we did in Texas. I'm not sure I can disabuse them of that notion ... nor am I sure I want to, at this point."

"Understood, Nathan. But when I said 'temporary,' I was thinking ... under the circumstances—this being a legitimate national emergency, per the president himself—we might make an exception to the usual rules. Say, commission them on a short-term basis, their commission agreed to expire once the present crisis is resolved."

Nathan thought about that a moment, and nodded, "Yes ... that might work. But I'd like to see that in writing ... ideally in a telegram from the Secretary of War. I'll not have my men getting into anything that'll come back to bite them later."

"Agreed. Lieutenant Allen ..."

"Already on it, sir," the young man said, taking his seat and beginning to tap away at the telegraph.

An hour later General Saxton received his reply from the secretary, approving the temporary commissions for any rank lower than colonel, to be doled out at General Saxton's discretion as needed, and to expire upon resolution of the present crisis at Harpers Ferry, or earlier as the general saw fit.

Saxton handed the telegram to Nathan, "Satisfied, Mr. Chambers?"

"Yes ... that'll do nicely. I'll gather the men who are currently present, though I have a few still out scouting."

"That'll be fine ... we'll use the ones you've got here for now, and deal with the others whenever reasonable and prudent—it may very well be their scouting abilities are more valuable than anything else at the moment."

"Yes ... very likely so," Nathan answered, but then smiled at a thought he had ... that he somehow couldn't quite picture either Stan or Billy being officers, even should they return in time to do so.

ಬಿಬಿ೫ಥಿಬಿಬಿ೫ಥಿಬಿಬಿ೫ಥಿ

An hour later Tom, Jim, William, and Zeke were standing against the wall in General Saxton's kitchen office, looking puzzled. With Georgie and Jamie out scouting, and Billy and Stan still unaccounted for, they were all the old Mountain Meadows men that Nathan had, save Tony. And since freemen were not yet eligible to enlist, he stood next to Nathan as directed.

Nathan hadn't bothered to explain to the general that Zeke, one of the original Mountain Meadows farmhands, had never served in the army before. Nathan figured the time Zeke had spent around the other soldiers, target practicing, helping to train up the freemen, and fighting his way out of rebel held territory made him more qualified as an officer than ninety-nine percent of the men who'd already been commissioned, many of whom were political appointees who had never even fired a gun before.

"Gentlemen, thanks for coming," Nathan began. "Seems with all the rush to get soldiers out here to head off General Jackson, we are presently suffering a serious shortage of officers. So General Saxton has asked if he can *borrow* you men for the duration of the current crisis to serve as field officers, to which I've agreed, pending your own consent. The secretary of war himself has approved the temporary arrangement, to automatically expire when the crisis is over, or at the general's discretion. Of course … if you *wish* the commissions to be permanent …" he shrugged, "that can likely be arranged."

The men all nodded their assent without hesitation.

"Thank you, Mr. Chambers," the general said. "We'll have to see what we can do to provide you with uniform tunics in a few moments, but for now I do have the officer's shoulder patches to give you as the symbol of your rank. When I'm done handing them out, I will have you all say the oath of office together, to save a little time," he smiled.

Then the general stepped up in front of Tom. "Mr. Clark, I would like to commission you as a lieutenant colonel reporting directly to me as overall quartermaster for this army. Because of my own previous extensive experience in that regard, I had assumed I would not need a quartermaster, but … such has not proven to be the case," he said, and smiled ruefully.

"I'll be happy to help, sir," Tom answered, shaking hands with the general, and accepting the shoulder patches General Saxton handed him, bearing two silver oak leaves, the insignia of a lieutenant colonel. He looked over at Nathan and rolled his eyes — he'd just gone directly from a sergeant to an officer of a higher rank than Nathan had ever attained in all his years of service. Nathan smiled and chuckled quietly.

Next Saxton moved over in front of Jim, and said, "Jim Wiggins … I am also offering you a commission as lieutenant colonel, but in your case, I find myself in need of a commanding officer ... for the 102nd New York Infantry Regiment."

"*What?!* Beggin' your pardon, sir ... but what does a sergeant from Texas know about coloneling a whole passel o' New Yorkers? Ain't never been a commanding officer before ..."

But it was Nathan who answered, "Mr. Wiggins ... we're about to have a battle ... and you know more about fighting a battle than just about anyone I know ... so, just ... *fight the battle.*"

"Oh! Yeah ... well, I reckon I can do *that,*" he answered, somewhat sheepishly, then grinned and shrugged.

"Oh, and that reminds me," Saxton said, "Colonel Clark, I will need to ask you to also serve double-duty as quartermaster for Mr. Wiggins ... another of the many officers the 102nd is currently lacking."

"Will do, sir," Tom replied.

Then Saxton stepped up to William, and handed him a set of shoulder patches, each with two *gold* oak leaves, the insignia of a major—the rank in between lieutenant colonel and captain. "William Jenkins, I understand from Mr. Chambers that you are the finest physician he has ever known, and previously served with distinction in Texas. I would like to offer you a major's commission and place you in command of all surgical personnel in this army. Please begin preparing proper hospital facilities and equipment as you see fit and as appropriate for the major engagement we deem likely."

"Yes, General. I ... I will do my best," William said, his voice a little shaky.

Finally, General Saxton moved in front of Zeke. "Ezekiel Benton—" he began, but was immediately interrupted.

"Uh ... just *Zeke,* sir," Zeke said, and grinned.

Saxton returned an amused smile, "Very well ... *Zeke* Benton, I wish to offer you a captain's commission and ... hmm ... let's make it backdated to the start of the war so you'll outrank all other captains out there on the basis of seniority. Mr. Clark will review the lists of the various regiments and assign you to the command of a rifle company or other command position where the need is greatest."

"Thank you, sir," Zeke said, trying hard to suppress a growing smile. He too glanced over at the Captain and raised an eyebrow, then over at Tony, giving him a wink. Tony couldn't suppress a smile, appreciating the significance of this event to the men—all of whom he now considered his comrades in arms—and how it reflected well on the Captain. Nathan just smiled and nodded at Zeke and the others.

"Nathan, when your other men return from scouting, if there is still time, I will also commission them captains, and have Colonel Clark assign them to regiments as needed."

"That sounds fine, General," Nathan answered, then turned to the men and said, "Congratulations, gentlemen ... and well deserved. I know y'all will make me proud."

Then Saxton lined them up and had them raise their right hands, and repeat after him, "I, *state your name* ... appointed an officer in the Army of the United States, do solemnly swear ... that I will bear true allegiance to the United States of America ... and that I will serve them honestly and faithfully against all their enemies ..."

⇗⇗⇗

Jamie and Georgie returned early in the afternoon, and after informing Nathan they'd never seen anything of Stan and Billy, he brought them straight in to General Saxton to give their report.

"Sirs," Georgie began, "we ranged as far as we could, several miles out past Charlestown, in various directions. Never could get sight of Jackson's main column, though. He's got cavalry out in force in all directions, screening his army. We'd o' had to shoot our way past 'em to get a better look ..." Georgie shrugged. "We didn't figure you'd be wanting us to do *that*, sir," he concluded, looking directly at Nathan, who nodded.

Saxton, looking thoughtful, said, "The fact that he has cavalry out screening his advance is telling ..."

"Yes," Nathan agreed, "it's a good bet he's preparing to move in our direction soon ..."

"Oh ... and speaking of ..." Jamie said, "after we were done with our scoutin' and passin' back through Charlestown we had a chat with some o' the locals. Several shared an interesting rumor with us …"

"Yes?" Saxton asked.

"The rumor has it, sirs," Jamie continued, "that General Jackson has been heard to say he intends to eat his breakfast in Harpers Ferry … *tomorrow!*"

Saxton and Nathan shared a serious, concerned look. Then the general turned back toward Nathan's two scouts and handed each a set of shoulder patches—rectangular, blue with gold trim, and a set of two gold bars on each end.

Georgie looked up with a shocked expression, "What's this, sir?" he asked.

But Nathan chuckled and said, "that's to sew onto the shoulders of your new uniform … *Captain* Thompson!"

☙❧☙❧☙❧☙❧☙❧☙❧

An hour later *Captain* Jamie O'Brien stepped up to where his new command was stationed, just in time to witness the inaugural address by the regiment's new commanding officer—to his everlasting amusement.

"Gentlemen … my name's Sarg—uh, that is … *Lieutenant Colonel* Wiggins," the commanding officer announced in a booming voice. And Jamie had to admit, *Sergeant* Jim looked and acted the part—barrel chested, red-bearded, and supremely confident—already a long-time veteran soldier though still only in his mid-twenties.

The eyes of the eight hundred some men gathered around, many so young they'd never before shaved, were riveted on their new commander, eager to hear what he had to say.

"General Saxton has asked me to take y'all under my wing—so to speak—so I reckon that's what I'm fixin' to do. Now … y'all will find I've got little truck with etiquette and protocol … Me bein' an old Indian fighter from out West, I'm much more concerned about whuppin' the enemy and winnin' the battle than about how shiny your Goddamned buttons are.

"And I've got no patience for cowards or shirkers … But if y'all follow your orders, do your duty, and stand up to the enemy like

men … well, then I reckon we'll get along just fine. Company …
dismissed!"

Later that evening, Nathan, General Saxton and his senior
officers were gathered around the kitchen table in Saxton's office
reviewing their current troop dispositions and preparations. Tony
stood "at ease" behind Nathan's chair, and Harry the Dog lay
under the table in front of him.

And despite the pessimistic rumors, Stonewall Jackson had *not*
yet launched his attack, so apparently his breakfast in Harpers
Ferry would have to wait at least another day.

In the midst of the meeting, Saxton's assistant, Captain
Anderson, poked his head in the door and said, "General, sir,
there's a Lieutenant Daniels here to see you. Just arrived from
Washington on the train."

"A *lieutenant?* I've no time for him now, Captain."

"Sir … you *will* want to speak with *this* one," Captain
Anderson said, with a look that clearly meant something to the
general.

"*Oh!* I see. Very well, send him in then."

Nathan met eyes with General Cooper sitting across from him,
and raised an eyebrow, but Cooper just shrugged. He had no idea
what it might be about either—why General Saxton would agree
to meet with a *lieutenant* in the middle of planning the defense of
the city with his senior officers.

A young man, appearing to be in his mid-twenties, with light
hair and mustache stepped into the room, snapped to attention,
and saluted General Saxton.

"General Saxton, sir! Lieutenant Charles Daniels, United States
Navy, reporting for duty, as ordered."

This announcement, along with the distinctive uniform
accompanying it, came as a great surprise to all present.

"At ease, Lieutenant," Saxton responded after returning the
salute. "Navy? A bit far afield for the Navy, aren't you?
Considering we're something like a hundred unnavigable miles
up the Potomac."

Daniels relaxed and assumed the formal "at ease" stance, legs apart and hands behind the back. He grinned at the general's question.

"Yes, sir; seems we've been … blown a bit off our usual course, one might say."

"And who, may I ask, has ordered a *Navy* lieutenant to report to this *Army* post for duty?"

The lieutenant continued to grin, as if he found the whole situation quite amusing. "Well, sir … it's my understanding the order came directly from his excellency, Abraham Lincoln, President of these United States and Commander in Chief of all armed forces—by way of the honorable Edwin M. Stanton, Secretary of War, of course."

This statement caused a stir in the room, and everyone suddenly was attentive and sitting up in their seats.

"Please … *do* go on, Lieutenant; tell us exactly what it is you are here to *do*."

"Oh, as to that, sir; I'm just here to … render assistance as required. That is, if you're willing to put up with, house, and feed me and my crew of 300 or so sailors and marines."

"And … pray tell, why would I want to do *that*—orders aside?"

"Well, sir. I guess it could be out of the kindness of your heart."

Saxton scowled at him.

"Or it could be because … we've brought you a little *gift*, sir. Just a small token of our esteem … and a thanks for your hospitality, so to speak."

"A gift?"

"Yes, sir. I've brought with me a collection of fine-looking Dahlgren guns, sir. Nice and shiny—barely broken in. And a full naval artillery crew to man them."

"*Oh!* Our promised artillery at last! Why didn't you just say so, Daniels? I'd have likely kissed your backside for joy instead of giving you a stern grilling."

"I'm happy you're pleased, sir!" Daniels continued to beam, clearly delighted to deliver what he assumed was exceedingly good news to a group of otherwise desperate officers.

"Naval guns, eh? *Dahlgrens* you say? 'Soda bottles,' I believe they're sometimes called," Saxton said.

"Yes, sir; *soda bottles* indeed, on account of their distinctive shape. But these bottles are big'ns, sir, and they've got quite a *pop* to them!

"I think you'll especially enjoy the big momma of the family; she's a nine-inch rifled gun meant for mounting on large warships or shore batteries. The old gal can hurl a seventy-pound ball 3,450 yards with good accuracy; that's nearly two miles for those not mathematically inclined. Or 1.7 *nautical* miles, for those of us more used to shipboard measures.

"And I've brought a goodly supply of high-explosive shells with me. Since I assumed we're talking defensive, anti-personnel support, that seemed more useful than solid balls—assuming, of course, we won't need to sink any warships or batter down any stone walls."

"Yes, yes, that should be perfect. This is *excellent* news, Lieutenant, thank you!" Saxton answered, suddenly buoyed up and smiling. "And the only 'stone wall' we'll need to batter down is one with a beard who rides a horse," he chuckled at his own attempted humor.

The lieutenant thought about that a moment, and then laughed, "Oh, well done, sir. *Well done!* Yes, let's see if me and the boys can't set an explosive shell right down on top of good old Stonewall's rebellious head!"

The others laughed.

"The only downside to our big gun is—at over ten feet long and weighing a svelte 9,000 pounds—she's a bugger to move around. We've brought our own mule team and plenty of muscle for the task. Wherever you want me to put her, sir, we'll put her; but I'd prefer not to move her around much thereafter."

"Yes … I should think *not.*"

"The other six guns we've brought aren't so bad; twelve-pounder rifled boat howitzers, only weighing 880 pounds apiece. We've taken the liberty of mounting these on wheeled carriages. But though they're smaller, they can still reach out and—none-too-politely—greet the enemy at better than a mile."

"That will be a Godsend, Lieutenant. And your timing is impeccable; at first light we plan to head out and reconnoiter the defensive line, assuming Jackson hasn't overrun us before then. Please do accompany us and help decide where to best position your battery."

"With pleasure, sir."

"Lieutenant, allow me to introduce my senior officers ... General Cooper and Colonel Miles. And this is Mr. Chambers, from the *Restored* Virginia Governor's office."

The lieutenant shook hands with the officers, and then Nathan.

"Mr. Chambers is also an Army man—a West Pointer and Mexican War veteran. Soon to join the ranks of us generals, I should think, once he tires of playing at building new states for Mr. Lincoln," Saxton chuckled.

"Ah ... *West* Virginia, isn't it? I've not heard much about it, other than it's being put together by a bunch of loyal Unionists who wish to tell Richmond to stick the secession back up its ass where it came from!"

"Yes ... that's a fair description," Nathan answered with a chuckle. He immediately liked this young officer. Daniels not only had an easy sense of humor and seemed relaxed among older, superior officers; he clearly knew his business. Nathan hoped he was as good under fire as he was at handling generals!

Nathan then introduced Daniels to Tony, introducing him as his aide de camp, and using his "free name," Mark Anthony, which seemed to please him greatly. The two shook hands, and Tony said, "just call me Tony, sir."

Daniels looked back toward Nathan and said, "Hey, that's quite a hound you have there, Mr. Chambers!" noticing the large animal lying next to Nathan for the first time.

"Yes, he's unique, that's certain. And ... it appears he *likes* you, Lieutenant."

"Oh? How can you tell, sir?"

"Well, for one, he's hasn't bitten your arm off ... *yet.*"

Daniels chuckled, "Oh! Well ... that's mighty decent of him." He gazed admiringly at Harry but resisted the urge to reach out and pet him.

Wednesday May 28, 1862 – On the Kanawha River, Virginia:

Evelyn's two-day trip down the Ohio River to Point Pleasant, at the confluence of the Kanawha River, had been uneventful, for which she was grateful. The smooth, easy voyage by steamboat had given her time to rest and try to clear her mind of all that'd happened recently.

At Point Pleasant they switched to a smaller steamboat specifically built to ply the shallower, narrower Kanawha River which flowed east to west across the bulk of western Virginia. During the sixty-five-mile voyage to Charleston, Virginia the only excitement was at a place called Red House Shoal.

Back in the 1700s the river had only been navigable to just below the shoal, it's rapids impossible for steamboats to traverse. But in the early 1800s, men had undertaken an ambitious project to extend steamboat access all the way to Charleston by blasting a channel through the rapids, providing a fast-flowing shoot through which steamboats could travel. But the shoot was narrow and the current strong, so it took a highly skilled captain and a powerful steam engine to successfully make the run.

When Evelyn's ship neared the shoals, the captain announced its imminent approach and asked the passengers to either be seated or to hang onto something as he made the run. Evelyn couldn't sit still for it, and wanted to watch, so she leaned out, holding tightly to a handrail as the boilers were brought to full steam and the boat's paddlewheels amidships churned the water in an impressive display of power, sending a mist of spray wafting across the boat, coating her hat and her shoulders with fine droplets.

She found herself holding her breath as the ship entered the narrow channel at full speed, bouncing perceptibly as it began the ascent. At first it seemed the ship would have no trouble with the run, surging ahead mightily. But soon Evelyn could detect a slackening of their pace, even as the paddlewheels continued to churn and the smokestacks belched prodigious wafts of smoke and steam.

And then, just as she felt the ship would surely lose its battle and begin inexorably drifting backwards, they were through the shoot and back into flat smooth waters.

Evelyn laughed out loud at the sudden release of tension and for the thrilling joy of the little ship's heroic victory over the river. She glanced back at Nigel standing a few feet away, and he also laughed, enjoying her enthusiasm. They shared a happy smile, but when Evelyn looked away again, Nigel breathed a heavy sigh, and slowly shook his head, continuing to gaze in her direction with a smile that refused to leave his face.

They debarked at Charleston two hours later, and there they spent the night at a boarding house. While Evelyn settled in, Nigel went out to arrange their transportation for the next leg of their journey overland to Gauley Bridge—a reasonably comfortable covered coach with a driver for hire.

The information Nigel had been given by Jonathan had said the Confederate-controlled territory started somewhere between Gauley Bridge and Lewisburg, some sixty-five miles distant. So, he'd intended to send the carriage back once they reached Gauley Bridge and switch to riding, figuring he could purchase horses and any supplies they'd need to camp outdoors at the small town there. They'd then have to reconnoiter and determine the most expedient way to cross over to the Confederate side so they could meet Jonathan's agent in Lewisburg.

Nigel carried forged government papers for both sides, so he could pass himself off either as a Union Undersecretary of War, or a Confederate Assistant Secretary of State, as exigencies required. And he'd practiced his Virginia accent on Evelyn until she assured him it could not be distinguished from the real thing, even by a native such as herself—the benefits of him being a skilled actor!

But when they stopped at Gauley Bridge for the night, they learned there had been a battle at Lewisburg a week earlier. The Union army had been victorious, driving the rebels completely out of the town. The surviving Confederate forces had retreated east, passing over the Greenbrier River at Caldwell, then burning the covered bridge behind them, making the river the new *de facto* boundary between the two belligerent forces. Evelyn was saddened when she heard the picturesque covered bridge at Caldwell had been destroyed; she had fond memories of crossing over it, sitting next to Nathan in his carriage.

Forced to change plans, they continued on toward Lewisburg in the coach, still hopeful they could connect with Jonathan's agent there.

But after two fruitless days waiting at the agreed meeting place—a boarding house on the eastern edge of Lewisburg—they were forced to conclude the agent could not reach them, doubtless stuck on the far side of the river in Confederate territory.

Now they were faced with a fateful decision—to turn back and look for another way into eastern Virginia, or to somehow attempt a dangerous crossing of the Greenbrier River under the guns of both armies.

Chapter 10. The Fateful Lightning

"He hath loosed the fateful lightning
of his terrible swift sword,
his truth is marching on."
- *Julia Ward Howe*,
lyrics to
"Battle Hymn of the Republic"

Tuesday May 27, 1862 – Harpers Ferry, Virginia:

At first light in the morning, Nathan, Saxton, and Lieutenant Daniels rode out to Bolivar Heights, about a mile and a half west of the Harpers Ferry train station. Harry the Dog trotted along behind Nathan's mare, Milly, as usual followed by Tony looking very uncomfortable on one of the Captain's geldings. He'd had very little experience riding horses, so it still made him nervous, though he was doing his best not to show it.

Their goal was to inspect the Union lines to assess their readiness for an assault, and to discuss where to position the lieutenant's battery of naval guns. They'd brought Colonel Miles along with them. Him being the former commander of the station, he knew the terrain surrounding the town better than any of the other officers.

All along the Bolivar Heights ridgeline, Union soldiers worked like so many industrious ants, digging trenches, erecting log barricades, and clearing trees on the far slopes to open up firing lanes and deprive the enemy of cover.

Nathan had to laugh when he caught sight of Jim Wiggins barking orders at captains and lieutenants like an old field general with a burr under his backside.

When they reached the highest point along the ridge line they paused and looked back toward town. Nathan's keen, highly trained military eye took in the view and immediately began analyzing how a battle might play out. "What's that high spot about a mile away, on the west edge of the downtown area, Colonel?" he asked.

"It's called Camp Hill, Mr. Chambers," Colonel Miles answered. "And the little village of houses between here and there is named Bolivar, same as the ridgeline behind us."

Nathan gazed around the valley, then said, "The village should be evacuated of civilians if hasn't been already—whatever happens, they will very likely be in the very heart of a battle if they remain there."

He continued scanning the valley, then said, "Camp Hill should be our fallback position if it becomes necessary, General. The peninsula narrows considerably there, so we'll be able to concentrate our defenses and help eliminate the enemy's advantage in numbers."

Saxton gazed a moment, then said, "Yes … could be. But I'm loath to give up Bolivar Heights without a fight. I fear if Jackson holds it, he'll be able to shell the town and there'll be little if anything we can do about it."

But Nathan grinned, "Oh … *not so*, General … that's why we have Daniels here!"

At the mention of his name the young naval lieutenant perked up, "Oh … yes, indeed, Mr. Chambers." He stood up in his stirrups and gazed about from side to side of the valley. "I reckon we can cover the entire valley with our Dahlgrens, if we position them correctly. Maybe on your Camp Hill, do you think, Mr. Chambers?"

"Hmm … maybe, but … that's still lower than we are here, so Jackson's guns will have the high ground if he manages to take this position. Colonel, what's that steep ridgeline across the Potomac on the Maryland side called?"

"It's called Maryland Heights, appropriately enough," Miles answered.

Nathan gazed at it intently for several moments, then seemed to concentrate on a particular spot. He raised his spyglass and focused in on the spot. He lowered it and looked over at Miles. What's that open space … about halfway up the slope, just to the left of the confluence?"

Miles gazed in the direction for a moment, then shrugged, "I'm not sure what you're referring to, Mr. Chambers ..."

"Here," Nathan said, leaning across to hand Miles his spyglass, "start at the bridge tunnel and move slowly to the left. You'll see what appears to be a cleared area about halfway up the slope."

Miles peered at the slope for several minutes, then said, "Ah ... now I see it," then he lowered the spyglass and handed it back to Nathan. "That's the old coal mine. Not sure when it was last worked ... hasn't been active since I've been here, anyway."

"Coal mine, huh? That means there must be ..." Nathan began, once again putting the spyglass to his eye, "... a road up to it ... *Ah ha!* There it is, just as beautiful as can be."

He lowered the spyglass and looked over at Daniels, grinning brightly. "Mr. Daniels ... I believe we've found your gun position. Look for yourself," he said, handing Daniels the spyglass.

General Saxton was already gazing at the site through his binoculars.

A moment later Daniels said, "Oh ... yes, indeed, Mr. Chambers ... It's really quite a lovely location. Beautiful view of both rivers, the valley below, and the surrounding heights. Good access, and already cleared so it's ready for further development. And best of all ... no noisy neighbors to speak of," he concluded, lowering the spyglass, handing it back to Nathan, and beaming.

"Yes, that'll work nicely, I believe," the general agreed. "I've already had the carpenters plank the railroad bridge between the rails, so men, horses, and artillery can cross the river as needed, which should make your task all the easier. And we can run a telegraph line from the town, across the bridge and up the road to the battery so we can coordinate our actions."

"That'll be perfect, General," Daniels agreed, "I'll get started as soon as we get back to the train station," he concluded, standing in his saddle and gazing from the proposed gun position on Maryland Heights back to where they now sat their horses on Bolivar Heights. "Yes, sir ... we can certainly make it uncomfortable for General Jackson from there ... warms my heart just thinking on it," he said, continuing to smile brightly.

Thankfully, for reasons known only to himself, Jackson chose not to attack that day as well, and by early afternoon Lieutenant Daniels, his sailors, and their mule teams had wrestled the heavy guns into position, leveled and aimed them, and stacked heavy sandbags to their front to help protect them from potential return fire.

It was an exhausted but well-satisfied Lieutenant Daniels who tested out the newly installed telegraph line by sending a message to General Saxton at his headquarters:

Naval Battery, Maryland Hts.
May 27, 1862

General Saxton, Harpers Ferry:
Guns in place, and ammunition stocked. We await your pleasure, sir. Please give my regards to Gen'l Jackson when you see him, and tell him our Dahlgrens are eager to give him a proper reception.

Charles Daniels,
Lieutenant, US Navy
U.S.S. Harpers Ferry (in drydock!)

Wednesday May 28, 1862 – Harpers Ferry, Virginia:

By Wednesday morning, General Saxton was pacing the floor in his anxiety, having slept very little the night before. Not knowing where Jackson was, nor when he would finally launch his assault was beginning to gnaw at the general.

He ordered a reconnaissance in force out toward Charlestown, seven miles to the southwest, consisting of the 111th Pennsylvania Infantry Regiment, the First Maryland Cavalry, and a section of the First New York light artillery battery.

Nathan and Saxton, with Captain Anderson, Tony, and Harry the Dog in tow, accompanied the reconnaissance column out to Bolivar Heights. From there they awaited its return, gazing through their spyglasses for anything they might see in the distance. An hour and a half later they heard cannon fire out toward Charlestown—first only a smattering, but eventually what sounded like a full-blown artillery duel, lasting some twenty minutes before abruptly cutting off.

So General Saxton sent out reinforcements in the form of the Seventy-Eighth New York Infantry and the remainder of the First New York Artillery.

A few hours later they could make out the Union force falling back in good order, with a brigade-sized rebel column pursuing at a safe distance. But as the Union reconnaissance force neared Bolivar Heights, the rebel advance halted and turned back; apparently they'd seen the massed Union lines on the ridgeline and thought better of getting any closer.

But as the returning reconnaissance column passed by their position, Nathan was elated to recognize two of the horsemen—one a very giant of a man, and the other diminutive, but with a fierce look in his eyes—Stan and Billy, at last!

"Gentlemen ... so good of you to join our little party here at Harpers Ferry," he called out, smiling brightly and waving.

Stan looked over at the familiar voice and grinned, turning his horse in their direction. Billy followed suit.

When they pulled up their horses in front of Nathan and General Saxton, they saluted, and both Nathan and the general returned the salute. Nathan could see they were dirty, ragged, and tired looking.

But General Saxton was impressed at the sight of them, thinking they fairly bristled with so many weapons they looked capable of taking on a division all by themselves—each carried two rifles in saddle sheathes, a quiver with bow and arrows tied onto their horses, plus a pistol holster on each hip, and two more up under their shoulders. And finally, a large knife in a sheath attached to a strap across their chest.

"Captain ... it is good to be seeing you," Stan said and grinned, "you too, Tony."

Nathan introduced the men to General Saxton, and asked them to give their report right there on the spot.

Billy started, "After we sent you the telegram about Jackson's fake camp at Harrisonburg, we tracked him across the valley and northward to a town called Front Royal. But by the time we got there the Union garrison had already been destroyed."

"Yes, was nothing left of them," Stan said, shaking his head.

"So we followed the main column of Jackson's army north, toward the town of Winchester," Billy continued.

"Was big battle there," Stan said, "but Union general was beaten like naughty stepson … and ran away from fight, leaving much equipment behind … was disgrace."

"We decided the rebels were likely heading north from there," Billy said, "so we got out ahead of them by traveling at night."

"Yes … but they are many, and we have not always been able to sneak by," Stan said, then shrugged, "so we have had to kill a few …"

Billy looked at him and scowled, "*No* … we have killed *many*, Captain … I believe after a time they began to know we were out there killing their scouts, so they sent cavalry soldiers to track and kill us."

But Stan just grinned and said, "Yes … but we are being very hard to kill! Though, I am having to admit … will be good to be for a while where all men are not trying to kill us all the time."

During this narrative General Saxton looked from one to the other, with an amazed look, slowly shaking his head. Finally he said, "Mr. Chambers … your men … *these* men … are like something out of a Wild West dime novel … I've never seen the like."

"Nor likely ever will again, General," Nathan said with a grin, reaching into his pocket for a cigar and lighting up.

Stan gazed up and down the Union lines on Bolivar Heights. "Is good you have so many soldiers. How many are here, Captain? Twenty … thirty-thousands?"

"No … closer to seven," he answered.

Stan gave him a concerned look, "Is only seven? Is not enough, Captain … not enough by many. Jackson is having …" he looked over at Billy and shrugged, "twenty thousands at the least …

twenty-five maybe … more or less," to which Billy nodded. "And plenty big guns … fifty … a hundred? Maybe more …"

Saxton groaned, then said, "And have you any idea where his main column is at the moment?"

"Not precisely," Billy answered, "but it must be close. The brigade that just drove your men out of Charlestown is one they call the stone wall. It is never far from General Jackson himself, from what we've seen."

Saxton took a deep breath and looked up at the sky, "The Stonewall Brigade!" he said.

"Yes … is correct," Stan said, "Billy and I came to Charlestown with stone wall soldiers fast behind us. So we were warning Union men to get out before the slaughter, and most did as we said. Was close thing, though, as stone wall men are much better with big guns than Union men. Would have gone very bad if reinforcements had not come along to help."

Then he looked at Saxton and tipped his hat, saying, "Was good move, General."

Saxton nodded, then looked up at the sky, and sighed, "Too late for Jackson to get here and launch an assault today. But I'll issue a general order, that all Union forces be on the alert, and prepared for potential enemy action come first light in the morning."

🙪🙪🙲🙲🙪🙪🙲🙲🙪🙪🙲🙲

Thursday May 29, 1862 – Harpers Ferry, Virginia:

But first light came with the morning, and still no attack by General Jackson. Saxton sent another reconnaissance force out from Bolivar Heights, this time the Fifth New York Cavalry. But the cavalry got no further than Halltown, a small village to the west just a few miles past the foot of the rise, before taking heavy fire from the enemy and being forced to retreat back to the heights.

Saxton feared this meant an assault was imminent, so he ordered the Union Army drawn up in line of battle. Brigadier General Slough, who'd arrived by train from Washington just the

264

evening before, had been given command of a brigade on the Union left, and the remaining troops under Brigadier General Cooper formed into a brigade on the right.

General Saxton ordered the New York light artillery to open fire on Halltown, but what effect that may have had on the enemy was impossible to see—so very likely little, if any. He soon called a halt to the bombardment to save ammunition.

A tense hour passed, and still no response from the enemy. Nathan Chambers gazed out to the southwest and suddenly paused, raising his spyglass to his eye. "Look, General—out past Halltown …"

Saxton raised his binoculars in the direction Nathan had indicated, then immediately lowered them, a concerned look knit his brow as he continued to gaze out into the distance. "A large cloud of dust … drifting into the sky between Charlestown and Halltown …" he said in a quiet, quavering voice—the voice of a man who had just witnessed his own doom fast approaching.

Jackson's vast main column had arrived at last.

☙☙☙☙☙☙☙☙☙

Tensions ran high all along the Union lines. Officers paced nervously, soldiers gazed intently out to their front, rifles loaded and raised, bayonets fixed. Army chaplains moved among the troops, giving encouragement, and loudly reciting appropriate Bible passages to motivate the men.

But as afternoon drew on toward evening, and no attack came, it began to look like Stonewall Jackson would once again fail to make his expected appearance.

General Saxton was in a high state of anxiety, pacing restlessly, stopping to gaze out toward the enemy position, and occasionally putting his binoculars to his eyes and peering out expectantly. But as the sun set and night fell, he issued his general orders—all officers and men were to stay at their posts, and sleep on their arms, expecting a large-scale assault by the enemy at any moment.

Saxton had earlier ordered the telegraph line extended out to the heights, and had set up a command tent there, so he would never be far from the action when it occurred.

And though he was anxious himself, Nathan was now fairly certain Jackson would not launch his attack this night, so he retired to his own tent, intending to be up and pacing the lines well before dawn. He shared the tent with Tony, each with his own folding cot.

But dawn came early for Nathan and Tony; a few minutes before midnight one of Saxton's staff officers poked his head in the tent flap and said, "Mr. Chambers ... Mr. Chambers, sir ..."

"Hunh? Yes, Captain ... what is it?"

"General Saxton sends his compliments and requests you come to his command tent on the double, sir."

"*Oh!*" Nathan said, springing to his feet. He had slept in his clothes, so only had to pull on his boots, strap on his pistol holster, and put on his hat before heading out the door. Tony, who'd likewise been sleeping fully clothed in a cot on the other side of the tent, was already waiting at the tent flap when Nathan was ready to go.

When Nathan and Tony entered Saxton's command tent, they saw General Cooper and Colonel Miles were already there, seated around a small folding table. Saxton had a concerned look, but did not appear panicked.

In a moment General Slough arrived, followed closely by Tom Clark. Both took seats at the table.

"Gentlemen," Saxton began, "sorry to disturb you at this late hour, but I fear it is absolutely necessary. I have called this council of war because we have just acquired fresh information concerning General Jackson's likely intentions. A little over a half-hour ago, a deserter from the rebel side turned himself in to our sentries, who brought him directly to me. I have interrogated him thoroughly, and believe he is telling the truth ... at least as far as he himself knows it.

"The deserter believes, from what he has heard from his own officers, that Jackson intends to cross the Potomac upstream, then capture Maryland Heights, and launch an artillery attack upon us from above, in coordination with an all-out frontal assault on our present position."

General Cooper was the first to respond to this dire news, "But sir … if he does *that*, he may very well seize our own naval guns and use them against us!"

"Yes, precisely … and it gets worse … the man assures me he knows for a fact Jackson has already placed an infantry regiment and artillery battery on Loudoun Heights across the Shenandoah. They will also be able to bombard us from there."

This pronouncement brought a shocked silence over the room. If Jackson seized the high ground and captured the naval battery, the Union forces guarding the town would have nowhere to hide and would be completely annihilated.

It was Nathan Chambers who broke the silence, "General … firstly, we've got to save those naval guns or we're all dead men. And then … I believe it's time we move our line back to Camp Hill."

Saxton thought on this a moment, then nodded, "Agreed, Mr. Chambers. General Cooper, march your brigade, along with whatever light artillery you can manage, up to the top of Maryland Heights above our naval guns. You must prevent the rebels from seizing the high ground at all costs!"

Cooper stood, and snapped a salute, "It will be done, sir!"

"Colonel Clark, see that all the equipment and ammunition General Cooper needs is transported to his position as quickly as it may be arranged."

"Yes, sir!" Tom answered, also rising to his feet.

"And General Slough," Saxton continued, "with the shorter line at Camp Hill, your brigade should be able to dig in and hold the position even without Cooper's men—likely with better troop concentration than you both together can manage here on the heights."

"Yes," Nathan added, "and that'll also force Jackson to attack across the open valley where the Bolivar village sits in between the two ridge lines. And when he does that—"

"Lieutenant Daniels will finally get to use his beloved Dahlgrens," Saxton finished Nathan's thought for him, and they both nodded.

"Speaking of ..." Nathan continued, "General, may I suggest that Daniels fire a few target shots first ... say over across the Shenandoah toward Loudoun Heights?"

"*Ah!* Excellent suggestion, Mr. Chambers. I will see that it is done."

"Let's move, gentlemen, I fear time is *not* our ally," Saxton concluded, and they all pushed back their chairs and headed for the door of the tent.

☙❧☙❧☙❧☙❧☙❧☙❧

It took most of the night to get the 3,600 men of General Cooper's brigade across the Potomac and up onto the top of Maryland Heights, along with their horses, artillery, ammunition, and equipment.

Despite General Saxton's prescient order to plank the railroad bridge, they'd also had to utilize every boat at their disposal to ferry men and equipment if they were to have any hope of completing the move before morning.

And to make matters worse, shortly after 2 a.m. an unexpected incident threatened to derail the entire maneuver.

Colonel Maulsby's First Maryland Regiment had been assigned guard duty over the huge stockpile of supplies accumulated at the old armory near the train station. Their duty was to guard the railroad crossings and warehouses against possible spies or saboteurs.

But when the green Maryland troops started seeing General Cooper's brigade crossing the railroad bridge into Maryland they panicked, incorrectly believing it was a general retreat in the face of Stonewall Jackson's overwhelming force that was approaching. They feared they were being left behind to be killed or captured, so they rushed the bridge and tried to force their way across. The result was utter chaos, as Cooper's brigade, with men, horses, and artillery, vied for space on the narrow bridge against the panicked Marylanders.

Assistant Secretary of War Peter Watson, who'd arrived days earlier and had been assisting Tom Clark in acquiring the additional equipment and ammunition needed from the War

Department, saw what was happening and heroically stepped onto the bridge in an attempt to intervene and stop the stampede. But his efforts proved in vain, and he was nearly pushed off the bridge and into the river.

The situation on the bridge was so chaotic that several cavalry horses panicked and fell off the bridge into the water, some forty feet below. Fortunately, the river was deep under the bridge, and the horses quickly re-emerged and swam safely back to shore, where they were collected by the soldiers.

General Saxton finally arrived on the scene and confronted Colonel Maulsby in a great fury. But Maulsby explained that his Marylanders had signed on under the promise they could do all their fighting within their own home state. He begged Saxton not to force them to return to the Virginia side, and that he, Maulsby, could not force them to do so.

In great disgust Saxton agreed to let the Marylanders stay on their side of the river and guard the bridge, deeming them too cowardly and incompetent to be of any use on the Virginia side even if he forced them back.

When dawn began to lighten the eastern sky, it was a weary and footsore regiment under General Cooper that finally formed up at the top of Maryland Heights, preparing for an attack by Stonewall Jackson, expected to hit them at first light.

Other than the fiasco with the Marylanders, their all-night slog across the river and up the hillside had only been briefly interrupted by a sudden salvo of artillery from the naval battery halfway up the slope, which was apparently aimed out across the Shenandoah toward Loudoun Heights, lighting up the night sky with thunderous bright flashes and smoke. But what effect, if any, those shots had had upon the enemy over on Loudoun Heights, they had no way of knowing.

ೞೞഐഈೞೞഐഈೞೞഐഈ

Friday May 30, 1862 – Harpers Ferry, Virginia:

General Saxton had left only a small contingent of pickets and light artillery at the top of Bolivar Heights when he'd withdrawn the rest of the army to Camp Hill the night before. The token force was only intended as a trip-wire—to give warning when Jackson's main column began approaching in earnest. Shortly after dawn, the federal pickets were pushed back by a massive force of rebel infantry coming up the hill. When the Union pickets retreated to the position of the light artillery, their cannons fired a salvo of cannister at the approaching rebels to slow them, then quickly packed up and retreated to Camp Hill.

The battle for Harpers Ferry had begun.

ಬುಬ್ಬು)ಬಿ)ಬುಬ್ಬು)ಬಿ)ಬುಬ್ಬು)ಬಿ)ಬು

Nathan Chambers and Brigadier General Rufus Saxton now stood at the top of Camp Hill, looking out across the valley toward Bolivar Heights, now invested by Stonewall Jackson's army. They could see a mass of men, many on horses, gathered at the top of the ridgeline. But for an hour or more there was no further movement, as the expected assault seemed to take a long pause.

Nathan turned to Saxton and snorted a short laugh, "I'm envisioning my old friend Thomas Jackson arriving on the scene, looking out at our position, and noticing our battery of naval guns up on Maryland Heights. He's an old artillery officer from the Mexican War, so he well understands the significance of what we have managed to assemble there. He knows what those guns can do to his army if he tries to cross the valley."

Saxton nodded, gazing out at the rebels through his binoculars, but kept his thoughts to himself.

A few minutes later they saw a rebel force move down into the valley. This force was mostly cavalry with some infantry and a small amount of light artillery—only about a brigade size in total. This group of soldiers did not immediately attack, however, but seemed to be slowly moving through the valley—milling around, as if searching through the village for something.

"What are they about, Mr. Chambers?" Saxton asked, "Why is he sending only this small force … and that only at a very slow pace?"

Nathan gazed at them through his spyglass for a long moment before answering. He lowered his spyglass and looked over at

Saxton, "It's a trap, General. He's seen our big guns and doesn't want to risk sending his whole army out to get chewed up by them, so he's decided to try baiting us … make us think he has only brought a brigade-sized force to Harpers Ferry, to make you believe you have him outnumbered. He wants you to charge out into the valley to attack his brigade, at which point he will launch his entire army, kept back behind the ridge … and he will utterly destroy you."

Saxton nodded and said, "I believe you're right Mr. Chambers. Captain Anderson!" he called out, and his assistant was quickly at his side.

"Sir!"

"Anderson … send the word down the line, and directly to General Slough … hold position … do not advance. Understood?"

"Yes, sir!" Anderson said, "hold position and don't advance."

"Oh, and Anderson … have the telegraph signal to Lieutenant Daniels … 'Please give General Jackson a proper good morning.'"

"Yes, sir!" Anderson said, now grinning as he snapped a salute, then ran off to relay the orders.

Saxton turned back to Nathan and smiled thinly, "I think this time … I would likely have done the same thing even without your advice, Chambers … I am so nervous about Jackson's approach I doubt I would've ventured out to attack him in any case."

Nathan returned the grin and said, "We're in agreement there, General. I'm feeling the same."

A few minutes later they heard a loud *WHUMP* to their rear and a second later a tremendous *BOOM* out across the valley, accompanied by a brilliant flash of light and a great cloud of smoke.

Nathan raised the spyglass to gauge the effect of Daniels first salvo. "A little short … but they got the message … they're no longer advancing, and the infantry is seeking cover," he said.

Saxton, who was also gazing at the scene through his binoculars, nodded his agreement.

Eight more projectiles were hurled at the enemy in rapid succession, each round still falling short, but each landing incrementally closer. These explosions were slightly smaller than the initial blast, and Nathan guessed that first one had been the large nine-inch gun, and these were the smaller twelve-pounder boat howitzers. Nathan now understood Daniels was intentionally "walking" the explosions ever closer to the exposed enemy formation, an absolutely terrifying and demoralizing experience for the men under bombardment, and also an effective exercise for finding the proper range.

"Daniels knows his business," Nathan said, nodding appreciatively.

"I can see that," Saxton said, returning the nod.

There was a pause in the firing, presumably while the large guns were being reloaded.

Jackson's proffered bait being rejected, and at risk of annihilation by the naval guns, he quickly withdrew it to the heights, and Daniels called a halt to the bombardment.

And though Bolivar Heights was within the theoretical range of the naval Dahlgrens, the rebels had good cover there, and could shelter back behind the ridgeline, so any effort to bombard them while they maintained that position would likely be no more than a waste of ammunition. Even so, Saxton had to force himself to resist a very strong urge to order it.

After that, a waiting game ensued, with no further action by either side for the remainder of the morning, and well into the afternoon and evening. Union forces stayed on high alert, and men were served out cold rations mid-day while standing by their rifles in their hastily dug trenches and behind their makeshift log barricades.

By late afternoon, Nathan was beginning to feel annoyed by Saxton's nervous pacing. "Please, General, do try to relax. You're like to wear out the ground beneath your feet if you keep this up."

Saxton stopped and met eyes with Nathan, smiling ruefully. "I don't know how you manage to stay so calm, Mr. Chambers. I feel like a schoolboy sitting on an anthill."

Nathan snorted a chuckle, "I'm not as calm as you think, Rufus. Why do you think I ran out of cigars several hours ago?"

The two continued to wait, anxiously gazing out across the valley. Nathan noticed the sky, now overcast, had suddenly gotten very dark, though it was only 6:00, and sunset wouldn't be until 7:30.

"Looks like a storm coming on, General," he said.

Saxton looked out and said, "Yes … there's a storm coming all right … and it's got General Thomas Jackson's name on it."

Nathan nodded his agreement.

☙☙◊◖◖✦☙☙◊◖◖✦☙☙◊◖◖

When it was almost 7:00, Nathan experienced a sudden premonition, and he turned to Saxton, "General … I've just been thinking … I believe Jackson is going to try to attack us right at nightfall, to avoid our naval guns. He's had time to reconnoiter the valley, and he probably believes he can successfully cross it under cover of darkness and then overrun our lines with a quick rifle volley and bayonet charge."

"Do you really think so? That would be a bold move … and almost unprecedented, I believe—to launch an assault at night over unfamiliar enemy ground. Although … Jackson *has* been in Harpers Ferry before, and he *is* known for his bold actions. So—"

But Saxton was interrupted by a deep rumble in the distance. Both men turned and looked out toward the valley.

"Artillery?" Saxton asked.

"No …" Nathan answered, "thunder, General. That storm's coming closer."

"Ah … yes … I see that now," Saxton answered.

They were both quiet for a moment and listened as another peal of thunder echoed in the distance, and the sky became nearly as dark as night.

"They're coming, sir!" Captain Anderson called out, from his position a few yards off to their right.

Both Nathan and Saxton immediately raised their spyglasses and looked out. Nathan confirmed the captain's report; the enemy was now pouring into the valley down the slopes of Bolivar Heights, rank upon rank—horses, men, and light artillery, even as the darkness was about to obscure them entirely from view.

"Tell Daniels to fire for effect," Saxton called out, "and all formations stand to their arms and prepare for battle!"

But even as he shouted these orders the night seemed to close in on them like the lid of a cook pot.

Captain Anderson shouted back from the command tent, where the telegraph operator sat at his machine, "Sir ... Lieutenant Daniels reports he cannot target the enemy on account of darkness and asks if he should rather fire for illumination."

But even before Saxton could answer there was a tremendous flash and explosion overhead, out above Bolivar Heights, and for a moment the ridgeline was lit up in dazzling white against a pitch-black horizon. At first, they assumed Daniels hadn't waited for Saxton's reply, but Nathan shook his head, "Lightning sir ... it's going to be one hell of a storm ..."

There was immediately another lightning flash, and another, this time out above the valley between their position and the advancing enemy. These flashes were followed by two quick concussions that shook the earth. Then they heard a familiar *WHUMP* back behind them, and a bright flash and *BOOM* out across the valley, this time followed by a small, drifting cloud of smoke.

Captain Anderson shouted out, "Lieutenant Daniels says, 'Never mind, we'll target them in the lightning flashes!'"

But when Nathan turned back to look out at the valley the skies opened up and a deluge of rain suddenly beat against the top of his hat and upon his shoulders. Tremendous drops poured down in great sheets, thoroughly drenching the Union men as they stood awaiting the advancing enemy, even as another bright flash lit up the night and shook the earth.

ঃ৾৲৲৲৶৶৶৲৲৲৲৶৶৶৲৲৲৲৶৶৶

Jackson's army had to cross more than a mile of open ground from the base of Bolivar Heights to the beginning of the slope that climbed Camp Hill. The only cover the rebels would have during that trek, taking the better part of an hour, were the few trees, hedgerows, houses, and outbuildings of the small village of Bolivar near the midway point.

And Lieutenant Daniels and his naval gunners did their best to punish the rebels the entire way, using their nine heavy guns and high explosive shells to devastating effect.

As lightning continued to torture the skies with great rending, twisting streaks of light, a deadly cat and mouse game ensued between the soldiers of the approaching army and the gunners on Maryland Heights. Each flash would light up the Confederates' current position for a fraction of a second, after which complete darkness covered their progress until the next flash. During that darkness Lieutenant Daniels and his fellows would try to anticipate where the enemy would be by the time they adjusted their guns and fired. And with eight guns at their disposal, they could generally bracket the enemy in a deadly spread of incoming rounds. The rebels, for their part, would try to alter their course or their speed to avoid the deadly blasts they knew were coming.

Nathan and Saxton stood shoulder to shoulder, gazing out at the spectacle in awestruck wonder. Never had either imagined such as scene, let alone witnessed one. As powerful and earth-rattlingly concussive as the huge naval guns were—hurtling huge, high explosive shells at thousands of feet her second—they were dwarfed almost to insignificance by the tremendous power, light, and noise of the thunderstorm—the very artillery of God!

And though Daniels' Dahlgrens performed heroically, and likely inflicted devastating casualties upon the enemy, it soon became apparent to the Union officers watching that it would not be enough, and that the bulk of the enemy army would reach the base of Camp Hill still intact. At that point the naval guns would have to cease firing—they would no longer be able to see the rebels on the back slope of the hill, and their shells would become a deadly danger to their own lines at the hill's crest.

And to make matters worse, the slope fell off so steeply that even the light artillery of the New York battery would not be able to target the enemy, the barrels unable to be lowered far enough.

Nathan and Saxton exchanged a serious look. They knew in a few short minutes the only thing standing in the way of Jackson's

20,000-man army would be just over 3,000 Union rifles and three hundred yards of hillside.

Saxton resumed his pacing, knowing he had done all he could do. Now it would be up to the courage and grit of the Union soldiers to hold the line against overwhelming odds.

ઇઉઇઉ૭ઇ૭ઇઉઇઉ૭ઇ૭ઇઉઇઉ૭ઇ૭

As Nathan leaned against the log barricade in front of him looking out toward the enemy, water streaming off the brim of his hat, he wasn't surprised to see Tom settle in beside him on his right side. He looked over, they met eyes, and shared a quick smile. No words were necessary between them. Nathan had always known, no matter Tom's duties, they would stand side by side once the shooting started. Tom handed Nathan a rifle, bayonet already fixed. Nathan examined it and saw that it was already loaded, then looked back at Tom and nodded his thanks.

Tony stood next to Nathan on his left side, and Stan and Billy were beside him. Nathan noticed Tony had his hand in his pocket—imagining him nervously fondling the handle of his Colt revolver.

And then Nathan was amused to see Harry the Dog sitting between the men, seeming unconcerned by all the noise and commotion, and that Tony, who'd been terrified of the dog in the past, stood next to the large beast, seemingly at ease. But even as Nathan watched, the hound stood up on his hind legs and gazed out at the lightning battle with a curious expression, his front paws on the log barricade, his head as tall as any of the men, save maybe Stan.

Stan also noticed the dog and laughed, reaching out to stroke the raised fur along the hound's back until Harry looked over at him, and dropped back down on all fours. Stan then reached over the dog and patted Tony on the back, "Is good having you here, Tony," he said. But then he looked Tony over and said, "But … where is rifle, Tony?"

"Captain said us freemen can't fight yet, and can't be seen holding weapons. So …" he shrugged, "he gave me one o' his Colts to carry in my pocket … just in case."

276

Stan snorted, "Tiny Colt is not *real* weapon for big battle ... here, take one of mine," he said, handing across his spare rifle, already loaded with bayonet fixed. "Keep next to you. If enemy comes over this wall, then nobody will care what color you are being."

Tony took it, and leaned it against the log wall, "Thanks, Stan," he said.

Stan chuckled, and said, "You can thank me by poking rebel with it."

Nathan looked over at his men and smiled. He decided if he had to die today, this was a good way to go, fighting with stout-hearted men he knew well, and respected. It was the way a soldier *should* go.

His only regret was that he would never see Evelyn again. She was the person he loved most in this world, and the thought that his last words to her had been in anger haunted him. He prayed he might live long enough to gain her forgiveness.

ᏃᏀᏆᏓᏃᏀᏆᏓᏃᏀᏆᏓ

When the enemy finally reached the base of the hill there was a pause, as if the Confederate soldiers needed to catch their breath. The rebels were no longer exposed to the naval guns, and were in no real threat from the Union rifles, being three or four hundred yards away yet, so they seemed to take a moment of respite before launching the expected assault up the hillside.

General Saxton sent orders down the line for coordinated volley fire whenever the rebels attacked—all three thousand guns on the first volley, followed by staggered partial volleys thereafter, to allow more volleys than the time it would typically take to reload all the guns.

Five minutes passed, and then ten, with no movement from the rebels. The lightning continued to light up the battlefield, but had noticeably slackened in intensity, so Lieutenant Daniels was now adding to the illumination by lobbing shells out over the Bolivar village, intended to provide the defenders with a brief glimpse of the enemy, should they decide to attack. Nathan continued to be impressed with Daniels' competence—he was clearly staggering the shell bursts such that the enemy would not be able to time them and launch an assault in the gaps between rounds.

But at thirteen minutes past the time when the rebels had arrived at the base of Camp Hill, there was a bright flash, and a loud *boom*, followed by a rapid, rolling series of the same, as the enemy unleashed his artillery against the Union position above. But though a few of the rounds struck in front of the dug-in Union lines, or banged against the logs of their fortification—shaking the earth and rattling nerves—most of the shells sailed harmlessly overhead to impact well back of their lines, inflicting no casualties.

After a few minutes of this bombardment, it suddenly ceased. Nathan wondered whether Jackson had decided it was ineffective given the circumstances, and he was better off saving his precious ammunition, or he had something else in mind.

That question was quickly answered, as only a minute went by before the sky was once again lit by the flash of gunpowder, and the air shuddered from a thunderous noise, this time unleashed by thousands of rifles fired simultaneously. The bullet rounds buzzed overhead like a swarm of angry bees and impacted against the log barricade in front of the Union lines like the hammering of a thousand carpenters. But thankfully the enemy volley was entirely ineffectual, as no Union soldier had exposed himself to present a target for the enemy.

Then they heard a loud, eerie high-pitched yell, what had come to be known as the "rebel yell"—the calling card of the Confederate army in full attack, and the Stonewall Brigade in particular. The Union officers immediately responded per their pre-arranged orders and called out down the line, "Present ... arms!"

Nathan and the other men stood up, leaned out over the log barricade and extended their rifles.

"*Aim!*" the officers shouted out.

Tony, who was leaning out over the log to watch, said to himself, *Aim at what? It's complete blackness!* But fortunately at that very moment there was another flash of lightning, and Tony could make out the rebel soldiers, shouting at the top of their lungs, racing up the hill toward them.

"Fire!"

A tremendous concussion, flash of fire, and pall of smoke surrounded Tony and shook the earth.

"Reload!" Union officers were calling out.

Tony shook his head, deciding that particular order was ridiculously unnecessary—he couldn't imagine anything in life the soldiers would want more at that very moment than to reload their rifles, no matter what anyone else might have to say about it!

In a few seconds he was back at the log barricade, ready to watch the Union side unleash another volley. But the order to fire never came. He glanced over at the Captain, and saw him gazing through his spyglass, with General Saxton leaning in next to him.

Nathan said, "They've gone to ground … it was a feint, likely. To see if we would stand our ground or run … and to count our rifles."

Tony wasn't sure he understood all that strategy, but he was happy the enemy had stopped coming. In the brief flash of lightning he had seen *so* many enemy soldiers … he couldn't imagine any possible way that the few Union men standing on this hill could ever stop them.

And then … nothing. For more than an hour there was no movement from the enemy … no sound, no action.

And then, with no warning, another thunderous volley from the enemy, deafening in its suddenness. And another rebel yell.

Then, as before, the Union officers called out, "Present arms … aim … *fire!*" and the Union army answered, with three thousand guns of their own.

And once again, the enemy did not press the attack, and another long silence ensued, with only the occasional lightning strike or artillery burst to disturb the silence. Even the pouring rain had abated and was now only a light drizzle.

An hour later it began again with a sudden rifle volley from below, but to Nathan's trained ear there was something different this time, and he turned to General Saxton and shouted, "Have the men hold fire and keep their heads down!"

Saxton turned to Captain Anderson and gave the command, which was quickly repeated down the line.

"What is it, Chambers?" Saxton asked, sliding back in next to him.

"They only fired a fraction of their guns this time. They're baiting us into standing up to return fire, and then they will hit us with the rest …"

"Ah … I see. Thank you, Mr. Chambers."

And as Nathan predicted, ten seconds later a second volley was fired. But it was also only a fraction of the guns. And after another ten seconds, there was a third volley.

"What are they about, Nathan?"

Nathan quickly leaned up and peered out over the logs with his spyglass, ducking back down after only a few seconds.

"They're advancing up the hill at the march, staggering their volleys to force our heads down. When they get close enough they'll launch an all-out bayonet charge, and we will be overrun and slaughtered."

ↈ

"What are we to do, then?" Saxton said, his anxiety threatening to overcome him, "Pull back and defend the river, do you think?"

Nathan reached in his pocket for a cigar before remembering he'd run out hours ago. Then he chuckled; if he'd had any cigars left in his pocket they'd have been totally soaked anyway, along with the matches.

"General … it's too late to fall back—the enemy is too close. If we turn our back on them now, it'll turn into a rout, and your army will be utterly destroyed.

"Aside from which … I've never been too keen on showing my back to the enemy—I much prefer facing him and showing no fear. I say let's give him a taste of the death that awaits him on this hill."

Saxton remained wide-eyed, but he nodded.

"Have Daniels hold off shelling until you give the command. Then once he starts, have him fire for illumination as rapidly as he can. Then send the word down the line—staggered volley fire, every fourth rifle company at a time. Have them raise up and fire immediately after the enemy fires his volleys, then duck back down."

Ten minutes later, with the rebel advance now nearly halfway up the slope, a shell burst in the sky, illuminating the advancing enemy lines, and a few seconds later, the rebels fired another partial volley. But this time there was an immediate response from the hilltop, "*Present … aim … fire!*" and nearly eight hundred guns opened up on the advancing rebels.

A few seconds later another rebel volley was fired, with the same response from the Union soldiers above, all the while shells continued to explode out over the valley, lighting up the night sky.

Nathan and his men fired their rifles on the fourth volley, and then … silence. This time the enemy did *not* respond, and only Lieutenant Daniel's continuing artillery fire disturbed the silence.

☉ℬ☉ℭℛℭℬ☉ℬ☉ℭℛℭℬ☉ℬ☉ℭℛℭℬ

Saturday May 31, 1862 – Harpers Ferry, Virginia:

When dawn lit the sky, Nathan peered out over the log barricade with his spyglass, scanning the hillside below, then out across the valley, and up to the Bolivar Heights ridgeline.

"What do you see, Nathan?" General Saxton asked from where he sat on the ground with his back to the log wall.

"Nothing."

"What?"

"Absolutely nothing, General. Not a man, not a horse, not a gun. Nothing. Not even a dead body. Just … nothing."

Saxton jumped to his feet, leaned out over the logs, and put his binoculars to his eyes. After a few moments, he turned and gazed at Nathan wide-eyed, then turned and trotted over to his command tent, "Captain Anderson!" he called out.

Anderson came out of the tent, looking bleary eyed, "Sorry, sir … must've dozed off for a moment …"

"Never mind that … tell General Slough to send out a reconnaissance force … cavalry and light artillery … to see where the rebels have gone. And send another up Loudoun Heights to make sure they're not up there. Oh … and ask Lieutenant Daniels if he can see anything from his vantage point. Then ask for a report from General Cooper up on top of Maryland Heights. Though we heard and saw nothing from that direction all night, I still want to confirm his status!"

Nathan turned to Billy and Stan, and said, "Men … would you mind—"

But Billy said, "We are already going, Captain. We will find Jackson and learn what he is up to now."

Stan just grinned and nodded.

Then Nathan added, "But Billy … this time don't follow him. If he has retired out past Charlestown, it means he won't be coming back, and he is no longer our concern. I would prefer you were safely back here."

Billy nodded, then the two of them trotted off to get their horses.

"*'He hath loosed the fateful lightning of his terrible swift sword,'*" Tom said, gazing out across the battlefield of the previous night.

"I don't recognize *that* Bible verse, Tom; though it's very apropos, I must say!" Nathan said.

"That's because it's not from the Bible, sir. It's a line from a new song William was playing on his violin a few weeks ago. Written by a woman who's an abolitionist; wanted to inspire the Union side in the war. She calls it *'Battle Hymn of the Republic.'*"

"*Fateful lightning,* indeed!" General Saxton said, gazing out across the valley through his binoculars. "God has helped us stem the tide with his timely storm, of that there can be no doubt! Without it, we'd have been mostly firing blindly into the darkness, unable to see the enemy until he was upon us with his bayonets!"

ஐ௸௸௸ஐ௸௸௸ஐ௸௸

The recon force sent back word in the early afternoon that they had advanced into Charlestown, but the enemy was gone. The locals reported the rebel column had passed through town in the darkness of pre-dawn, heading south on the road toward Winchester.

The regiment deployed to the top of Loudoun Heights sent a lieutenant back to report what they had discovered. "Sir, we found no rebels, not even any bodies, but we did find the remains of their camp—broken artillery carriages and shattered guns, burned out tents, wagons that had been splintered into a thousand pieces and then burned, and several dead mules," he said. "And most telling, sir … we found a number of large, blood-splattered areas and pools of blood in the dirt and on the vegetation all around the camp—clearly the enemy incurred a large number of casualties, but apparently has hauled them away as they have withdrawn," he concluded.

Saxton looked over at Nathan and raised an eyebrow, "More of Lieutenant Daniels' handiwork, I presume?"

Nathan nodded, and said, "Sounds like he landed a shell from his nine-inch gun right on top of them—from a mile and three quarters away! Like I said before, the man knows his business."

Saxton nodded his agreement, then shook his head in wonder at the young naval officer's undeniable artillery expertise.

And a few hours later Billy and Stan also reported back to camp, confirming the news. They had ranged several miles further along the Winchester road, discovering what appeared to be a large pit hastily dug and re-filled with dirt—they suspected it was a mass grave where the rebels had buried their dead before moving on.

"I … don't understand, Nathan," Saxton said, trying to digest this news. "Why didn't Jackson press the assault? Why has he left? Though I couldn't be prouder of our men and their resolute courage under fire, still … if Jackson had come on with all his might there is nothing we could've done to stop him. Surely he had little fear of defeat at our hands; we were simply too few."

But Nathan smiled, "We didn't have to beat him, General … we just had to make his victory too costly to bear. I had a good notion he wouldn't press the assault after that first rifle volley. It became clear to me that his goal was to drive us away, not to fight us. But when we refused to run, he knew we were determined to give him a fight."

"So … you knew all along he would not overrun us?"

"No, General," Nathan said, contentedly puffing on a dry cigar he'd found in his pack, "I figured *that* would be one of *two* possible outcomes … the other being he would go ahead and kill us all as punishment for our impertinent defiance.

"Either way, as long as we stood our ground, we were going to win, the only question was whether or not we'd live to enjoy our victory—if he'd pressed the attack, he would've destroyed us and taken Harpers Ferry all right, but his army would've been too depleted by our resistance to mount a march on Washington."

Saxton slowly shook his head, taking it all in. "This is why I am not a field commander, Nathan. You are made of stern stuff, sir … utterly fearless."

But Nathan shook his head, again recalling his greatest fear of the night before, that he might never see Evelyn again, and he said, "No, General … not *completely* fearless, it turns out."

"At any rate, congratulations to you, Rufus, on a great victory."

But Saxton shook his head, "And who will celebrate, I wonder? We suffered only one casualty in the battle, some poor unfortunate fellow who stuck his head up at the wrong moment. And Jackson has taken his dead and wounded away with him, so he will deny having suffered any losses in the action. Likely he'll claim he simply changed his mind, and moved off in a different direction. The whole event won't even warrant a mention in the newspapers—they only believe a battle is of interest if tens of thousands are killed."

But Nathan smiled, and patted him on the back, "But you and I know what has been accomplished here by holding this station. And more importantly … the *president* knows."

Saxton returned the smile and nodded.

☙❧☙❧☙❧

At noon on the third day since their arrival in Lewisburg, Nigel announced he was going out to reconnoiter the Greenbrier River to see what the Union troop dispositions looked like, and determine if there was any feasible way one might cross undetected after dark.

Evelyn wanted to go with him, but he argued that would look odd and out of place—he had the papers of a mid-level government official from the Union War Department to prove he had a reasonable purpose for being there. But it would be very strange for him to bring his "wife" along into a potentially dangerous war zone.

She had to acknowledge the logic of his reasoning, and so as he departed, she steeled herself to sit and await his return. And since it was a one hour walk to the river, plus however long it took him to reconnoiter, and then walk back again, she settled in for a long afternoon.

He finally returned a few minutes before six in the evening, and she could tell by the gleam in his eye that his mission had been a success.

"What did you find, Nigel?" she asked, eager to hear the news.

"As we feared, both sides of the river are heavily patrolled, though nobody expects an attack is imminent. Seems the recent Lewisburg battle took a bit of the wind out of both armies, and they are content to 'rest and refit,' for the time being."

She nodded, but let him continue.

"Oddly … the soldiers I spoke with were more concerned about enemy spies than enemy soldiers."

She raised an eyebrow at this, and he smiled and nodded in response. "Yes, I know … exactly what *we* are … though ironically *not* the enemy of the Union side."

Evelyn snorted, "Tell General McClellan that!"

Nigel smiled. "Anyway, as I was searching for a means of crossing, I came upon a small creek emptying into the river a few hundred yards north of where I first came to the river's edge, and it occurred to me it would accommodate a small rowboat. And then I started thinking that a person with a house along that stream might keep just such a boat on hand so they could go fishing in the river if they had a mind. So I followed it upstream and … sure enough, not fifty yards from the big river there was a small farmhouse with a two-person rowboat pulled up on the grass of the bank—oars and fishing poles still in it!"

"Ah … that sounds hopeful … and no soldiers patrolling near there?"

"No … they are all positioned closer to the main riverbank. The trick, of course, will be to slip past them on the small stream and into the river without being noticed. But the good news is the clouds have been steadily thickening, so whatever moon there would normally be ought to be completely blotted out tonight. That should make for a very dark night, so as long as we just float along, not making any noise, we should go unnoticed. We won't start using the oars until we are well out into the river. And by the time we reach the far shore I will have switched to my Confederate papers, so when the rebels catch us, we can just explain how we got caught on the wrong side of the river when the Lewisburg battle took place, and only just now figured out how to get across to our own side. Given all our recent experiences, and the quality of the papers I carry, I'm feeling very confident I can convince them it's true."

They had dinner at the boarding house, but Evelyn found she was too wound up to eat much. The time seemed to crawl awaiting sundown, but finally darkness arrived and they set out.

Evelyn carried her small carpet bag, and Nigel a satchel, such as a government official would carry containing official papers. She noticed he'd also strapped a pistol holster to his waist, which she'd not seen him do since he was disguised as a Union major back at the prison.

Though it was almost completely dark, Nigel carried a small oil lamp of the kind that could be shuttered except for a tiny opening when needed. He now shone a small sliver of light ahead to illuminate their path as they walked.

Earlier, on the way back, he'd scouted out the more direct route along the road to the rowboat's farmhouse so they'd not have to go anywhere near the main river on their way. They hoped this would prevent them from encountering any soldiers. And even if they did, they'd already agreed on a story they'd spin to talk their way out of it.

As they walked along the road, Evelyn noticed the change in the weather Nigel had been talking about—not only had it clouded over, but the temperature had dropped perceptibly to the point Evelyn was wishing she'd worn her shawl instead of packing it in her bag. A cool, fitful breeze had picked up that was making her shiver.

They followed a gravel road, winding through the trees, passing several small houses along the way until Nigel stopped and waved toward a house on their left. He briefly flashed the light across the yard, and in that instant she saw that the grass sloped away from them and seemed to disappear down an embankment. But the most important thing she saw was the prow of a small rowboat sticking up out of the grass of the slope.

They moved quickly to the boat and set their things inside. Nigel removed the fishing poles and set them aside on the grass. Then he reached into his pocket and pulled out a $20 gold coin, which he set down on the grass between the two poles. He leaned over to her and whispered, "I may be a thief, but I'm an honest one," which made Evelyn smile and shake her head.

He gestured for her to get in the boat and sit in the back, then handed her the lamp. He picked up the small tie-down rope attached to the front of the boat and set it inside, noting it hadn't even been tied on the shore side. He bent down, took hold of the prow, lifted and shoved at the same time. The boat slid easily down the slope—almost too much so, as he had to run and jump in at the last second or he'd have been left behind. They were soon drifting along with the stream, which was a dozen or so yards wide with a slow but steady flow and no ripples or rapids. They each held an oar, ready to push off if they ran up against the bank. But the stream ran a relatively straight course, and they encountered no obstacles until they approached the Greenbrier River, looming in the darkness ahead of them. They could hear the movement of water in front of them, though it wasn't especially swift in this section.

They slid into the main flow of the river, and then something bumped hard against the port side of the boat, causing it to lurch and rock violently—Evelyn's mind's eye suddenly recalled the image of striking the sunken ship with the fishing boat while floating down the James. She shuddered at the unpleasant memory.

But Nigel reached across, shoved with his oar and they were moving again. It'd been nothing more than a small, grassy island just yards from the shore, partially blocking their route to the main flow.

But then Evelyn flinched as she heard a voice, only a few yards away, "Hey … did you hear that, Willard? Someone's out there. Who's goes there? Show yourselves or we'll open fire …" the voice called out.

But Evelyn and Nigel stayed silent, not daring to move, trusting in the darkness to conceal them. Then Evelyn noticed they were sliding past another island, this one on their right. It was from this small island that the voices were coming.

"Maybe just a turtle or something," a different voice said.

"Hmph … biggest turtle ever," the first voice answered, then seemed to change the subject completely, "Damn this wind. It's getting nasty cold out here on this water."

And Evelyn noticed he was right, the wind had suddenly picked up, and the temperature had taken another precipitous drop. But she resisted a strong desire to wrap her arms around herself, not daring to move as they drifted past the soldiers only a few yards away.

After several more minutes she felt she could breathe again; they'd floated far enough downstream as to no longer be easily heard by the soldiers on the island. Nigel appeared to agree, as he moved over and carefully slipped his oar into the oarlock on the starboard side. Then he took Evelyn's oar and slid it into place on the port side. He took a seat between the two oars, and slowly dipped them into the stream and pushed, turning the boat slowly toward the far bank.

Evelyn was impressed at how quietly he was able to perform the task, imagining it would be nearly imperceptible on the far shore—especially with this wind. This wind! All of a sudden it had gone from chilly and fitful to strong and gusty, rocking the small boat perceptibly with each gust. It was now appearing that Nigel's fortuitous "cloud cover" from earlier in the evening was swiftly becoming a full-blown storm. But other than being uncomfortable, and that they'd likely get a good dousing if it rained, she figured it could only be for the good, masking any sounds they might happen to make in the boat.

Nigel continued to stroke, now more vigorously, no longer fearing the noise it might make under cover of the howling wind. And even in almost complete darkness Evelyn could still just make out the outline of the horizon above each shore. She estimated it was just over a hundred yards wide at this point and decided they were already nearly halfway across. She began to relax and feel confident they were going to make it.

And then everything changed in a flash—a dazzling flash of white light that illuminated the bank on the Union side in glittering sharp relief, revealing a row of soldiers with rifles gazing out toward them across the river. *Boom!* a noise like a thousand cannons shook the world and rocked their tiny boat, drawing a gasp of shock from Evelyn. The first flash was followed almost immediately by another, and another tremendous booming roar. And then another.

But to Nigel's credit he had not stopped rowing, in fact he now worked the oars with a new sense of urgency—desperation even, Evelyn realized—as they were now clearly visible from the shore in the flashes of lightning. And Nigel had noticed what she had not: the third flash and boom had been closely followed by distant *popping* sounds and zipping, whistling noises mixed with the howling of the wind. The Union soldiers were firing at them!

The lightning flashed again, and this time a bullet impacted against the wood of the boat's bow, causing Evelyn to flinch and squeal in surprise and shock. Then to Evelyn's surprise, Nigel suddenly shipped the oars and unholstered his pistol. In the next flash he fired off a few shots toward the Union soldiers.

"Nigel!" she yelled, "stop that! Those are *our* soldiers!"

But he looked at her and grinned, shouting back, "Don't worry, Evelyn … I'm a terrible shot; I'll never hit anyone anyway!"

The lightning flashed again while Evelyn was still looking at Nigel's face. His eyes suddenly widened, and he grimaced, clutching at his chest before dropping the pistol and sliding down in his seat.

"Nigel!" she screamed, and scrambled over to where he now lay face-up on the floorboards. His eyes were still open and blinking, but only a gurgling sound came from his mouth.

"Nigel … Nigel, how can I help? What can I do?" she shouted, feeling around where his hand clutched at this chest, but she felt something warm and wet all around his hand, and when she brought her own hand back up it was covered in blood.

She gasped … "*Nigel* … what can I do for you?" she yelled into the howling wind. He looked up at her and for a moment his eyes seemed to focus on her face, and she could see his lips moving, so she put her ear up to his mouth and listened.

"Kiss me …" he whispered in a weak, raspy voice, choked with his own blood, "a kiss … finest woman … ever known … love … you …" he said, and then twitched and shook, unable to say more. She leaned forward and kissed him on the lips, tears streaming down her face. And even as her lips lingered on his, she felt the life leave him and he went entirely limp.

And then, as if in answer to her grief, the heavens opened up with a blinding sheet of rain that pounded her body and violently shook the little boat. But Evelyn was so distraught she barely noticed, so overwhelmed with pain and despair she could barely think or move.

But then a spark of defiance lit the tinder of anger in her, which quickly grew into a flaming rage, and she reached down, picked up the pistol and turned toward the far shore, pulling back the hammer and firing over and over, no longer concerned that the soldiers there were on "her side." They'd killed Nigel—not knowing who he was, or why he was there, they'd thoughtlessly murdered him. She hoped every one of her shots hit their mark …

but she would never know for certain. And then in the final throws of her spent anger and grief she shouted an unintelligible curse and threw the now empty pistol at them, though it sailed through the air only a few yards before sinking into the river with a splash.

Then she heard a new sound—the popping and banging of rifles, but now much louder … and coming from the opposite direction. She realized it was coming from the shore behind her—the Confederate side. And then she noticed the boat was nearly there. The Confederates had heard the noise, of course, and were now targeting the Union soldiers, returning fire across the river.

Then several men were in the river next to the boat, chest deep in the water, pulling the vessel to shore. "Are you all right miss?" one of them asked her.

"Yes … yes," she tried to say, but her voice had become so strained and dry from screaming and shouting that nothing intelligible came out, so she just nodded.

"It's all right, miss. We've got you … y'all are safe now … we'll get you in to shore."

And then she felt the bottom of the boat grind against the dirt of the bank, and a man was helping her step to the shore. Two other men jumped in and lifted Nigel, carrying him out and then laying him down on the ground. Another man immediately knelt down and examined him with a lantern, checking for a pulse in his neck, before looking up and sadly shaking his head. "Sorry miss … I'm afraid he's gone."

Chapter 11. Empty Homecoming

"I suspected, however, that I wasn't homesick
for anything I would find at home when I returned.
The longing was for what I wouldn't find:
the past, and all the people and places there,
were lost to me."
- Alice Steinbach

Monday June 2, 1862 – Wheeling, Virginia:

Nathan's homecoming from the successful defense of Harpers Ferry was not at all the happy, even joyous event he'd envisioned. Instead, he was met with the shocking news of Walters' attack on the farm, his nearly successful capture of Margaret, and the serious and possibly mortal wounding of Phinney.

And even as his tightly wound emotions were festering over these events, Miss Abbey pulled him to the side, handed him a letter, and quickly told him of Evelyn's visit. This was, in some ways, even more emotionally gut-wrenching than the other news.

First things first, he decided, and immediately went to see how Phinney was doing, bringing William along, of course. Margaret accompanied them and gave her version of events as they walked up the stairs to the farmhouse room he'd been laid in. She spoke in such a breathless flurry that Nathan worried she was still suffering a good deal of emotional trauma over it.

When they talked with Phinney, still lying in bed and looking very much in pain, Nathan met eyes with William, who frightened him with the serious look he returned. Nathan wished Phinney well and led Margaret away by the arm, leaving William to do what he could for their wounded comrade.

Nathan's next order of business was to ensure the threat from Walters was truly over, at least for the foreseeable future. The obvious course there was to send Billy out to investigate and see if he could discover where the villain had gone after the attack. As usual, Stan went with him, though this time he hadn't been asked.

Nathan spent the next hour sitting with Margaret, alone down by the river. He gently prompted her about what had happened, but this time more from the perspective of how she was *feeling* about it and how it was affecting her now that it was over. He mostly listened, allowing her to vent her emotions, letting her cry on his shoulder, and generally just being supportive and understanding. He stalwartly resisted a very strong urge to apologize for the whole incident—after all, he could hardly have been in two places at once, regardless of the urgency.

He then met with the freemen of the watch, congratulating them on their successful defense of the farm, and thanking them profusely for it, contrasting their dangerous and deadly action against the—as it turned out—lack of any real fighting for Tony and the other men at Harpers Ferry. This was met with very gratifying laughter, pats on the back, and smiles from the men.

When he was satisfied the needs of the farm and everyone on it had been met—at least for the time being—he finally took time to deal with his own feelings. He climbed the stairs to his room, threw his hat on the chair, sat heavily on the bed, and pulled out Evelyn's letter:

> *May 26, 1862*
> *Belle Meade Farm*
> *Wheeling, Virginia*
>
> *Dearest Nathan,*
>
> *Words cannot express the rapturous joy I felt when our eyes met and we finally embraced at the train station in Harpers Ferry. As long as I live, I will treasure that memory as one of the happiest in life. Nothing that happened after can possibly dull or dim the warmth and intensity of that glorious moment.*
>
> *Being with you again, no matter how briefly, reaffirmed the depth of my feelings for you and my certainty that I*

wish to be with you always. And please believe me when I tell you it was the most painful and difficult thing I have ever done, leaving you there alone ... my heart still aches from the dreadful emptiness of it.

But I take solace in knowing I am doing the thing I must do, even if nobody else in the world appreciates this need in me, not even you. I pray someday you will come to understand me, or at least to forgive me.

And I choose to believe, despite the angry words at our parting, that you still love me even as I still love you, with all my heart. And believe me when I say, living with you is the one thing I want most in this life; but my Daddy used to tell me when I was a small child, "Evelyn, we can't always have the things we want ... or at least not without working hard for them," which I have always thought was a good twist on the age old saying. Perhaps I just have to work hard a while longer before this thing that I want above all else finally comes to pass ...

Sitting here at your lovely new farm by the river, I am reminded of the words the pastor said at Mountain Meadows' Big Wedding. He said, "The Lord granted us three great gifts: faith, hope, and love." And I believe that you and I must have <u>faith</u> that everything will work out for us, and never lose <u>hope</u> that this terrible war will end with the outcome we so greatly desire. That we may begin our lives together in peace, even as God has intended.

And then the pastor said, "But of these three most gracious gifts, the greatest is <u>love</u>." That I truly believe, Nathan, my dearest, for I can feel the strength of your love even a thousand miles away. My most fervent prayer is that our love will always shine like the brightest star, and burn like a raging fire that may never be quenched.

Your forever love ... and wife to be?

Evelyn

When Nathan finished reading, he groaned, crumpled up the paper, and threw it across the room, muttering, *"Damn you, Evelyn!"*

He covered his face with his hands and cried as he hadn't done for as long as he could remember. Not even when she'd left him the first time. Not even after Maria died, now countless ages ago.

But after several minutes, he sat back up, wiped his face on his sleeve, stood and retrieved the letter from the floor. He laid it out gently on the desk, and neatly smoothed out the wrinkles. He read it again, then raised it to his mouth and gently kissed it before folding it and placing it in the desk drawer.

Then he pulled over the inkwell, grabbed pen and paper, and began his response. He remembered the potential danger to her if he was too direct in his letters, and briefly debated writing something innocuous, such as "I entirely agree with the opinions you expressed in your letter of May 26 last," but even *considering* that idea raised his ire.

He quickly decided it was time he poured his heart out to her on paper, even as she had just done to him; he'd figure out how to get it to her later. Perhaps Tom could send it via their old friend Joseph in Richmond—he was entirely trustworthy and reliable and likely could hand-deliver it to her safely.

ಬಜ಼ೞಐಛೞಬಜ಼ೞಐಛೞಬಜ಼ೞಐಛೞ

William asked Cobb and Georgie to attend him. Cobb because he was Phinney's best friend, and Georgie because he'd been around gunshot wounds before and could be trusted to follow orders without hesitation. William needed two assistants, and these men were as stout-hearted and reliable as any he knew.

He'd considered including Margaret—after all, she'd likely saved Phinney's life with her level-headed actions at the time of his wounding—but then he'd thought better of it. She'd already been through enough in that regard; he could tell from her description of the event that the images of it still haunted her. There was no need to traumatize her any further—this would be unpleasant and painful. Not a thing one wanted burned into one's

295

memory if it could be helped. For William there would be no help for it, but he steeled his heart to it, as he always did.

"Phinney, I know you're not feeling well," William began, not bothering to ask it, but rather making the obvious statement. "But now I am going to help you start feeling better."

Phinney nodded, but said nothing. Sweat poured down his face in streams, and he shuddered from time to time, his coal black face knotted in a grimace of pain.

"Phinney … you must now trust me, because there is going to be no easy way to say this or to do it. The arm is already gone … it's dead and we must remove it, or you too will die. Do you understand me?"

Phinney's face knotted up, and he shook his head emphatically. But William locked eyes with him and kept his gaze. "I know what I'm saying, Phinney. I've seen too many of these cases … if we don't remove the arm, it will fester, and you will die—I'm sorry, but there is no other way."

"Then … then just let me die …" he said, in a rasping, shaky voice, barely above a whisper, such that William had to lean over to hear him clearly.

William looked up at Cobb, and then Georgie, both of whom held fearful but determined expressions. Then he looked back at Phinney, "Not today, Phinney … not today. I'm not going to let that happen …"

Then William looked up and gazed out at the horizon, taking off his glasses and cleaning them as he did. He'd had the men carry Phinney out to a sturdy wooden table set on the lawn in the sunlight so William would have enough light to see what he was doing. And though it was already June, thankfully it was not yet unpleasantly hot.

William tried to think of what the Captain might say at a moment like this, and sighed. After a long moment he spoke in a quiet voice, "Phinney … I am seeing a day far off in the future … a bright, sunny day when the world is a better place than it is today … a peaceful day when all the fighting is over. I see you sitting in a chair on a wide, wooden porch in front of your own home. You have grandchildren with you … one on each knee.

Your beautiful wife and daughter look on and smile. Then your little grandson, the younger of the two, looks up and says, 'Tell me again, Grandad … how did you lose your arm, anyhow?' You gaze down at him, smile and say, 'Well son, I lost that arm back in the great war that we fought to free all our people. Lost it when a wicked slaver shot me … just before I shot the villain dead with my own rifle!'"

William paused a moment, looked back at Phinney, then continued, "I have seen the kind of *man* you are, Phinney: a fighter—*lionhearted*—not any kind of shrinking coward."

Phinney now had tears streaming down his face. They continued to stare at each other for several more heartbeats before Phinney nodded.

"Cobb, give him a shot of that whiskey, and then that stick to bite down on," William ordered, "then the two of you hold him down hard; I must saw away the sharp end of the shattered bone. Phinney, this will hurt for a few moments, but then after … you can finally start feeling better again."

Cobb did as he was bid, and after two good swallows from the whiskey bottle, Phinney bit down hard on the stick and began breathing hard, eyes wide. Then William looked up at Cobb and Georgie and nodded. They reached down and took hold of Phinney's shoulders, pinning him to the table as William picked up a small, razor-sharp saw he kept for just this purpose.

〰〰〰〰〰〰〰〰

Other than a brief hello, William had not had any time to speak with Margaret since returning home. Along with the Captain, he'd listened intently to her hurried recounting of the events the night Walters attacked and Phinney was wounded, but had known instantly there was no time to lose in amputating the shattered arm if he was to save Phinney's life.

But now that the operation was over, there was little more he could do—Phinney would either recover, with the grace of God, or he wouldn't.

William finally had a moment to breathe, so he worked up his courage, entered the farmhouse, climbed the stairs, and knocked on Margaret's bedroom door.

He felt anxious, not knowing what he'd say, or how she'd greet him given their previous unhappy parting. He knew he'd done what he *had* to do, and yet … he'd also promised to protect her, but he hadn't, and that'd very nearly been disastrous. Not only that, but ironically his medical skills had been more urgently needed back here at the farm than they'd been needed in the so-called battle at Harpers Ferry. He knew she had every reason to give him a piece of her mind—and likely he deserved it.

But when she opened the door, she smiled warmly, and he instantly felt a great sense of relief. "William! Please … come in. Is it over?"

He nodded, knowing she was referring to Phinney's amputation. "Yes, everything went well. And though the arm was clearly dead, there was no sign of festering in general, so God willing, he should make a swift recovery. It's a frightful thing for a man to endure, but he was very brave—I am very proud of him."

She smiled brightly, "Oh, thank you, William. That's such good news. And … thank you for taking care of him, William … I'm so happy you're here."

He returned her smile, feeling the familiar warmth and happiness of his relationship with her returning, such as he'd not felt since their parting. "You're welcome, Margaret. And … I never had time to tell you before … I greatly admired how you took charge when he was injured. Cobb told me the whole story, and I'm certain Phinney would've died within minutes if you'd not been there and did what you did. That was well done, Margaret, truly."

She looked down, and shook her head, then looked back up, "William … it was the scariest thing I've ever done … even more so than anything to do with Walters … and I hope to never have to do it again."

"Amen to that, Margaret," William replied.

"But, William … I've been wanting to tell you … when I saw the pain Phinney was in … and the desperate need in his eyes … all I could think of was you. All the things you do with such seeming ease and courage … things we all take for granted, except when you're not here. And it made me think of all those frightened young soldiers, wounded on the battlefield and how much they need you in their darkest hour.

"I … I have felt very foolish and selfish for the things I said to you before we parted. I now know you did the right thing, regardless of what happened here; your proper place was on the battlefield helping the wounded soldiers, even as you said."

She looked down, no longer meeting his eyes. He was shocked—it was exactly the opposite of what he'd expected her to say, and it caught him speechless. "I … I thank you for that, Margaret … but I … I do feel guilty now that it turns out I was needed more urgently here than there, both for your protection and for taking care of Phinney."

She looked back up and they met eyes, "That may be so, William, but there is no way you could've known that ahead of time. You made the right choice and did the right thing," she concluded, nodding emphatically, gracing him with a very sincere look.

There she goes with those pretty eyes again, William thought, and this time decided to take the initiative, leaning in to kiss her. She closed those pretty eyes and accepted his kiss with affection. They lingered there a long moment, moving into a soft, warm embrace in the meantime.

When they pulled apart, she had a serious look on her face. "William … when you were gone, I had this terrible fear you would be killed in the fighting, and I would never see you again, and our last words to each other would've been in anger.

"And then when Walters arrived, and I was held by his man, I knew he would kill me, and I was surprised that my greatest fear and regret at that moment was that I would never see you again— never be able to tell you how I truly felt. So, I wish to tell you now—how sorry I am for my angry words … and …"

"Yes?"

"William … it has made me think … either one of us could've been killed this past week. And next week we could be as well, or the week after … or even the one after that."

"Well … that may be true, but it's not a very happy thought—" he began, but she put her finger to his lips to stop him talking.

"Please … let me finish, or I shall lose my courage … William, we don't know what tomorrow will bring, but I don't want to die never knowing love … never knowing the love of a man that I love in return. William, I want to know *that* kind of love … with you … *now*."

His eyes widened, and he could think of nothing to say to this. But it turned out no words were required; she reached out and pushed the door closed, then took him by the hand and led him to her bed.

ജയയയയയയയയ

Tony stepped up to the door of Rosa's tent and reached out his hand to knock, but before his knuckles hit the wood the door flew open and something came rushing out with a squeal, hitting him in the chest and nearly knocking him over backward.

Once he'd recovered his wits and his balance, Tony realized it was Rosa, who'd wrapped her arms around his neck and was now squeezing like a vise.

He laughed and spun her around in a circle until she was giggling like a little girl.

When he stopped, she loosened her grip just enough to lean back and gaze into his eyes, before leaning forward and kissing him with great affection.

When they finally came apart again, and Tony was able to catch his breath, he said, "Oh my! Reckon that was about as fine a greetin' as a man could ever hope to get! What's got into you, girl?"

She beamed, "Reckon I was missin' you, is all."

"Well … figure maybe I ought to leave more often if that's the greetin' I get when I return."

She scowled, "Now … don't you go makin' me think better of it …"

He smiled, and laughed, "I's just teasin', Rosa. I didn't like bein' away from you any better'n you liked it."

Then he took her hand and said, "C'mon ... let's go for a walk down to the river ..."

She smiled and nodded.

As they strolled along holding hands she said, "Tony ... I never felt so afraid before ... not knowin' if you was gonna get killed or somethin'. When Miss Abbey got that telegram from the Captain sayin' the battle was over and y'all were okay, I finally felt like I could breathe again."

He chuckled, "Sounds like things was more dangerous around here for y'all than it was for us as was out there soldierin'. The Union army fired its rifles a few times, but them rebs never made their final attack."

"*Oh?!* How come?"

He grinned, and said, "Well ... reckon they saw *me* standin' up on that hill and thought better of it."

She scowled at him, and punched him in the arm.

"Ow! Damn ... you're stronger than you look, Rosa!"

She giggled.

"We did see plenty o' fireworks, and heard plenty o' noise though, on account of a big ol' lightning storm that started up at the beginning of the fight and mixed with the big guns goin' off. It was quite a show all right."

"Tony, when you tell it like that ... I can almost see it."

They were quiet then for a few minutes as they continued down the path.

"Hey Rosa ... on the way back riding on the train I got to thinkin' 'bout the whole jumpin' the broom thing."

"Oh yeah?"

"Yeah. And I want to do it as soon as may be."

She smiled, nodded, then looked at him sidewise and said, "You sure you thinkin' 'bout jumpin' the broom ... and not just 'bout what comes *after*?"

He looked over at her, and tried to suppress a smile, but with little success, "Well ... maybe just a *little* ..."

She laughed, then gave him a coy look and said, "Well ... maybe you won't have to wait that long ..."

That evening at dinner, Miss Abbey asked Nathan a question she'd been wanting to ask for several days, but hadn't been able to due to his absence. It concerned something she'd read in the newspaper.

"Nathan ... Megs and I have been wondering if we should stop working so hard on our flower garden, after all."

"Oh? Why would you think that, Momma?"

"Well, while you were gone we read in the newspaper that the Union Army has won a battle at Lewisburg and now controls Greenbrier County. So we were wondering ... if we might return to Mountain Meadows sometime soon."

He nodded, then said, "Ah ... I see. I heard about that too, of course, so had General Saxton make some inquiries ..."

"And?" Megs asked, leaning forward.

"Turns out they *did* drive the rebels out of Lewisburg. But the Confederate Army burned the covered bridge next to the Caldwell Place to prevent the Union Army crossing. Now the rebels control the east bank, and the Greenbrier has become the de facto border between the two sides. So ... Mountain Meadows—"

"Is on the wrong side ..." Miss Abbey finished his sentence for him, with a groan.

"Yes, 'fraid so, Momma ... Megs ... sorry. But even if they'd pushed the rebels back farther, I'd still have to say 'no.' It's just too close to the fighting, and I'd not put my family at risk in that way. It's just not worth it at this point."

"Too bad ..." Megs said, and sadly shook her head.

"Well, look on the bright side," Nathan said, "... now you can keep working on your new flower garden! Speaking of which, please give me a tour, if you would ... I've been eager to see the progress you've made while I've been away ..."

They all pushed back their chairs and headed toward the back door for a tour of the new Belle Meade flower garden.

Billy's investigation had quickly led back to the late neighbor Ward's farm. Though he and Stan approached the farmhouse cautiously, with guns drawn, Billy determined that nobody was home, nor had they been for several days. Upon entering the house, they discovered a man's body, laid out on the kitchen table—the same table Ward himself had been seated at when he was killed several months earlier. The man on the table had been shot in the belly with a large caliber rifle bullet and had clearly bled out and died there. Likely his comrades had been unable or unwilling to do anything to save him.

After a thorough search of the barns and other outbuildings, Billy did a cursory search along the main road, but quickly concluded there would be no way to track the assailants on the hard gravel surface after several days of traffic on it.

He and Stan returned to report their findings to the Captain, who listened quietly and nodded, but seemed unsurprised by the revelations. He ordered his men saddled up and ready to ride out at first light the next day, giving Sergeant Jim some specific instructions on particular items to bring with them.

Nathan's men laid the body out on the drive of Ward's farm, folding the man's hands across his chest respectfully, with his hat covering his face.

Sergeant Jim stepped up to Nathan and said, "That makes four of the varmints killed to only the one wounded on our side. Helluva nice little gunfight, I'd say, sir."

"Yes, Mr. Wiggins ... and a testament to the training, capabilities, and downright courage of the freemen."

"That it is, sir. That it is. They're gonna make some damned fine soldiers once Mr. Lincoln decides to set 'em loose on the rebs."

Nathan nodded. "Jim ... let's go ahead and bury this fellow out in the woods, like the freemen did with the others. No need to give our enemies any fodder for false accusations against our men. They've done heroic service, and I'll not have them suffer any injustice for it just because they're black men and these scoundrels were white."

Tom and Jim nodded their agreement, but said nothing. The others also stood by silently, waiting for the Captain to give them the orders they were fairly certain would be coming, given the particular items he'd ordered brought with them.

Nathan slowly smoked a cigar, gazing at the shabby farmhouse. Harry sat next to him, gazing in the same direction, panting heavily. Nathan turned to his men, and said, "Gentlemen ... this place has become a house of evil, far too close to our peaceful new home. I would purge our neighborhood of its ill presence."

He turned to Jim and said, "Mr. Wiggins ... have you brought the kerosene?"

"Yes, sir! I brought four cans, though two ought to be more'n enough to do the job."

Nathan nodded, then gazed back at the house a moment and sighed, "I suppose we should do this proper and legal after all ..."

He turned to face the house as if speaking to it. Then in a formal tone he projected his voice as if addressing a large audience, saying, "By the power vested in me by the Restored Government of the Commonwealth of Virginia as its Chief Law Enforcement Officer, I hereby declare this property forfeit due to its illegal and treasonous usage as a place of safe harbor for individuals intent on overthrowing the rightful government and murdering its peaceable citizens. And so, in order to preserve and maintain the peace and security of the state and of the Union, and in the name of the honorable Francis H. Pierpont, Governor of the Commonwealth of Virginia, I hereby order these premises to be destroyed forthwith ..." then he looked over at his men and concluded in a quieter tone, "and so on ... and so forth ..." to which he received appreciative grins.

"Tom ... when we get back, please write this up ... perhaps using more appropriate legal language ... then I'll sign it and file it with the governor."

"Very good, sir," Tom said. "I assume the governor knows of this, then?"

Nathan gave him a wan smile, "He *will* … once I file the papers."

Tom rolled his eyes and shook his head, but said nothing.

"Mr. Wiggins … if you please …" Nathan said.

Jim snapped a salute, "Sir!" then went over to the pack mule and unstrapped two of the kerosene cans. Georgie and Jamie trotted up and said, "We'll take those, Sarge."

"Oh, thank ye kindly, men. Be sure and open up the windows. Then just splash it all around on the inside … furniture, walls, and … oh, hell, you know what to do."

"Yes, sir, Sarge," Georgie said, "the army never skimped on our training in that regard." Then he chuckled, which Jamie echoed; the army out in Texas had regularly employed the tactic of burning down hideouts, cabins, houses, and any other suspect buildings in an attempt to discourage outlaws.

Georgie and Jamie entered the house while the others waited outside. It was not a large place, so in just over five minutes they came out again, with Jamie backing out the door, pouring the last of the kerosene from his can into a puddle on the top wooden step, so that all one had to do was drop a match into it and the whole place would go up in flames.

Jim then turned to the Captain to await his command to commence the operation. But Nathan hesitated a moment.

He turned back toward the men and said, "Gentlemen … I believe it would be appropriate to call upon divine providence at this moment, and ask that our Lord remove the taint of this foul den of wickedness from our midst, replacing it with his divine wholesomeness." He removed his hat, and the men did likewise. "In the first book of Peter, chapter three, verse twelve it says, *'For the eyes of the Lord are over the righteous, and his ears are open unto their prayers: but the face of the Lord is against them that do evil.'* Amen."

"Amen," the men echoed.

Then Nathan replaced his hat, turned to Jim and nodded. But Jim surprised him by stepping forward and extending his hand, "May I, sir? Somehow it seems ... appropriate."

At first Nathan didn't understand what he meant, then it came to him, "Oh! Yes, certainly," he answered, taking the lit cigar from his mouth and handing it to Jim.

Jim smiled and nodded, "Thank ye kindly, sir." Then he stepped up to the porch and set the cigar down right on the edge of the pool of kerosene Jamie had poured there. In a moment a wisp of smoke curled up, followed by a flickering yellow flame that quickly grew.

When the house was well engaged, with smoke curling up vigorously out all the open windows, Jim stepped up to Nathan and asked, "What about the barn and other outbuildings, sir?"

Nathan looked over at the sorry looking barn with its sagging roof, and multiple missing shingles. Then he gazed around at the other outbuildings, all equally dilapidated and in need of serious repair. Then he caught a sudden movement between two of the buildings—only a cat, chasing after a mouse or rat.

"Have the men search the buildings and chase out any cats or other creatures ... hmm ... please look for owls and such in the rafters ... any other of God's innocent creatures ... then burn the buildings. Burn them all. If someone later wants to make something of this place, better that he rebuild it from scratch ... yes, it should either be a clean start, or none at all."

"Yes, sir! It'll be done even as you say."

ഇ഻ഇ഻ഇ഻ഇ഻ഇ഻ഇ഻

Later that same day, Nathan once again sought out Billy, and after asking all around the farm, finally found him sitting with his back to a tree on the riverbank, gazing out at the broad stream rolling by.

"Hello, Billy."

"Captain. You have become good at tracking me ... I must be more careful from now on," he said, and smiled with his eyes.

Nathan chuckled, "Oh, I'm sure if you didn't want to be found, I could never do it. Billy ... I have another mission for you ..."

"Yes, Captain," he answered, sitting up a little straighter and becoming more attentive.

"Yes ... I want you to track down General Jackson's army once again. But this time not just to report back on their position ..."

Nathan reached into his pocket and pulled out what appeared to be a letter, sealed with a blob of red wax—the familiar mountain-like MM stamp—for Mountain Meadows—clearly visible. "This time only to sneak a letter into their mail bags so that it might be delivered to Richmond.

"But before I ask this of you ... I want you to know ... that I am reticent about doing so ... not because I think you incapable or have any doubts about your ability to perform the mission. Rather, I feel it is important that you know ... this message is *not* critical to the Union, nor to the war, nor to the new state. Not even to the safety of this farm, nor for the benefit of its inhabitants. This mission is *only* important to me. The only thing contained in this letter ... is my very beating heart."

Billy tilted his head and looked toward the sky a moment, then looked at the Captain and nodded. "Show me on your map where Jackson was last seen and where you think he is going next," was his only answer.

As they walked back toward the farmhouse to have a look at the map, Nathan said, "I suppose Mr. Volkov will insist on going with you again?"

"Yes, Captain. And I doubt you and I together are strong enough to stop him if he wants to go."

"True ... nor foolish enough to try!" Nathan said, and they shared a smile.

❧❧❧❧❧❧❧❧❧

Monday, June 2, 1862 – near Lewisburg, Virginia:

"General ... do you really mean to interrogate me? *Now?*" Evelyn asked. I've just lost my husband—killed trying to escape from those ... *horrible* ... Yankees. An officer and Southern gentleman ought to ... ought to ... have better manners," Evelyn choked out the words, scowling angrily even as she sobbed and

307

wiped away tears with a handkerchief. And for once she wasn't just putting on an act—she was venting the anger, frustration, and gut-wrenching grief she was genuinely feeling over the senseless killing of Nigel.

"Miss Eve … I don't mean to be … *indelicate* … in your hour of grief, but there are certain things I simply *must* know," he answered coolly.

Confederate General Henry Heth was tall, lean and handsome, with dark hair and mustache—somewhat reminiscent of Nathan, she decided, though with a more severe, stern look. She wondered if the man had seen so much death and loss recently that it no longer had any effect on him and it was no longer able to touch his emotions. She prayed she never came to such a pass.

"I've never heard of your husband, *Assistant Secretary of State Nigel Smith*, Miss Eve, and I never saw him before, during all the time we were stationed in Lewisburg. You must forgive me if I'm a little confused about who he is, why he is here, and why *you* are here," he said, continuing to show the same complete lack of sympathy he'd displayed ever since his soldiers had brought her to his "command office"—a room in the Caldwell Place, a roadside inn that she'd visited a few times with Nathan on the way home from church when she was staying at Mountain Meadows.

"I believe *I* can answer that, General," a man said, stepping into the room unannounced. He was tall, lean, middle-aged, and neatly groomed, wearing a fine, dark suit and matching bowler style hat. And his was a face Evelyn recognized immediately and knew well—*Joseph!*

But she said nothing and had to resist a very strong instinct to jump to her feet and embrace him right there on the spot. The last time she'd seen him was on the wharf in Richmond, surrounded by rebel soldiers. And until this very moment she hadn't known if he yet lived or had been killed in the fight. She was gratified to see he looked as healthy and vigorous as ever.

"And … just who might *you* be?" the General asked, not bothering to get up from his chair to greet the stranger.

At that moment a slightly overweight sergeant poked his head in at the door, and said, "Sorry sir ... I told him you were busy but ... somehow he slipped past me, sir."

But the General just waved the back of his hand at the sergeant, and said, "Never mind that, Sergeant ... it's all right. I'd like to get to the bottom of this matter, and it seems this gentleman may be of assistance in that regard. You may go now."

"Yes, sir. Thank you, sir!" the sergeant said, saluted, and disappeared back into the hallway.

Joseph removed his hat, stepped into the room and said, "I am Joseph Miller, assistant to the Secretary of War, here from Richmond, having been sent out to meet with Mr. Smith. The reason you had not seen him in Lewisburg is that he was not *in* Lewisburg during your time there. Some months ago he was tasked with working his way down the Kanawha Valley, meeting with citizens there who are loyal to our cause—taking the pulse, as it were, of their support for a general offensive in that direction should we deem it tenable. The secretary wanted to explore the possibility that a relatively small force could launch an attack and that it might stimulate an uprising that would serve as a force multiplier of sorts.

"Unfortunately, your recent little ... *setback* ... in Lewisburg disrupted our plans to meet, and I was stuck on *this* side of the river, while Mr. Smith became stuck on the other."

"All right then, but why bring his wife along? And why not tell me about this matter?"

"You weren't told because it was none of your concern, General, to put it bluntly. And Miss Eve could not tell you as she was sworn to secrecy with instructions only to report to the secretary on the matter. Clearly plans for a potential offensive are not to be discussed willy-nilly, even with high-ranking officers such as yourself. I am only obliged to do so now in order to straighten out this unfortunate matter of Mr. Smith's untimely demise, and with the trust that you will share it with no one else.

"As for Miss Eve's presence, I should think it would be obvious, sir; Mr. Smith needed to appear innocuous and beyond suspicion. What better way than to have one's wife along. But

Miss Eve is also an aid to him in her own right—very knowledgeable and resourceful—a great help to her husband in his various dealings.

"And … I believe, if I'm not mistaken, you will find among his papers, documents—forged of course—proving him to be in the employ of the Union War Department, allowing him to get past their roadblocks and into their garrisoned towns."

"Ah … that explains it … I must confess I was baffled as to why he carried such papers. Now it all makes more sense. Hmm … I am sorry about what happened to him. And my apologies to you, Miss Eve, and my condolences on your loss."

"Thank you … apology accepted," she said, still snuffling, and not trusting herself to say more.

"Thank you for being understanding, Miss Eve. Mr. Miller, thank you for straightening out this matter. And unless there's something more I can do for you …"

"No, but I thank you, General. I shall … see to the arrangements for transporting Mr. Smith's remains back to Richmond."

"Very good, sir. I thank you for that as well, and for trusting me with your explanation concerning this affair. I shall keep the matter strictly confidential, even as its gravity demands."

"Excellent, General—very gratified to hear it. Have a good night, sir."

As they left the general's office and walked down the hallway, Evelyn suddenly felt the full impact of the stressful events of the day, an exhaustion that went to the bone. Joseph must have sensed it, taking her arm to steady her, for which she was grateful.

Fortunately, she didn't have far to go as Joseph had rented a small room at the inn earlier in the day, to start working on his own plan for getting across the river. He'd intended to wait for them in Lewisburg, but when he'd arrived the battle was already over and the bridge burned. He'd dressed in his vagabond disguise and loitered around the neighborhood on the east side of the river, hoping some opportunity presented itself, or some news arrived from the Employer. But today he'd decided to try a different approach, perhaps enlisting the aid of Confederate soldiers, so had switched to his government official attire and checked himself into the Caldwell Place.

As soon as they entered his room and closed the door Evelyn turned and embraced him, hugging him tightly, and sobbing. He held her gently for a long time, allowing her the time she needed to let her emotions flow.

Eventually she pulled away, turned, and sat in the one chair in the room. Joseph moved over and sat on the bed facing her.

"I was heartbroken to learn about Nigel," Joseph said, "from all accounts he was a fine young man."

"Yes … yes, he was—very capable, brave, and loyal …" Evelyn added, once again becoming choked up. "And … and I can't believe our own men—Union soldiers—killed him! It's … just too horrible to think about."

"Well … I know it doesn't help, but they had no way of knowing you two were on their side. Given you appeared to be running away—escaping to the enemy side—it was natural to assume you were enemy spies. It has been a problem in war from the beginning of time—what is now often termed 'friendly fire.' Very tragic and sad, but unavoidable, I'm afraid."

Evelyn nodded and gazed down at her feet, suddenly feeling guilty about shooting Nigel's pistol at the Union soldiers in her frustration and rage. She now prayed she hadn't hit anyone—and given the distance, her state of mind, and the severe rocking of the boat, she thought it most likely she'd not even come close.

Joseph sadly shook his head, "I dread having to tell Jonathan that his beloved young cousin is dead …"

"No, Joseph … that responsibility isn't on you … Nigel died trying to help me … to help me get home. I should be the one to tell him."

Joseph nodded, but said, "I'll agree to that … *if* … you'll agree not to make his death your responsibility. Don't forget Jonathan recruited him to help you, and everything he did from that point forward was of his own volition, and nothing you asked of him. Besides, it isn't fair to him to say he died just trying to help you … rather we should say he died for a bigger cause—that of preserving the Union, and ultimately putting an end to slavery."

She sighed heavily, then nodded, "You're right, of course—as usual."

She was quiet and thoughtful for a long moment, before suddenly looking up and saying, "Oh my dear God, Joseph! With all that's happened I have been remiss in not saying how terribly happy I am to see you again! And that you are looking so well! Until just a few moments ago I'd had no news of you whatever, and didn't even know if you yet lived or were dead.

"Please … before saying anything more, you must tell me what happened back there on the wharf in Richmond after I left."

He smiled, and chuckled. "Well … it actually worked out better than expected—as well as it possibly could have, actually, now that I think back on it.

"Fortunately for me, I was taller with a better reach and was also a more practiced, experienced boxer than the sergeant. He was, however, younger, stronger, and more vigorous. It made for a very even match, for which I was grateful, as it prolonged the bout making your escape all the more likely.

"And, as one might expect, the young soldiers gathered around greatly enjoyed the entertainment, and started a betting pool as to which of us would prevail, further distracting them from your getaway.

"After several minutes of pounding on each other, which seemed more like hours to us two taking the punishment, we both ended up sitting on the ground, gasping for air, and rubbing our sore limbs. I confessed I'd been known to become belligerent when I'd had too much liquor and likely had been in the wrong on this occasion. Then he laughed and admitted he had, in fact, been ogling my wife, but could hardly be blamed on account of her good looks.

"Just then one of the soldiers came trotting up to report that the fishing boat was gone. The sergeant gave me a serious look and for a moment I thought my number was up. But then he shrugged and said it was a decrepit old tub and likely the rats had chewed through the tie lines, and it had just drifted away. He looked back at me, stood up, tipped his hat and wished me a good evening."

The next morning at first light Evelyn and Joseph were dressed and ready to depart from the Caldwell Place after a less than restful night. Joseph had given up his room to Evelyn and had spent the night sleeping in a chair in the common room, so was aching and stiff. Evelyn, being exhausted, had fallen asleep quickly, but had suffered terrible dreams of death and drowning, so awoke in the morning feeling worn and groggy.

They headed east along the main road in an open wagon drawn by a single mule—a mode of transportation Joseph had requisitioned from the army, using his leverage as a war department government official. Nigel's body lay in the back of the wagon, wrapped up in a blanket, as there had been no time, materials, or carpenter available to fashion a proper casket.

"We'll not be able to take him all the way back to Richmond," Joseph said. "If we bring his body back to Richmond now, Jonathan will feel obligated to take charge of the arrangements, and that will put him at risk of being tied to what just happened here, and that must be avoided. At some point they may discover we were not who we claimed to be, and Jonathan must not have any association with that. Also, we're going to be traveling over some rough country backroads on the way back, so we'll not be able to bring the wagon, and will have to ride."

"Backroads? Why?" she asked.

"The railroad from Covington to Richmond is no longer available, as the Union now controls much of the territory it traverses. And right now northern Virginia and the peninsula are embroiled in warfare, making the main road east from here potentially very problematic for civilian travel. Fortunately there is currently no fighting south of Richmond, so if we take the more rugged, southerly route through the mountains we will avoid the conflict altogether. Ironically, it will be the very same route Mr. Chambers and company took when he escaped from Richmond just after the secession. Though we'll not be chased by hooligans trying to shoot us, thankfully," he smiled.

"Oh! Well, that all makes sense I suppose. Though I haven't any clothes suitable for riding a horse."

"Well, at the risk of being immodest, I suggest you simply cut a seam up the front and back of your skirts so you can ride astraddle the horse. Or … you can just ride *sidesaddle* …" he grinned at the scowl she gave him in return for *that* suggestion.

"Yes … cutting the skirt will work, she said. "I can even stitch them back together around my legs like a kind of very loose-fitting britches. Shouldn't show much even when I'm walking around."

"Perfect. Anyway, as I was implying," he continued, "we will need to find a place to bury Nigel where we can find him again — someplace off the beaten path, but easily mapped or identified later so that his body may be disinterred and returned to the family for a proper burial when circumstances allow."

Evelyn was quiet and thoughtful for a moment, then said, "I know the proper place …"

❞❞❞❞

Two hours later, Evelyn was slowly walking up the stairs of the Big House at Mountain Meadows, Joseph following respectfully behind. She paused at the top of the stairs and gazed out across the fields of the farm, now weedy and unkempt looking. She sighed, turned, and walked to the front door.

She tested the doorknob, and couldn't decide if she should be surprised or not that it was unlocked. She opened the door, and walked in.

She slowly walked around the house, from room to room, gazing at the walls and the ceiling. The memories came flooding back in a rush, and she suddenly felt light-headed. She thought she heard the echo of a far distant voice muttering, *Who am I?* But she ignored it and continued on. Everything looked just the same, only … empty. The house was still the same: solid, elegant … *magnificent*, just as she'd remembered. But it was entirely empty. Not a single stick of furniture, picture on the wall, book on a bookshelf, or drapery around a window. The house had been completely stripped of its furnishings, down to the last teacup.

Joseph came in behind her, gazed around, and whistled, "It's … quite impressive … beautiful, really."

But she gave him a sad look and said, "Not like it used to be … filled with life and love … now it is just … an empty house." She sighed.

After a few minutes she turned and walked back out the front door, Joseph following close behind. When she closed the door again, Joseph could see she had tears in her eyes. He looked away, allowing her to mourn what she had lost in her own way.

Then she said, "We will bury Nigel in the Chambers' family cemetery, just over there next to the duck pond. I believe Nathan would approve … even should it prove to be the permanent location for Nigel."

There was a simple dirt road leading to the cemetery, purposely built for just such an occasion, and after they brought the wagon over, Joseph pulled out a shovel—also requisitioned from the Confederate Army—and began to dig. When he was about a third of the way done, he paused to rest and have a drink from a canteen he had in his pack. Evelyn grabbed the shovel and hopped down into the hole.

"What are you doing?" he asked.

She snorted a laugh, "I know how to use a shovel, Joseph—just one of the many practical things my Daddy taught me." She proceeded to dig until the hole was nearly complete, and her hands were sore and blistered. She found it a good release for her pent-up emotions, and didn't notice the pain in her hands until after she had paused for a rest.

Joseph took over and finished digging, then together they lifted Nigel in, still wrapped in the blanket, and took turns filling the dirt back in. Neither of them could think of the proper Bible words for a burial, so they decided it wasn't necessary since it would likely be a temporary location anyway. Whenever Nigel was re-interred, a preacher could say the proper words.

When they were finished, Evelyn walked over to the pond and dipped her hands in the cool water to ease the burn of the blisters. Joseph followed her and splashed some water on his face, which had become drenched in sweat and caked in dust from his exertions.

Then Evelyn became quiet and stood gazing off across the pond with a thoughtful look. Joseph noticed her eyes were watery, and guessing she was thinking of Nigel, turned away and left her to grieve in silence.

Why? she thought. *Why did he have to die ... for me? It's so unfair ... And why did he have to go and fall in love with me? Did I unintentionally do something to lead him on, though I meant not to? With Jubal I knew what I was doing, playing him ... but Nigel? Why?*

She was thoughtful for a moment, then turned and gazed at Joseph, who was discreetly looking the other way. *And what about you, Joseph? I even kissed you once, though it was clearly not for romantic reasons. Are you going to suddenly fall in love with me, and throw your life away on my behalf, like the others?*

But to this question, she had no answer.

"Joseph ... I think we should go now," she said.

He turned and gave her a serious look, as if debating with himself whether or not to say something that might ease her pain. But finally he just nodded and said, "Yes ... let's do."

☙☙☙☙☙☙

Saturday, June 7, 1862 – near Harrisonburg, Virginia:

Stan waited anxiously for Billy's return, lying flat on his belly on top of a low rise overlooking the rebel camp below, gazing at it through the Captain's brass spyglass. A loaded rifle lay next to him, and four revolvers were strapped to his hips and up under his shoulders. At the first sight or sound of a disturbance below he was ready to rush to Billy's aid, guns blazing.

But it had been completely quiet since Billy's departure a half-hour earlier. And try as he might, Stan already knew he would never be able to see Billy through the spyglass–the man was just too good at moving unseen. Stan had not even argued when Billy had said he would do this part alone, knowing he could never match the Tonkawa Indian when it came to stealth.

It had taken all his skills to get this far, having to first cross the Union lines of General Fremont's force just north of the town of Harrisonburg, and then slipping past the outer ring of scouts for General Jackson's army a few miles south of town. They had witnessed a battle inside the town the day before, which seemed to have been won by the rebels, though afterward they moved off to the south. As another engagement seemed imminent, both armies were on high alert.

But knowing it made sense for Billy to go it alone from this point didn't make the waiting any easier, and he suppressed the urge to groan in his impatience. He continued to reconnoiter the camp, watching the slow movement of the sentries in the glow of campfires and torches as they made their rounds.

He heard movement behind him and whirled around, drawing a pistol and cocking the hammer. But he sighed in relief, lowered the hammer and re-holstered the pistol—Billy at last.

"Successful mission?" Stan whispered, as Billy settled in beside him on the ground.

"Yes … though I couldn't tell which wagon is carrying mail, I placed the letter where it will be easily found, so hopefully one of the soldiers will mail it. Any sign of movement?"

"No … all is still. Was good job, Billy … like always."

Billy just shrugged, and said, "Let's go."

In a heartbeat they were on their feet, moving down the slope and quietly off through the trees toward where they'd stashed their horses and gear.

⁕⁕⁕⁕⁕⁕⁕⁕⁕⁕

Monday, June 8, 1862 – Cross Keys, Virginia:

The air was thick with gun smoke, making it almost painful to breathe for the four young Confederate soldiers hunkered down behind the trunk of a fallen tree. Union artillery shells screamed by overhead, exploding only a few dozen yards beyond their position, and seemingly coming closer every minute.

Confederate artillery, farther back behind a ridgeline, dueled against the federals, their own high explosive shells detonating with a distant *pop*, a quarter mile or so away, across the narrow valley over toward the Union lines.

Jeremiah Taylor glanced back just in time to see the latest Union high-explosive shell hit just under what appeared to be a supply wagon, about fifty yards away, toppling it over, and setting it on fire.

His stomach growled for the hundredth time today, reminding him he'd had nothing to eat since yesterday, and skimpy, near-starvation rations for as many days as he could remember before that. He pictured the wagon full of food, and the thought of that priceless sustenance going up in flames made him groan out loud.

"What is it, Jer?" the young man lying next to him, Isaac Green, asked.

"They done hit a supply wagon. I'm fixin' to go see if it has any food in it 'fore it all burns up."

"No … it's too dangerous just now, Jer. Wait 'til this shelling stops or moves on."

"By then it'll be burnt up," Jeremiah argued, then jumped up and sprinted toward the wagon, doing his best to keep his head down as he ran. He'd left his rifle back with his mates, figuring that'd let him run faster, and carry more rations if he found any.

He made it about halfway to the wagon before another incoming shell burst, its noise almost deafening. But it was further back, beyond the fallen wagon, and all he felt from it was a sudden short gust of wind, so he continued on. When he got to the wagon, he went straight to the back so he could check the contents. Since the shell had hit just under the wagon, the wood planking and wheels were afire, but the canvas top and its contents were still intact. Thankfully there'd been no mules or horses attached to it when it was hit—he was softhearted when it came to animals, and cringed at the thought of seeing them killed in their traces, or even worse, badly mangled but still alive.

He reached inside the tailgate and started pulling out sacks that were now all piled onto the side that'd tipped onto the ground. He pulled them open, dumping them onto the ground one by one. But to his dismay, he found no food. The first carried only woolen blankets. The other bags were just as disappointing, overcoats, and more woolen blankets—useless in the current hot weather.

He gazed back down the road and for the first time noticed there were no other wagons in the immediate area—apparently already hauled off to get their precious cargo out of harm's way. Likely the teamsters had realized the contents of this one were basically useless and had simply abandoned it.

He turned and looked back toward where he'd left his fellows, and could see Isaac staring back in his direction, waving for him to return. He braced himself for the sprint back, but happened to glance down and saw a letter laying on the dusty ground. It had apparently been in amongst the bags he'd pulled from the wagon. He saw it was addressed to a man in Richmond … his own hometown …. So, he leaned down and snatched up the letter, stuffing it into his trouser pocket before taking off at a run. But he'd gone only a dozen yards when another shell burst, this one directly overhead. Shrapnel tore through his body, and he fell—utter darkness mercifully embracing him before he ever felt any pain.

ഇ

Lieutenant Jubal Collins led a rifle company of the Twenty-Seventh Virginia up a rutted, dusty dirt lane toward where Confederate command was gathering men for a counterattack against the approaching federals. The company was moving at a trot, not wanting to be late for the attack and getting left behind.

They passed a burned-out wagon, and then a short distance farther Jubal saw a man lying face down in the road. He stopped and knelt to check if the man was still alive, but immediately realized that was impossible; his head had been nearly split in two by shrapnel from a high explosive shell.

As he stood, he noticed the corner of an envelope sticking out of the man's pants pocket and it instantly brought to mind his precious letters to Evelyn. He leaned back down and grabbed the letter. He saw it was addressed to a man in Richmond and it was sealed in red wax with the symbol of a mountain on the stamp. A letter to the man's father most likely … possibly the last words his kin folk would ever hear from him. Jubal stuffed the letter inside his shirt, then signaled the men to resume their double-quick march.

ℰᏏᏬᏇᎦᏇᎦᏏᏬᏇᎦᏏᏬᏇᎦᏏᏬᏇᎦᏏᏬᏇᎦ

Thursday, June 12, 1862 – Richmond, Virginia:

It had been a hot, dusty, tiresome week and more in the saddle from Mountain Meadows Farm to Richmond, winding through the backcountry mountain roads, and Evelyn was feeling it in her bones, and in her backside. She was ready to get home, take a hot bath, and sleep in her own bed for the first time since the end of March—three and a half months earlier! But she knew before she could rest she would have to perform the duty she'd been dreading the whole way home; she would have to stop by the Hughes' house and give them the painful news about Nigel.

She and Joseph had agreed to split up a few miles short of town to avoid being seen riding together. She arrived at the Hughes' house alone. Being dirty and crudely dressed, and entirely undignified—riding astraddle a horse with her modified skirts—she just couldn't picture riding up to the grand front door, knocking, then walking in through the elegant, marbled foyer. So, she went around back to the alleyway, tied her horse in the small stable they kept there, and slipped in through the back door.

She was met inside by their elderly black freeman butler Sam who, if he was surprised to see her, didn't show it. Joseph had sent a telegram from the hotel at White Sulphur Springs, just a few miles beyond Mountain Meadows, so the Hughes had a reasonably good idea of when she would arrive.

Nonetheless, Jonathan and Angeline greeted her with great enthusiasm and affection—so much so that Evelyn was soon crying like a baby, which didn't help when it came time to tell them about what had happened to Nigel.

Angeline cried along with Evelyn when she'd finished her tale, but Jonathan took it stoically, though watery eyed, saying only, "He was a good man ... and proved himself magnificently capable and heroic. I shall miss him dearly."

320

And as much as they were eager to hear the whole story of Evelyn's adventures since departing Richmond on the fishing boat down the James, she had begun to wilt in her chair. They bundled her into a carriage and had one of their drivers take her home. She promised to come back in a day or two when she was rested to tell the whole tale and to more properly celebrate her homecoming with them.

When she finally entered her own front door and closed it behind her, she stood in the entryway and gazed about at the dark and quiet house for a long moment. Then she let out a great sigh.

She had finally made it home … but in that moment she realized it was an entirely empty house that perfectly reflected her entirely empty life. She went up the stairs to her bedroom, stripped off her hat and shoes, lay down on her bed, and cried herself to sleep.

跼迋

The next morning she was feeling much refreshed, impressed with how much better she'd slept being in her own bed in her own home. She dressed, ate a quick breakfast of what little food she had left in her travel pack, then went to the mirror see what could be done about her hair.

Every chance she'd had since meeting up with Joseph, she'd washed it thoroughly with soap and water, trying to get the black dye out and the proper color back in, before arriving in Richmond. She knew she'd have enough explaining to do concerning her long absence without having to explain the black hair as well. And though Nigel had said it would only last a couple of weeks, it had proven stubbornly resistant to her efforts. It was now much improved, but was still a noticeably darker shade of blonde.

She pinned it up, put a hat on over it, and looked herself over in the mirror. She decided it was not too noticeable, and regardless, it would have to do.

Her first stop after leaving the house was the post office to collect three months' worth of mail. When she asked the postmaster for her mail, he frowned at her, and came out carrying a box which he set down heavily on the counter with a *thump*.

She carried the box outside and sat on the steps, thumbing through the letters to see what had arrived. Happily anything that required her to pay out money had already been taken care of by Jonathan, so she had no fear of letters from angry vendors.

But her heart sank when she got to the bottom of the pile and there was no letter from Nathan.

And she cringed when she saw the stack of letters from Jubal. *The poor dear man … out there fighting all this time and never a letter from me. He must be just devastated and thinking I have entirely abandoned him … which reminds me, I need to go see Angeline right away and ask her what story she has made up to explain my long absence … that should be a good one.* She smiled at the thought, wondering if she'd been recovering from the bubonic plague, or maybe had been kidnapped by pirates or something!

She quickly opened and read through Jubal's letters, relieved in the third or fourth letter to read that none of the soldiers had been receiving any letters on account of all the marching around they'd been doing for General Jackson—the mail service just couldn't keep up with them. At one point Jubal actually apologized for not being able to read any of the letters he was sure she'd been sending! She smiled and shook her head at the irony of *that* one.

But when she read the last letter, her breath caught upon reading the last paragraph, and she jumped up, rushing off to see Jonathan and Angeline straightaway.

June 7, 1862
Harrisonburg, Va.

Dear Evelyn,

I've lost track of how many miles we've marched and how many battles we've fought since this Shenandoah Valley campaign began. And we have won nearly every fight, despite being outnumbered pert-near every time.

Yesterday we fought against forces of Yankee Colonel Kane and his Pennsylvanians in a town called

When Evelyn met with Angeline a short time later, she shared
Jubal's letter with her, confessed to hiding the correspondence,
and apologized for not telling her about it earlier. But Angeline
was understanding and thanked her for the information. That
Jackson would soon be marching south was another critical piece
of information that needed to be forwarded to the Union War
Department straightaway, even with General McClellan no
longer to be trusted.

And Evelyn felt great relief when she asked Angeline about
Jackson's attack on Harpers Ferry and received only a blank look
in response. Apparently, Jackson had turned away from Harpers
Ferry at the last moment for unknown reasons, and there had been
no battle after all. So for the moment at least, Nathan and his men
were safe, for which she felt thankful.

Then Angeline shared with Evelyn the cover story she had
invented and spread around town concerning Evelyn's long
absence.

According to Angeline's story, Evelyn had run out of slaves to train for her business, slaves being in such high demand in support of the army's war efforts. And so she had traveled to Goldsboro, North Carolina where she'd heard a wealthy, aristocratic family had tragically lost their master and his two sons in the war, and were forced to sell their farm and all its slaves at auction—including several experienced house servants. But while she was on her way to Goldsboro by train, the Union Army under General Burnside had advanced farther than anticipated and cut the rail line, forcing her to debark and seek shelter while the war raged. And then the yellow fever swept through the small town she was in and—though she thankfully never took ill—she helped out in the hospital until the scourge relented. After that she was forced to make her way back to Virginia cross country, as the train service was now disrupted. She'd eventually made it back to Richmond after her long ordeal, but sadly had been unable to acquire the slaves she'd originally sought. So, at some future date, she might be forced to undertake another such mission.

Evelyn shook her head in amazement, "That's a good one, Angeline—very, very good. So good, even *I* would believe it, and I know better!" she said, and they shared a laugh.

—————

The next day, Evelyn went to see her friend Belinda for the first time since returning, but she had sent a message earlier letting her know she was back in town, so her visit wouldn't be a total shock. After a tearful and joyous reunion at Belinda's house, they put their hats on and walked down the street to where Lydia Johnston was now staying. In Evelyn's absence, Belinda and Lydia had become friends on account of the connection of their husbands, Belinda's Oliver being a major on the staff of Lydia's husband, Major General Joe Johnston.

But Evelyn had learned General Johnston had been wounded in the peninsula campaign at a place called "Seven Pines," and was now recuperating at a friend's house in downtown Richmond where Lydia was now staying with him.

After yet another happy reunion, with Lydia this time, Evelyn and Belinda were ushered into the library of the house, where General Johnston sat in a chair, dressed in a robe and house shoes, reading a page of what appeared to be a stack of letters on the table next to him. He looked pale, and in ill health, but Evelyn assumed it was a good sign that he was out of bed and sitting already, given the reported seriousness of his injuries.

"Joseph, darling … I thought you could use a little company. No, no … don't you dare try to rise, you ridiculous thing!" she scolded teasingly when the general set down the paper he was reading and braced his arms for the task of rising. But then he relaxed, and smiled thinly at his wife's reprimand, settling back into his chair.

"Good afternoon, ladies … a pleasure to have you," he said.

"Joseph, you remember Major Boyd's wife, Belinda of course," Lydia said, and Belinda curtsied right on cue.

"Yes, yes, of course, of course … so good to see you again, Miss Belinda. Come in, come in …"

"And this is the wonderful young lady Evelyn I've told you so much about … you remember … she's the one who lent me Julia to help run the household while you were away?"

"Oh! Oh, yes … that was wonderfully kind of you Miss Evelyn. Thank you so much for looking after my Lid while I was out fighting the wars." He smiled and seemed genuinely happy for the interruption, though Evelyn thought there was a good deal of pain reflected in his countenance as well.

"It has been my great pleasure to get to know your wonderful wife, General … and if I was able to make her stay here in Richmond more comfortable and less burdensome, then I am honored to have been of service," Evelyn said, and also curtsied. "And may I also say what an honor it is to meet you, sir. I have heard no end of stories concerning your personal heroics, not to mention your brilliant leadership of our armies."

He nodded, but waved off the compliments with a wan smile.

"I was so saddened when I heard you'd been wounded," she added, "so it has lightened my heart to see you up out of your bed, sir." She looked at Lydia, "That must be a very good sign of his speedy recovery, is it not Lydia?"

"Yes, yes, the doctors say he is made of very stern stuff ... which I knew already, though I also know how soft he is on the inside ..."

Johnston rolled his eyes and said, "Only soft toward you dear ... some other folks ... *pah!* Not so much."

"Now dear ... don't get started, you're like to burst your stitches when you get yourself all worked up over what's going on."

"Hmph ... and why shouldn't I get worked up ... General Lee's reckless tactics are decimating our troop reserves! He acts like Confederate soldiers grow on trees!"

"Oh!" Evelyn said, "I was under the impression General Lee was being quite effective in driving back the Yankees. Was I ... misunderstanding the current state of affairs?"

Evelyn's interest was now piqued—was General Johnston really going to divulge Confederate war strategy right to her face? What a rare opportunity to gain valuable information. And that there might be a rift at the very top levels of command was also an interesting development.

"Well ... no ... you weren't misunderstanding," he answered, suddenly looking glum and pouty, "it's just ... I've come to realize McClellan is so unbelievably cautious that any decent commander could beat him, despite his overwhelming numbers. And there's no need to throw our troops at him as if there were no tomorrow. Those young men's lives are worth more than that!"

"Oh ... I see ... that doesn't sound so very commendable. But I'm also surprised to hear you speak of General McClellan in that manner ... from what I'd been reading in the papers, he sounded like the very scourge of the North—the 'young Napoleon,' I believe the Yankees have been calling him."

"*Pah!*" Johnston snorted, "Only George McClellan could have failed to conquer Richmond with the golden opportunity we gave him. While we scrambled to get our defenses organized, he waited, and he dithered, and now he has totally lost the initiative and is on the retreat. Do you know he took an entire *month* to take

Yorktown—and then by *siege?!* When he had us outnumbered nearly ten to one?!"

He shook his head, "Unbelievable … But now everyone thinks Lee is the hero, and I'm all but forgotten."

"Oh, that's not *true* dear!" Lydia said, "As soon as you're back on your feet, I'm sure Jefferson will put you right back in command of the armies."

Johnston snorted derisively, "Jeff Davis! What a fool he's turned out to be. We used to be friends … *good* friends … but no more!"

"*Joseph!*" Lydia scolded.

"No, no, it's true," he argued, "He's stabbed me in the back one too many times. No, Lee's his man now … thinks he walks on water … there's no going back. No … when I'm well they'll give me a desk job, or else ship me off to Texas or somewhere to get me out of their hair."

There was an embarrassing and awkward silence after this, as no one could think of anything to say that might mollify the general. Lydia changed the subject and shortly thereafter made the proper excuses, and the ladies departed the room.

When they were back at the door, Lydia said, "I apologize for that … he's been in an ill humor since he was wounded, and who can blame him. It's just so very sad … all his sacrifice and service just to be tossed aside because he was injured."

"Yes … it doesn't seem fair," Evelyn answered. "But perhaps when he's feeling better, he can … patch up his friendship with the president …?"

But Lydia frowned and shook her head, "You know … that's what I thought too … but last week when I went to visit Varina Davis I was shocked at how cold she was toward me after we've been such good friends for years. And she even hinted at Joseph not performing up to expectations in his command! Well, as you can imagine that didn't sit well with me, and I fear I may have reacted a bit too strongly."

She shook her head sadly, "Now I'm afraid the rift between the men has spread to us ladies as well … when I departed, she made it clear I was no longer welcome in her home."

"*Oh dear!*" Evelyn said, genuinely shocked and saddened to hear this news.

"Yes … I'm afraid it's true," Lydia said, looking downcast. But then she looked up at Evelyn and Belinda and smiled brightly, "but we shall still be friends, and for that I am most grateful."

"Of course, of course, Lydia," Evelyn answered, and Belinda nodded her agreement.

But as she walked down the stairs, and toward their waiting carriage Evelyn felt a growing sadness. Despite the odd circumstances, Evelyn had developed a genuine liking for Lydia—much more so than for the enigmatic Varina Davis—and considered her a good friend. But now … she would be forced to break off that friendship; Varina Davis was just too important in her espionage plans to risk offending.

છલૠિઝલૠિઝલૠિઝલૠ

The day after her visit with Lydia Johnston, Evelyn received a message delivered by one of Angeline's couriers, summoning her for another meeting as soon as possible. When she arrived an hour later, she detected a much more serious tone in Angeline's greeting than in the last two meetings.

"Thank you for coming to see me so promptly today, Evelyn."

"Of course, Angeline. It's always my pleasure to meet with you, anytime you wish."

Angeline nodded and smiled. But then her expression turned serious.

"My dear … I'm going to get right to the unpleasantries. But before I do, let me preface it by saying nobody has died; it's not *that* kind of bad news."

"Thank the Lord for that."

"Indeed … Evelyn, you know I greatly dislike telling you hurtful news; but we've agreed from the beginning … and recently renewed our promise … not to keep any secrets from each other."

"Yes … of course, Angeline," she answered, but felt a growing sense of dread about where this conversation was heading.

"Then please know I'd especially rather not tell you what I am about to tell you. I even considered not doing so, despite our agreement. But ... other people know of this ... *incident*, and eventually word might get back to you. And by then who knows what the story might have grown into. Better to hear the truth straight from me and be done with it.

"I want you to know I have received this information from an impeccable source who witnessed the events in person; so, I have no doubts about its authenticity."

Evelyn had a sinking feeling about where this was going and could feel a knot of anxiety forming in her stomach. She nodded, but said nothing, not sure her voice would cooperate anyway.

"Evelyn, our people have been tracking a particularly elusive and productive Confederate spy for some months now. This spy had been personally responsible for providing vital intelligence on Union defenses to General Stonewall Jackson even as he was planning his attacks throughout the Shenandoah Valley. It is not too great an exaggeration to say this spy was responsible, to a great degree, for Jackson's seemingly unstoppable string of successful raids this spring. But fortunately, this nefarious activity has come to an end—largely thanks to Nathan Chambers."

"Nathan? Has he been hurt? Did this spy harm him?"

"Mr. Chambers is fine, as far as I know—at least he was at the time of the incident. But he *was* instrumental in uncovering the espionage and having the enemy's infiltrator arrested at Harpers Ferry. This individual is now safely tucked away somewhere in a Northern prison, there to sit out the rest of the conflict, thank God."

Evelyn nodded, having a pretty good idea which prison *that* was. "Well ... that all sounds to the good. What is the *bad* news, then?"

Angeline didn't immediately respond but stood and paced across the library toward the window. She pulled back the drapery, stood and gazed outside a moment before turning back toward Evelyn.

"Evelyn, this spy was a young woman."

"Oh!"

"And … Mr. Chambers discovered her traitorous business and identity … after spending the night with her in Harpers Ferry."

Evelyn suffered a sudden shock, like a kick in the stomach. She felt tears forming, and her throat constricting, "He … *slept* with her?" she managed in barely a whisper.

"Yes … I'm afraid so."

Evelyn looked away, no longer meeting eyes with the other woman.

Angeline moved her chair closer to Evelyn and sat, reaching across to clasp her hands. "My dear, I know this is hard, but please try not to take it too … personally."

"Not take it *personally?* How can you say that?! How can one not?"

"Well … I don't say this to excuse the man's behavior, but … such liaisons don't mean as much to a man as they would to a woman. Believe it or not, it doesn't mean he loves you any less. 'The spirit is willing, but the flesh is weak,' Jesus said. And truer words were never spoken, I think, especially when it comes to young men."

But Evelyn continued to shake her head and fight back the tears. So, Angeline tried a different tack.

"Think of it this way, dear. Leaving moral considerations aside, a physical union of this kind must mean more to a woman for pure biological reasons, if nothing else. If a man sleeps with a woman, and rides away, never to see her again, there are no physical ramifications for him. He is guaranteed to be exactly the same before as after—discounting certain unmentionable diseases, which are always possible.

"But a woman must always consider the possibility of getting with child. Any time she beds a man, at least in the back of her mind she must consider, 'am I willing to have this man's baby? And if he's honorable, to marry him? And if he's not honorable, to raise a child all alone … a child out of wedlock, who will always be despised for it, along with the mother?'

"The possible consequences are such that a woman must be more … *choosy.* Whereas a man can be more casual and thoughtless about it."

Evelyn nodded her understanding but continued to wipe back the tears. "Thank you, Angeline," she sniffed, "for telling me the truth. And ... for trying to make me feel better about it. But ... I think I should go now."

"Of course, dear, of course. We will speak again another day, when there will hopefully be more pleasant matters to discuss."

🙰🙰🙰🙰🙰🙰🙰🙰🙰🙰

When Evelyn returned to her house she walked straight to her bedroom, closed the door, and threw herself on the bed, sobbing.

"The filthy trollop!" she said aloud, "Shameless whore! I'll ... I'll ... punch you bloody ... *damn you!*" She pounded her pillow, imagining it was the woman's face. "Sleeping with ... *my Nathan!* How dare you?!"

She planted her face in the pillow and sobbed again. For the first time in her twenty-one years of life she understood what gut-wrenching jealousy felt like. Evelyn had never slept with the man she loved because of their odd circumstances, despite a burning desire to. But now this ... *person* ... he didn't even know jumped into bed with him at the first sight. It wasn't ... *fair!* Her chest ached with the stinging, burning pain of it.

And then she thought of Nathan. *How could you? I thought you loved me. I thought we meant something ... something special to each other? How could you just ... sleep with that brazen ... hussy ... without a second thought? Ohhhh ... I hate you, Nathan ... I hate you!*

Then she cried long and hard, eventually falling asleep.

When she awoke in the morning, her head hurt from crying. She felt drained of emotion, and finally sober after the previous evening's emotional inebriation.

And with that sobriety came a cold, hard reckoning. *It's my own fault. Not the trollop's. Not Nathan's. Mine. All mine.*

I could have been with him dozens of times when we were at Mountain Meadows, but I chose not to. I thought it best to wait ... but then ... then ... "who-am-I" happened.

And then again at Harper's Ferry ... he practically begged me to spend the night with him and then return with him to Wheeling and marry him there. But I had to come back here ... back to ... what? An

331

empty house filled with pain and tears? Lying to and betraying people who believe I'm their friend? And a war that will never, ever end …

What a fool I've been. What did I expect?! What did I think was going to happen?! He's a young, strong, handsome, and virile man; women are drawn to him like a magnet. What did I think he was going to do? Behave as a priest the rest of the war?!

And then despite herself she chuckled. The mental image of Nathan Chambers dressed up in priestly robes, meekly walking around praying and doling out absolution, was just too amusing. The absurd thought helped break the spell of her despair.

She sat up from the bed and wiped the crust of dried tears from her eyes. She still felt blue and hurt, but knew she must deal with it and get on with her life. After all, there really was no other choice …

And despite all that'd happened, she knew she still loved him. *God help me, but I still do,* she thought, and sighed.

☙❦❧☙❦❧☙❦❧

Tuesday, July 1, 1862 – Malvern Hill, Virginia:

Union Brigadier General Fitz Porter took in a deep breath of satisfaction as he gazed across the battlefield from his vantage point atop Malvern Hill. Though it was now almost completely dark, the sun having set a half hour earlier, through his binoculars he could still make out the hunkered down Confederate lines in the flashes of shell bursts from his own artillery. The smoke from the ongoing Union artillery bombardment hung thick like a wreath around the crest of the hill, intermittently illuminated by the shell bursts.

And though he now knew the rebels were thoroughly beaten and would launch no further assaults this day, he'd ordered Colonel Hunt, his artillery officer, to continue shelling the enemy for another half hour just to put a punctuation mark on the stunning defeat he had just dealt them. He meant to send the rebels a chilling message—that the Union artillery was so powerful and so well stocked with powder and high explosive

332

shells it could afford to continue bombarding them long past the point where it could possibly be to any effect.

As he lowered the binoculars and gazed around at his own troops—standing by in good order, rank upon rank, rifles in hand, faces turned toward the enemy—his heart soared. This day he had personally orchestrated a nearly picture-perfect victory. The kind all generals dreamed of, but few ever achieved.

With General McClellan off reconnoitering their next fallback position aboard the U.S.S. *Galena* with Commodore Rodgers, and the commanding general having failed to appoint an overall commander in his absence, Porter, who was officially commanding general of just V Corps, had found himself *de facto* commander over the entire army.

When he realized General McClellan had no intention of being present at whatever action might occur, Porter decided it was time to step up, use every ounce of his intelligence, training, and suppressed courage, to position and use the army to its greatest potential. And maybe … just maybe … win a battle!

He knew this might be his only chance to get out from under McClellan's shadow and show what he could do without McClellan's domineering presence.

His once promising career—graduating near the top of his class at West Point, receiving a promotion to brevet captain for bravery at Molino del Rey during the Mexican War—had somehow gone terribly wrong after his assignment to the Army of the Potomac under McClellan.

And oh, the glory of today! Today he had made amends and finally lived up his potential and won a great victory, perhaps even the decisive victory that would ultimately win the war.

His staff officers standing around him shared his excitement and enthusiasm, joking, smiling, and patting each other on the back enthusiastically, a thing he'd not seen since their arrival on the peninsula more than four months earlier. Colonel Henry Hunt, Army of the Potomac's chief of artillery, had joined them, and the officers congratulated each other on a brilliant victory.

They were joined shortly by Brigadier General Erasmus Keyes along with several of his staff officers. Keyes, whose IV Corps had held down the Union right flank during the action, was also smiling brightly, and shook hands with Porter and then Colonel Hunt with great enthusiasm.

Porter and Keyes congratulated each other and agreed their next move should be an all-out counterattack at first light in the morning.

But at that moment, Captain Brown of Porter's staff stepped up next to him, leaned in close and spoke in a low voice, "General McClellan, sir ..."

"*Oh!*" Porter said, looking in the direction Brown had indicated with a nod of his head. Major General McClellan came striding up the hill, three staff officers in tow.

"The commanding general!" Porter announced, and all present came to attention facing the arriving general, then saluted as McClellan stepped up and stood facing them.

"Good evening, gentlemen," he said, smiling brightly. "I understand we had a good time of it today."

And though Porter continued to smile, and nodded at McClellan, he suffered a sudden realization—that McClellan would likely claim all the credit for the victory, even as he would have denied any blame if things had gone wrong. *The advantages of being away somewhere on a gunboat while the actual fighting is taking place ...* he thought.

"Gentlemen ... I can't be more pleased with your heroic actions today, preserving our great army," McClellan said. "And to continue the good news of today, I have reconnoitered our next fallback point, and have determined it will make an excellent defensive position in which to encamp the army."

Porter felt a shock roll through his body and a knot forming in his stomach. "*Fallback,* sir? You ... *do* realize we have just won a resounding victory here today, entirely decimating the enemy's forces while most of ours are still fresh and ready to fight? That likely Lee and Jackson are so depleted that it is highly unlikely they can do anything to halt a quick march on Richmond?"

Keyes and Hunt nodded their agreement, but McClellan just smiled, then scoffed, "Come now, gentlemen ... one battle does not a campaign win. I appreciate that we have done well today ...

and as I said before, I can't be more pleased that you officers have saved the army, preventing the enemy from overwhelming and destroying it while I was necessarily away seeking a more defensible position for the morrow. But gentlemen ... despite our heroic deeds of the day, the enemy still has us *vastly* outnumbered, and a march on Richmond at this point would be nothing short of a disaster. Lee's willingness to throw his men at us in one reckless frontal assault after another proves the truth of what I'm saying, gentlemen — clearly he has more troops at his disposal than he knows that to do with."

"But ... sir, allow me to at least lead a counter-attack in the morning. If we aren't immediately successful, we can always fall back then," Porter pleaded.

But McClellan was unmoved, and just shook his head, gazing off into the distance as if envisioning events yet to come. "No, Fitz ... and I'll brook no more argument on it ... I'll not risk this army on a pumped-up, headlong dash forward just because we have had one good day of fighting.

"Tonight we start our pullback to Harrison's Landing, just as quickly as it can be arranged — we'll march all night if we have to. And I have a nagging fear we've not a moment to lose, as the enemy is likely to launch a fresh attack with overwhelming force at first light in the morning."

Then he grinned, "But he's in for a nasty surprise ... when he springs his trap, we will no longer be here. Once we are safely up against the river, we can be resupplied from the water, and defended by our own gunboats. The enemy will dare not attack us under those circumstances."

"But sir," Keyes said, "what then? Won't it be that much more difficult to attack Richmond from down there, tucked in behind a large bend of the James and ... some twenty-five miles or so from the city?"

"What we will do there, General Keyes, is rest our worn-out men, re-equip, and refit. Then we shall await reinforcements."

"Reinforcements?" Colonel Hunt asked.

"Yes ... I intend to ask our incompetent masters in Washington to do their duty — for once — and finally give us the manpower we so desperately need in order to re-start this offensive. I've been thinking … another 100,000 men ought to be a good starting point …"

After McClellan and his staff officers departed, and General Keyes walked slowly away, shaking his head and muttering to himself in apparent disgust, Colonel Hill stepped up to Porter, and the two exchanged a serious look.

Porter said, "I can't believe it … he acts as if the army is beaten."

But Hunt shook his head and answered with a scowl, "The army's not beaten … just *him*."

Friday, July 4, 1862 – Harrison's Landing, Virginia:

Captain James Hawkins sat down on his bunk in his tent with a heavy sigh. He was feeling very low, discouraged, and disgusted, but had no one to talk to who wasn't feeling the very same, so he decided to pen a letter to Nathan Chambers, since he hadn't done so in some time:

> *July 4, 1862*
> *Harrison's Landing, Va.*
>
> *Dear Mr. Chambers,*
>
> *The Seventh finally arrived on the Virginia Peninsula by boat on July 1, and the next day went into action against Confederate forces under General Jeb Stuart who were attempting to position artillery on the high ground above the landing so as to shell our camp here. You would've been proud of the Seventh, sir, as our men charged resolutely across an open field, exposed to the enemy's fire, then displayed great coolness and undaunted courage, rushing the enemy's position, driving off their cavalry and infantry, then capturing four cannons—securing the high ground.*

Yesterday we fought a sharp skirmish against our old nemesis, the Stonewall Brigade, whom we had dueled against recently all the way up the Shenandoah Valley. They approached the landing, likely to assess our current strength, but we drove them off. There was scant satisfaction in it, though, as they did not press the assault.

But despite the regiment's exemplary performance, we are in a state of disheartenment, as it seems General McClellan has all but given up on the idea of capturing Richmond. From talking to officers who took part, it seems as if our army won a great victory at Malvern Hill the day we arrived, annihilating the Confederate forces sent against us, and very likely destroying their ability to defend Richmond. But despite all that, the General ordered a retreat to this place, from which it will be nearly impossible to launch an attack against the enemy's capital.

My respect for General McClellan, which was already at a very low point after the inexcusable death of General Lander, has now reached the very lowest of depths. Today he issued a proclamation to his army praising them for their "successful and extremely difficult" maneuver making it into this camp. Yes, maybe ... but a successful <u>retreat</u>! Hardly the stuff of legends, nor deserving of praise in my humble opinion.

And to top it off, this place is miserable—hot, damp, and disease-ridden, which only adds to the bitterness of the situation we find ourselves in. I pray that things will improve, and some unforeseen circumstance will reverse our present fortunes before we are forced to withdraw and return northward to an entirely bitter and empty homecoming.

Your loyal friend and servant,

James Hawkins
Captain, Seventh Loyal Virginia Regiment

Chapter 12. Joyful Surprise

Thursday, July 3, 1862 – Wheeling, Virginia:

Nathan waited for Margaret just inside the front door of the Customs House after a long day of meetings, mainly concerning how to best "sell" the new West Virginia constitution to President Lincoln and the Republican-controlled congress—a mission made exponentially more difficult due to the new constitution's failure to address the slavery issue, despite Nathan and Margaret's best efforts.

He was startled by the sound of someone running down the hallway toward him from the direction of the post office, and turned to see who it was and what it might be about. Harry the Dog also turned toward the noise. Nathan was surprised, and mildly amused, to see it was Tom, holding a sheet of paper up in his hand, grinning brightly.

When he came closer, he called out, "She's coming, Captain ... she's finally coming!"

Nathan didn't have to ask who "she" was; clearly Tom had just received good news in a letter from Adilida.

Tom pulled up in front of Nathan, nearly sliding into him on the smoothly polished granite floor. He was almost out of breath, but waved the letter in front of Nathan and repeated, "She's coming, sir."

Nathan smiled and raised an eyebrow in amusement, "Do tell, Tom ..."

"Edouard has completed an agreement to sell both his house and business, to a Union Naval officer, if you can believe it. And he's booked Addie and himself a ride on the steamship that carries the Union mail. They'll depart New Orleans on the tenth of this month—well … that's just a week from today! Expecting to arrive in Baltimore on the eighteenth."

Nathan extended his hand, and Tom shook it firmly, "Congratulations, Tom. I am so very happy for you; that is just *marvelous*—the best news we've had all this year, by far!"

"Thank you, sir … I'm … I'm … about to burst …" he said, trying his best to suppress a smile that threatened to crack his face in two, but failing utterly.

"I wanted to ask you, sir … if you would consider coming with me to Baltimore … you know, to greet her when she arrives."

"Of course, Tom … I would love to—and have been hoping you'd ask whenever the time came. It would be an honor and a privilege."

"Thank you, sir, thank you!" he said, grasping Nathan's hand and pumping it once again, before turning and trotting out the door, gazing at the letter as he did, nearly bumping into the door frame on his way. Harry the Dog tilted his head and watched as if trying to fathom why this normally stolid and reliable man was suddenly acting so erratically.

At that moment Margaret stepped up and took Nathan's arm, "What's that all about?" she asked, gazing after Tom as he slid out the door and headed down the outside stairs.

Nathan gazed at her a moment, smiled and said, "*Love,* … I believe."

⇚⇛

Saturday July 5, 1862 – Wheeling, Virginia:

Miss Margaret stepped out onto the front porch at Belle Meade after Megs had come to her room and mysteriously informed her that "someone" wished to speak with her outside, refusing to elaborate.

Phinney stood there, at the top of the stairs, smiling at her with his old felt hat clutched in his remaining left hand. His empty right sleeve had been sewed shut about a foot below the shoulder.

Margaret returned the smile easily, and said, "Phinney! You are looking *so* much better! How are you feeling?"

He nodded, continuing to smile brightly, "I's feelin' very much better, Miss Margaret, thank you for askin'."

"That's wonderful news, Phinney … we were so worried about you when you … weren't feeling well."

"Well, thanks to Mr. William I'm now well on the mend, and not even much of any pain left to speak of. But …" he looked at her, then looked down, as if suddenly shy.

"What is it, Phinney?" she asked.

He looked back up, "It's just … I never done thanked you proper like, Miss Margaret … at first I was in such fear and pain, and then Mr. William come home and … well, you know the rest. Anyway, I wanted to thank you *now*, Miss Margaret for … well, for savin' my life, I reckon is about the size of it. Cobb done told me if it weren't for you, I'd o' bled out that night right there where I lay, as nobody else knew what to do.

"Anyway … I thank you kindly, Miss Margaret," he said, then chuckled as a sudden thought hit him, "… and my *grandchildren* thank you as well."

She smiled, and wiped away a tear, "Well, you're very welcome, though I don't think I did so very much … I'm just grateful to see you doing better. But, Phinney … your *grandchildren?!* I didn't think you were even married …"

He laughed, "Not *yet*, Miss Margaret … but you never know how the future world may be!"

She nodded and shared the smile with him, thinking of her own situation with William and wondering if they'd ever be married with grandchildren of their own. But she shook off the thought and kept her focus on Phinney.

"So, tell me, Phinney … are you becoming accustomed to … *you know* … doing things with just one arm?"

He grinned, and nodded, "Oh, yes ma'am. I can do darned near everythin' I used to now. Oh, at first it was real hard … and to tell the truth, I was gettin' a might down and frustrated on account of it. But then ..." he chuckled, "you know what that rascal Cobb done?"

She shook her head.

"He comes up to me one morning with his right arm behind his back. Well, I was a bit miffed, thinkin' he was makin' fun o' me or somethin'. But then he turns around and I see he done tied the arm behind his back so's he couldn't move it.

"'What'd you go'n do that for?' I asks.

"'So's we can figure out this danged one-armed thing together,' he says and grins. And damned if he don't go all day with that arm tied there like that, doin' everything that a way. We laughed so many times that day it made my face hurt—just tryin' to do all the stupid little things that used to be easy," he shook his head and beamed at the memory of it.

Margaret smiled, "Now *that*, Phinney, is a good friend," she said.

He nodded, "Yep ... I reckon you're right about that, Miss Margaret. Made me stop feelin' sorry for myself and realize I got it pretty darned good—havin' a friend like Cobb ... and a big ol' family like this here," he waved his left arm out toward the tents, taking in the whole farm with the gesture.

❦❦❦❦

Friday July 18, 1862 – Richmond, Virginia:

Evelyn stood in the office of her house, gazing out the window at the woods beyond the back yard. It was another beautiful, sunny day, and the bright green leaves flickered and swayed in a gentle summer breeze. But in Evelyn's heart it felt like the dead of winter ... and for the hundredth time today she reproached herself for not sitting down at the desk to begin the pile of paperwork that'd been accumulating since before her return. And for the hundredth time today she sighed, and continued to stare out the window, entirely unable to motivate herself.

She knew she needed to pull herself out of this very low place she was in, but she couldn't figure out how. *Perhaps I'm still just exhausted from my long journey*, she lied to herself one more time.

And she was not just struggling to complete tasks that were normally simple, she knew she was also being surly with her helpers, and had even been snappish and impatient with the last group of "travelers" that'd come through her house—runaway slaves being smuggled out of Virginia via the Underground Railroad. She cringed when she recalled *that*; the last thing these poor, frightened people needed was someone treating them sternly and with lack of empathy.

The problem was she didn't know what to do about it. No matter how many times she promised herself she would stop it— be kinder, and more understanding—something else would set her off, and she'd be back where she started ... and feeling guilty about it.

She sighed again. Then thankfully her dark thoughts were interrupted by a soft knock on the doorframe. She sternly reminded herself not to react harshly to the interruption and to treat whomever it was kindly.

But when she turned, she was surprised and genuinely pleased to see the person standing there.

"*Joseph!* Please ... come in, come in," she said, and actually smiled—perhaps for the first time that day.

"Good afternoon, Miss Eve," he said, returning her smile, and removing his hat—this time the simple hat of a common laborer, matching his current "role." She never knew how he would appear when next she saw him—he had any number of different personas he would adopt for various tasks and scenarios in his clandestine line of work—but she always knew his face, no matter how cleverly he might disguise it.

"Miss Eve ... I have been intending to stop in to see you for some time, but ..." he shrugged, "somehow duties always seem to interfere."

"Never mind that, Joseph ... I'm always happy to see you. Did the Employer send you to check up on me?" she asked with a rueful grin. "I know he's been worried about me ... he thinks I haven't properly recovered from my little ... *adventure.*"

Joseph gazed at her and tilted his head with a thoughtful look. "And ... is he *wrong?*" he asked, softly.

She looked down at her feet, shook her head, and said, "No ..." fighting down the tears that always seemed to be lurking, just the next dark thought away. She sank slowly into the desk chair, continuing to gaze at the floor.

He sat in the chair opposite the desk and gazed across at her in silence, allowing her to elaborate—or not—as she saw fit.

"Joseph ... it has been so hard to just ... pretend like nothing happened and go back to doing things as before. I feel like ... like my journey of over a thousand miles and several months was not just an utter failure, but an absolute disaster. General McClellan failed to secure a victory despite the information we provided, I was forced to kill a man—and possibly others," she shrugged, "... and a good man died helping me—yes, I know, I know, *I mustn't take responsibility for that* ... but I can't help how I'm feeling about it.

"And then there's Nathan ... I feel like I've ruined that too ... have pushed him into the arms of another woman by rejecting him and running away ... and I have tainted my good feelings for him in the process. Now I switch between loving him and resenting him on a daily basis.

"I'm sorry Joseph ... I shouldn't be dumping all this on you, but ... there's no one else to talk to who understands what I've been through ... and I just feel so ... so ... *terribly low* ..."

He slowly nodded his head, then said, "Well ... I am honored you feel you can confide in me ... *truly.* But I didn't just come here so you could vent your ill humor on me. I have actually come here because I believe I might be of some help to you concerning it."

"Oh? As much as I appreciate the *thought*, Joseph, I can't imagine what you can possibly say to make me feel better, after everything that's happened."

"It's not what I'm going to *say*, my dear, but rather what I am going to *do* ..." he smiled, reached into his pocket, pulled out a folded sheet of paper and handed it across to her. She looked it over and saw it had been sealed in red wax at one time, but the seal was long gone. The outside of the sheet was dirty, crumpled, and slightly torn. It had a man's name written on the outside that she didn't recognize, with the address simply "Richmond, Va."

She looked up at Joseph with a puzzled expression, "What's this?"

"As you can see … this is a letter that has literally 'been through the war,' which is why it is so ragged, and why it has taken more than a month to arrive. I suspect it's something of a miracle it has made it here at all."

Her eyes widened, and she held her breath—but she dared not ask … if it was from … *him*.

But Joseph smiled and nodded, as if reading her thoughts, "Yes, it's from Mr. Chambers, as you have surmised. And I must apologize for having opened it and read it already. It was addressed to me, you see, under one of my several assumed names—this particular one I'd provided to Tom Clark in case he ever needed to get a message to me."

But she shook her head, and said, "It's all right, Joseph. You've done so much for me that it'd take a lot more than *that* to make me even begin to think the least bit ill of you."

Then he stood, replaced his hat, smiled, and said, "Thank you for that, my lady. I will leave you now … may peace and joy be with you."

She gazed up at him, but could think of nothing to say in response, other than, "Thank you, Joseph … and also with you."

She sat staring at the ragged, folded sheet of paper in her lap for several minutes, struggling with conflicting emotions—shock and trepidation battling against hope and excitement. Finally she unfolded the paper, straightened it out on the desk, and began to read:

June 2, 1862
Commonwealth of Virginia

My Dearest E.,

I am filled with remorse and shame for how I treated you when last we were together just prior to your departure on the train. I must now admit I was wrong concerning almost everything I said to you on that occasion, and I beg you to accept my most humble apology. My only defense is that I had been missing you so terribly for such a long time that I was not thinking clearly. The idea of being together with you again, and of finally becoming your husband, was so overwhelmingly joyful it clouded my better judgment.

I now realize there are things in life that you must do in order to be able to stand tall and feel proud of the person you see in the looking glass, even as I am so very proud of you.

But now I must tell you of something that happened on the night we parted, hopefully before you hear an incorrect and hurtful version of events from someone else. If you already have, I sincerely apologize for the unnecessary pain it has no doubt caused you. I swear on the Bible, and my word of honor as a gentleman, that what I'm about to tell you is the whole truth.

After you left that evening, I went to the common room of our inn, in a foul humor. I sat with Tom, drinking whiskey, but I was ill company, and after a time he retired to his room. I continued to drink, and I will confess it was likely more than was good for me. Some hours later a young lady entered the inn in search of a room, but there were none available. She was very friendly and talkative, and explained she'd been forced to flee her home just south of town in fear of the advancing rebel army.

I offered her my room for the evening and told her I would bunk up with one of my men, which she accepted. But when I escorted her to my room, intending only to collect a few personal items for the morning, she made advances on me – pressed up against me and kissed me. I'm afraid in my inebriated state, and after having spent a good part of the day thinking of nothing but you, my mind became confused and for a moment I imagined myself once more in your arms.

But then I realized it was not so; rather she was a total stranger. I pushed her away, telling her I was in love with and even betrothed to another woman. Then I left the room. Not wanting to disturb Tom, and it being a mild evening, I went outside and slept under a bush with Harry the Dog.

In the morning I discovered she had rummaged through my government papers. Then I remembered a story Tom had told me of a female rebel spy and I made the connection. She knew I was working for the loyal Virginia government and thought to pry military secrets from me.

When I confronted her and had her arrested, she made an embarrassing display in the common room and inferred that we had slept together, which was untrue. Other than the kiss which she initiated, and which frankly caught me by surprise, I never laid a hand on her and behaved as a proper gentleman should. But I'm afraid her unladylike performance was witnessed by one of the Employer's men, whom I talked with afterward, and it wasn't until later it occurred to me that he may have been led to believe her slanderous tale.

I have never been unfaithful to you since first we met, and I never will be. And I could not agree more strongly with everything you said in your letter about the glory and strength of our love for each other; it is truly a gift from God, the greatest feeling I've experienced in life. I know you can feel it in your heart, but I am compelled to say it anyway—I love you more than words can say.

Every day I pray for your continued good health and safety, and for a swift end to this war so that we may finally be together.

Your true love—and future husband,

N.

Evelyn jumped to her feet and made a loud, unintelligible sound, halfway between a shout and a squeal, then began dancing around the room, alternating between clutching the letter to her breast and kissing it with her lips, tears streaming down her cheeks.

Oh Nathan, Nathan, my dearest—you still love me! You still love me! Oh, thank God; thank dear, sweet, Jesus and all his saints and angels!

Nathan my love ... my darling ... most beautiful of men ... you have brought my heart back alive!

☙℘ℰℭ℥☙℘ℰℭ℥☙℘ℰℭ℥

Friday July 18, 1862 – Baltimore, Maryland:

Tom paced nervously at the foot of the gangplank as the passengers debarked. He scanned those still queueing up on deck but hadn't yet spotted Adilida and Edouard. Then suddenly he saw them, and Adilida waved enthusiastically, flashing her beautiful smile. His heart leapt, and he could feel it pounding in his chest like it would burst. He thought he'd never seen a more beautiful sight, and was almost happy the Captain hadn't yet arrived, sure he looked anything but dignified, smiling from ear to ear and waving furiously like a small child, fighting back tears of joy.

The line seemed to crawl. Several older people moved cautiously down the thin, wobbling gangplank, clutching the handrails as if their very lives depended upon it—which they probably did, Tom decided.

347

And then the moment he had anticipated and dreamed about for the better part of two years finally arrived. Adilida stepped down off the gangplank, and ran to him, leaping into his arms and wrapping her arms around him. She squeezed him so hard he thought he'd lose his breath. But he squeezed back almost as hard. Then she leaned back and put her lips on his and kissed him like he had never been kissed before, not even when they were alone in the hotel back in New Orleans. He felt like his head was swimming, and when he released her, he was surprised he had a hard time seeing for the tears in his own eyes.

"Hello Addie," was all he could think of to say, after all that.

She laughed, and hugged him again, "Oh, my dear, sweet Thomas. We are together again at last, my love!"

Tom remembered the first time she had called him that, and he felt an involuntary twitch down deep in his body.

But then he remembered his manners, and released her, turning toward Edouard, and extending his hand, "It is so good to see you again, sir. Thank you so much for coming … there's no way I can thank you enough for bringing my dear Adilida back to me!"

But Edouard smiled brightly, "Oh, think nothing of it, my dear boy! It would not be an exaggeration to say it is one of the greatest pleasures of my life!" and then he laughed, and fondly patted Tom on the back.

"Captain Chambers should be here shortly, then we can depart. We ran into an old friend of his on the way here, and he felt obliged to visit with him for a bit before coming down to the docks."

"Oh, never worry, Thomas," Adilida said.

When she said that, it reminded him how much he loved the way she said his name, like "Toe – MOSS."

He resisted a very strong urge to kiss her again, feeling a little self-conscious in front of Uncle Edouard.

"We must also wait, Thomas … You see … I have a little surprise for you."

"Oh, what's that, Addie?"

"Wait a moment, and you will see. Oh! There he comes now."

Tom looked back up onto the deck, and saw a handsome young man with dark hair, dressed as a fine gentleman, complete with top hat. Tom immediately recognized him as the man who was hugging and kissing Adilida on that fatal day back in New Orleans. Cousin Phillipe, at last!

"Oh, I remembered you saying Phillipe might come! I'm so happy he has joined you. Now we can finally settle our score!" he smiled good-naturedly at Adilida, but he thought she had a strange, anxious look about her suddenly. Surely, she didn't think he was angry with Phillipe and might treat him unkindly?

He looked back up toward the ship, and saw Phillipe stepping onto the gangplank. It was then he noticed the man clutched something in his arms, something he held close against his chest. When Phillipe was about hallway across Tom realized it was a small child, about two years of age. Tom was surprised the man would bring such a young child on such a long journey. And … where was the mother, he wondered?

Phillipe stepped down from the gangplank and walked over to where they stood.

He extended his hand to Tom, "Thomas … I am so happy to finally meet you. I am Phillipe … the … infamous 'other man'!"

They shared a smile, and Tom gripped his hand and shook it firmly.

"No fault to you for that, Phillipe! The fault was all mine for making one of the world's worst, false assumptions! Never before in the history of being wrong, has a man been so wrong about something, it seems."

"Well, now I pray we shall make amends and become the very best of friends," Phillipe said with a warm smile.

"I couldn't agree more, Phillipe. And … I must say this young man is a handsome looking fellow. Takes after his father, I see."

Phillipe didn't respond right away, just smiled. He turned the boy, so Tom could clearly see his face, then said, "Thomas … I would like you to meet … Nathaniel."

Tom looked at the child and thought him a fine-looking boy. He had dark hair and eyes, and a perfect, unblemished face. The boy was wide awake and gazed back at Tom with a curious look.

"Well … isn't that something. I know someone … someone very close to me named Nathaniel. How old is your son, Phillipe?"

"Oh, the boy is sixteen and a half months old, Thomas. But … *I* am not his father."

Tom was confused and looked up at Phillipe. "Well then …"

But before he could say more, Phillipe held up his hand, and said, "Thomas … allow me to make formal introductions. Thomas Clark … please meet … Nathaniel … Thomas … *Clark!*"

The words went in Tom's ears, but it took a few moments to register. His jaw dropped with a shocked expression. He turned to Adilida. She had tears in her eyes, and smiled in a tentative way, not knowing how he would react. She nodded.

"Then he's … he's …" Tom looked at the child, then back at Adilida, "… my son?"

Tears now streamed down her face, and she couldn't speak, but managed a whisper, "Yes."

He looked back at the boy. Then slowly reached out and took the child from Phillipe's arms, and held him up at arm's length, gazing at him.

"Addie … he's … beautiful … just like his Momma."

"No, Thomas … he is handsome … and strong, like his Daddy!" Then she began to weep in earnest.

But Tom continued to gaze at the boy. The child stared back at him, unflinchingly, with a slight grin, before looking over at his Momma, who nodded to him encouragingly. The boy looked back at Tom and said, "Daddy?"

Tom chuckled, nodded his head, and said, "Yes … I reckon I'm your Daddy, Nathaniel … *my son.*" He finished in a soft voice, lowering the boy to his chest, hugging him close, and patting him gently on the back. Then he reached out his right arm and pulled Adilida in toward him, so the three of them joined in an embrace.

They stayed that way for a long time, Tom with a smile on his face, and Adilida with tears streaming down her face, clutching Tom with all her strength.

Edouard turned to Phillipe, reached out his arms, and the two men embraced, surreptitiously wiping away tears, thoroughly caught up in the emotions of the moment.

Several of the passengers, picking up on what was happening stood around smiling, whispering, and pointing at the happy spectacle.

Just then Nathan walked up with Harry the Dog following close on his heels.

Tom saw him approaching and looked up, releasing Adilida, and stepping back, still holding the boy.

"Captain! You've already met Mr. Edouard Boudreau, but I should like to introduce his son, Mr. Phillipe Boudreau, and ... Adilida Boudreau."

Nathan walked up, smiling broadly, "Of course, good to see you again, Edouard. Phillipe, Adilida ... your fine reputations proceed you. I am entirely delighted to meet y'all at last."

"Monsieur Chambers," Edouard responded, "I greatly enjoyed your company that evening when we met, back at the St. Charles. I was very impressed with your tales of the wild west, as I recall, though I thought ... they sounded vaguely familiar, somehow ..."

Nathan laughed, "Yes, I understand Tom and I were telling the same tall tales that evening!"

They shared a good-natured laugh as they shook hands, after which he shook hands warmly with Phillippe, and then kissed Adilida's hand with a bow, which she returned with a curtsy, "A pleasure to meet you at last, my dear."

"Oh, thank you ever so kindly, sir, but the pleasure ... she is all mine!" and she smiled up at him brightly.

"I can see Tom's description of your beauty and charm was not exaggerated in the least!" Nathan said.

She blushed, "Oh ... it is so kind of you to say, Captain Chambers."

But then Tom caught Nathan's eye, and Nathan could see Tom had a serious look.

"Sir ... I would like you to meet someone else. Captain ... this is ... Nathaniel ... Thomas ... Clark—my son."

Now it was Nathan's turn to be shocked. His jaw dropped, and he stared at Tom, then at the boy, and finally over at Adilida. Her bright, tearful smile seemed to snap him out of it, and he looked back at Tom and grinned, "Well … that's the best news I've heard in a month of Sundays! Congratulations, Tom … Adilida! That's just … *absolutely wonderful!* Praise God from whom all blessings flow! In a world of darkness and despair, you two have managed to shine a bright, happy light! God bless you!"

"Thank you, sir. But … Addie … please now, tell me, how is it you came up with this … *particular* name for the boy?"

"Oh … well, we planned to arrive just after the child was born so you and I could decide the name together, but then the war came. And, as you know, there was no way to sail to you. Uncle and I talked of what I should do, but finally decided it wouldn't be fair to tell you of the child when we had no way to come together. So we waited … until finally the Union navy recaptured New Orleans. But that took a whole year! A child cannot go without a name, my dear! I wanted to name him Thomas, after his Daddy, but Uncle said some men didn't like that idea, that it causes confusion in the family about who is who. So we talked about other names, and I remembered how much you loved and admired your Captain. I decided on Nathaniel for the first name, and your name, Thomas for the middle, as is common, I understand, amongst the English-speaking people."

"Well … that was … brilliant, my dear." Tom looked over at Nathan, who continued to smile, "I had often thought … if I ever had a son, I'd like to name him after *you*, sir. Though I always envisioned asking your permission first …"

"Well, consider it granted!" Nathan said. "I feel truly honored, such as no medal on a uniform could ever have bestowed! Thank you sincerely, Adilida! I feel *blessed* … truly."

"Oh, thank you so much, dear Captain! I can see now why Thomas loves you so. You are such a beautiful and kindly man!"

Nathan blushed, and smiled warmly.

They began to walk away from the docks when Adilida stopped suddenly, and said, "Oh! In all the excitement introducing young Nathaniel, I nearly forgot … I have something else I must tell you, Thomas, dear."

They stopped, and everyone turned to look at Adilida.

"Thomas … now I must confess … after we met, and then parted … when I realized I was … with child, I didn't know what to do."

Tom shook his head, "I'm so sorry, Addie … I didn't know …"

"Never you mind that now, Thomas … you had no way of knowing. But, well … you know how it is for a child born … out of wedlock; it is very hard. People will say cruel things … they will treat him as … a lesser being, no?"

"Yes, I understand. Addie, I would never have allowed that if I'd have known …"

"I know, Thomas. But please, let me finish. I didn't know how you felt, after you left so suddenly, so … I … took certain … liberties."

"Liberties?"

"Well … you see …"

"It was *my* suggestion," Edouard said, gravely.

"Yes … Uncle, *sagely* suggested … we should tell everyone … you and I fell in love and were secretly wed when we met in New Orleans. Thomas … since then we have told everyone you and I are married, and you had to go to the East on business. That I planned to join you later but had to wait for the child's birth first. And then, of course, the war came.

"I hope you are not angry with me, but … I have been using your name these past two years, even before the child was born. Now everyone in Thibodaux knows me as Adilida *Clark*—that is, Mrs. Thomas Clark!"

Tom looked at her, then gazed up at the sky. After a long moment he looked back down, smiled and said, "That was well done, Addie. 'Righteously done,' we would've said back at Mountain Meadows. All I have to say about that is … let's find a preacher and make truth of the lie as soon as may be."

Adilida burst into tears and had to sit down on the cobblestones of the walkway. Tom sat down next to her, still holding the child in his left arm, wrapping his right arm around her as she leaned into him and sobbed.

Nathan, Edouard, and Phillipe stood above them, smiling, shaking hands, and wiping tears from their eyes.

<End of Book 6>

If you enjoyed *Invasion,*
please post a review.

Ready for more of Nathan Chambers, Evelyn Hanson, and the ever-growing Mountain Meadows family?

EMANCIPATION
ROAD TO THE BREAKING BOOK 7
is coming in 2022.

In the meantime, to show my appreciation for all the loyal readers of Road to the Breaking, please visit my website for a *FREE* **short story** about how Nathan Chambers' particular "Band of Brothers" first came together. I think you'll enjoy it:

ADVENT
A ROAD TO THE BREAKING
SHORT STORY

To download your free copy of **ADVENT** please use the web address below:

https://www.chrisabennett.com/advent

ACKNOWLEDGMENTS

Special thanks as always to my editor, Ericka McIntyre, who keeps me honest and on track, and my proofreader and fellow Tolkien fanatic Travis Tynan, who makes sure everything is done correctly!

And, last but not least (at all!), the experts at New Shelves Books, featuring my trusted advisor on all things "bookish," Keri-Rae Barnum. You are the best!

RECOMMENDED READING

For a serious, well-deserved, and utterly devastating "dressing down" of Union Major General George B. McClellan, please read *McClellan and Failure: A Study of Civil War Fear, Incompetence and Worse*, by Edward H. Bonekemper, III.

For a good overview of the actions of the "Stonewall Brigade" please read *The Stonewall Brigade: The History of the Most Famous Confederate Combat Unit of the Civil War*, by Charles Rivers Editors. And for a very interesting and compelling first-hand account of the same, I recommend *Four Years in the Stonewall Brigade*, by John O. Casler.

To learn more about Lydia Johnston, her husband C.S.A. Major General Joe Johnston, and their tumultuous relationship with Jefferson Davis and Varina Davis, see *Joseph E. Johnston: A Civil War Biography*, by Craig L. Symonds.

If you wish to read Union Brigadier General Rufus Saxton's official account of the events at Harpers Ferry in May, 1862 which led to his being awarded the Congressional Medal of Honor—including the riveting actual transcripts of the telegram communications between his command in Harpers Ferry and the War Department (many of which are reproduced in this book) and the exciting battle in the lightning storm—search online for U.S. Congressional Serial Set Document Number 2322, 48th Congress, 2nd Session, 1884 - 85, House Miscellaneous Documents #12, starting on page 626.

Get Exclusive Free Content

The most enjoyable part of writing books is talking about them with readers like you. In my case that means all things related to *Road to the Breaking*—the story and characters, themes, and concepts. And of course, Civil War history in general, and West Virginia history in particular.

If you sign up for my mailing list, you'll receive some free bonus material I think you'll enjoy:

- A fully illustrated **Road to the Breaking Fact vs. Fiction Quiz.** Test your knowledge of history with this short quiz on the people, places, and things in the book (did they really exist in 1860, or are they purely fictional?)

- **Cut scenes from *Road to the Breaking*.** One of the hazards of writing a novel is word and page count. At some point you realize you need to trim it back to give the reader a faster-paced, more engaging experience. However, now you've finished reading the book, wouldn't you like to know a little more detail about some of your favorite characters? Here's your chance to take a peek behind the curtain!

- I'll occasionally put out a **newsletter with information about the Road to the Breaking Series**—new book releases, news and information about the author, etc. I promise not to inundate you with spam (it's one of my personal pet peeves, so why would I propagate it?)

To sign up, visit my website:
http://www.ChrisABennett.com